FOUND

ALSO BY H. TERRELL GRIFFIN

Matt Royal Mysteries

Fatal Decree
Collateral Damage
Bitter Legacy
Wyatt's Revenge
Blood Island
Murder Key
Longboat Blues

Thrillers: 100 Must-Reads: Joseph Conrad, Heart of Darkness
(contributing essayist)

FOUND

A Matt Royal Mystery

H. Terrell Griffin

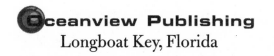
Longboat Key, Florida

ISBN: 978-1-60809-099-0

Published in the United States of America by Oceanview Publishing,
Longboat Key, Florida
www.oceanviewpub.com

2 4 6 8 10 9 7 5 3

PRINTED IN THE UNITED STATES OF AMERICA

This book is dedicated to the memory of my personal heroes

Sion P. Griffin
Seaman Second Class, United States Navy
USS *John Paul Jones* (DD-230)
World War II
Battle of the Atlantic

and

Henry Alden Higgins
Private First Class, United States Army
Fifth Infantry Division
World War II
Campaigns: Normandy, Northern France, Rhineland,
Ardennes-Alsace (Battle of the Bulge), and Central Europe

ACKNOWLEDGMENTS

The gang at Oceanview Publishing spends their days making life easier for the writers. Patricia Gussin, Robert Gussin, Frank Troncale, and David Ivester are always available to lend a hand in editing, story ideas, launch parties, publicity, and so many other things that we writers need from time to time.

Pat Gussin, the company's president, who is herself the author of several novels and also edits my work, must never sleep. She is the busiest person I know, and she always makes my books better. The indispensable Susan Hayes also edits my work and makes sure that I'm actually writing in the English language and not in some indecipherable gibberish. She smooths out the prose and makes it more readable.

Bob Gussin, a true gentleman and the other busiest person I know, is always upbeat and supportive. He makes me want to write, just to hear his compliments when the manuscript is done.

It is my good fortune to have three friends, voracious readers all, who find time to read and edit my manuscripts as I'm writing them. Jean Griffin, Peggy Kendall, and David Beals are quick to point out errors and inconsistencies and, most preciously, provide encouragement and good cheer. They never let me go so far with the story that it becomes implausible. Peggy is particularly good about nagging me when my muse deserts, and I don't turn out at least some copy on a regular basis. Their insights and, yes, their nagging, are invaluable and much appreciated.

I get a great deal of pleasure out of writing; spinning tales that I hope will give readers a few hours of enjoyment. My readers are the ones who really make the whole process of writing worthwhile. Without you, I would have no reason to write. I hear from some of you on a regular basis, and I encourage you all to e-mail me with your thoughts and comments on the books. I answer all my e-mails, and I have found that the positive criticism I receive makes me a better writer.

Nothing in my life would be complete without my wife, Jean Griffin, the woman who encourages me, helps me, edits me, and loves me. She is my polestar, the light that has guided me since I was a college student. She has also put up with me, and I suspect that has not always been an easy job. She has done it all with patience and grace and a smile that brightens my world and assures me that life is immeasurably good.

CHAPTER ONE

The photograph of the dead woman bounced about the ether, from cell phone to switch to satellite, and back to earth. It rested briefly, perhaps a nanosecond, at the cell tower behind the fire station on Cortez Road before finding its way to its programmed destination. One photograph sent as a text message, one of hundreds of millions transmitted every day, but this one would change lives and bring pain and death and grief to some good people.

Jennifer Diane Duncan's cell phone pinged, alerting her to the arrival of the text message. She was driving her Camry west on Cortez Road, the sunroof open, windows down, enjoying the sun and salt-laden air of a Tuesday morning in February. She ignored the phone. She'd be home in a few minutes, and the message could wait until then. Traffic slowed and finally stopped as she approached the Cortez Bridge that spanned the Intracoastal Waterway. The draw was rising to let a large sailboat pass through. J.D., as she had been known since infancy, was stopped on the bridge, the third car in line behind the crossing gate, giving her an expansive view of the bay and the boats anchored in the lee of Anna Maria Island. She never tired of the vista that always welcomed her back to her islands, even when, as on this morning, she had only been gone for a couple of hours.

She'd had a meeting with a young Manatee County prosecutor at the courthouse in Bradenton. He was anticipating the trial of a burglar whom J.D. had arrested on Longboat Key, where she was the entire detective division of the local police department. They were "getting ready for trial," the lawyer had said with some pride. J.D. wondered if this was his first time at bat by himself in a felony courtroom.

J.D. watched as the graceful sailboat came onto a course that would take it directly under the raised span. Its sails were furled and its small diesel engine's exhaust burbled at the stern. The boat was barely making way, the captain cautious, probably unsure of the currents.

J.D. settled in for the wait. She reached over to the passenger seat and took the phone from her purse, opened it, and looked at the text message. It was a photo of a woman, holding what appeared to be a newspaper. The picture was too small to give much detail. J.D. pressed a couple of buttons and forwarded the picture. She pressed another button, waited for the answer, and said, "Matt, I just forwarded a photo to your e-mail. It came in on my phone and it's too small to make out any detail. Can you pull it up on your computer and see if you recognize the person in the picture?"

"Sure. Are you on your way?"

"I'm stopped at the Cortez Bridge waiting for a boat to go through. I should be at your house in about fifteen minutes."

"See you then."

CHAPTER TWO

My name is Matt Royal. I'm a lawyer who retired early, fed up with the rat race that the once honorable profession of law had become. I moved to Longboat Key, a small island about ten miles long and perhaps a half-mile wide at its broadest point. It lies off the southwest coast of Florida, south of Tampa, about halfway down the peninsula. Sarasota Bay separates the key from the mainland. Anna Maria Island is to the north, the islands connected by the two-lane Longboat Pass Bridge. The southern end of the key is attached by a bridge to Lido and St. Armands Keys, which in turn are connected to the city of Sarasota by the soaring John Ringling Bridge. The Gulf of Mexico's turquoise waters lap gently on our beaches and the sun almost always shines. A cold day is a rarity, even in February. I live in paradise.

I'd been a trial lawyer in Orlando, made a few bucks, saved my money, lost my wife to divorce, said the hell with it, and retreated to the simpler life of Longboat Key. I live in a bayside cottage in Longbeach Village, the community that hugs the north end of my island. It's known simply as "the village" and is a neighborhood of small houses, bungalows, and cottages, many of which date to the 1920s. I don't have a lot of money, but it's enough to last my lifetime if I'm careful.

I stand six feet tall, weigh one hundred eighty pounds, and have a head full of dark hair and a face that I'm mostly satisfied with. I run four miles a day on the beach, take weekly martial arts lessons, and generally stay in good shape. Before I went to law school, I was an infantry officer in the United States Army Special Forces, saw some combat, came home, and tried to put it out of mind.

Oh, and I have a sweetie. I don't call her my sweetie to her face, because I value my hide. She tends to be a bit independent. I'm not sure what to call her, but I know she wouldn't find "sweetie" acceptable. "Significant other" rings a little too pretentious and "girlfriend" sounds like we're still in high school. It's not really an important issue since titles or descriptions don't matter much on the key. Everybody knows we're a couple. But in my heart, Detective J. D. Duncan is my sweetie.

J.D. and I had only been a couple since Christmas, although we'd been friends since she arrived on the island about a year ago. She'd been a cop in Miami for a dozen years, rising to detective and finally to assistant homicide commander. Her mom had lived on Longboat Key and when she died, J.D. inherited her condo on the bay. J.D.'s patience with Miami crime had worn thin, and she was ready for a quieter life. Bill Lester, the Longboat Key chief of police, had jumped at the chance to hire her. She was tall, slender, and beautiful with dark hair worn shoulder length and emerald eyes that flashed with humor or anger, depending on the situation.

I opened the text message J.D. had forwarded to my computer. The photo showed a thin, attractive woman who appeared to be in her mid-thirties, sitting in a straight-back wooden chair in a bare room. Her dark hair was cut short and framed a pretty face. She was wearing jeans and a white tank top. She was not smiling, but did not seem distressed, just pensive. She was holding a copy of the *Sarasota Herald-Tribune* so that I could see the date. The headline was the one I'd read while drinking coffee on my patio that very morning. There was something written across the front page in large black ink, perhaps by a magic marker. It read, "Good morning Jed."

The woman in the picture was a complete stranger to me. I was pretty sure I'd never seen her. Maybe she was somebody J.D. had known in Miami during the years she had lived there. I had no idea who Jed was.

I saved the picture and checked my e-mail. It was mostly spam, but there was a short note from my lifelong best friend, Jock Algren, telling me that he was still in Europe. He'd finished his assignment and was taking a few days in Rome. He planned to fly straight to Sarasota this weekend without stopping at his home in Houston. He and Logan Hamilton, my friend who lived on the key, were entered in a golf tournament that started the next Monday at the Longboat Key Club. I didn't play, but they let me drive the beer cart.

CHAPTER THREE

I heard a car pull to a stop in front of my cottage, and a few minutes later J.D. came through the front door. She'd spent the night with me and left early for an appointment in Bradenton. I'd slept in and was dimly aware of a morning kiss on my forehead as she'd left. My first sight of her every morning was like a burst of light that warmed the cockles of my heart and today was no exception. Whatever cockles are.

"Good morning," she said, grinning. "You look kind of rough."

"Had a bad night. Didn't get a lot of sleep."

"Maybe I ought to spend more nights at my condo."

"Nah," I said. "I used to be a soldier. I'm tough. I can take it."

She laughed. "Did you get the picture?"

"Yes. I don't know the woman. Take a look."

J.D. peered at the picture on my monitor, studying it closely. Suddenly, the color drained out of her face, and I heard a sharp intake of breath. "My God, Matt. That's Katie Fredrickson."

"Should I know her?"

"She's dead."

"What are you talking about?"

"She died more than a year ago. At least we all thought she did."

"That's today's paper she's holding."

"I know."

"Who's Jed?" I asked.

"Me."

"I don't get it."

"Katie and I went to college together. When I was a sophomore, she was a freshman. We met during rush week when all the freshmen are taking a look at the fraternities and sororities. I was wearing a name tag and at first she thought the 'J.D.' read 'Jed.' She called me that all night, until somebody told her my name was J.D., not Jed. She pledged my sorority, and I became her big sister. Do you know what that means?"

"She became your protégé."

"Yes. I had to guide her through the pledge rituals and keep an eye on her. We became good friends. She called me 'Jed' as an inside joke. I think the message in the picture is to let me know that it's really her."

"Why do you think she's dead?"

"She married a law student from the University of Miami named Jim Fredrickson, and when he graduated, they moved to Sarasota. He went with one of the silk stocking firms and had made quite a name for himself representing big-time white-collar criminals. He'd also gotten pretty rich."

"I remember that story," I said. "Happened early last year. They lived in a big house on the bay south of downtown. He was murdered and his wife disappeared."

"That's it. It was in January. She and I had kept up with each other and, when I heard about the murder, I came over to Sarasota and met with the detective on the case. He opened up his file to me. Jim had been shot in the head at close range with a .22-caliber revolver. The medical examiner found the slug in his brain during the autopsy and the forensics people found the bullet casing in the living room. There was also a lot of blood that belonged to Katie."

"But no body."

"No. She was gone, but the medical examiner thought that the volume of blood she'd lost would make it unlikely that she survived."

"Any theories on why the killer would have taken her body?" I asked.

"None. It appeared that she'd been raped, so maybe the guy was just a weirdo."

"What made the cops think she'd been raped?"

"The crime-scene techs found vaginal fluid on the sofa and all that blood on the floor. Both belonged to Katie."

"Semen?"

"No. If there was a rape, the guy must have used a condom."

"I take it the rape is just speculation," I said.

"Yes. Without a body, the medical examiner said he couldn't make a finding of rape."

"Who was the Sarasota detective on the case?"

"It was run by Captain Doug McAllister, the chief of detectives at the Sarasota P.D. He's the one I met with when I first came over to look at the file. He took a personal interest in the case. Apparently he and Katie's husband were golfing buddies and McAllister took Jim's death hard."

"Nobody ever heard from Katie after the murder?"

"No. Not even her parents. That's the reason we think she's dead. She wouldn't have just disappeared. She was close to her parents and would never have put them through this."

"You're sure that's a picture of Katie?" I asked.

"Yes. Katie had long blonde hair and wasn't as thin as the woman in the picture. But hair dye is cheap and people can lose weight. Her face is Katie's, and she's the only one I know who would have reached out to me by calling me Jed."

"Where are her parents?"

"They live in the Orlando area, Winter Park. That's where Katie grew up."

"Maybe the parents have heard from her recently."

"I doubt it," J.D. said. "I talk to them every month or so, and the last time I called them they hadn't heard from her. I think they would have let me know if they had."

"You probably ought to get in contact with them."

"I'll call them tonight, but I don't want to tell them about the picture. I'll see if the phone company can tell me where the text originated."

"How would Katie have known your cell number?" I asked.

"It's the same number I've had for years. She would know it."

"If she's alive, why would she just now be getting in contact with you?"

"Good question. Maybe she was kidnapped and is just now able to make contact."

"Why would she contact you instead of the police?"

"I am the police."

"You've got a point. You want some lunch?"

"Sure, but let me get the phone company working on finding out where this text originated."

CHAPTER FOUR

During season, that time of the winter when the northerners flock to the island, the population of Longboat Key swells from about 2,500 people to 20,000. That makes having lunch out a dicey proposition. The restaurants are full to overflowing and there are always waiting lines. It's not a time for the casual diner. One has to be either ravenous or a bit crazy to join the throngs, wait in line, endure less-than-great service, and settle for food left too long in the warming pans.

We were neither crazy nor ravenous, so we stopped by Harry's Deli and got a couple of sandwiches, Diet Cokes, and potato chips and drove across the Longboat Pass Bridge to Coquina Beach. I pulled a couple of canvas beach chairs from the Explorer, and we sat on the sand bordering Longboat Pass and ate and watched the boats go by.

We were chatting when I heard a faint noise in the distance, a high-pitched warble that I realized was a siren. It caught J.D.'s attention as well, and she stopped talking in mid-sentence. The siren was growing louder, coming toward us from the Longboat side of the bridge.

"Wonder what's up," she said.

"Speeder?"

"Must be more than that. Speeders usually stop when the siren gets their attention."

The siren grew louder as it neared the bridge. We sat quietly waiting for whatever was coming. The bells on the bridge began to clang, warning motorists that the span was about to rise. A couple of cars came to a stop as the crossing gates came down blocking the travel lanes. We watched as a vehicle moving at a high rate of speed came around the slight curve just to the south of the bridge. It was a new Jaguar, traveling north toward Anna

Maria Island. As it approached the stopped cars, the driver moved into the southbound lane, never slowing. Suddenly, the driver hit the brakes, hard. He was past the line of cars, now between the first car and the rising span. He must have just figured out that the span was on its way up. I glanced at the channel that ran under the bridge. No boats. None waiting on the other side. The bridge tender was helping the cops, raising the span to stop whoever was in the Jaguar from leaving the island.

The Jaguar's tires were making that squeegee noise that comes with the hard application of disc brakes. The driver was in control, the car braking hard but staying on a straight-line course and within its lane. I was thinking he would not be able to stop before he hit the span when the noise from the braking tires stopped and the car accelerated. I heard the slight roar of the muffled engine and watched as the driver turned the steering wheel hard left. The car hit the curb that separated the vehicle lane from the bike and pedestrian path and went airborne, barely missing the bridge tender's shack. The Jag's undercarriage sliced off the top half of the bridge's concrete railing, taking it into the channel below. The car's trajectory took it a few feet from the bridge and into a flat landing in the water, where it briefly floated before beginning a nose-first descent toward the bottom. I knew this channel and knew that the water was about fifteen feet deep.

The cop car pursuing the Jaguar came to a stop behind the second car waiting for the drawbridge. I saw a uniformed officer throw open the driver's side door and run toward the breach in the railing. J.D. was on her feet, shucking her equipment belt.

"What're you doing?" I asked.

"I've got to get to that car. Maybe the guy's still alive."

I grabbed her arm. She shook loose. "No, J.D.," I said. "You've got an outgoing tide, a strong current, and that car's on the bottom with fifteen feet of water above it. You can't save him."

"I'm going to try."

"No," I said. "He's dead. Let's go to the bridge and see what's going on." I looked at her and saw challenge in her face. She didn't like a mere man telling her what to do. Then it was gone and she shrugged, picked up her equipment belt, and started for my car. I followed.

By the time we reached the road, there were several cars stopped in the southbound lanes. A Bradenton Beach police cruiser was coming to a stop on the berm just before the bridge. I parked behind the cop. The officer recognized us as we got out of my car and walked toward him. "Hi, J.D.," he said. "Matt."

"Hey, Ned," J.D. said. "Do you know what's going on?"

"Not much. We got a call from Longboat P.D. asking us to intercept a Jaguar coming our way. I guess the bridge was going up to block the car, but it looks like the Jag went into the water."

"Yeah," J.D. said. "We saw him go in. Looked like it might have been deliberate. I'll check in. Can you get these cars turned around and headed in the other direction? We'll have a crime scene on the bridge."

"No problem."

The cop turned and walked toward the stopped cars.

The people were not going to be happy. It was a long drive back across Anna Maria Island, over to Tamiami Trail, down to Sarasota and back to the southern end of Longboat Key.

J.D. made a phone call, talked for a minute, and hung up. She turned to me and said, "They're setting up on the other side of the bridge, sending people back the way they came. I told dispatch where I was and she said the bridge would be lowered in a few minutes and we can walk over and meet the Longboat guys."

"What's going on?" I asked.

"That was Steve Carey chasing the Jag. The driver shot and killed somebody down around mid-key. A witness saw him get in the car and called 911. Steve was just down the street when he got the call and started the pursuit."

CHAPTER FIVE

J.D. and I had walked across the lowered bridge span and were standing with a group of Longboat Key police officers and a very distressed bridge tender. Divers from the Manatee County Sheriff's office had been called and a wrecker was on its way.

"Do we have an ID on the victim?" J.D. asked Chief Bill Lester.

"A preliminary one," the chief said. "His name was Ken Goodlow, according to a woman who lives in the condo complex where he was killed. He was an elderly guy who lived in Cortez and had stopped by to see her. He was leaving when the shooter pulled into the parking lot and shot him in the head. We have a couple of officers on the scene waiting for the medical examiner and the forensics people."

"What about the witness?" J.D. asked. "Can she tell us any more about the victim?"

"The cops on the scene haven't talked to her in any detail. She's very upset and is with a neighbor."

"I need to get a statement from her while it's still fresh," said J.D.

"Go ahead," said Lester. "I don't think there's much you can do here until we get that car out of the drink."

"I was with Matt. His car's at the other end of the bridge. My car's at his house."

"Get one of the officers to drive you to your car," said the chief.

J.D. turned to me. "Will you be all right?"

"Sure. Go on. I'll stick around here until they clear the bridge."

"That'll take at least a couple of hours," said Lester. "We've got a wrecker coming over from the mainland to pull the car up on Coquina Beach. The crime-scene people are going to want to take a preliminary look at it before they haul it to the sheriff's garage. They also have a lot to do here on the bridge."

"You've got a lot of work ahead of you. I'll walk home. I can come back for my car when you reopen the bridge."

"We can drop you at home," said J.D.

"No, thanks. I'll stick around for a bit and see what happens. Call me when you finish."

"That might take a while." She and a cop walked toward the parked police cruisers, got into one, and backed down the bridge until they could turn around and head south to my cottage in the village.

The bridge tender had broadcast a warning to boats not to cross under the bridge and within a few minutes the Longboat Key Police boat and one from the Manatee Sheriff's Marine Unit were on the scene to quarantine the area around where the car had sunk into the channel.

A wrecker drove onto the beach and backed up as close to the water's edge as he dared. A police diver was in the water and attached a cable from the wrecker to the submerged car. I told Chief Lester that I was leaving, and he said he'd call me when the bridge reopened and I could come get my car.

I started walking south on the bridge, heading toward Longboat. The water in the pass was green and flat and dappled by the sun's reflection, its face rippled in places where fish broke the surface. Boats rode at anchor, their occupants drinking beer and watching the police activity, waiting patiently for something to happen. A cooling breeze blowing in from the Gulf brought a hint of winter and brine, reminding me that it was February and the water was cold.

I pulled my windbreaker a little tighter and walked past the police cars stopped in the northbound lane and stepped off the bridge and onto the bike path that bordered Gulf of Mexico Drive. Ten minutes later, I was at Tiny's Bar, a dimly lit tavern run by Susie Vaught, an island legend. She called the place "the best little bar in paradise," and it was.

I ducked inside, got the hug that Susie dispenses to all the regulars, and took a stool next to my buddy Logan Hamilton. "Starting early?" I asked.

"Indeed," said Logan.

"Did you have lunch?"

"I did. With my paramour, the beautiful and saintly Marie Philips."

"Sounds like you may have drunk your lunch."

"The bartender at the Mar Vista has a way with a Scotch bottle. Pours a bit heavy."

"And that suits you."

"It does."

Susie put a cold Miller Lite on the bar in front of me. "What brings you in here this time of day, Matt?"

"J.D. and I were having a picnic at Coquina Beach, down by the pass. A car went off the bridge, and the police have closed it to traffic. My car's on the other side. I was walking home."

"I guess that explains the sirens," said Susie.

"Steve Carey was chasing the guy who went off the bridge," I said. "They think he shot somebody at mid-key. J.D. went down there to interview a witness and get the investigation started."

"Did the guy make it out of the car?" asked Logan.

"No."

"That's good," said Logan. "Saves the taxpayers the cost of a trial."

"You're pretty cynical today," I said.

"I think Marie is about to dump me."

I was surprised at that. Marie was a wealthy woman who lived in a high-rise condo on the south end of the key. She and Logan had been together for more than a year, and it seemed to work for both of them. "Why?" I asked.

"Why is she about to dump me or why do I think she's about to dump me?" The precision of the nearly drunk mind.

"Why do you think she's about to dump you?"

"You know how women act when they start to pull away from you?"

I thought about that for a beat. "I guess so."

"They get kind of twitchy," Logan said.

"Twitchy?"

"You know. They don't always return your calls. You go out to dinner and they say good night at the door. No inviting you in to spend the night. That sort of thing."

"How long has this been going on?"

"Since yesterday."

"You might be jumping the gun, buddy. What do you think, Susie?"

She grinned. "Logan's full of crap, as usual."

Logan swished the ice in his glass, looked at it, and held it out to Susie. "One more."

Susie shook her head. "It's not even two o'clock, Logan, and you've already got a load on. Maybe you ought to let Matt take you home for a nap."

Logan chuckled. "I don't need no stinkin' nap."

"Logan," I said, changing the subject. "You hang out some over at Annie's. Do you know a man named Ken Goodlow?" Annie's was a bait-and-tackle shop on the bayfront at the mainland end of the Cortez Bridge. It had a tiny bar that sold beer and wine and provided a small menu that included some of the best hamburgers and fried clams in the area.

"Yeah. Neat old guy. Comes in for a beer most afternoons. Lived in Cortez all his life."

"He's the one who was shot."

"Dead?"

"Yeah."

"Damn," said Logan. "That's too bad. He had a lot of stories. He was a soldier back in World War II. Military police, I think. Worked the fishing boats when he came back after the war. When he got too old for the boats, he drove the water taxi until that went belly-up. His wife died years ago and he never got remarried. Used to say he was too ornery for any one woman to put up with."

"Sounds like an interesting guy," I said.

"Yeah. I hope the son of a bitch who shot him died a slow death in that car."

CHAPTER SIX

Ann Kuehnel was in her late seventies, tall and what one might call "stately." Her skin was lightly tanned and her face smooth, so smooth that J.D. suspected the hand of a skilled surgeon had molded it. Her upswept hair was a reddish-blonde, her dress expensive, her necklace diamond, her voice cultured. She stood in the doorway of a condo unit that cost several million dollars.

"Mrs. Kuehnel? I'm Detective J.D. Duncan."

"Please come in, Detective. This has been a terrible day."

J.D. was led into a large and exquisitely decorated room overlooking the Gulf of Mexico. A middle-aged woman was standing in the center of the room. "Detective Duncan," said Mrs. Kuehnel, "this is my neighbor, Cheryl Loeffler."

"Don't mind me, Detective," the woman said. "I was just leaving."

"Thanks for sticking around, Cheryl. I'll call you later," said Ann.

"Before you go, Ms. Loeffler," J.D. said, "can you tell me if you saw the shooting?"

"No, thank goodness, but I think I heard it."

"What did you hear?"

"Just a pop. I didn't think anything about it. Figured it was a car out on the road. When I heard sirens and saw the police cars pull into our lot, I came out to see what was going on and saw Ann talking to the police. We came back up here to wait for you."

"Thank you, Ms. Loeffler," said J.D., handing her a business card. "If you think of anything else, please call me."

"Certainly," said Cheryl. "Ann, call me if you need anything. I'll let myself out."

"Please, have a seat, Detective," said Mrs. Kuehnel. "Can I get you some iced tea or a glass of wine?"

"No, thank you. I'd like to ask you some questions about the shooting you saw."

"Of course. Ken Goodlow was a friend. I'll do anything I can to help."

"I understand he was visiting you."

"Yes."

"Have you known Mr. Goodlow long?"

"A few years."

"I don't mean to pry," said J.D., "but I have to ask you about your relationship."

"Oh, dear. There was no relationship. Not in the way you're implying."

J.D. smiled. "I didn't mean to imply anything, Mrs. Kuehnel."

"Well, then, I didn't mean to jump to conclusions. Ken was very much involved in the Cortez Historical Society. I met him some years ago because of my interest in local history."

"Do you know his family?"

"I don't think he had any. His wife died years ago and they never had any children. I think all his other relatives died out a long time ago."

"What about his friends?"

"I only know the ones involved with the historical society."

"What was your interest in Cortez?"

"My husband, God rest his soul, died ten years ago and left me more money than I'll ever be able to spend. I have a number of charitable causes and one of them is the Cortez Historical Society. Ken Goodlow was the president. He'd lived his whole life in the village, except for some time out for military service during World War II."

"So you give them money?"

"Yes. Not a lot, because they don't require much. I just do what I can to support their efforts to maintain the memories of a way of life that has just about disappeared from Florida."

"You mean the fishing?" asked J.D.

"Yes. The commercial fishing has pretty much died out. The net ban that took effect some years ago just about killed a whole way of life. Cortez may be the last village in the state that maintains itself with fishing. And the number of fishermen is declining every year. The old people are dying out and the young ones don't want anything to do with fishing for a living. Soon, Cortez will be just a dim memory. We need to make sure that memory survives."

"Do you know of anyone who would want to hurt Mr. Goodlow?"

Ann sighed and her eyes welled with tears. She wiped them away and said, "No. He was a sweet and harmless old man."

"Tell me what you saw," J.D. said, switching gears.

"Ken took the elevator downstairs, and I was standing on the balcony overlooking the parking lot watching him go. He was getting into his truck when the man in the Jaguar drove into the parking lot and said something to Ken. He walked over to the car, and the driver shot him in the forehead and took off."

"Did you notice from which direction he came on Gulf of Mexico Drive?"

She was quiet for a few moments, thinking. "No. In fact, I'm not even sure he came into the parking lot from that direction, from GMD."

"There's no other way to get in, is there?"

"No. As I think about it, he may have been parked in the lot when I first saw his car."

"Do you remember where he was parked?"

Ann was quiet again. "His car was moving when I first saw it. He was coming out of a parking space and driving toward Gulf of Mexico Drive when he stopped and called to Ken. I don't think I noticed which parking space he was in, but I think he was backed in, facing GMD. All he had to do when he saw Ken come out was drive forward. He just stopped, shot Ken, and drove off."

"What did you do after the shooting?"

"I had my cell phone in the pocket of my sweater and I immediately called 911 and asked for an ambulance. I told the operator about the man in the Jaguar and that he took off north on GMD. I heard a siren almost immediately. I guess it was the officer chasing the Jaguar. One of your young officers told me about the man going off the bridge."

"Can you describe the man in the Jaguar?"

"No. I didn't get much of a look at him. I don't think I saw anything except an arm coming out of the window."

"Why did Mr. Goodlow come to see you today?"

"He wanted to show me some snapshots he'd come across that were taken shortly after the war. They were of a group of young people, most of whom are dead now. I think Bud Jamison was the only one still alive."

"Do you know Mr. Jamison?"

"Oh, sure. He's involved in the history projects. He's lived in Cortez since the war. He and Ken Goodlow were the best of friends. Bud's going to take this hard."

"Do you have an address for Mr. Jamison?"

"No. But I can give you his phone number."

J.D. wrote the number in her notebook. "Can you think of any more friends of Mr. Goodlow who might be able to shed some light on his murder?"

"I'm sure he has a lot of friends in Cortez, but Bud Jamison will be able to tell you a lot more than I could."

"Did anyone know Mr. Goodlow was coming to visit you today?"

"I doubt it. He called a few minutes before he stopped by. Said he was in the neighborhood and had some old pictures he wanted to show me."

"Anything else you can think of that might help us?"

"No, but I'll call you if anything comes to mind."

J.D. thanked her and left. The medical examiner's van that had been in the parking lot when she arrived was gone. The crime-scene people were packing up, getting ready to leave. She walked over to one of them. "Hey, Loren," she said. "Find anything?"

"Hey, J.D. Just a casing from a nine millimeter. Probably from the slug that killed the old guy."

"Not much to go on."

"There's a security camera up there." He pointed to the corner of the building. "The manager gave us a disc with the footage from all day. We'll go through it. Never know what might turn up."

"I'll want to look at that as soon as possible."

"I'll make a duplicate and drop it by the station this afternoon."

"Did you find any photographs? Old ones?"

"Yeah. There was an envelope in the car that had some pictures in it. We left it there. The people back at the lab will have them."

"I'd like copies of those as soon as you can get them."

"Not a problem. I'll get some copies made and bring them with the surveillance CD."

"Thanks, Loren. See you later."

CHAPTER SEVEN

I declined another beer. I had missed my morning run, so I needed to get home, change, and jog my daily four miles on the beach. "You want to go run with me?" I asked Logan.

He looked at me as if I'd slipped a gear. Logan had recently retired from the financial services company he'd worked for since he graduated from college. He had made a lot of money, and, as he said, he'd never wasted it on a wife or kids. He was young for retirement, but so was I, and maybe that's what made us such good friends. Logan stood about five feet ten and had lost most of his hair. What was left had turned white, so he looked older than he was. He had gained some weight since he gave up working for a living and, if he wasn't careful, he would become one of those retirees who did nothing but drink and watch television. I was worried that he was drinking too much, but he seemed to have a large capacity for alcohol and he was never a sloppy drunk.

"You go ahead," he said with a grin. "I'll catch up."

"Right."

The door to the parking lot opened, letting in light and a little fresh air and Cracker Dix. He greeted us in his English accent, took a stool, and ordered a glass of white wine. "Matt," he said, "you're here a bit early. What's up? J.D. dump you?"

"Not yet, Cracker. I just stopped in to rescue Logan."

"It'll happen," Logan said.

"What'll happen?" asked Cracker.

"J.D. will dump Matt's sorry ass. Soon, probably."

"Ah," said Cracker, "a match made in paradise. Can't go wrong."

"You hear about the mess on the bridge?" Susie asked.

"Yes," said Cracker. "I also heard that the asshole who went off the bridge killed old Ken Goodlow." News travels fast on our small island.

"Did you know Goodlow?" I asked.

"Yeah. I met him when I first came to the island. Used to drink with him over in Cortez. He got me a job on one of the boats that used to work out of the fish houses over there."

"I didn't know you worked the boats," I said.

"Sure did. Lasted one whole day. Wouldn't have been that long if the captain hadn't refused to bring me in early."

Cracker Dix was an expatriate Englishman who had lived on Longboat Key for thirty years without losing his English accent. He was in his late fifties, bald as a cue ball, and dressed, as usual, in a Hawaiian shirt, cargo shorts, flip-flops, and a single-strand gold necklace. He had a gold stud in his right earlobe and an IQ that rested somewhere in the stratosphere.

"Any idea who'd want to kill him?" I asked.

"None. Everybody liked the old codger."

"Did he have a family?"

"No. His wife died some years ago and they never had kids. The closest thing he had to family was Bud Jamison. Those guys were tighter than a virgin's—"

"Don't say it," interrupted Susie.

Cracker grinned. "Well, you get my meaning."

"We all got it," said Susie.

"Anyway," said Cracker, "they've been buds since World War II."

"Is Jamison married?" I asked.

"No. I think he was once, years ago, but his wife died before I met him."

"I'll pass this on to J.D.," I said. "She'll probably want to interview him."

"She probably already knows," said Cracker. "Everybody in Cortez knew those guys were close. But, there was something that happened two or three years back."

"Like what?" I asked.

"Don't know."

"Then what makes you think something happened?"

"Back then, there were still several of the old guys left, and they had coffee every morning at the Cortez Café. I was seeing a woman who lived nearby and when I'd spend the night with her, when her husband was traveling, I'd join the old guys for coffee."

"Cracker," Logan said, "did you ever have a woman who wasn't married?"

Cracker was quiet for a moment, thinking. "A couple," he said finally. "But you know, they get all clingy, want to spend all their time with you. It's smothering. Married women are more appreciative and are not unhappy to see me leave in the morning."

"So," I said, "you were having coffee with the old gentlemen."

"Yeah, and they loved to talk about the old days, back when fishing was a real industry. They were a pretty tight-knit group. One day I stopped by and they weren't there. I didn't think much of it until a few days later when I went in again. Their table was empty. I asked the waitress about them, and she said they'd just stopped coming in. She didn't know why."

"Did you ever find out why they stopped? Did they start going somewhere else?"

"Never did find out, but there's no place else nearby for them to have coffee. I think they just gave up their morning ritual."

"Did you ever see any of the guys again?" I asked.

"Sure. I'd have a drink occasionally with Ken and sometimes Bud would be with him. I asked about the coffee klatches, and they just gave me some vague answer."

"Did you ever see any of the other men?"

"No. They started dying off. Both of them and they died within a year."

"Natural causes?"

"I think so, but actually I never heard. Maybe I just assumed they were natural deaths."

"Do you remember the names of the other two?"

"Not offhand, but I probably wrote them down in my journal."

I was surprised. "You keep a journal?" I asked.

"Sporadically."

"I'm not sure I get the significance of keeping a journal sporadically. Isn't a journal like a diary?"

"Exactly like a diary."

"Then wouldn't you want to keep it up on a daily basis?"

"I do that during the times that I keep it."

"I'm not following you, Cracker."

"It's my love journal."

"What the hell are you talking about?" Logan asked. He'd been listening intently.

"It's like this. When I'm wooing a new woman, I like to keep a record of the relationship. I can go back years later and read about it and enjoy the affair all over again."

"Got any pictures?" asked Logan.

"You're a pervert," said Cracker.

"I'm not the one keeping a record of my conquests," said Logan.

"If you did, you could have written the whole thing on a napkin," said Cracker.

"Sadly," said Logan, "there's truth in that statement."

The conversation moved on to island gossip, and I gave in and ordered another beer. There'd be no run on the beach that afternoon. A couple more of the locals came in, ordered drinks, and joined the group. The afternoon wore on, friends enjoying a lazy day of drinking and talking. About the time I finished my third beer, J.D. called.

"Are you at home?" she asked.

"No. I'm at Tiny's. Are you finished for the day?"

"No. I've got to stop by the station and then I'm going over to Cortez to interview one of the victim's friends."

"Bud Jamison?"

"Geez," she said. "Tiny's telegraph."

It was an old joke. Tiny's was the gossip center for the north end of the key. Somebody had once described the place as the north-end clubhouse, and I guess it was. Secrets are hard to keep on a small island, and gossip was the lifeblood of our little community of year-rounders, those of us who did not flee north with the coming of summer's humidity.

"Yeah," I said, "Cracker was filling me in a little. He knew the victim."

"If you're going to be there for a while, I'll stop by when I finish up in Cortez."

"No. I've had three beers. Time for me to go. Come on by the house."

"See you then," she said.

I paid my tab, said my good-byes, and walked out into the late afternoon. There was a slight chill in the air, a precursor of the cold that would envelope the island during the night. It would be a good evening for a fire in the fireplace, and a bottle of wine with my sweetie. My phone rang. Bill Lester calling to tell me the bridge had been cleared and I could come get my Explorer. I turned around and retraced my steps to the end of the island.

CHAPTER EIGHT

By the time J.D. drove north to Anna Maria Island, the bridge had been cleared and Matt's Explorer was gone. She turned east onto Cortez Road and crossed the Cortez Bridge. The village of Cortez perches at the eastern end of the bridge, abutting Sarasota Bay. It boasts a Coast Guard station, a couple of working fish houses where the boats sell their catch, and two boatyards that can repair everything from expensive yachts to ancient diesels that power some of the older fishing boats. The narrow streets are paved with crumbling asphalt and bordered by small houses, most of which were built before World War II. The people who live here work hard, take care of their families, and mostly ignore the wealthy people who populate the islands at the other end of the bridge.

J.D. turned off Cortez Road onto 123rd Street, following the directions Bud Jamison had given her on the phone. She found his small house nestled under a stand of trees next to one of the boatyards. A twenty-year-old Chevrolet sedan, with a current sticker attached to the license plate, was parked in a carport abutting the house.

An elderly man met her at the door. He was tall and lean and stood erect. He had a head full of iron-gray hair, clear blue eyes, and a small scar high on his left cheek. His face had the weathered look of a man who had spent years at sea.

"Detective Duncan, I presume. I'm Bud Jamison. Please come in."

J.D. followed the old man into a living room. He had a noticeable limp, perhaps an injury of some sort to his right leg. He motioned her to a seat on an old leather sofa. He took a chair across from her. "What brings you to this little village?" he asked.

"I'm afraid I've brought some bad news. Ken Goodlow was killed today. I'm sorry."

A look of pain crossed the man's face. He put his hand to his forehead and sighed, pushing the pain away, J.D. thought. She watched him as he composed himself, mentally shaking off the bad news.

"How did he die?"

"Murdered," said J.D. "Shot at close range by a man driving a Jaguar."

Jamison sat quietly for a few moments, as if trying to digest the fact that his friend had been murdered. Finally, he shook his head. "Do you know who the man was?"

"Not yet, but he drove his car off the Longboat Pass Bridge. He's dead and, as soon as the techies get finished with the car, we'll get some fingerprints and figure out who he is."

The old man sighed. "I've lived too long, Detective. I'm the last one."

"Last one of what, Mr. Jamison?" J.D. asked kindly.

"The last of the young men who came back from the war and went to work on the boats. We fished for our living, a hard life, but a good one. The work was honest and it paid the bills. Men could take care of their families, raise their children, love their women. It was a good life."

"Were you in the war, Mr. Jamison?"

"No. I was Four-F, medically disabled. I'd injured my leg in a motorcycle accident before the war, and the military wouldn't take me. I came here in 1942 and found a job with old Captain Dan Longstreet. He's been dead for years now. There weren't many young men around to do the jobs then. They were all off fighting or training and getting ready to fight."

"Where did you come here from?"

"Washington, D.C."

"Why here?"

"No particular reason. My parents had died and the military wouldn't take me, so I came to Florida. I was the only child and I had sold their house, so I had a little cash. I thought I'd travel a bit and then try college or find a job. I was in Tampa and running low on funds, and somebody told me that there were jobs available in Cortez. I got a job and stayed."

"How did you come to know Mr. Goodlow?"

"He came back from the war and went to work on Captain Long-street's boat. We became good friends and that friendship lasted until today. Almost a lifetime. An entire lifetime for him, I guess."

"Do you know anyone who would want to hurt him?"

"No." But he said it too quickly or too emphatically or too something. J.D. caught it, even if she didn't know quite what it was. Something just didn't ring true. The old man was lying, but she'd let it go for now. Try to figure it out later.

"Does Mr. Goodlow have any family here?"

"No. His wife died some years ago and they never had any children. He had a brother, but he was lost at sea not too long after the war. He had a couple of cousins, but they died years back."

"What do you know about his work with the historical society?"

"Wasn't much to it. We both volunteered at the museum, recorded oral histories of some of the older folks around here. Ken and I recorded our own histories."

"Do you know anything about some photographs he was taking to show Ann Kuehnel?"

"I suppose you're talking about the old pictures he found in a trunk in his attic. Taken in the late forties. Those the ones?"

"Yes. Mrs. Kuehnel told me that Mr. Goodlow had stopped by her condo to show them to her."

"Yeah. I'm pretty sure those are the same ones he showed me yesterday. He was real excited about the find. They were black-and-white and taken with an old Brownie box camera that somebody had. I remember the day they were taken."

"Was there any significance to the photos?"

"What do you mean?"

"Anything that would make somebody want to kill Mr. Goodlow?"

"I can't imagine that to be the case. They were just pictures of a bunch of us at a fish fry here in the village. I think it was a Fourth of July celebration, probably 1948. We were all young, late twenties and early thirties. Just folks having a good time and not even thinking that someday life would end. Now they're all gone. Except me."

"When's the last time you saw Mr. Goodlow?"

"This morning. We had coffee over at the café."

"Did he say anything about going to Longboat?"

"Yes. He had some business over there and if he had time he was planning to stop by and show Ann the pictures. He wanted them to go to the museum, and Ann was putting together an exhibit of pictures taken here over the years. He thought she could use some of them in the display."

"What kind of business did he have on Longboat?"

"He was going to try to see a lawyer. A man named Royal."

"Matt Royal?" J.D. registered surprise.

"Yes. Do you know him?"

"I do. Do you know what that was all about?"

"No. Ken didn't say." There it was again. Some shadow passing over the old man's face or maybe a slight change in his eyes. J.D. couldn't place it, but she knew she'd just been lied to again.

"Did Mr. Goodlow know Matt Royal?" she asked.

"I don't think so. Royal was recommended to him by the bartender over at the Seafood Shack. Nick Field."

"Did Mr. Goodlow have an appointment with Royal?"

"I don't think so. Ken said he couldn't talk about anything on the phone, and Nick told him how to get to Royal's house. I think he was just going to stop in and try to see him."

"Did he mention to you that he was having trouble with anybody?"

"No. Ken got along with everybody."

"Would you mind if I asked you a couple of personal questions?"

The old man smiled. "Don't mind at all. I might not answer them, but you can ask away."

"Is Bud your real name?"

"No, but I've been called that most of my life. My real name is John, no middle name."

"Have you ever been married?"

"Yes. Once. My wife died many years ago."

"Any children?"

"A daughter, but she died, too."

"I'm sorry for your loss."

"Thank you."

J.D. stood. "Thank you for your time, Mr. Jamison. I'm sorry I had to bring you such bad news." She handed him a business card. "Would you call me if you think of anything that might help me solve Mr. Goodlow's murder?"

The old man stood. "I thought you had the guy who did it. The one who went off the bridge."

"We've got him, but this doesn't feel like just a random shooting. I want to know why someone would want Mr. Goodlow dead. I want to know if anybody else is involved." She was staring him squarely in the eyes, waiting for a reaction, any reaction, to her statement. There was a slight tightening around Jamison's mouth, nothing more. Did that mean anything? Probably not, she decided.

As she drove away, J.D. glanced into her rearview mirror. The old man was standing stock-still on his front stoop, staring at her, his face as blank as an overcast sky. A black Toyota Corolla pulled out of a parking space in front of the neighboring boatyard and, unnoticed by J. D., followed her as she drove toward Cortez Road.

CHAPTER NINE

J.D. drove across Cortez Road and into the parking lot of the Seafood Shack. She walked down the dock and entered the restaurant overlooking the bay. Nick Field was behind the bar polishing glassware. It was not yet five o'clock and there were no customers.

"J.D.," said Nick, "long time, no see."

She took one of the empty stools and said, "You know how Matt is. Hard to get him off the key."

Nick laughed. "That's for sure. I spent my whole life trying to figure a way off that island." Nick had been born and raised on Longboat Key and had spent most of his adulthood there. He knew almost everybody on either side of the bay. He was an affable sort, now in his early fifties. "What can I get you?" he asked.

"Nothing, thanks. I'm still working."

"That sounds a bit ominous. What brings you across the bridge?"

"Did you know Ken Goodlow?"

"Sure. He's one of my regulars."

"I'm sorry to tell you, Nick, but Ken was killed on Longboat earlier this afternoon."

"Crap. He was a good guy. Been here all his life. He and my dad used to hang out together. I've known him ever since I can remember. I tried to get him to give up driving. He wasn't real steady anymore. Did he hurt anybody?"

"It wasn't a car wreck, Nick. Somebody shot him."

"You're kidding. Who the hell would want to hurt that old man?"

"I've just come from Bud Jamison's house," J.D. said. "He's taking it pretty hard. He told me you had suggested that Mr. Goodlow go see Matt about some kind of legal problem."

"Yeah. A couple of days ago. Ken told me he had a legal problem and asked if I knew a lawyer who worked cheap. He didn't have much money, but he said he needed help. I know Matt helps out some of the islanders when they need a lawyer and can't afford it. I thought he might be able to help Ken."

"Was there anybody else in the bar when you talked about the lawyer?"

"Yeah. There were three or four. I remember Devlon and Mynu Buckner were here. Do you know them?"

"I don't think so," said J.D.

"They used to live in Sarasota. They're both pharmacists up in the Tampa area now, but they come down for dinner every few weeks. They were on the other side of the bar and probably wouldn't have heard anything. A couple of men I'd never seen before were also here. They might have heard something."

"Do you know what kind of problem Mr. Goodlow had?"

"No. I pried a little, but he wouldn't say anything. Said he needed to talk to somebody who couldn't pass on what Ken knew. Said he didn't want me to get in the line of fire, whatever that meant. I gave him Matt's number, but he said he couldn't talk to him over the phone. He was afraid somebody had bugged his line. I told him where Matt lives."

"Do you know of anybody who'd want to hurt Mr. Goodlow?"

"I sure don't. I hope you get the bastard who shot him."

"We already have him. He drove off the Longboat Pass Bridge right after the shooting. We'll know who he is as soon as we get his prints from the medical examiner."

"Did Ken ever talk to Matt?" Nick asked.

"I don't think so. Matt didn't mention it to me. Bud Jamison said Ken was going to Longboat today to try to see Matt. I don't think he ever made it."

"It's a damn shame," said Nick. "Ken was one of the good guys."

J.D. got off the stool and started for the door. "Call me if you hear anything, Nick."

"I will. You take care."

J.D. drove west across the Cortez Bridge and into the setting sun, a big orange ball just beginning to disappear into the Gulf of Mexico. She smiled, thinking about Matt who was still as excited by the sunsets as the newest tourist. She wondered if he was at home or down at the Hilton watching the day end. She'd call him as soon as she made a stop at the police station.

As she turned south on Gulf Drive, her phone rang. Martin Sharkey, her deputy chief. She answered. "Tell me we've got an ID on the shooter," she said.

"Afraid not," said Sharkey. "His prints aren't in the system."

"What about the car?"

"Stolen yesterday in Sarasota."

"Dead end. Did you find the weapon used in the shooting?"

"We found a .22-caliber pistol on the floorboard on the passenger side. Untraceable. The serial number was filed off. Ballistics will run it to make sure it was the murder weapon, and we'll put it in the federal database. See if anything turns up."

"Nothing on the car or the weapon?"

"No, but we found a bunch of documents in the trunk. They were in a waterproof briefcase, so they're in good shape."

"Did they give us any leads?"

"Don't know yet. We're going to have to have them translated."

"Translated? From what?"

"German. And get this, some of them are in Arabic."

CHAPTER TEN

It was dark when J.D. called from the police station. "I'm about done," she said. "I'm finishing up a report on what I did today. Got to keep the files current, you know." She chuckled ironically.

The files were one of her least favorite things about police work. The paperwork was important, but it took a lot of time that she thought could be better spent on the investigation. On the other hand, she understood the importance of getting the day's information into writing while it was still fresh in her mind.

"You need a secretary."

"Yeah, right. The chief will probably put that in next year's budget if I ask nicely."

"Do you want to meet somewhere for dinner?"

"Are you at the house?"

"Yes."

"You got any food there?"

"A couple of steaks, some salad, and garlic bread in the freezer."

"Wine?"

"Sure."

"Feel like grilling?"

"Sure."

"I'll be there in ten minutes."

"Sure."

"I love you."

"Sure. You'll say anything for a finely grilled steak."

"Sure," she said, and hung up.

• • •

Dinner was a quiet affair, devoid of any talk of murder and loss. My sweetie wanted some downtime, she said, and would tell me about her day after dinner. I'd grilled the steaks on the patio, wrapped up in an old sweatshirt to ward off the cold wind that was blowing down the bay. J.D. kept me company, sipping wine and talking about unimportant things. When the steaks were nearly done, she tossed the salad and sliced the garlic bread that had been warming in the oven. We ate and talked and then cleared the dishes and sat by the fire I'd built in the fireplace, letting the warmth of the room lull us into a state of near lethargy. We were on the sofa and she was snuggled into the crook of my arm, her head resting on my shoulder.

J.D. stirred, picked up her wine glass, and disengaged herself from me. "I need more wine," she said and padded barefoot toward the kitchen. "You ready for another beer?"

I nodded. When she returned, she handed me a cold can of Miller Lite and took the chair across from me. "I want to bring you up to date on my investigation and get your feel for what's going on."

"You can't do that from over here?"

"If I stay over there on the sofa with you, we'll end up doing something other than talking."

"Is that bad?"

"No. That's good. Maybe later."

"Maybe?"

"Well, probably."

"I can live with that."

She smiled. "Did you know that Ken Goodlow was trying to meet with you?"

"No. I don't think I'd ever heard the guy's name until today. What's that all about?"

"I talked to Bud Jamison this afternoon. He told me that Nick Field had given Goodlow your name to handle some kind of legal problem. Nick confirmed that. Said Goodlow didn't have much money and needed a cheap lawyer."

"Inexpensive," I said. "Not cheap."

"Well, anyway, Jamison said Goodlow didn't want to talk to you by phone because he thought there might be a listening device on his line. He was just going to show up at your door. That's apparently the reason he came to Longboat today."

"I never saw him," I said. "If he came, it must have been after we left for our picnic."

"Maybe he was planning to stop by after he saw Ann Kuehnel."

"I guess we'll never know. Did you get anything from the other witnesses?"

She told me about her meetings with Ann and Jamison. "I think Jamison was lying to me about not knowing anybody who would want to hurt Goodlow."

"Why do you think that?"

"Just a feeling. Cop's intuition, I guess. That's what my gut was telling me."

"Then you're probably right. But why would he lie to you?"

"The answer to that question may be the key to solving this case. I've got a CD of the pictures Goodlow took to show Mrs. Kuehnel and another of the security camera at the condo where he was killed. Can we take a look?"

I booted up my computer and put the first disc into the drive. It was a black-and-white clip from the security camera. "The time stamp puts the start of this about an hour before the shooting," she said. "I told the forensic guy to give me one hour on either side of the murder. The time stamp will give us an exact time of the murder."

"Are you looking for anything specific?"

"I want to know when Mr. Goodlow and the Jag came into the parking lot."

"What kind of car was Goodlow driving?" I asked.

"An old pickup truck. A red Ford, probably ten years old."

I fast-forwarded the video until we saw the truck enter the lot. "There we are," I said, and slowed the CD. We watched as an elderly man got out of the truck and went into the building.

"The time stamp puts that about thirty minutes before the shooting. Run it forward some more."

Ten minutes later, according to the time stamp, the Jaguar pulled into the lot. The driver found a parking space directly across from Goodlow's truck, backed in, and sat. Ten minutes later, a man in a T-shirt, shorts, and flip-flops came out of the building and talked to the man in the Jaguar, got into a black Acura SUV that was parked in the lot, and left.

"Who was that?" I asked.

"I don't know. Might be a resident. Can you get a better look at him?"

I fiddled with the mouse and isolated the best view we had of the man in flip-flops. I enlarged it until it started to blur, backed off a bit, and then homed in until I had a reasonably decent picture of the man. I printed two copies.

"Can you get another of his car?" asked J.D.

I repeated the process and isolated a picture of the car. I manipulated it some more and it began to blur. "I can't get the license plate. The camera's resolution isn't good enough."

"If the guy's a resident, it shouldn't be a problem. There're only about ten units in that complex."

"Even if he was a visitor, you should be able to get an ID from the other owners. I wonder why he didn't come forward and let you know that he had talked to the man?"

"Maybe he was gone for the afternoon. I'll follow up tomorrow. I'll find him."

We watched some more and finally came to the shooting itself. Goodlow came out of the building and walked to his truck. The Jag started to move out of its parking space. It drove toward Goodlow and stopped. The driver's side window glided down, and the man behind the wheel leaned his head partially out. Goodlow turned, as if the man in the Jag had said something that caught his attention. We watched the old man toss an envelope through the open window of his truck and walk toward the Jaguar. As he got close, the man in the Jag raised a pistol and shot Goodlow in the forehead. The old man fell to the pavement, and the Jag sped out of the lot, turning north onto Gulf of Mexico Drive.

I put the other CD into the drive and pulled up a page containing a dozen thumbnail pictures. They were black-and-white and showed several young men and women at a party on a bayside beach. I clicked on the first picture and blew it up to full-screen size. There were three men and three women dressed in summer clothes sitting at a picnic table eating from plates heaped with what appeared to be fried fish. They were smiling and looking into the camera. Another group of people was in the background, huddled around a brick-bordered fire pit. A large pot was suspended over a fire and a man was stirring it with an oar that had likely come from one of the small Jon boats beached nearby.

"Do you see anybody that looks familiar?" I asked.

"No, but I wouldn't expect to. Look at their clothes and that car in the background. A long time ago. Ann Kuehnel said Goodlow told her these were taken soon after World War II. Those people are all either dead or very old now. Bud Jamison said he thought they were from a July Fourth picnic in 1948. He can probably tell us who they are, but I don't see how they would be important. I doubt they had anything to do with Goodlow's death. They're just pictures of dead people."

"It's kind of sad, isn't it?" I asked.

"What?"

"The people in these pictures were all young and had most of their lives ahead of them. They were happy and enjoying a day on the water. The camera caught them in an instant in time, one very minute portion of their entire lives. And yet, here we are, in a sense reliving that very second that happened well before we were born. I wonder how their lives turned out, what kind of joy or hurt they experienced before their lives ran their courses."

"Yeah. Life doesn't last very long, does it?" she said. "Let's look at the rest of the pictures."

I scrolled through the remaining photos. They were all of the same group, maybe twelve or fourteen in all, an equal number of men and women. The shadows cast by the trees in some of the photos indicated they were taken in late afternoon. J.D. didn't see anything that seemed to have any significance to Goodlow's murder. I put the CDs back in their plastic cases and put my computer in sleep mode.

"Did you hear anything from the phone company about the picture you got this morning?" I asked.

"Yes. It's confusing. The photo was sent from a disposable phone in Detroit, but there's no record of that phone receiving any text messages.

The phone was only activated this morning and the only thing it was used for was to send me that one text."

I chewed on that for a couple of beats. "That can be explained if the picture was taken with a camera in the phone."

"That was a real cheapie bought in Atlanta. It didn't have a camera," she said.

"Then the picture would have to have been uploaded from a computer or another phone."

"But what's Katie doing in Detroit?"

"If that was Katie."

"It was her," J.D. said.

"There are a number of computer programs that could have put that picture together so that it looked like Katie. They could have easily inserted a copy of today's paper into the picture."

"I know. But what about the message? Nobody would know about her calling me Jed."

"Your sorority sisters would, wouldn't they?"

J.D. frowned. "I guess. And maybe some other people we knew back then, but somebody would have to go to a lot of trouble to figure that out."

"Maybe not, if the person was still friendly with Katie."

"Why would somebody go to all that trouble to send me that picture? It doesn't make sense."

"I agree. We need to know a lot more than we do now."

"Matt, would you be up to doing me a big favor?"

"Of course."

"Would you go to Orlando tomorrow and meet with Katie's parents? I've got too much on my plate with this murder to be going out of town, and I want to get to the bottom of this thing with Katie. If that picture wasn't just somebody's bad idea of a joke, she needs me."

"I'll be glad to go. You ready for bed?"

"Yes. You need a good night's sleep."

"Well, that, too."

CHAPTER ELEVEN

The drive to Orlando on Wednesday morning was boring, mile after mile of interstate highway. J.D. had called Katie's parents, George and Betty Bass, before I left. They were expecting me shortly after lunch.

Orlando traffic is a testament to poor planning. Interstate 4 winds through several sharp curves as it approaches the city, the result of politicians' insistence fifty years before that the highway come through downtown. The curves slow traffic between the giant attractions such as Disney World and Universal Studios and the city center. Add fifty-two million tourists every year to the mix of harried commuters and you get chaos. I timed my trip to miss the worst of it and pulled into downtown Orlando two hours after leaving Longboat Key.

I ate a quick lunch at the Wall Street Cantina, a restaurant I had frequented when I practiced law in the city, and then headed for the upscale suburb of Winter Park. The Basses lived on a tree-shaded brick street near the Rollins College campus in an old house that had been refurbished and modernized. The neighborhood was expensive and quiet and exuded an air of gentility.

I was greeted at the door by a tall, thin man with gray hair, a large Adam's apple and a patrician nose. He appeared to be in his mid-sixties and had kept in good shape. He invited me in, and I followed him to the back of the house to a room that that was mostly glass. It was shaded by the overhanging oak trees and looked out over a garden filled with azalea bushes. They would bloom soon and bring, for a short time, a blast of color that would overwhelm the senses.

Betty Bass was sitting on a sofa, sipping from a glass of iced tea. She stood and shook my hand. She was a petite woman with a pretty face just developing the lines that would soon give away her age. She had dark hair going to gray that she wore just short of shoulder length. "May I get you a glass of tea, Mr. Royal?" she asked. I declined and took a seat in a chair facing the sofa. George sat beside his wife.

I smiled. "I guess you're wondering why I'm here."

Betty returned the smile. "When J.D. called this morning, she said you were a lawyer and a friend of hers and that you were looking into Katie's case."

George said, "I don't think we ever met, Mr. Royal, but I knew you by reputation. I was a stockbroker in Winter Park before my retirement."

"I don't know if that's good or bad, Mr. Bass," I said. "My reputation, that is."

He laughed. "Your reputation was sterling. An outstanding trial lawyer and an honorable man."

"Thank you for that," I said.

"Mr. Royal," George said, "Betty and I only had one child. Katie was the light of our lives. When she disappeared, I didn't think we would survive. We have, but it's been tough. I think it'd be easier if we knew she was dead, if we could find a body and put her to rest. We've given up on finding her alive."

"Mr. Bass," I said, "I don't want to give you any false hope. I don't have any idea that Katie is alive. Since J.D. joined the Longboat Key Police Department, she is perhaps in a better position to investigate Katie's case. She's in the area where it all happened. She can follow up on what the Sarasota Police may have given up on. What she'd like to do is find out what happened to Katie and who murdered her husband."

"What's your interest in this?" asked George.

"J.D. asked me to help."

"That's it?" George asked. "Why would a detective ask a retired lawyer for help?"

I held it for a beat, trying to decide how to answer. It was a reasonable question. "J.D. and I are more than friends," I said finally.

Betty grinned. "I thought so. There was something in J.D.'s voice when she talked about you."

George said, "She's a sweetheart. She's kept in touch with us over the years. Checks in regularly."

42 H. TERRELL GRIFFIN

"Mr. Bass," I said, "I know you've been asked some of these questions a thousand times, but I'd like to go over some things, if you'll indulge me."

Both Basses nodded.

"Okay," I said. "Have you heard anything from the Sarasota Police in the past year?"

"Captain McAllister calls every couple of months," George said. "He never has anything new to tell us. He mostly wants to know if we've heard from Katie."

I was surprised at that. "Has he said that he thinks Katie's alive?"

"No," said George. "He says he's just covering the bases. Since they never found her body, he wants to make sure she hasn't turned up somewhere and contacted us."

"Did you know Captain McAllister before Katie's disappearance?"

"Not really," said Betty. "We had heard his name because he was a friend of Katie's husband, Jim. But that was just in passing. We didn't know much about him. I don't think we even realized he was a policeman."

"Were you and Katie close?" I asked.

"Yes," said Betty. "We talked by phone a couple of times a week and she visited us regularly or we went to see her in Sarasota."

"When was the last time you talked?"

Betty was quiet for a moment and then shook her head. "A week before the incident. That's what George and I call it. The incident."

"Phone call?" I asked.

"No. She drove over to visit. She stayed the night."

"Anything unusual about the visit?"

"No. Nothing. She seemed a little stressed out, but that was about it."

"How long did she stay?" I asked.

"Just the one night. She came over late in the afternoon, watched some television with us, and went to bed early. I made breakfast for all of us and then had to go to my regular shift at the hospital."

"You work at the hospital?"

"I volunteer four hours a week. I'm a pink lady. I work in the gift shop."

"How was she when you got home?"

"Oh, she'd already left for Sarasota. She told George she had to get back because she and Jim were leaving on a cruise. Said she'd call when they got home. I never heard from her again."

"Did you ever hear about anybody who wanted to hurt either Jim or Katie?" I asked. "Anybody mad at them or that they'd had a spat with?"

"No," said George. "Of course, Katie probably wouldn't have mentioned anything like that to us. Not unless she thought she or Jim were in danger. She didn't like to worry us."

"Where is Jim's family?" I asked.

"There isn't one," said George. "His parents died while he was in college, and he didn't have any siblings."

"What about their friends in Sarasota?" I asked. "Do you know who they were?"

"No," said George. "I think they socialized a lot with other members of the law firm. They probably had other friends, but I don't think we ever met any of them."

"How often would you go to Sarasota to visit Katie?"

"Not often," said Betty. "Maybe a couple times a year. She usually came here."

"You never met any of her friends when you were visiting?"

"No," said George. "Normally, we'd drive over one day, spend the night, and come back the next day."

"How did the marriage seem to you?" I asked.

"Good," said Betty.

"I'm not so sure about that," said George.

Betty turned to him, a look of consternation on her face. "Now George, you don't have any basis for that opinion."

"You're right, honey. It's just a feeling, but I think there were some problems that Katie never mentioned to us."

"What makes you think that, Mr. Bass?" I asked.

"I'm not sure. She just didn't seem happy. There's nothing tangible I can put my finger on."

"I think it was just the normal ups and downs of marriage," said Betty.

"It was more than that," said George. "I think maybe she was being abused."

"George," said Betty, anger tingeing her voice. "Jim would never have hurt Katie."

"I don't mean physical abuse," said George. "But Jim was an intense guy. I think he was pretty controlling. Katie wanted children, but Jim wouldn't have anything to do with that. Wouldn't even discuss it."

"He worked hard," said Betty. "His job put a lot of pressure on him. If the marriage was as bad as you think, George, Katie would have divorced him."

"Maybe not," George said. "Katie would have seen that as a failure. And, more importantly, she would have thought that we would have seen it as a failure. She never wanted to disappoint us."

I changed the subject. "Did Jim's parents leave him any money?"

"No," said George. "They had a small citrus operation over near Avon Park, but I don't think it amounted to much. They made enough to live on, and that was about it. Jim went to college and law school on scholarships."

"Were they growers?" I asked.

"In a small way," George said. "They owned a grove, but I heard from someone that it wasn't very productive. Jim inherited it when his parents died, and he had some people running it, but I'm sure it didn't bring in much income. A hurricane came through there several years ago and took out most of the trees. The land must have had some value because Jim sold it just before he died."

"Who stands to inherit Jim's estate?" I asked.

"Jim's will left everything to Katie, and if she didn't survive him, it would come to us. I hired a lawyer over in Sarasota to probate the will and everything's just sitting there. Jim had named a lawyer in his firm to be the executor, and he sold the house. Turned everything into cash in accordance with the will. Now the cash just sits in a bank until there is some determination that Katie is dead. I guess we'll get it sooner or later, but we're going to give it to charity. Maybe set up a scholarship in Katie's name."

"Do you know how much cash there is?" I asked.

"Something over twelve million dollars," George said.

That was a bit of a shock. A lawyer in Jim's league would do okay, but

I didn't think he would have accumulated twelve million dollars in cash in the ten or twelve years he'd practiced law. "Would you mind telling me how that much cash came to be?"

"The house sold for almost a million, and I was told that the grove in Avon Park went for about ten grand. I think all the other money was from cash assets."

"Were there any stocks, bonds, mutual funds, that sort of thing?"

"No. I went through all that with the administrator. Just the house, the grove, and cash."

"Do you have any idea where all that cash came from?"

"I assumed he made it. He was a pretty prominent lawyer."

Not that prominent, I thought. "Do you know who was running the grove for Jim?"

"Yes. Hold on and I can get you the name and a phone number." He stood and left the room.

Betty sat quietly for a few moments and then looked at me with tears welling in her eyes. "George may be right, you know," she said. "About Katie and Jim. She wasn't happy during the last years. She was coming here more often and staying longer. Never more than three or four days, but before that she'd only been staying for one night, or two if Jim was out of town. There was something sad about her that I couldn't figure out. She always denied that there was anything wrong, but a mother knows."

"What about friends here in Winter Park? Did she see anybody regularly?"

"No. She pretty much withdrew from all her high school friends. I'd see some of them occasionally and they always asked about her, but she never got in touch."

"Did that happen when she went to Miami to college?"

Betty thought about that for a bit. "No, I don't think so. I remember times when she came home on breaks and the house was full of her old friends."

"When did that change?"

She thought some more, and I watched as a tear finally broke loose and rolled slowly down her right cheek. "About the time she got serious with Jim."

"Did that seem strange to you?"

"Not really. I guess I always thought she was just growing up and moving on."

"Was there ever a time when she cut off contact with you and George?"

"No, but there was a time after they got married that we didn't see much of them. Her excuse was that they were busy in Sarasota. Jim was just starting out and trying to build a practice."

George returned to the room and said, "I'm sorry. I can't put my hand on the information about the people helping Jim out in Avon Park. Is it important?"

"Probably not," I said, "but if you do run across it, I'd appreciate your letting me know." I stood. "I appreciate your hospitality, and I hope I didn't dredge up too many bad memories."

"No," said Betty. "We appreciate your help."

"I'll keep you posted if we find out anything."

Betty walked me to the door and reached up, gave me a hug, and whispered in my ear, "Take care of J.D."

I smiled at her. "Yes, ma'am."

CHAPTER TWELVE

J.D. was again sitting in Ann Kuehnel's living room. Pleasantries had been exchanged and now they were sipping freshly brewed coffee. "Ann, I need to show you a picture and ask if you can identify the man in it."

"Is he the murderer?"

"No. But he may be a witness. I think he might live here." She gave Ann a copy of the picture captured from the security video.

"Yes, I know him. That's Porter King. He lives in 3B."

"His car wasn't in the parking lot this morning, and I had a patrol car check periodically during the night. It doesn't look as if he came home."

Ann laughed. "He has a girlfriend over on the mainland. I think he stays over sometimes."

"Do you know how I can get in touch with him?"

"I'm sorry, J.D. I don't know his girlfriend's name. Our manager would probably have his cell phone number, though. You could try that."

"Thanks. I'll check on my way out. What can you tell me about Mr. King?"

"Not much, I'm afraid. He's a number of years younger than most of the people who live here, so he doesn't spend much time with us. I've heard he was in the oil business in some way and he made a small fortune and retired."

"Do you know where he's from?" J.D. asked.

"New York City, I think. But I'm not sure about that."

"Do you know how long he's lived here?"

"About a year, I guess. He bought the place from Clara Johnson's estate after she died. She was one of the original owners, like me."

"Can you think of anything else about the murder?"

"Sorry. I wracked my brain all night, but there's nothing more I can tell you. I couldn't sleep. I never saw anybody killed before. And Ken was a friend. It was just awful. I don't know if I'll ever get it out of my head."

"I'm sorry you had to see all that, Ann. I'd better go. I need to get back to the station. If you happen to see Mr. King, will you give me a call? I really need to talk to him."

"I'll call you the minute I see him."

The women chatted for a few more minutes and J.D. left, stopping by the manager's office on her way out. She sat for a few minutes in her car, thinking, and then called Martin Sharkey, her deputy chief. She asked him to run Porter King's name through the databases and see if anything came up. She wanted to know all she could about King before she talked to him.

She called the sheriff's forensics office and asked about any results on the car they pulled out of Longboat Pass or any information on the man that was in it. Nothing. She sat for a few more minutes, frustrated at the pace of officialdom. She picked up her phone again and called Bert Hawkins, the chief medical examiner of the Twelfth Judicial Circuit, identified herself, and was put through.

"Ah, my favorite detective," said Dr. Hawkins. "You must need something."

"Now, Bert, what if I called just to hear your voice?"

"Then I'd think you had finally come to your senses and dumped Matt and were coming on to me."

J.D. laughed. "If you were single, I'd probably do just that. As it happens, I do need something."

"What can I do for you, J.D.?"

"We pulled a John Doe from Longboat Pass yesterday. He should be in your morgue. I was wondering if you could get to his autopsy today."

"Already done. I got to it first thing this morning."

"I guess the sheriff doesn't have your report yet. What can you tell me about him?"

"Not much. He was in good health, probably in his mid-thirties. He didn't drown. No water in his lungs, but his spinal cord was severed up in the neck area. Died instantly."

"Is that an unusual injury?"

"Very common in car wrecks. Usually we see it in high-speed rear-enders. The lawyers call it whiplash, which isn't very scientific. It's a flexion-extension type injury. The head is knocked to the rear and then immediately to the front. If the force is sufficient, it can sever the cord."

"This wasn't a rear-end collision."

"I know. I think it probably happened when he hit the bridge railing. He wasn't wearing a seat belt, and the force of hitting the railing would have thrown his head into the steering wheel. There was an abrasion on his forehead consistent with that theory. The steering wheel stopped his head's forward progress, but his chin would have kept going. That would have thrown his head back at an awkward angle, snapping his neck."

"Did he have any marks on his body, any wounds, tattoos, surgical scars, anything that would give me a lead on his identity?"

"He'd been shot sometime in the past, but it looks like a pretty good doc cleaned him up."

"How so?"

"The bullet went into his abdomen and ruptured his colon and took a part of his liver. Whoever took care of him got everything fixed."

"Any idea how long ago?"

"Probably years."

"Did you get some blood samples for DNA?"

"Of course, and I put a rush on them for you. You should have some results tomorrow."

"Will you ask the lab to test for any genetic markers that could tell us where he's from?"

"That's a little more complex, but we can do it. Probably narrow down his ethnicity, but we won't be able to tell you where he's from. He could have been born in Sarasota, and we couldn't tell you that, but we could tell you if he is of Chinese extraction, say."

"Is he Asian?"

"No. Not in appearance. I was just using that as an example."

"Thanks, Bert. Call me when your wife kicks you out."

He was chuckling as he hung up.

J.D. shook her head in frustration. She was no closer to identifying the shooter than she had been when she woke up that morning. Sharkey called before she could start her car. "King lives at the same address as the murder yesterday, drives a black Acura SUV, and is fifty-two years old. No warrants and nobody's looking for him. His record is clean as a whistle and he's lived on Longboat for a little over a year. Does that help?"

"It confirms what I know. So I guess that's a help."

"What's your interest in King?"

"The security video showed him talking to our shooter just before the murder. King was gone by the time Goodlow was killed, but I want to talk to him."

"Do you think he's got something to do with the murder?" Sharkey asked.

"Probably not, but I'll interview him. See what he does know. I'll keep you posted."

J.D. hung up and pulled out onto Gulf of Mexico Drive, heading north toward her condo. It was time for lunch and she didn't want to fight the crowds. She'd make a salad and get back to work.

She gradually became aware of the black Toyota a couple of car lengths behind her, driving at the same speed she was. Nothing out of the ordinary about that, except that she'd seen the same car, or one just like it, behind her as she was leaving Matt's house that morning. She picked up her phone and called dispatch. "Who's on road patrol this morning?" she asked.

"Steve Carey is the only one working right now. The other guy is in court in Sarasota."

"Do you know Steve's location?"

"He just radioed in. He's watching traffic in front of the Catholic church."

"Thanks," said J.D. and hung up.

She dialed Carey's cell phone. "Steve, it's J.D. I'll be passing you northbound in about three minutes. There's a black Toyota Corolla following me. I've seen him twice today. Will you pull in behind him and run his tag for me?"

"Sure. You want me to pull him over?"

"Let's check on the tag first. If it turns up as stolen, get him. If not, stay with him, but call me back with a name."

"Got it."

J.D. passed the parked patrol car and gradually slowed her speed by ten miles per hour to give Steve a little more time. She decided she wouldn't turn into the road that led to her condo, but keep driving. If Steve didn't get back to her, she'd keep going and cross the bridge onto Anna Maria Island. Her phone rang.

"J.D.," said Steve, "the car's registered to a corporation named SMI, Inc., based in Tampa. No reports of it being stolen."

"I want to know who's driving that car. I want you to drop back way behind him."

"I've already done that. Didn't want to spook him."

"Okay. I'm going to speed up to about sixty miles per hour. If he wants to stay with me, he'll have to break the speed limit. You get him and give him a ticket for speeding and let him go. Treat it like any traffic stop. His license will tell us who he is."

"If it's not a fake."

"That's the best we can do for now. I don't want him to realize I've made him. I'm up to sixty now and he's keeping pace."

"I'll have him in a minute," said Steve, and J.D. heard the wail of the siren cutting through the cool air.

CHAPTER THIRTEEN

Dusk shrouded the islands as darkness swallowed the day's final moments, the last traces of light bleeding slowly from the sky. I drove across the bridge and onto Longboat Key, glad to be home, tired from the drive, and in need of a cold beer. I'd called J.D. from the road and arranged to meet at Tiny's.

The place was quiet, a few locals enjoying the short interval between the time the afternoon crowd left for home and the evening crowd began to stir. J.D. was at the bar talking to Logan Hamilton and his girlfriend, Marie Phillips. She apparently hadn't dumped him yet.

A cold bottle of Miller Lite appeared on the bar as I sat down next to J.D. She kissed me on the cheek. "You have a good day?"

"I did. How about you?"

"Made some progress on the murder, I think," she said. "Were the Basses any help?"

"Maybe. Did you ever get the impression that there was trouble in Jim and Katie's marriage?"

"Not really. She'd complain about him sometimes, but I always thought that was just the usual ebb and flow of marital bliss. Why?"

"I'll fill you in later. Hey, Logan, Marie."

"Matt," Logan said, "heard you were off-island."

Our key leaks information, most of it no more exciting than the comings and goings of the islanders. "Just for the day," I said.

"Where'd you go?"

"Orlando."

"That doesn't sound real exciting."

"It wasn't. How're you, Marie? Still putting up with my buddy, I see."

"He needs supervision, Matt," Marie said, "and I'm the only one crazy enough to take on such a long-term project."

"You guys want to go to dinner?" Logan asked.

"I don't know," I said. "Too many people this time of the year."

"We could go to the Haye Loft," he said. "Pizza and dessert. If we go now, we'll beat the crowd."

I looked at J.D. "Sounds good to me," she said. "I need to make an early night of it."

Pizza and beer topped off with a calorie-laden piece of key lime pie had lulled me into a near torpid state. J.D. and I were huddled on my sofa, the sound of her voice pushing me closer to sleep. "And so," she said, "I stripped naked and jumped on top of old Bob, just about giving him a heart attack."

"What? Who the hell is Bob?"

"Are we awake now?"

"Geez, yes. What the hell are you talking about?"

"Fantasy, dear. Nothing more, but it appears to have woken you up."

"Sorry," I said. "I was kind of dozing off." I sat up straight. "So tell me about your day."

"Not a lot to report. I found out the name of the man we saw on the security tape talking to our shooter. Porter King. He lives in the complex, but apparently is out of town. I'll try him again tomorrow. The big surprise was that somebody was following me today."

"Following you? How?"

"In a car, dummy. A black Toyota Corolla."

"I'd think a black Lincoln Town Car would have been more intimidating."

"Probably, but the Corolla was bad enough."

"Any idea who it was?"

"A private investigator from Tampa."

"You been fooling around with a married man?"

"Not lately."

"Any idea why he was following you?"

"No. I had Steve Carey pull him over for speeding and find out who he is. I don't think he would have connected the traffic stop to me. I'm going to find out a bit more about him before I do anything."

"Want me to go talk to him?"

"No. Not yet, anyway."

"I could send Jock to see him."

J.D. laughed. "The guy would die of fright. When's Jock due in?"

"Sometime this weekend. He'll let me know when his plans gel. He's taking a little downtime in Rome."

"Must be nice."

"He's been doing agency work," I said, "so I don't know what kind of shape he'll be in when he gets here."

J.D. was quiet for a moment. "Matt, if he needs you, I'll stay at my place. Let you two do what you do. Get him clean. I'll stay out of your hair."

"Thanks, but I hope it won't come to that. He and Logan are supposed to play in a golf tournament next week at the Longboat Key Club, so maybe it won't be too bad. I appreciate your understanding, though."

"I love him, too, you know."

"I know you do."

"He's family."

I smiled. "He is."

"So, what did you find out in Winter Park?"

"I'm not sure. I think there was trouble in Jim and Katie's marriage." I filled her in on my discussion with the Basses. "Do you think Jim was abusive?"

"I never thought about that," she said. "But it did seem that Katie withdrew during the three or four years before she disappeared."

"How so?"

"She hardly ever called. For a long time, we talked every week or so, but then the calls almost came to a halt. When I called her, she always seemed to be in the middle of something and couldn't talk more than a few minutes."

"Did you see much of her during that period?"

"No. She almost never came to Miami, but I used to visit her in Sarasota a couple times a year. The invitations stopped about the same time as the phone calls. I didn't attach any significance to it. I just figured she was building a new life here with Jim and I wasn't part of it. Friends do grow apart, you know, so I thought that was what was happening."

"The same kind of thing was going on with her parents. George seemed to think she was being mentally abused. They didn't think it was physical."

"Jim was always pretty intense. Maybe the pressures of the law practice were making him worse."

"Did Katie ever talk to you about having children?"

J.D. smiled. "Yeah. She wanted a houseful. I don't know why she didn't start a family. I thought it might be a physical problem with one of them, but it wasn't my place to ask."

"Did she ever say anything about Jim not wanting kids?"

"No."

"She told the Basses that Jim didn't want children. Apparently he was adamant about it."

"Katie never said anything to me."

"Do you know why Captain McAllister would still be calling the Basses to ask if they'd heard from Katie?"

"No, but I assume he hasn't given up. He and Jim were buddies, and there is always one case a cop can't solve and can't let go of."

"Do you have any of those?"

"A couple, but when I left Miami, I put them behind me. I wouldn't be able to work the cases from here, so I had to let them go. But they still haunt me."

"I think you might want to have another talk with McAllister," I said. "See if he's found out anything more."

"I plan to do that. I've been debating whether to show him the picture of Katie."

I thought about that for a minute. "I don't think I would. Not yet, anyway. That's kind of our ace in the hole. If Katie's alive, she's either being kept somewhere by somebody or she's intentionally hidden herself away from her world. If she's reaching out to you after all this time, there must be a reason."

"You're probably right."

"I guess you're no further along in your investigation of Ken Goodlow's murder."

"No. I went to see Bud Jamison again this afternoon after I got away from the P.I. He gave me the names of all the people who were in the picture from 1948, but the ones he knows about are all dead. There were a couple of people who moved away over the years and he lost contact with them, so he doesn't know whether they're dead or alive."

"Cracker Dix knew Goodlow," I said. "He used to have coffee with him, Jamison, and two other old men over at the Cortez Café. He said they all just stopped showing up for coffee, and Ken never would give him an answer as to why."

"Did Cracker know any of them by name?"

"He didn't remember them, but he said they might be in his journal."

"Cracker keeps a journal?"

"You don't want to know. He did tell me the men died over the past couple of years. Goodlow and Jamison were the only ones left. Do you think they may be important?"

"I doubt it, but I need to cover all the bases. I'll talk to Cracker tomorrow, show him the old pictures. If he knows the names of the old guys he had coffee with, he can tell me whether they were part of the crowd back in '48."

"Why don't you just ask Jamison?"

"I will. But if I know the names of the old gents and those guys were in the pictures, I can tell if Jamison is lying if he says they weren't."

"Why would he lie to you about something like that?"

"I don't know. It's probably not pertinent to anything."

"Sounds like you're just scratching around."

"That's half the job."

CHAPTER FOURTEEN

The night often brings disquiet and dreams of dead soldiers and jailed clients, the ones I couldn't save, the ones who didn't deserve death or incarceration. That night, I dreamed of Jock Algren. We had grown up together in a small town in the middle of the Florida peninsula, best buddies who struggled with dysfunctional families and survived the trials of our teen years.

When Jock graduated from college, he joined the most secretive agency of the federal government, one so secret it didn't even have a name. Over the years, he had become one of their top agents and he reported directly to his director and to the president of the United States. Jock had extraordinary powers given to him by the president and Jock gave the president deniability, cover from any mission that blew up in the politicians' faces. So far, that hadn't happened.

Jock was called on to do many things in fighting terrorists and other enemies of the United States. Sometimes he killed the bastards in cold blood, and while every one of them deserved his fate, when the body count reached some sort of undefined critical mass, the actuality that it was he who sent them to hell would sporadically slam Jock into a state of wretched self-loathing. He would slink onto Longboat Key and hole up in my cottage on the bay, watching the boats and birds and people and slinging back glass after glass of good bourbon. He'd talk and tell me about the horrors he'd seen, the men he'd killed, the destruction they had wrought that made them undeserving of mercy or due process. Just death at the hands of an assassin they had not seen coming. And when he'd drunk himself into a stupor, Jock would crawl into bed and sleep for hours. Some nights I'd hear him sobbing through his pain, and the next morning he'd attack another bottle of bourbon.

Three or four days would pass without my leaving him. I made sure he ate enough to survive and I listened as he poured out the details of a life that was his personal scourge. And on the fourth or fifth morning, he'd wake up early, shower, and drink glassfuls of water. "Ready to run?" he'd ask, and I would know it was over, the bad days that we called the "cleansing time."

We'd run the beach, pounding the booze out of his system, and then we'd go to the Blue Dolphin Cafe for a huge breakfast and lots of coffee. The old Jock would be back, the self-assured man with the ready smile and a kind word for everybody. He'd stay a few more days, play golf with Logan, drink his nonalcoholic beer at Tiny's or the Hilton or Pattigeorge's, joke with his many friends on the island, and then fly off to Houston and home until the wars again came knocking on his door, bidding him to join up and start the terrible process all over again. It was Jock, and men like him, who stood between us and the devils who crashed planes loaded with civilians into buildings filled with office workers. His work was honorable, but I knew that he left a little of himself on the battlefield after every skirmish. Someday, there would not be enough left of Jock Algren for me to help rehabilitate. And then my friend would die and a large piece of my life would go to the grave with him. I wasn't sure how I'd survive that.

I tossed and turned in the bed, the dreams and thoughts crashing around in my turbulent brain. I felt J.D.'s hand on me several times, her quiet whisper letting me know she was there. Finally, I got out of bed and went into the kitchen to make coffee. Four a.m. on a dark Thursday morning. A time when predators roam the earth.

I took my cup into the living room and sat in the dark, staring at the bay through the sliding glass doors that opened onto the patio. The security lights on my dock cast shadows on the black water, providing an unsettling sense of dread.

I crept back into the bedroom and retrieved a pair of shorts, a sweatshirt, and my running shoes. I put a note for J.D. on the kitchen counter and left the house. The only way to rid myself of this creeping anxiety was to run it out of my system. I jogged down Broadway to Gulf of Mexico Drive and headed south, past Cannons Marina and the Euphemia Haye

Restaurant. I turned around at the Centre Shops and picked up speed as I ran north toward the village. I slowed to a walk when I reached Broadway and ambled toward home. It was still dark, and the coolness of the early morning was quickly drying the sweat I'd exuded during the run. The endorphins had kicked in and my mood was definitely on the upswing.

A car turned onto Broadway from Gulf of Mexico Drive, its headlight beams startling me for a second. I moved to the left edge of the road, giving it plenty of room to pass. I could hear the car as it approached and knew it was slowing. I looked over my shoulder, but the headlights' glare obscured my view. I stepped onto the grass berm, looking for an escape route. I had no reason to fear a strange car in my own neighborhood, but the adrenalin was beginning to flow into my system. I told myself I was being stupid, imagining things, finding threats where there were none. Still, better safe than sorry.

I was a step or two from bolting into the yard of a dark house, when the car came to a stop and a familiar voice said, "Hey, Matt. You're out early."

I turned to see a Longboat Key Police squad car and an officer I'd known for years. "Morning, Joe. Just running off last night's pizza. How's the night shift working out for you?"

"Kind of quiet, but I did see a black Corolla that's on my 'watch for' list. The same one that was tailing J.D. yesterday."

"Where?"

"Parked a couple of houses down from yours. I ran him off, but I've been driving by every half hour or so to make sure he hasn't come back."

"Was it the same driver Steve Carey stopped yesterday?"

"Yeah. Some private eye from Tampa named Ben Appleby. Said he was working a case but wouldn't tell me anything else. I had no reason to hold him, but I told him it would be in his best interest to get off the island until daylight."

"When was that?"

"A little after two. He hadn't been there long. I drove by an hour or so before, and he wasn't in the area."

"Thanks, Joe. I'll tell J.D. I wonder what this guy's up to."

"No telling. Take it easy, Matt." The window slid up and the car moved on.

CHAPTER FIFTEEN

It was still dark and J.D. was fast asleep when I returned to the cottage. I looked at my watch. Almost six. I took a shower in the guest bathroom and put on a pair of shorts and a T-shirt I found in the dirty clothes hamper. They would probably last one more day. I drained the coffee pot and made fresh, poured myself a cup, and went back to the sofa.

Why was Appleby watching my house in the middle of the night? Maybe it was time to pay him a visit. If J.D. was in danger, I needed to know about it. Should I tell her I was going to Tampa? Not a chance. She'd think I'd gone into protective mode and that would piss her off. She had told me often enough that she didn't need my protection. I'd have to think on that some more.

"You're up early," said J.D. as she came out of our bedroom. Her hair was tousled and the left side of her face was a bit wrinkled from where it had rested on the pillow. She was barefoot and wearing nothing but the old T-shirt she slept in. "Couldn't sleep?"

"Not well."

"Want to go for a run?"

"Already been."

"Wow, aren't we industrious."

"Want some coffee?" I asked. "I just made it."

"That'll help." She disappeared into the kitchen and returned with a mug bearing the logo of the Miami-Dade Police Department. "What's on your agenda today?" she asked.

"Not sure." I hated lying to her, but I thought it'd be better than starting an argument. "What about you?"

"I'll see if I can get with that witness Porter King and then I think I'll go have a conversation with Captain McAllister. See if there's anything new on Katie."

"Are you going to tell him about the photo you got?"

"No. At least not yet. I need to know more about what's going on."

"I ran into one of your cops this morning, Joe Carson. He said he'd had to run off that P.I. from Tampa, Appleby, about two this morning."

"Where was he?"

"Parked down the street."

"Doing what?"

"According to Joe, he was just sitting there. Maybe watching the house. I don't know."

"I don't like that."

"I don't either," I said. "Maybe you ought to talk to him."

"Maybe, but I'm not sure I want him to know that I know he's following me."

"What's the downside?"

She thought about that for a couple of beats. "I don't know, come to think of it. Maybe I ought to let him know I'm on to him. That might scare him off. But I'm so jammed up with this murder and Katie, I just don't have time to go see him."

"What if I set up a meeting with him? I could drive up to Tampa this morning."

She was quiet for a moment and then nodded. "I don't see why not. Do you mind?"

"Not at all." I smiled to myself. There's more than one way to skin a cat.

"I'll see if our dispatcher can run down a number for him."

I was at the apex of the Sunshine Skyway Bridge, one hundred seventy-five feet above the ship channel that runs through Tampa Bay. I always get a bit nervous as I cross this beautiful span. It's a long way down.

I was on my way to a meeting with Ben Appleby. I and the Rohrbaugh R9's 9mm pistol in the holster I carried stuffed into my pants at the small of my back. I wasn't sure what I was going to run into and I thought the little six-shot weapon would provide me with a bit of confidence.

I'd called Appleby an hour before and apparently awoken him from a deep sleep. "Mr. Appleby," I said. "My name's Matt Royal. Does that mean anything to you?" He might already have connected me to J.D., since he was parked outside my house. I'd decided it didn't matter. Either he'd meet me or I'd go find him.

"No. Should it?"

"Probably not. I'm a lawyer and I need some investigative work done. You were recommended. Can I meet with you this morning?"

"Recommended by whom?"

"I don't remember. Somebody I met at a bar luncheon recently."

"What's it about?"

"Some surveillance on an errant husband."

He laughed. "Guy fucking around, huh?"

"Something like that. I need some dirt as soon as possible."

"Okay. Meet me at eleven."

"Give me your office address."

"I'll come to your office."

"Sorry," I said. "That's not possible. I'll explain when I see you."

"Okay. I don't actually have an office. I pretty much work out of my car. Can you meet me out by the Tampa airport?"

"Not a problem."

"Okay. There's a Denny's on Highway 92 about three blocks north of its intersection with I-275. How will I know you?"

"Don't worry. I'll find you," I said. J.D. had given me a photo taken from Appleby's Department of Motor Vehicles file, the one that shows up on his driver's license. It was not what I expected.

I had envisioned Appleby as a small, dark man, but he was actually blond, tall, and thin as a rail. He was sitting in a booth in the back of the restaurant, a cup of coffee in front of him. He looked tired. The midnight surveillance wasn't working too well for him.

"Mr. Appleby?" I asked. "I'm Matt Royal."

"Sit down. You want coffee?"

I shook my head and took a seat across from him. "What I want is to know why you're following Detective Duncan."

A look of puzzlement crossed his face. "What? I thought we were here to talk about a divorce case."

"Listen to me," I said, my voice low and hard. "I want to know why you were following Detective Duncan yesterday and why you were parked in front of my house in the wee hours of this morning."

"I don't know what you're talking about," he said, moving to extricate himself from the booth.

"Yes, you do, and if you get out of that seat, I'm going to follow you to the parking lot and beat the shit out of you."

He leered at me. "That might be harder to do than you think."

"I doubt it."

"You're not a cop." A statement, not a question.

"I'm not."

"Who are you?"

"I told you. I'm a lawyer."

"I'm not impressed."

"I'm also Detective Duncan's, how shall we say, boyfriend."

"Ah."

"Yes. Now why don't you simply tell me why you're following her and sitting outside my house in the middle of the night?"

"You don't want to know."

I leaned back in the booth, sighed, and smiled. "I want you to try and follow this logic, Mr. Appleby. If I actually didn't want to know, I wouldn't have asked the question. How difficult can that be?"

"Look, Royal, the people I work for are not the kind of people you want to fuck with."

"They're fucking with me."

"I doubt they know you exist."

"When they fuck with my woman, they fuck with me."

He laughed. "That's brilliant."

I had to laugh. "That did sound a bit stuffy," I said, "but in stuffiness there is sometimes truth."

"And you're a philosopher as well as a tough guy."

"Okay," I said. "You're not as dumb as you act, and I'm not really a tough guy. Philosopher either, for that matter. All I'm trying to do is find out who's interested in my girlfriend and why."

"And I can't tell you that."

"Can't or won't?"

"Doesn't matter. Either way, I'm not telling you jackshit."

"Can you deliver a message for me?"

"Sure."

"Tell your employers I want to talk to them." I gave him my cell number.

"I don't think that's a good idea."

"Maybe not, but will you do it?"

Appleby sighed. "I'll do it, but I don't think you'll like the reaction you get."

"And you stay away from Detective Duncan."

"Or what?"

"You don't want to know."

"Are you playing tough guy again?"

I grinned. "No. But the Longboat law will find some reason to arrest you if you show back up on the island. I can promise that, and by the time all the paperwork finds its way up the proper channels, you will have spent a week or two in the Manatee County stockade."

"That sounds a little extralegal."

"Yeah, but you know how it is. The cops always take care of their own."

"My people will just send somebody else."

"Then tell your people to send someone who won't mind spending a couple of weeks in jail."

CHAPTER SIXTEEN

Porter King was sitting in the waiting room of the Longboat Key Police Station. It was not quite ten in the morning and he had been there less than five minutes when J.D. came through the door that led to the bowels of the building. "Good morning, Mr. King. I'm Detective J. D. Duncan."

King rose. He stood a little under six feet tall with a compact body that didn't seem to hold any fat. His face had that creased look that gives middle-aged men a rugged appearance. His brown hair was sprinkled with gray. His clothes were casual and expensive, his voice inflected with the cadence of his native New York City. "Nice to meet you, Detective. I'm sorry I was so hard to get hold of."

"Well, you're here now and I appreciate it. Come on back. Can I get you a cup of coffee or something else to drink?"

"No, thanks. I'm fine."

J.D. led him to a small room that had four chairs placed around an oval table that held a laptop computer. "Have a seat, Mr. King," said J.D. "I want to show you a surveillance tape from your condo complex and ask you some questions."

"This must be about the man who was killed in the parking lot on Tuesday."

"It is. Let me show you the tape and then we'll talk." She put the CD in its slot and called up the video that showed King walking out of the building and stopping to talk to the man in the Jaguar. It only took a minute or so for the scene to run its course. "Do you know this man?" J.D. asked.

"No. I'd never seen him before. Was he involved somehow?"

J.D. ran the tape forward as they watched Ken Goodlow come out of the building, stop at his truck, and walk back to the Jaguar. King flinched as the man shot Goodlow.

"That's the killer?" he asked.

"Yes."

"He's the guy who went off the bridge?"

"Yes. Can you tell me about your conversation with him?"

"It wasn't much. I saw him sitting in the car when I walked out, and I stopped to ask if I could help him in any way."

"What was his reaction?"

"He told me that he was a real estate agent and was waiting to meet a client interested in one of the units. I told him I didn't know one was for sale, and he said that the owner wanted everything to remain confidential. I didn't push it. Just wished him a good day and got in my car and left."

"Tell me about his voice. Any accent, speech impediment, that sort of thing?"

"Not so I noticed. He may have had a slight regional accent, like from Maine or somewhere in New England, but it wasn't foreign. He sounded very American. Why? Do you think he came from somewhere else?"

"We don't know who he is, Mr. King. That's what we're following up on. Did you notice a gun in the Jaguar?"

"No. He was just sitting there, minding his own business."

"Do you mind if I ask where you've been for the past couple of days?"

"Not at all. I spent Tuesday night in Sarasota with my girlfriend and we drove down to Naples yesterday morning. We spent the day and drove back last night. I dropped her off and came back to my place late last night."

"Would you mind giving me your girlfriend's name?"

"Be glad to."

J.D. wrote it down along with an address and phone number. She'd follow up, but she was pretty sure that was a dead end. King assured her that he'd be around for the next couple of weeks at least and if he wasn't at home, she could reach him on his cell phone.

"I tried that for the past couple of days," she said.

He gave her a sheepish grin. "Sorry about that. I ran off and left the damn thing on my dresser. By the time I realized I didn't have it, we were halfway to Naples."

J.D. ushered him out of the station, shook his hand, and watched him walk to his SUV. She went back to her office and called Captain Doug McAllister. "Good morning, Doug. This is J. D. Duncan."

"J.D. A pleasant surprise. How have you been?"

"I'm well, thank you. I wonder if you'd have time to sit down with me today to talk some more about Katie Fredrickson."

"I'm pretty well backed up around here. Have you got any news? Has anybody heard from her?"

"Her parents tell me they haven't. I've got a little time on my hands and I thought I might go back over the file and see if I can come up with anything. That is, if you don't mind."

"J.D., I'm always glad to have the help. I'm not one of those guys who guards his turf like a mama bear."

"I know, Doug, and I appreciate that."

"Look, I had a luncheon conference with the chief set for today, but he had to meet with the mayor or somebody. Have you got time for lunch? I'll bring the file."

"I can certainly do that."

"How about Marina Jack at noon?" he asked.

"Great. Thanks, Doug. I'll see you then."

J.D. sat at her desk for a few minutes thinking about Katie's case. She'd been through the Sarasota P.D.'s file a couple of times and had talked with Doug McAllister on many occasions. He'd always been cooperative. J.D. knew he was a good cop and thought he was a pretty good guy to boot. However, there was something nagging at the back of her mind about the property Jim Fredrickson had inherited over near Avon Park. She'd never heard of that before Matt told her about it. It probably wasn't important, but it was a loose end that McAllister should have rolled up, and she'd seen nothing in the file to suggest he had.

She picked up her phone and called the Basses' house. George answered. "George, it's J.D."

"Hi, sweetheart. Great to hear from you. I met your boyfriend yesterday."

"He told you he was my boyfriend?"

"Well, he said you were more than friends."

J.D. laughed. "I guess we are. I'm practically living with him."

"He seems like a nice guy. I knew him by reputation when he practiced law in Orlando. It was all good."

"Glad to hear it," J.D. said. "I'd hate to think he could fool a real live police detective."

George chuckled. "You'll have to bring him over sometime. We miss seeing you."

"Thanks, George. I'll do that. I was calling about something else though. Matt said you had looked for the name of the caretaker of the grove that Jim owned in Avon Park. Did you find it?"

"No, but I didn't look any further. Matt didn't seem to think it was that important."

"It's probably not, but I'd like to talk to him."

"I'll look some more and see what I can find."

"And, George, I know this is going to sound funny, but if you talk to Doug McAllister, I'd prefer that you not mention this or that Matt came to see you."

"What's up, J.D.?"

"Probably nothing, but I'd like a little time to check some things out for myself."

"Do you think there's any chance Katie's alive?"

"I don't think that's likely, George, but I want to make sure that somebody has covered all the bases. I want to find the killer. I don't think we'll find Katie."

After she hung up, she felt like a little girl who'd just lied to her father. She wanted to tell the Basses about the texted picture, but she didn't want to give them any false hope. They'd been through that special hell reserved for parents who outlive their children, and she didn't want to send them back into it. She knew she was right, but sometimes being right doesn't make it easier.

CHAPTER SEVENTEEN

Captain Doug McAllister was in his mid-forties and had been a Sarasota cop for more than twenty years. He was well known and respected in the law the enforcement communities that dotted the Suncoast. He stood a little over six feet tall and had the body of an aging linebacker, with muscles in the process of turning to fat. His face was wrinkle free, but wide and flat with dark eyes set a bit too far apart, heavy eyebrows, and a cleft chin. His head was covered with hair that was too gray for his age. He was walking across the restaurant toward J.D., a grin breaking out as he spotted her. He had a large file folder in his hand.

"Good to see you, J.D.," he said as he pulled a chair up to her table. "Have you ordered yet?"

"No. I got here two minutes ago. It's good to see you, too."

McAllister put the file folder on the table. "I've made a complete copy for you. I'd like it back when you finish with it."

"Not a problem. I appreciate your going to all this trouble."

"Glad to do it. Sometimes a fresh pair of eyes will pick up something I've missed."

"Are you still actively looking into the case?" J.D. asked.

"Not really. I pull the file out occasionally just to refresh my memory, but there hasn't been anything new since we finished the initial investigation."

"Do you have any theories about what happened to Katie's body?"

"Speculation is all we have."

"It's strange that the killer would have taken her body and left Jim's at the scene."

"We think maybe he was afraid he'd left some evidence, like DNA, on or in Katie's body," said McAllister. "Maybe she was still alive when he pulled her out of that house. Maybe he wanted to make sure she didn't live to identify him. We never have come up with a good answer to that, J.D. You know she was raped, right?"

"I know the medical examiner said that might fit the evidence, but he couldn't be more definitive."

"Right. And we're only speculating about the reason for taking the body, but that is the only thing we can come up with that makes any sense."

"So what happened to the body? Any guesses?" asked J.D.

"Who knows? Probably dropped into the Gulf. This is an easy place to lose a body. Lots of water."

"Have you considered that she might not have been killed? That she might still be alive somewhere?"

"Unlikely. There was a lot of blood at the scene."

"Are you sure it was all Katie's?"

"Yeah, and it was enough that Doc Hawkins thought she probably wouldn't have survived that big a loss."

They ate their lunch and discussed theories about the reason for the murders. They reached no conclusions, just two experienced homicide cops passing the time of day. They were wrapping up when McAllister said, "I know you and Katie were close. Looking back at it, did she ever say anything to you that didn't mean anything at the time, but may have some significance to the murders?"

"No. We'd drifted apart over the years. I didn't talk to her regularly toward the end of her life. She was pretty caught up in her life here in Sarasota."

"Jim and I were good friends, you know. Played golf every Saturday."

"Didn't you find that a bit of a conflict of interest? You know, cop and criminal defense lawyer?"

"Not really. Jim didn't do the nitty-gritty cases that I usually work. He handled mostly white collar crimes. Fraud, embezzlement, that sort of thing. Criminals who could pay his big fees. Not the dirtbags I deal with every day. And if we did get on the wrong side of a case, we just didn't talk about it. Friendly adversaries, I guess you could say."

"You didn't see any of this coming?" J.D. asked.

"Not a hint. Jim was hardworking and happily married. He was doing well financially and had built a good reputation around here. Had a bright future. His murder was a big shock to everybody. I'm beginning to think it was just a crime of opportunity. Some junkie wandered into his house and snuffed out two lives."

"I don't remember that anything of value was taken," said J.D.

"Nothing was. We think Jim and Katie may have surprised the intruder, and he panicked and killed them and got the hell out of there."

"But he stopped long enough to rape Katie? That doesn't hold up too well."

"I know."

"Could the killer have been interrupted? Somebody knocking on the door, the phone ringing?"

"We never found any evidence of that."

"You never came up with anybody who might have had reason to kill Jim? Former client? Somebody like that?"

"Nobody that didn't have an alibi."

"A contract killing, then? Paid for by one of the people with an alibi?"

"We worked that angle but came up empty. And if it was a contract killing, it was done by an amateur. The scene was too messy and the rape doesn't fit a pro's MO."

J.D. looked at her watch. "I've got to go, Doug. Paperwork is calling my name. I appreciate your letting me in on this one. I'll get the file back to you by the first of the week, and if I come up with any bright ideas, I'll give you a call."

J.D. was crossing the John Ringling Bridge on her way back to Longboat Key when her phone rang. Bert Hawkins. "Hey, beautiful. I've got your DNA results. Nothing on the ethnicity yet, but if he's in the system, this will tell us who he is."

"That was quick. I appreciate it, Bert. Can you e-mail the results to me? I'll run them through the system and see if anything comes up."

"It'll be on its way in a few minutes."

"I've got another question for you," said J.D.

"Shoot."

"Do you remember the murders of Jim and Katie Fredrickson?"

"Sure. I knew them. It was a terrible shame, losing two young people like that."

"Can you tell me about Katie?"

"What's your interest in this? I thought this was Sarasota P.D. territory."

"Katie and I were close friends in college, and Doug McAllister has been good enough to keep me in the loop. I'm just taking another look at everything."

"You don't think he would mind my talking to you?"

"Not at all. I just had lunch with him. He gave me a complete copy of his file. You can call him if you like."

"No need. I'll take your word for it."

"What makes you think Katie was raped?"

"The techs found vaginal fluids on the sofa. The DNA matched the blood on the floor. The same woman who secreted the fluids on the sofa left a lot of blood on the carpet."

"And that matched Katie's DNA."

"Yes. At least it matched the DNA we found on what was apparently Katie's toothbrush and strands of hair we found in her hairbrush."

"Do I detect a bit of uncertainty in your voice?"

"Maybe. We didn't have a body to match it to, so we had to assume that the toothbrush and hairbrush belonged to Katie. They were found in her bathroom, so I think it's a pretty good assumption, but still an assumption. That bothers the scientific part of my brain."

"What about her parents? Wouldn't you have been able to match their DNA to Katie's?"

"The Basses were not Katie's biological parents. They adopted her as an infant. She'd been left at a fire station in Orlando when she was about three days old. There was no way to track her biological parents."

"I didn't know that," said J.D. "I can't believe as close as we were that she wouldn't have mentioned that."

"She didn't know," said Hawkins. "I talked to her parents myself. They never told her."

"That's cruel," said J.D., anger flashing in her voice.

"Yes, it is. But I think the Basses' hearts were in the right place. They didn't want Katie to grow up thinking her biological mother had abandoned her like a sack of garbage."

J.D. was quiet for a beat. "Are you satisfied that she was raped?"

There was hesitation on the other end of the call. A sigh. Then, "No, I'm not satisfied."

"Why?"

"The vaginal secretions could have been the result of consensual sex. The only thing that pointed to rape was the blood on the floor indicating that the woman had been killed."

"So you wouldn't conclude that she had been raped."

"Not definitively. Again, my scientific brain gets nervous when it doesn't have enough evidence to prove the hypothesis."

"Bert, I read your reports in the Sarasota P.D. files some time ago, but I don't remember there being anything in them about Katie's adoption."

"There wasn't. The police were content with the rape scenario and weren't excited about my doubts. They thought I was being too pedantic in trying to tie up all the loose ends. I followed up with the Basses after the reports were filed and didn't see any reason to amend them. It wasn't going to make any difference in the investigation."

"So McAllister doesn't know about that."

"I've never told anyone other than you. I don't know whether he might have found that out from the Basses himself."

"Should I tell McAllister about this?"

"That's up to you."

"Did Katie bleed enough that you're confident she couldn't have survived?" J.D. asked.

"The average human body contains about ten pints of blood, maybe less in a woman of the size and weight of Katie. If she were to lose forty percent of that blood volume, she'd not likely survive without immediate medical attention."

"What actually causes death?"

"If the loss is very quick, and it probably was in this case, there's just not enough blood left to circulate. The blood pressure drops and organs start shutting down. It goes very quickly, and she was probably almost immediately unconscious."

"Thanks, Bert. I'll talk to you later."

"Are you going to tell McAllister about my reservations?"

"If what you're telling me is that the victim may not have been Katie, that could change the course of the investigation."

"I'm not saying that. I have some scientific quibbles with the conclusions the police are drawing, but all the evidence would suggest that the victim was Katie. It's just that in the absence of DNA proof, I can't be sure."

"And you don't think the DNA you found in the blood and secretions was Katie's."

"Now you're reaching conclusions not supported by the evidence. Look at it this way. In all likelihood, the victim was Katie. Think about how hard it would have been to fake her death. One, somebody would have had to go to some lengths to plant somebody else's toothbrush and a hairbrush with the same person's hair in it. Two, the murder happened in Katie's house. Three, no other woman who could have been the victim has been reported missing. Four, if Katie wasn't in the house the night of the killings, where was she? Five, where has Katie been for the past year? If she were alive, don't you think she would have let us know, reached out in some manner? Certainly, she would have been in touch with her parents. It goes on and on. I think the detectives got it right. There's just that little issue about not having a direct DNA match from either a body or a close family member that nags at me like some minor hangnail."

"Let's keep this between us for a bit," said J.D. "Thanks, Bert. Talk to you later."

As she pulled into the station parking lot, J.D. was thinking that Bert had made a good case, except that now Katie had reached out. With a texted photograph.

CHAPTER EIGHTEEN

I'd just exited the causeway on the south side of the Sunshine Skyway Bridge when my phone rang. I didn't recognize the number and thought about ignoring it. I answered.

"Mr. Royal?" a deep voice came over the hands-free speaker.

"Yes."

"I understand you want to talk to me."

I was stumped. "Who is this?"

"My name's not important. Ben Appleby gave me your number."

Okay. Contact. "Thanks for calling."

"What can I do for you, Mr. Royal?"

"We need to talk."

"We're talking now."

"Face-to-face."

"Why?"

"Why not?"

The voice laughed. "You're a piece of work, Mr. Royal."

"I've heard that before."

"Where do you want to meet?"

"Your choice," I said. "I'm almost to Bradenton now. Just coming off the Skyway. Let's make it a public place."

"I'm a little jammed up today. How about in the morning? Starbucks at Cortez Road and Seventy-Fifth Street. Ten o'clock."

"That'll work. What's your name?"

"You can call me Tony." He hung up.

I called J.D. "Where are you?" I asked.

"At the station. I had a productive lunch with Doug McAllister."

"Anything new?"

"Some stuff I didn't know. Most of the new stuff came from a telephone call with Bert Hawkins."

"Sounds interesting. I had a meeting with your P.I. buddy. Not very productive, but it did get me in touch with the people who hired him."

"Who?"

"Some guy named Tony is all I know. He just called. We're going to meet at Starbucks on Cortez Road in the morning."

"I'm not sure I like the sound of that."

"I'm not sure either, but maybe I can turn over some rocks. See what crawls out."

"What's on your agenda for this afternoon?" J.D. asked.

"I haven't eaten lunch yet. I think I'll stop by Moore's and then curl up with a book. What do you want to do about dinner tonight?"

"I haven't thought about it. I'll call you later. We'll think of something."

Moore's Stone Crab Restaurant sits at the end of Broadway in the village. It has been there for more than forty years and occupies one of the most scenic points on the key, with views twelve miles down the bay to the City of Sarasota. It was after two and the lunch crowd had mostly cleared out. I spoke to Allen Moore on the way in the door, walked through the nearly empty dining room and into the bar. Barb, the bartender, was talking to a couple I didn't recognize who were seated on the far side of the U-shaped bar. I took a seat near the door.

"Hey, Matt," Barb said. "Miller Lite?"

"Not today, thanks. I need some lunch and a Diet Coke."

"Menu?"

"No. Just whip me up a hamburger and an order of onion rings." For a seafood restaurant, the place serves a surprisingly good burger and the rings are the best on the island.

Barb sent the order to the kitchen and came back to chat. "I guess J.D.'s been real busy with the murder," she said. "Is she making any headway?"

"Some, but it's slow going."

"I knew old Mr. Goodlow. He was a good guy."

"I never met him. Did he come in a lot?"

"Not here. I met him over at Annie's. My husband and I go over there for the burgers some afternoons. He was there a lot, I think. Liked to tell stories of the old days in Cortez, back when fishing was the community's lifeblood."

"Did you ever meet his buddy, Bud Jamison?" I asked.

"Tall guy, walks with a limp, has a small scar on his face?"

"I've never met him, but that sounds like J.D.'s description of him."

"Once or twice. He never said a whole lot. Kind of quiet."

"Did you ever meet any of the other old guys from Cortez? Cracker Dix told me there were four of them that hung out together until recently when the others died."

"If I met them, I didn't know who they were."

She left to get my food from the pass-through from the kitchen. She set it on the bar in front of me and refilled my glass of Diet Coke. "There was one thing that was a little strange," she said. "I didn't think about it until just now, but a few days ago we were in Annie's late in the afternoon and Mr. Goodlow and the man with the scar on his cheek were talking when we walked in. The man who runs the place was outside fueling a boat, and I don't think Goodlow was aware of us at first. He'd probably been there a while and had a pretty good load on. I heard him say something like 'They'll kill us all if you don't give them what they want.' "

"That's odd. Did either of them say anything else?"

"No. The conversation stopped when they realized we were there."

"And you're sure it was Jamison that Goodlow was talking to."

"Pretty sure. If Jamison is the guy with the scar on his cheek. He was the same one I'd seen in there before with Mr. Goodlow."

"I'll pass this on to J.D. She may want to talk to you some more."

"Glad to help. I heard Jock was coming for a visit."

I chuckled. No secrets on the island. "He should be here this weekend."

"Bring him in. He's a sweet guy." Two men came in from the docks that fronted the restaurant. I'd watched them maneuver a sailboat into a pier while Barb and I talked. She greeted them and went to take their orders.

I always found myself a bit amused about the islanders' view of Jock. A sweet man. He was that, but he was also a stone-cold killer when he had to be. I often wondered what his friends on the key would have thought if they'd known what he did for his country. The few people who did know held the secret close, and to the rest he was a gentle man with a big smile and an easy laugh.

I finished my lunch, paid Barb, and drove the couple of blocks to my house. I entered the front door and saw a large man sitting on the sofa in my living room. He stood as I walked in and said, "Hello, Mr. Royal. I'm Tony."

He was a big man, six feet four or so, with muscles that bulged from every part of his body. He was a bit intimidating, and I guessed that was the reason for all the bulk. He'd scare the hell out of people and he was probably as strong as the proverbial ox. We were about six feet from each other, eyes locked. If he decided to make a move, I'd see it in his eyes first.

"You're a little early," I said, "and this isn't Starbucks."

"I didn't think Starbucks would be conducive to the business we have to transact."

"And what would that be, Tony?"

"I'm going to have to hurt you a little. Just a warning, you know. Nothing too serious, maybe a couple of broken bones, but nothing that won't heal."

"Who sent you?"

"Sal Bonino."

"Ah," I said. "The Suncoast's own Mafia boss."

"There's no such thing as the Mafia."

"I've heard that. What do you call yourselves?"

"Organized crime."

"Surely your name's not Tony. I mean, that's like some kind of cliché. I'll bet it's Bob or Jim. Bart Simpson, maybe."

He tried for a scowl, but it came out looking more like a constipated ape might look when straining on the toilet. "You're not as funny as you think you are."

"I've been told that before. Just what is your role in all this?"

"I help Mr. Bonino keep people like you from bothering him."

"I see. And why does your boss have some dipshit investigator following Detective Duncan?"

"Mr. Bonino doesn't always confide in me."

"Tell me something, Tony," I said. "Do all those steroids you take really make your balls shrink to the size of a pea?"

He laughed. "You're a funny guy."

"But not as funny as I think, right?"

"Fuck you, Royal. Time to pay the piper."

"I also heard that stuff makes your dick wither up so that it's only good for pissing. Is that true?"

The laugh had died away. "Nobody likes a smartass," he said.

"A lot of people find me quite humorous."

"Not me. I might have to break a couple of extra bones just to take all the fun out of this."

"Tony, let me tell you something. You take a step toward me, and I'll have you charged with assault. As soon as you get out of the hospital, the cops are going to put you in jail, hold you without bond, and try you down at the Manatee County Courthouse. You'll get about forty years in a state prison. Nobody wants people fucking with their cops."

"You're not a cop."

"No, but J. D. Duncan is."

"Explain to me about how I'm going to go to the hospital."

"It's like this, numbnut. I'm going to royally kick your ass."

"Royally, huh. Is that a pun?"

"Yep."

He laughed again, and I saw it in his eyes. He was about to move. I took a step toward him and kicked at his groin. He was faster than I expected and turned his hip just enough that my foot bounced off it. He moved toward me again, coming faster. I sidestepped and threw a flat kick toward his knee. He danced backward, taking an end table and lamp with him. I missed completely. He grinned. "Tell me about that hospital again, Royal. While you can still talk."

This wasn't going well. He was big and strong and quick. Maybe he'd earned those muscles without the help of drugs. I reached around to my back and pulled the pistol from its holster. I shot him in the shoulder. He stepped backward with the impact and then shook it off and came at me again. The bullet had done no more harm that a horsefly's bite. But it made him mad as hell.

He was moving fast. I fired again, this time at his right knee. He took the bullet and lifted his weight off the wounded leg. He let out a bellow, sounding like I imagined a wounded elephant might. He kept coming. I fired again, taking out his left knee. That slowed him, put him down, and damned if he didn't keep coming, crawling toward me with his powerful arms, dragging his legs behind. I kicked him in the face and barely dodged out of the way as he tried to grab my leg. Blood and mucus spurted from his nose. I'd need to have the carpet professionally cleaned. He was stopped for the moment, his face showing the pain from his shoulder, both knees, and his nose.

"Look, Tony," I said. "The EMS people will come and take you to the hospital. But if you keep coming, I'm going to shoot you in the head, and it'll be the medical examiner's people who come to take you to the morgue. *Capisci?*"

He lay his head on the floor, then raised it and looked at me with the most terrifying hatred I'd ever seen. "Okay. I'm done for the day, but this ain't over, Royal."

"It is for you." I pulled my phone from a pocket and dialed 911, identified myself, and told the operator to send police and rescue personnel to my address. I hung up and sat on the sofa, my gun trained on the wounded giant.

There was quiet in the room except for Tony's labored breathing. He was tough, maybe the toughest man I'd ever met. Those knee shots would have had me screaming in pain. He didn't even moan.

I heard sirens in the distance, getting closer. Three vehicles coming my way. I heard them turn onto my street and come to a stop in front of my house. The first man through the door was Officer Steve Carey, gun drawn. "Don't shoot," I said. "I'm the good guy."

J.D. came running in, her pistol in her hand, a look of fear on her face. Steve said, "He's okay, J.D." She put her pistol back in its holster as she grabbed me in a bear hug. "Thank God," she said. "I was on my way here when dispatch called me about your 911 call."

Steve was standing over Tony, who seemed to have gone into hibernation. He lay quietly, sucking up the pain, showing us how tough he was. "Who's this guy?" Steve asked.

"His name's Tony. Works for Sal Bonino."

"The Mafia guy?"

Tony grunted. "There's no such thing as the Mafia."

"He prefers 'organized crime,'" I said.

"I want a lawyer," Tony said.

"What you need," said Steve, "is a doctor."

"Get me a lawyer."

The paramedics arrived, two of them pulling a gurney with a medical bag sitting on top. They began to check Tony's vitals, splinted his legs, and got him ready to transport.

Steve pulled a card from his pocket and read Tony his Miranda rights.

"I know all that shit," said Tony. "Now get me a lawyer."

"All in due time," said one of the paramedics as they got Tony onto the gurney and headed out the front door. "We're taking him to Blake," said the other paramedic, referring to a local hospital.

My front door opened again and Chief Bill Lester walked in. "You all right, Matt?"

"Yeah."

"Looks like you'll need a new lamp and a carpet cleaner. What happened?"

"Wait a minute," said J.D. "We're going to need a statement. Might as well do it now so he doesn't have to keep repeating things. You okay with that, Matt?"

"Sure."

J.D. went to her car and returned with a digital recorder, put it on the coffee table, and took me through everything, beginning with my meeting with Ben Appleby, the P.I.

CHAPTER NINETEEN

The night was cooled by a fresh breeze blowing down the bay, chasing the last vestige of warmth left by the day's sun. The palm trees bordering the pool at J.D.'s condo complex stirred in the currents of air. She and I were sitting on her sunporch, the sliding glass doors open to the night, enjoying the quiet that had descended upon us with the darkness. She was sipping a glass of white wine, and I was working on my second bottle of Miller Lite.

"You think Joy will be able to get that mess out of my carpet?" I asked. I'd called my friend Joy Fitzpatrick who owned a professional cleaning service and tidied up my house once a week. She came right over and did whatever she did with chemicals I didn't want to know about. She said that I should stay off the carpet for a couple of days until everything dried.

J.D. nodded. "She's good."

"Yes."

"How's the beer?"

"Fine. How's the wine?"

"Good."

"You're quiet tonight," I said.

"I'm pensive."

I was quiet for a moment. "What exactly does that mean?"

"It means I'm thinking, wistfully."

"About what?"

"About what might have been."

"What are you talking about?"

"Matt, when I got the call from dispatch today telling me you needed an ambulance and cops, a part of me just closed down. I don't know exactly what I was thinking, but I was seeing a future without you. It lasted only a moment or two, but it was terrible. I know it was selfish. I thought you were hurt or maybe dead, and all I could think about was my life without you."

"That's not selfish, J.D. If the person you love dies, he's out of it. He's either in an afterlife or oblivion. Whichever, he's okay. It's the one left behind who grieves, who has to face each day alone, who stares down across the years and knows life will never be the same."

"You've been there. When Laura died."

"Not in the same way. We'd been divorced for a long time, but I still loved her. When she died, a part of me died, too. But not a big part. She hadn't been in my life for several years. I'd gotten used to living without her, and I knew I was responsible for her leaving, for divorcing me. If something happened to you, I'm not sure I could go on. Maybe it'd be time for me to hang it up and see what's on the other side."

"Matt, promise me that if something does happen to me, you won't give up. Life is too precious."

"I guess it is. And besides, who'd look after Logan and Jock if I checked out?"

J.D. smiled. "Well, there's that. You just take care. There are a lot of Tonys out there. And I'm afraid Bonino's people will want some revenge for what you did to their buddy today."

"What are we going to do about dinner?"

"I've got chicken potpies in the freezer."

"That'll do. Why don't you tell me what you found out today about Katie? Then we'll eat."

I was intrigued by J.D.'s story. The police theory on the death of Katie hung together well and Bert Hawkins' reservation about the DNA was too little to change any minds. Except mine and J.D.'s. We had the photograph of Katie. Either she was alive, or somebody had gone to great lengths to make us believe she was. We couldn't come up with any reason why someone would do that. But, at the same time, we had no reasonable explanation as to why somebody would want the world to think Katie was dead.

My phone rang. Jock. "Matt, where are you?"

"I'm at J.D.'s. Are you on your way?"

"I'm sitting in front of your house."

"Come on over. I'll explain things when you get here."

"Be there in a couple of minutes."

I hung up and looked at J.D. "Jock's here."

"I'm glad. He might have a new perspective on what's going on around here. He can stay in my guest room."

"I hope he's okay."

"How'd he sound?" she asked.

"Fine. But you never know. It'll depend on how rough his last few weeks have been."

"If you guys need to be alone, I'll go bunk in with Marie Phillips."

"Logan's probably already there. A threesome?"

She looked at me. Pensively, I think. Then, "It's a thought. But I can also use her guest room."

"Good idea. Logan's heart probably couldn't handle both of you."

Her phone pinged. She pulled it out of her pocket, hit a couple of keys, looked at it, and handed it to me. The tiny screen was filled with another picture of Katie Fredrickson.

CHAPTER TWENTY

Jock was tired. He'd flown from Rome to Atlanta, cleared customs, and flown into Tampa, rented a car, and driven the sixty miles to Longboat Key. He preferred large airports to small ones like Sarasota-Bradenton, because of the anonymity they offered. He walked through the door, hugged me and then J.D. "Good to see you guys," he said.

He was dressed in black trousers, a black silk T-shirt, black socks, and black shoes, his usual traveling ensemble. He swore he wasn't trying to make a fashion statement, but that black hid all the food stains he'd acquire during a long trip.

Jock was my height, six feet, and had the wiry build of a runner. He'd lost most of his hair while still in his twenties and his bald head was set off by a fringe of black hair. His skin was deeply tanned from the many days he spent in the sun chasing our country's enemies, his face wrinkled by laugh lines, his eyes dark and penetrating.

"Glad you're here, Jock," I said. "You might as well get your gear. We'll be staying here for a couple of days."

"Oh? J.D. get tired of your dump?"

"Well," she said. "Sort of. His carpet is a little messed up right now."

Jock had a quizzical look, but stood silently waiting for an explanation.

"I shot a guy in my living room," I said.

"What?" The puzzlement turned to concern.

"A guy named Tony wanted to break some of my bones, so I shot him. Three times. This afternoon."

"Talk to me, podna."

"Sit down, Jock," said J.D. "I've got chicken potpies in the freezer. You hungry?"

"Starving."

"I'll put the pies in the oven. Want something to drink?"

"I'm fine for now," Jock said.

We sat and I told him everything I knew about the past three days. J.D. would chime in occasionally and fill in blanks in my narrative. When the pies were done, J.D. served dinner on the sunporch and we ate as we talked. Jock asked, "Do you think Katie's picture is a hoax?"

"No reason to think that," said J.D. "We've talked about it, but neither of us can come up with a reason why anyone would want to jerk us around."

"Who is this guy Bonino?" asked Jock. "You said he was the local Mafia. Do you have any idea how he might be connected to Goodlow's murder?"

"None," I said.

"Then there must be some other reason he's having J.D. followed."

"I think it may be more than that," I said. "I think this P.I., Appleby, was trying to intimidate her in some way."

"What makes you think that?" asked J.D. She looked at Jock. "This is the first time I've heard this."

"Think about it," I said. "He was parked near my house at two in the morning. He didn't recognize my name when I met with him. He must have known you were there and anybody with half a brain knows that the Longboat cops aren't going to let a strange person in a strange car stay on the key that time of the morning, much less one parked on a residential street. This guy's no dummy. He knew you'd be told about him."

She was quiet for a moment. "Maybe he was waiting for me to leave so he could follow me."

"At two in the morning?" I asked.

"If he didn't know I spend a lot of nights with you, he might have thought I'd leave after you'd had your way with me." She was smiling.

"Well," I said, "you do have a reputation for one-night stands."

She threw a napkin at me. "You may be right, Matt. Maybe he's trying to put me on edge. He certainly wasn't very subtle when he was following me on GMD. He should have known I'd make him."

Jock looked at me. "Maybe the whole reason the P.I. was following J.D. was to set you up for the beating Tony was supposed to give you."

"But remember, Appleby didn't know who I was."

"He wouldn't have to," said Jock. "He just went where he was told to go."

"Why go to all that trouble?" I asked. "He could have just shown up and beat the hell out of me."

"What message would that have sent?" asked Jock.

I was stumped. "None, I guess."

"And, what message did you get from his attempt on you?"

"Not to interfere," I said.

"Interfere with what?" Jock asked.

I thought about that for a minute. "It had to be something J.D. is working on. Tony's boss didn't want me to get involved in whatever it is."

Jock turned to J.D. "What are you working on?"

"Other than a couple of car burglaries, nothing but Goodlow's murder."

"And Katie's disappearance," said Jock.

J.D. sat back in her chair. "How could that be?" she asked. "Nobody knows about that except Matt and me."

"And the Basses," said Jock.

"They don't know about the pictures," I said.

"But you went to see them," said Jock. "Maybe somebody knows about that. It wouldn't be hard to tie the facts together, J.D.'s relationship with Katie and your relationship with J.D."

"Why would the Mafia be involved in a year-old disappearance?" I asked.

"Who knows," said Jock. "What was in the picture you just got from Katie?"

"It was nothing," said J.D. "Just a picture of her with a building in the background. I sent it to my computer if you want to look at it."

"I don't think she would have sent a picture that didn't have some meaning," I said. "If it did come from Katie."

"Let's take a look," Jock said.

J.D. brought her laptop to the table and booted it up. She found the picture and turned the screen so that we could all see it. The picture was taken from a distance. It showed Katie standing in front of a nondescript two-story building constructed of concrete block that could have been in any city in the country. Katie was wearing jeans and a sweatshirt, her short hair in disarray.

"Can you zoom in on Katie?" Jock asked.

J.D. manipulated the mouse. Katie began to grow on the screen until the picture started to pixelate. J.D. stopped the zoom feature, freezing the photograph. "That's the best I can do with the program I have. I think we could get a better picture with a more sophisticated program like the one we have at the station."

"Can either of you make out what's written on Katie's sweatshirt?"

J.D. peered closely. "Damn, I wish I had a bigger screen. I can't make it out."

"How big is your TV?" Jock asked.

J.D. grinned. "Forty-two inches, and it has a USB port. I'll plug the laptop into it."

She set up the laptop so that the TV sitting in the entertainment center in her living room became the monitor. The pixelation was no better, but the bigger screen gave us a picture on which we could make out more detail. "I'll be damned," J.D. said. "Those are Greek letters on the sweatshirt. It's our old sorority."

"Zoom out a bit," I said. "I think I saw some graffiti on that building."

J.D. played with the mouse and moved the picture around, zooming in on the paint defacing the side of the building. "Damn, again," she said. "Look at that."

The graffiti was garish, the letters stylized, but the message was clear. "JED." I looked at J.D. "I think she's giving you some more information, letting you know it's really her."

"But where the hell is she?" J.D. asked. "Why not just send me a message?"

"Probably because she's not sure yet who may be looking at her texts. She's being very careful."

"I'll have the phone company see if they can tell me where this one came from, but it'll have to wait until tomorrow. I'm off to bed. You guys do some catching up, and I'll see you in the morning. I'll leave the bathroom light on for you, Matt."

After J.D. left the room, Jock sat grinning at me. "You look happy, podna."

"I am, Jock. Happier than I can remember. How're you doing?"

"I'm fine."

"How was Europe?"

"Piece of cake. I spent a little time in Spain and some in Italy. Nobody died, and we gained some intel we didn't have before. I'm fine, Matt. Really."

"Glad to hear it. You look like you need a good night's sleep."

"Yeah. It's a long trip from Rome. You bunking in with me tonight?"

I grinned. "Not even if it was your last night on earth, old buddy."

CHAPTER TWENTY-ONE

It was still dark when the three of us left J.D.'s condo on Friday morning for our four-mile run. We stayed on the sidewalk that ran beside Gulf of Mexico Drive where the streetlights gave us some illumination. There was no chatter, just three people huffing and puffing as we ate up the distance, J.D. in the lead. At the two-mile mark we reversed our course. Light was seeping over the key as the sun reached for the eastern horizon, clawing its way into the dissipating night sky. By the time we returned to the condo, the sun was peeking over the bay, its rays painting brilliant colors on the clouds that skittered across its face.

Jock went to his room, and J.D. and I headed for her oversized shower. I soaped her down, taking more time than needed. Just making sure I didn't miss any spots that might need attention. "You know," she said, "Jock's going to be waiting for us to go to breakfast."

"He won't mind a few extra minutes."

"How few?"

"Does it matter?"

"Yeah. A lot."

"Then maybe we ought to wait until after breakfast."

"I've got to go to work."

"A nooner then?"

"Not today. Too much paperwork."

"After work?" I noticed a bit of desperation creeping into my voice. I hated to appear so needy.

"Jock'll still be here."

"I'll send him to Tiny's."

"He'll know why."

"He'll understand."

"That's kind of embarrassing."

"Nah. I've already told him you're insatiable."

She threw a washcloth at me and stepped out of the shower. "You might be right," she said, grinning. "We'll talk about it tonight."

"Are you thinking about more than talk?"

"Maybe."

I sighed. Sometimes hope is all you've got.

The Blue Dolphin Cafe was crowded, and we had to wait for a table. Such are the hassles of the season. Jock was a familiar face on the key and people missed him when he was gone. We spent our time with him catching up with some of his island friends and J.D. answering, to the extent she could, the many questions about Ken Goodlow's murder. I was generally ignored, but I've got thick skin, so it didn't hurt too badly.

After breakfast, J.D. left for work. She said she'd let me know what she found out about the origin of Katie's text. Jock and I took *Recess*, my twenty-eight-foot Grady-White fishing boat, out to a man-made reef about seven miles offshore. The fish ignored us, and after a couple of hours we gave up and headed in, running northeast toward the nearest inlet.

An offshore wind had kicked up and we were running head on into five-foot seas, the boat bouncing a bit as she cleared the tops of the swells. We made our way into the Passage Key Inlet, skirted the northern tip of Anna Maria Island, and found the channel into Bimini Bay. We pulled into the dock at Rotten Ralph's, tied up to the pilings, and went to a table on the deck overlooking the small bay.

"Great day," said Jock.

"Any day on the water's great."

"Beats golfing. Nobody keeps score."

"Are you and Logan going to practice before the tournament?"

"I called him this morning," said Jock. "He said he didn't need any practice."

I laughed. "He's a terrible golfer."

"He's so bad that a little practice isn't going to make much difference."

My phone played the opening bars from "The Girl from Ipanema," the special ringtone assigned to J.D.'s cell. "Catch any fish?" she asked.

"Not a one."

"Sounds about right. I got some interesting information on that text from Katie. It came from another burner phone in Detroit."

"I wonder what she's doing in Detroit."

"She may not be there. I got an e-mail on my office computer that was sent late last night. It came from an e-mail account of somebody I never heard of. It had a picture of a Tampa Police Department cruiser attached to it. The same building that was in the picture of her was in the background. The message said, 'This is the kind of patrol car I mentioned to you recently.' And the message was signed, 'Jed.'"

"She's telling us she's in Tampa," I said.

"I think so."

"We need to take another look at the building in the texted picture. Maybe there's something there that we were supposed to see. Something that'll give us a better location."

"I've already run the picture through the software here at the office. I didn't see anything that we missed last night, but maybe you or Jock can find something. I've sent the enhanced picture to your computer. Can you take a look at it and get back to me?"

"Yeah, but we're at Rotten Ralph's on Bimini Bay, so it'll be a while before we get home. Any chance of tracing that e-mail?"

"I asked our geek to look into it. He didn't sound very positive. We'll see."

"Anything new on your murder case?"

"Nothing. I just got the reports from the forensics people. I'll go over them and see if there's anything new. If not, I may go back to Cortez and talk some more with Bud Jamison."

"Was Cracker able to come up with the names of the two men he used to have coffee with?"

"Yes. He also told me about his journal."

"Think you might have a chapter in it?"

She laughed. "He assured me he'd destroyed that part. Said it was just too hot."

"What about the pictures?"

"He sold those to a magazine, you pervert. See you later."

CHAPTER TWENTY-TWO

Bess Longstreet was enjoying the coolness of the late autumn as she sat on the long front porch of her parents' home. A light breeze blew from the north, reminding her that winter was just around the corner. She'd trade her light blouses and skirts for sweaters and long pants, not much of a fashion statement, but one that fit the utilitarian life enjoyed by the fishermen and their families. It was late afternoon and she could hear her mother moving around the kitchen, the clang of pots and pans and dishes and bowls as she readied the evening meal. Bess's dad, Captain Dan Longstreet, was arriving soon, bringing his boat and crew in after two weeks at sea chasing the fish that drove the small economic engine that was the Village of Cortez.

She hoped her dad would be there for dinner. It was a ritual, this large meal prepared by her mom to welcome her man home from the sea. Sometimes the boat didn't return as scheduled, and most of the food would go into the icebox that sat on the small enclosed porch off the kitchen. Worry would set in. Boats were lost and men never returned. The sea could be vicious, taking those who worked it without warning, flinging them into its depths, never to be heard from again.

Bess had watched too many wives and children of fishermen in the days after their boats missed their scheduled return. They lived in anguish, their hope turning to despair and finally acceptance of the truth that the husband and father would not return, that their lives had changed and they would live out their days in the village as wards of their neighbors. It was a pact tacitly made among the people who fished the seas, that if one was lost, the others would come together to take care of the families. The widows would find work in the fish houses sorting the catch or in the coffee shops and cafés and bait shops that hung precariously to life in nearby communities. The boys would grow into teenagers and leave for the sea. Their sisters would wait a couple of years and then marry another of the young fishermen and spend their lives in the place where they were born.

Bess had seen the devastation that the war was bringing to the area. Many of the young men were in the military services and too often one of them would return home to Cortez, his remains hidden by a closed casket draped with an American flag.

The boats were crewed by men who were too old for the draft, but still young enough for the sea. Some of the older men, who had taken employment in the fish houses when they were too old for the boats, went back to sea, facing rigors to which their bodies were no longer able to adapt. Teenage girls and women, many of them married to men who'd left for war, replaced the old men in the fish houses, doing the work necessary to keep the small industry afloat in hard times.

It was time for Bess to help her mother in the kitchen. She was tired. She'd worked all day in the small office kept by her father, paying bills, balancing books, taking orders, the mundane minutiae demanded by any small business. The office was next door to the Longstreet house, sitting at the end of the long pier that was home to her dad's small fleet of three boats. Two of them were sitting idle, awaiting the time when Bess or her dad could find men to crew them.

She saw her dad's boat coming north from Longboat Pass, staying to the middle of the channel, its wake spreading out onto the flats that bordered the edge of the bay. A great sense of relief washed over her, the same one she felt every time she saw the boat coming home, another dangerous trip behind it, her dad and his crew alive. "Mom," she called. "Daddy's coming up the bay."

"Thanks, honey. You sit a while longer. I'll let you know when I need some help."

"Yes, ma'am."

Bess sat for a time, letting her mind wander. Life had always been hard for those who go down to the sea to take their living from an unforgiving ocean, but the war had made it worse. The village had been drained of young men, leaving young women who wouldn't find husbands. Some of the men would die and others, who were seeing the world outside their village for the first time, would decide to live elsewhere when the war ended. The life she had known since birth was being washed away like so much detritus of war.

She idly watched as a young man, a stranger about her own age, early twenties, walked up the crushed shell street that fronted her home, probably coming from the bus stop up on Cortez Road. He was tall and thin, angular in appearance, blond hair escaping from the Greek fisherman's cap atop his head. He walked with a noticeable limp.

He saw her, smiled, and stopped, standing in the street directly in front of her. He removed his cap and said, "Good afternoon, miss. I'm looking for Captain Longstreet's office."

"The office is closed, but I run it. I'm Bess Longstreet. Can I help you?"

"I guess I need to talk to Captain Longstreet."

"His boat came up the channel an hour ago. He should be here soon. He'll have stopped at one of the fish houses to unload his catch, but that shouldn't take too long. Why don't you come on up on the porch and wait for him?"

"If that wouldn't be an imposition."

"Not at all."

The young man climbed the three steps to the porch and took a seat in a chair facing Bess. "My name's Bud Jamison," he said.

"Nice to meet you, Mr. Jamison. Can I get you some iced tea or water?"

"No. I'm fine, thank you. Are you Captain Longstreet's daughter?"

"I am."

"I heard he might be hiring."

"He's always looking for good men. Have you ever fished the boats?"

"No, but I've had a lot of experience at sea. Sailboats, mostly."

"Where're you from, Mr. Jamison, if you don't mind my asking?"

"Washington, D.C."

"You're a long way from home."

"Yes."

"How did you wash up on our shores?" she asked, and then caught herself. "I'm sorry, Mr. Jamison, that was rude. We just don't see many new people around here. Forget I asked."

He smiled, showing two rows of very white and even teeth. She noticed a small scar on his left cheek that crinkled when he smiled. "It's a fair question," he said. "I've been traveling and had gotten as far as Tampa. I'm about out of money and was looking for a job. No luck in Tampa. I was hitchhiking toward Sarasota, and a man who gave me a ride said he'd heard that Captain Longstreet might be hiring."

"Do you know the man's name? The one who picked you up?"

"Mack Sweeney, I think he said. He lives on Anna Maria Island."

"I know Mr. Sweeney. He and my dad are friends. Why don't you stay for dinner, Mr. Jamison? Daddy's three crew members will be here with their wives, and we've always got room for one more."

"That'd be nice," he said, "if you're sure I wouldn't be intruding."

"Not at all. Here comes the *Miss Dolly* now."

Jamison turned to see a boat about fifty feet in length chugging up the narrow channel that led from the bay past the fish houses and the docks where the boats were moored when they weren't at sea. Its nets were folded on the deck, the booms standing straight up, as if at attention. A wheelhouse sat near the high prow just forward of a small deckhouse, leaving a large work area aft. A long blast of the ship's horn told the village that another boat had made it safely home.

Jamison watched as the captain eased the vessel into its berth, gently nudging the pilings as it came to rest. Crewmen jumped off the boat and slipped the dock lines over the cleats and bollards attached to the wooden pier. The engine shut down, and the crew brought out hoses to wash off the salt that had accumulated on the topsides during two weeks at sea.

Their work done, Captain Dan Longstreet and his crew trudged toward the house where the large meal awaited. Bess and Jamison stood as the four men approached. They were no longer young, and if there hadn't been a war on, they would probably be working a landside job, going home each night to their wives and family. They looked tired and worn, their clothes threadbare and caked with salt. Their skin was dark from the sun and wind, their hands gnarled by years of handling lines and nets, their bodies thin from the grueling work demanded of those who earned their living from the sea. They wore untrimmed beards and smelled of fish and body odor.

One of the men said, "We'll get cleaned up, Cap, and come on back with the womenfolk. I can smell Dolly's cooking from here. Tell her we'll hurry."

Three of the men continued down the shell street, leaving a tall gaunt man who turned toward his daughter, smiling. "Ah, Bess. Don't you look lovely?"

She went to him, hugged him, and kissed him on the cheek. "You need a bath, Daddy."

He laughed. "That I do."

"Daddy," Bess said, "I'd like you to meet Mr. Bud Jamison from Washington, D.C. He's looking for a job."

Longstreet shook hands with Jamison. "We can use all the men we can get," he said. "I've got two boats sitting idle because I can't find hands. What kind of experience do you have?"

"None fishing, sir, but I've had lots of time on sailboats. I know my way around a chart and can handle all the navigation equipment."

"Know anything about marine engines?"

"A bit. I used to help a friend of mine who worked on yacht engines at the marina where we kept our boat."

Longstreet laughed. "These ain't no yachts, young fellow."

"Yes, sir, but the principles would be similar. I can probably fix the little problems that come up from time to time."

The screen door of the house opened and a small woman wearing a dress and apron came through it. She ran to Longstreet and hugged him, holding him for a couple of extra beats. "I'm glad you're home, Dan. I've missed you."

"I've missed you, too, Dolly. What's for supper?"

She chuckled. "Just about anything you want, except fish. I figured you boys must have eaten about all the fish you can stand for a while."

"That's for sure. Will you join us, Mr. Jamison?"

"Mama," said Bess, interrupting, "this is Bud Jamison. He stopped by looking for a job, and I've already invited him to dinner."

Dolly said, "Glad to have you, Mr. Jamison. You might want to go wash up before this filthy person I'm married to ruins the bathroom."

"Yes, ma'am," said Jamison. "Thank you for having me."

CHAPTER TWENTY-THREE

THE PRESENT

Jamison answered the door wearing gray flannel trousers, a starched dress shirt, and a baggy cardigan sweater. The sky was overcast and a stiff wind blew down the village street and the air smelled of rain and salt. The old man invited J.D. into the chilly house.

"Sorry about the chill, Detective," said Jamison, as he pointed her toward a chair. "I keep the thermostat low during the winter. Helps with my power bills. Have you found out any more about Ken's death?"

"Do you know any Arabs, Mr. Jamison?"

"I don't think so. Why?"

"It appears that the man who killed Mr. Goodlow was an Arab."

"From where?"

J.D. shook her head. The forensic reports she'd reviewed didn't tell her much that she didn't already know. "Could be New Jersey for all we know. His DNA tells us he was of Arabic descent. He could have been from anywhere. I'd like to show you a picture of him. He's dead in the photo. Will that be upsetting?"

Jamison smiled, sadly. "I've seen dead people, Detective." He studied the picture for a couple of moments. "I don't think I've ever seen him before."

"Do you know if Mr. Goodlow had any Arabic friends?"

"Not that he ever mentioned."

J.D. pulled the prints she'd made of the old Goodlow pictures from her purse and passed them to Jamison. "Can you tell me which one of these is Mr. Goodlow?"

Jamison looked at one of the pictures and pointed to a young man standing next to a woman of about the same age. "That's him."

"Who's the woman?"

"My wife."

"What was her name?"

"Bess."

"Was she from Cortez?"

"Yes. She was the daughter of Captain Longstreet, the man I worked for."

"Do you mind my asking how she died?"

A cloud passed over the old man's face, a hint of sorrow, of what might have been. "In childbirth," he said. "May fifth, 1951."

"I'm sorry."

"Yeah. Me, too. We tried for a long time to have a child. It never occurred to me that it would kill her."

"You mentioned earlier that you had a daughter."

"Yes. Melanie. She's gone, too. Cancer. Died in August of '75."

"Do you have any other family?"

"No. I was an only child, and my parents died in an automobile accident before the war. The people in this village have always been my family. Now most of them are dead. Getting old, Detective, is hard."

"I keep hearing that age is just a number."

Jamison laughed. "Don't believe it. Age kind of creeps up on you and one day you wake up and realize that you're old, that what was once your future is now all in the past. Suddenly, you're staring into the abyss with nothing to look forward to but endless days of just surviving. I think some of us live too long."

"How do we know when that is?"

"When you're the last one left."

J.D. nodded. Maybe he was right. She pointed to two men who were seated at a table in one of Goodlow's pictures. "Do you know either of these men?"

"Sure. The one on the right is Mack Hollister and the other is Bob Sanders."

"Do you know what happened to them?"

"Yeah. They both died."

"When?"

"Why are you interested in that, Detective?"

"Just following up."

"On what?"

"If I'm going to solve this murder, I need to know everything I can about Mr. Goodlow and his friends, his life here in the village. I need to know if there are any people left who might bear a grudge against him for something that happened in the past. Something that might have gotten him killed."

"Are you going to ask me about every one of the people in these pictures?"

"I am. When did Hollister and Sanders die?"

"Mack passed about a year ago, Bob a month or two later. They were among the last of the old crowd to go."

"How did they die?"

"Are you asking me the cause of their deaths?"

"Yes."

"Old age. They just wore out."

J.D. paused for a beat, looking closely for a sign that Jamison was lying. Then she pointed to another figure in one of the pictures. "Who's this?"

Jamison identified the image, and J.D. asked about several more. Jamison told her the names and approximately when they died. Several of the people had moved away years ago, and Jamison had no idea what might have happened to them, whether they were alive or dead. But when J.D. pointed to one man standing near the fire pit, she noticed the same quirk she'd caught when she'd first interviewed him, that indescribable feeling that the old man had just lied to her.

"Who is this man? The one by the fire pit," J.D. said.

"That's Rodney Vernon. He moved to New Jersey back in the early '50s."

"Is he still alive?"

"I don't have any idea. I haven't heard from him since he left Cortez."

J.D. sat quietly for a moment, looking at her notes. "Mr. Jamison," she said, "I get the distinct feeling that you know more about Mr. Goodlow's murder than you're telling me. Why is that?"

"I don't know where your feelings come from, Detective, but I can assure you that you know everything I know."

J.D. stood. "Thank you for your time, Mr. Jamison," she said. "I can find my way out."

She drove to Matt's house and let herself in. The place was quiet, no one home. The spot on the carpet where Tony had left his body fluids had dried, leaving no sign of the fight. The overcast sky had not cleared, and the bay outside the windows was an expanse of gray water, slightly ominous in appearance. Drops of rain started to fall, splattering the sliding glass doors that led to the patio. A boat was coming down the bay, running at speed. It looked like *Recess,* Matt's boat. She watched as it came off plane, slowed, and began to make its way up the channel that led to the dock behind the house. She decided to let the men secure the boat. No need in her getting soaked.

She sat down at Matt's computer and pulled up the picture of Katie in front of the building in Tampa. She examined it closely, but could not see anything she'd missed before. She stared at the computer screen, mentally begging the photograph to reveal its secrets. Maybe there weren't any. She fiddled with the mouse and zoomed in on the picture. The resolution was much better after the department's geek had worked on it.

There was something on the back of Katie's right hand, a tattoo maybe. J.D. focused on the hand, zoomed in some more. The picture began to pixelate, just as it had the night before, but this time the upgraded resolution provided the image with much better definition. J.D. zoomed out in small increments until the picture cleared and she could read what was written on Katie's hand. It wasn't a tattoo, but something written in black ink. She studied the image, but could make no sense of it. Katie was trying to tell her something, but what? Why the subterfuge? Why not simply call her and ask for help?

J.D. studied the image, but couldn't make out the words written on Katie's hand. She downloaded the picture to a flash drive and inserted it in the USB port in Matt's TV. In the larger picture, she was able to read the inscription, but it made no sense. A letter and a number. "U166."

CHAPTER TWENTY-FOUR

We ate lunch as Jock told me about his mission in Europe. It was pretty run-of-the-mill compared to what he often had to do. I told him that my relationship with J.D. was ripening and that every day brought a new surprise, a new insight into this wondrous woman who loved me. "Life doesn't get any better than this," I said.

Weather was moving in as we left Rotten Ralph's. It had slipped up on us as we ate and drank a couple of beers. The sun had disappeared behind the dark clouds that were rapidly moving in from the north. The wind increased, bringing cold bursts of air that rattled the halyards of the sailboats docked at Galati's Marina next door to the restaurant.

"We'd better head for the barn," I said. "We've got a cold front coming in. It's going to get rough out there."

Jock agreed. We paid our check and climbed aboard *Recess*. I started the engines as Jock handled the lines. We motored out of Bimini Bay and into the teeth of the wind blowing south across Tampa Bay. We had a wet run with quartering seas until I found the intracoastal channel that led from the bay into Anna Maria Sound and down to Sarasota Bay. It was slow going all the way home. The wind had whipped up the surface so that even as we moved out of Tampa Bay and into the lee of Anna Maria Island, we had to contend with whitecaps. Visibility was dropping and the rain was pounding us as we approached the Manatee Avenue Bridge. The span began to rise in response to a signal from a northbound sailboat. I moved to the right of the channel, leaving plenty of room for the sailor. We sat while he slowly navigated under the bridge, fighting the wind blowing in his face. He'd have a rough time of it on Tampa Bay.

The rain came down harder, riding the wind blowing from the stern and robbing us of much of our visibility. I set the throttles to a slow speed, barely keeping the boat on plane as we ran south, skirting Palma Sola Bay and slowing for the Cortez Bridge. I picked up speed as we made the run for home. The rain had slackened a bit as we outran the worst of it.

As we made our way down the channel that led to my dock, I saw that the lights were on in my cottage. J.D., probably, but it might have been Logan or anyone of several other people who knew where I hid the spare key and were close enough friends to make themselves at home even when I wasn't there.

We secured the boat to the dock pilings and trooped up the walkway to the patio. We'd have to clean the boat and the fishing gear after the storm blew itself out. I could see J.D. inside, sitting at my computer, engrossed in whatever she was looking at. I knocked on the patio doors to get her attention. She came and unlocked the door to let us in.

"You're wet," she said.

"It's raining."

"Go change. I've got something to show you guys."

When we came back into the living room, J.D. pointed to the television screen that showed somebody's right arm and hand. "What's that?" I asked.

"Katie's hand. From the picture she texted last night. Look at what's written on it. Can you make that out?"

I stared at the screen for a moment, studying the hand. "Looks like it says 'U166.' Does that mean anything to you?"

"No. I thought you might have an idea."

"A rock band?"

J.D. laughed. "I don't think so."

"How about something to do with your sorority?" asked Jock.

"I doubt it," said J.D. "If it is connected to the sorority some way, I don't remember it."

"That's not a tattoo," I said. "Looks like somebody used a Sharpie to write it. Is Katie right-handed?"

"No. I already thought about that. She's left-handed, so she could have written it herself."

"It obviously has some meaning to her," Jock said.

"Apparently so." said J.D. "But why would she be trying to give me some information that I can't decipher?"

"Either she thinks it'll mean something to you or it's some kind of code," said Jock. "Maybe it's only part of a message."

"But why would she send me only part of a message?" J.D. asked.

"There's probably more to come," said Jock. "We'll just have to wait until she sends you another text."

"U166," I said. "What the hell is U166?"

CHAPTER TWENTY-FIVE

GULF OF MEXICO, JULY 30, 1942

U-166 was rigged for attack and running on the surface, racing at flank speed through the calm waters of the northern Gulf of Mexico, closing in on her target with the intensity of a cheetah going for the kill. The night was dark and hot and the German submarine was running without lights. Her target was blacked out too, no lights showing, but the lookout atop the U-boat's conning tower had the passenger freighter in sight. She was an American flagged ship, the *Robert E. Lee*, although the U-boat's captain, Oberleutnant zur See Hans-Günther Kuhlmann, had no way of knowing that. She was a medium-size American ship carrying passengers and cargo, and Kuhlmann didn't need to know her name.

U-166 was a new boat, launched in 1941. She was a IX C class *Unterseeboot*, one of the infamous U-boats that stalked the seas, killing Allied seamen, and sending millions of tons of seaborne cargo to the bottom. She was two hundred fifty-one feet of steel with a range of thirteen thousand nautical miles. She had left her home port of Lorient, France, on June 17 and was now forty-three days into her first combat patrol under the command of Captain Kuhlmann, a twenty-eight-year-old career naval officer.

Kuhlmann had been tracking his target for several hours, keeping to the depths, viewing the *Robert E. Lee* through his periscope. He could only make four knots while submerged and because of the need to recharge the batteries that propelled his boat while under water, it was necessary to surface more often than the captain thought prudent.

The U-166 had been patrolling the approaches to the Mississippi River, the captain sure that sooner or later a fat target would present itself, either coming or going from the Port of New Orleans. It had been late in the afternoon when Kuhlmann first sighted the lumbering freighter on the horizon. He quickly ordered the boat onto a course to intercept the target and returned to his place at the periscope. The U-166 was in position an hour later. The target was headed straight toward the U-boat as she approached the mouth of the Mississippi. Easy pickings, Captain Kuhlmann thought.

As the target grew larger in his viewfinder, Kuhlmann saw another ship moving up from astern of the freighter. It was faster than the target and in a few minutes Kuhlmann identified the new ship as a U.S. Navy patrol craft. He quickly checked his book of silhouettes and determined that she was a new type, a sleek warship one hundred seventy-eight feet long with a top speed of twenty knots. She carried four large guns and equipment to launch depth charges from either side and off the stern. She was escorting the merchantman, and Kuhlmann knew that once he fired at the target, the escort would come after him. If he didn't perform his killing mission with perfection, the depth-charge attack that was sure to follow might prove fatal to his boat and the forty-nine men under his command.

A surface attack with the U-boat's torpedoes provided the best chance to make the kill, but it also gave the American patrol boat a better chance to find and destroy the submarine. Kuhlmann's crew was anxious to sink something worthy of their efforts. The boredom of life at sea in a steel tube that spent all day underwater was taking its toll on their morale. They had only sunk three small vessels since they left France. Two of them had been too small to rate a torpedo and Kuhlmann had attacked on the surface, sinking them with gunfire.

The captain checked his position again. He was about forty-five nautical miles south of the entrance to the Mississippi River. The patrol boat had slowed and was now matching the speed of the *Robert E. Lee*, slogging along on her port side. Kuhlmann positioned U-166 so that he would be on the starboard side of the freighter as she came abreast of him. With any luck, he could get his torpedoes away and submerge before the patrol boat recognized the danger and came searching for the attacker.

Time seemed to creep by as the *Robert E. Lee* slowly sailed toward her doom, the patrol boat oblivious to the danger, unaware that a submarine lurked nearby. Kuhlmann looked at his watch, ten o'clock in the evening. He made a quick notation in his logbook and turned to the young Leutnant zur See sitting at the plotting table. "It won't be long now, Paulus. We'll take this one out and head for Texas."

Leutnant zur See Paulus Graf von Reicheldorf nodded. He was not a submariner. He was a courier for Admiral Wilhelm Canaris, chief of the Abwehr, the German intelligence agency. Captain Kuhlmann was the only man aboard the U-boat who knew of his mission. Von Reicheldorf had come aboard shortly before the boat sailed, and his presence on the patrol had not been explained to the crew.

The captain activated his microphone and spoke to the crew. "We're going after a cargo ship, but she has an armed escort. As soon as we fire the torpedo, we'll dive and begin evasive maneuvers. We're going to take some depth charges, but we've got a lot of water under us, so we should be fine. We surface in five minutes."

Reicheldorf was twenty-two years old and had been in the navy since he dropped out of Heidelberg University. He spent his first year as an officer aboard surface ships. He'd inherited the title of Graf, which was the equal to the continental counts or English earls, when his father was killed in the Royal Air Force's bombing of Hamburg on the evening of May 17, 1940. His mother had also died that night, leaving the young graf with no immediate family.

Admiral Canaris had been friends with the graf's dead father since they'd first met during their time as naval cadets. Canaris had remained in the navy following the First World War and eventually became head of the Abwehr. Like most of the men and women of that agency, Canaris was not a Nazi. Paulus's father had never accepted the party either, even though he served it as a diplomat. He saw himself as working for the greater good of his beloved Germany and thought that sooner or later the Nazis would disappear from the earth and sanity would again prevail in German politics.

When the elder graf died, Canaris plucked Paulus from the fleet and installed him in the Abwehr offices, thinking the new duty station would give him a better chance of surviving the war. The young officer worked for the agency for a year, acting essentially as a clerk. He chafed under the repetitive and boring tasks, and asked the admiral on several occasions to assign him work in the field. He completed some rudimentary courses, learning the basics of the spy trade, and hectored his boss to give him an assignment that would be more meaningful than filing documents sent by real field agents.

On a fine morning in early June in Berlin, when the sun shone over the city not yet destroyed by the incessant bombing of the British and American air forces, the young graf was summoned to the admiral's office. "Paulus," the admiral began, "you've been after me to send you into the field, and I've resisted those efforts."

Paulus smiled. "I'm aware of that, sir."

"I brought you into the Abwehr because I wanted to keep you safe. You've already sacrificed too much. You lost both your parents to the British bombers, and I wanted to make sure that you survive this madness. You come from a proud family with a long history. I think it necessary for those good names to survive this war. Somebody will have to run Germany after the war."

"Sir, I understand, but I think my father would want me to fight for the fatherland just as he did. Not spend the war shuffling papers."

"I agree, Paulus. I've put a lot of thought into this and I think your father would be unhappy with me for keeping you here. I've decided to send you on a mission."

Paulus sat back in his chair and drew a deep breath. "Thank you, sir."

"You have a command of the English language that we need for this mission and, frankly, I don't have any other agents available that can match that."

"Am I going to England, sir?"

"America," said the admiral.

"How?"

"A U-boat will be leaving Lorient, France, in a week, bound for a war patrol in the Gulf of Mexico. The captain's primary mission is to destroy shipping, but he can take you in close to the Texas coast near Galveston. From there, you'll be on your own."

"Texas?"

"Yes. We have a very active ring working in San Antonio, right in the middle of several important military installations. Your job will be to deliver some documents to them."

"How will I get from the coast to San Antonio?"

"Ah, my young friend, that is where your own ingenuity comes in. Since we don't know exactly where the U-boat will be able to safely put you ashore, we can't arrange a pickup. We don't want you using a phone to call San Antonio, so you'll have to make your own way. You'll be provided with documents making you an American citizen. I don't think it'll be that difficult for you to reach San Antonio and make contact with our people there."

"How far is San Antonio from where I'll land?"

"About four hundred kilometers, or two hundred fifty American miles."

"How will I get out when the mission's finished?"

"Our people in San Antonio have an escape route through Mexico already established. It's easy to cross the Mexican border into Mexico, but since the war started the Americans have beefed up their border security to the point that we cannot get anybody *into* the United States."

"How does it work?"

"You'll be taken across the border and then some Mexicans who sympathize with us will get you to the port of Veracruz. You'll board a neutral merchant ship and be taken to Spain. We'll get you home from there."

"Sounds like a lot of trouble for the delivery of some documents. They must be important."

"More than you will ever know," the admiral said.

The operation was well underway. The documents he was to carry to San Antonio were in a waterproof briefcase locked in the U-boat's safe. They were in code, a simple cypher that depended on page, line, and word number from a specific book to unlock.

He'd been at sea aboard the U-166 for more than six weeks and was anxious to get on with his mission. The documents section of the Abwehr had provided him with a fake identity, the papers establishing him as an American citizen. He had a passport, birth certificate, driver's license, American money, and a legend, the fabricated story of his life. His documents and money were in a waterproof money belt that he wore at all times. He did not want to take the chance of a crewman finding them. In a way, the documents for the group in San Antonio were not as critical to hide. Nobody would be able to figure out the code without the key, and Paulus was the only person other than the admiral who knew the name of the book that would unlock the code.

The sub carried a two-man rubber raft that Paulus would paddle ashore. The U-boat would come in as close to the beach as the water's depth would allow, but there would still be a lot of paddling involved. The plan was for him to land on a deserted section of the shore. A knife thrust would let the air out of the boat and he would bury it behind the dunes, dropping the small shovel into the hole before pushing the sand over it.

Von Reicheldorf would be wearing civilian clothes, and he knew if he was captured and his cover was blown that he would be executed, the penalty meted out to spies.

The two young officers, Kuhlmann and von Reicheldorf, found they had much in common, including a love of Germany and an abhorrence of the Nazis. They kept their anti-party feelings between them. One never knew if a crewmember might report them to the Gestapo over some careless remark. During the long days of the voyage from France, they'd formed a friendship that they thought would outlast the war. If they survived. But they both knew their chances of that were not good.

CHAPTER TWENTY-SIX

I was still staring at the hand on my TV screen when J.D. said, "I also talked to Jamison again."

"Anything new?" I asked.

"I went through all the pictures with him. He identified everybody in them, including the two men who used to have coffee with him and Cracker. Said both died of old age."

"What about the other people in the pictures?" Jock asked.

"The ones he knows about are all dead. Two of the people had moved away, and he said he didn't know what happened to them. He assumed they're dead, too. But I think he was lying again."

"About what?" I asked.

"He told me that one of the men who showed up in a couple of the pictures had moved to New Jersey back in the early '50s, and he didn't know what happened to him. I'm pretty sure he was lying about that."

"What makes you think he was lying?" I asked.

"Cop's intuition," she said. "I got the same feeling I had when I first met with him, and he told me he didn't know why Goodlow needed a lawyer. I can't put my finger on it, but he was lying. He knows more about this than he's letting on."

My phone played the first bars of the old Styx rock classic, "Renegade," the ringtone I'd assigned to my friend Sammy Lastinger, the bartender at Pattigeorge's. "Hey, Bro. Where are you?"

"At my house. Come on over."

"Nah. I'm at Tiny's, surrounded by horny women."

"It's three in the afternoon," I said. "There are no women at Tiny's this time of day."

"Well, Cracker's here and we're talking about horny women. The conversation conjures up visions of my misspent youth."

"I thought you were in the middle of your misspent youth."

"Maybe, but I feel like I'm misspending less and less of it every day."

"It'll get worse," I said.

"So I've heard. Matt, I overheard a conversation at my bar last night that might mean something to J.D."

"She and Jock are here with me. Let me put you on speaker." I fiddled with the phone and then said, "Okay. Can you hear me?"

"Sure."

"Tell us what you heard."

"Do any of you know Porter King?" asked Sammy.

"I've met him," said J.D.

"Well, he was at the bar with a man I've never seen before. I wasn't paying any attention to their conversation, but I did hear King say something about getting rid of Jamison. At least, I think he said Jamison. I figured they had to fire somebody. Then the new guy said something about the heat being all over this one. I thought they were probably talking about basketball, but I don't know any players named Jamison."

"Basketball?" J.D. asked.

"The Miami Heat? You know. The NBA team in Miami."

"Sammy," I said, "there's a large world out there that has nothing to do with sports."

"I know, but it's not real important."

"Did you hear anything else?" J.D. asked.

"No, but I was just asking Cracker if he knew who the hell they might have been talking about. Some player I never heard of, maybe. Cracker said there's an old guy in Cortez named Jamison and that J.D. might want to know about the conversation."

"I do, Sammy," said J.D. "Can you and Cracker keep this quiet? I don't think it would be in your best interest to let it be known that you overheard that conversation."

"This is serious, then," Sammy said.

"Very serious, Sam," said J.D. "I'll talk to you later." She hung up.

"Porter King is the guy who lives in the condo complex where Goodlow was killed," I said.

"And he was the one talking to the shooter just minutes before the murder," said J.D.

"What do you know about him?" asked Jock.

"Not much," said J.D. "We ran a background check on him, and he came up clean. Made a lot of money in the oil business. He was involved in exploration somehow. Never any trouble with the law. All his business dealings seemed legit, so I didn't follow up. I will now."

"Sounds as if Jamison might be in danger," I said.

"Yeah. I'll go talk to him. See if he's got somewhere to go that's safer than Cortez."

"What about King?" I asked.

"I need to find out more about him. I'll get somebody to run him through all the databases, see if anything pops up."

"You didn't find much before," said Jock.

"No. Unless there's a criminal history, we're not going to get a lot more than we could find on Google. I better get over to Jamison's."

CHAPTER TWENTY-SEVEN

The temperature had dropped and light rain was drifting on the north wind when J.D. parked in front of the Jamison house. She noticed that the old car that, on her last visit, she had seen ensconced in the carport, was missing. She knocked on the door and got no response. She waited for a couple of minutes and knocked again. No answer.

J.D. pulled her light jacket a little closer and walked next door. A middle-aged woman answered her knock. J.D. flashed her badge and said, "I'm Detective J. D. Duncan from Longboat Key. I'm looking for Mr. Jamison. Do you have any idea where he might have gone?"

"I'm Cindy Ferda, Detective. Come on in out of that wind."

"Thanks, Mrs. Ferda, but I'm in kind of a hurry. It's important that I get in touch with Mr. Jamison."

"I haven't seen him today, and he doesn't get out much anymore." She peered around the corner of the door. "His car's gone. He may have driven down to the Winn-Dixie at Seventy-Fifth Street. That's where he always buys his groceries."

"Any other place you can think of that I might find him?"

"He goes over to the Seafood Shack sometimes for a couple of beers. He usually waits for my husband, Joe, to come home and they go together."

"What about friends in the neighborhood?" J.D. asked.

"There're a few, but most of his buddies have died out. It's a shame. He seems lonely."

"You didn't hear his car drive off?"

"No, but I had the television on, so I probably wouldn't have heard it."

"Have you seen anybody around his house today?"

"You're starting to worry me, Detective. What's going on?"

"Nothing, really. I was here earlier today and spoke with Mr. Jamison. I got the impression he wasn't planning to go out in this weather."

Mrs. Ferda laughed. "Bud's his own man," she said. "He's lived alone for a long time. He tends to come and go when a mood strikes him. I think his biggest outing every week is the trip to the grocery store. But he's always home at night. He'll show up. Sometimes he stops for dinner somewhere, but he's always home by eight o'clock or so."

J.D. gave her a business card. "If you see him, will you tell him to call me immediately? It's important."

"Certainly, Detective."

J.D. walked back to her car thinking that there really wasn't any cause for alarm. Jamison had a life and there was no reason he wouldn't have gone somewhere to while away a dreary afternoon. If it wasn't for the threat Sammy had heard at the bar, she wouldn't be worried. But there had been a threat. She was sure that King was talking about bringing some harm to this old man. But why?

She called the station and asked for the department's geek. "Anything yet on King?" she asked when the phone was answered.

"There's not a whole lot. He owned a company that worked with oil companies that were drilling in offshore waters. His outfit contracted with the oil companies to find the best places to lay underwater pipe that would run from the drilling platform to the shore and then they'd build the pipeline. King sold his company to one of his major competitors three years ago and made a lot of money."

"Did you find any connection to Bud Jamison?"

"None. King bought his condo on Longboat a year ago and moved in. Before that he'd lived in New York City. They might have run into each other around here, but that'd be about it."

"Is he married?"

"Divorced."

"Any family?"

"None. At least not any close family."

"Okay. Thanks."

J.D. drove across Cortez Road and stopped in the parking lot of the Seafood Shack. It was getting late and she was worried about Jamison. She went into the bar to talk to Nick, the bartender. "Do you know a man from Longboat named Porter King?"

Nick shook his head. "Can't say that I do. Who is he?"

"He lives on Longboat Key. He may know Bud Jamison. King's middle-aged, about your height, brown hair going to gray, in good shape."

"If I've ever seen him, I don't remember it. Bud usually comes in by himself or with his next door neighbor, Joe Ferda. All his other old drinking buddies are gone. Ken Goodlow was the last one."

"Does Bud have a regular time for coming in?"

"No. He doesn't come in with any regularity, but he's usually here at least once a week or so. I think Joe Ferda kind of looks after him. They never have more than a couple of beers."

"If you see Bud, tell him to call me. I need to talk to him as soon as possible."

"I'll do it, J.D. Come back and bring Matt. I miss you guys."

J.D. drove back across the Cortez Bridge onto Anna Maria Island. A cold chill that had nothing to do with the weather was creeping up her spine. The old man didn't have a cell phone, or at least if he did, J.D. didn't have the number. She'd called him before on his landline. She'd try that number again later in the evening, and if she didn't get an answer, she'd drive back to Cortez.

She called Matt. "I'm crossing the Cortez Bridge. You and Jock want to have a drink at the Bridgetender?"

CHAPTER TWENTY-EIGHT

The Bridgetender Inn takes up a corner at Bridge Street and Bay Drive in Bradenton Beach, the southernmost of the three small towns on Anna Maria Island. The building has been there in different incarnations since the early days of the twentieth century and had over the years metamorphosed into a fine restaurant and bar.

J.D. was seated in the wood-paneled dining room in the older part of the building. She sat next to a window overlooking Sarasota Bay, a glass of white wine in front of her. She was staring out the window, a small frown creasing her face. It was nearly dark outside and the streetlights had just come on, giving the scene a slightly sinister look. The warm room was welcome shelter from the night and the rain and the wind. She looked up and smiled as Jock and I joined her.

I kissed her on the cheek. "Why the long face?" I asked.

"It shows, huh? I'm worried about old Mr. Jamison."

"What's up?"

"He wasn't home when I got to his house. Maybe he just went to the grocery store, but I'll feel a lot better when I know he's safe."

"Have you tried calling him?"

"Yes, just now. No answer at his house. I don't have a cell number for him."

"We can run by there before we go home," I said. "Maybe he'll be back."

J.D. shrugged. "I called the sheriff's office, and they put me in touch with the deputy that patrols the Cortez area. He'll ride by Jamison's house as often as he can and call me if the car's there. He'll also keep a lookout for it in the area, maybe parked at one of the restaurants or bars."

"He'll turn up," I said, but worry was creeping across my brain. Jamison would be an easy target for someone bent on killing him. And I was pretty sure that's what Porter King had been talking about at Pattigeorge's the night before.

"Did you find out anything else about King?" asked Jock.

"Not much. He had a business that mapped out routes for underwater pipelines running from oil drilling platforms in the oceans to shore installations and then installed the pipe. He sold out a few years ago for a lot of money and moved to Longboat about a year ago. Nothing on him that rang any alarms."

"Are you going to talk to him about the threat to Jamison?" Jock asked.

"I'm not sure yet that it was a threat. Maybe Sammy got it wrong. He's not right in the head, you know."

I laughed. "Sammy's fine," I said. "He talks a lot about his women and his sports teams, but a lot of that is just Sammy bluster. He's really a smart guy."

"I know," she said, grinning, "and you know I love him, but still, he's a real piece of work."

"That he is. And he's a damned astute observer of people. If he said he heard something, I'd take it to the bank."

"I know. That's the reason I'm so worried about Mr. Jamison."

"Did you get a look inside Jamison's house?" Jock asked.

"You mean when I went there this afternoon?"

Jock nodded.

"No," she said. "There was no answer at the door, and I didn't think I ought to just break in."

"Was the front door locked?" asked Jock.

"I didn't even check. I should have."

"Why don't Matt and I stop by his house and check the inside?"

"You mean break and enter?" asked J.D.

"I guess I do. We'd at least make sure that he's not inside hurt or worse. You don't need to be involved in it. I don't think there'd be reason enough legally for a cop to enter the house."

J.D. sat quietly for a few moments chewing on the possibilities. "Okay," she said. "If I don't hear from the deputy by the time we finish our drinks, I'll call Jamison again. If he doesn't answer, I'll go on home and you guys do what you need to do."

The house was dark and the carport empty. A streetlight partially lit the front yard, its feeble attempts at illumination mostly swallowed by the darkness. We parked a couple of houses down from Jamison's and waited for the sheriff's patrol car to come by. We didn't want to be arrested inside the house. Twenty minutes later the deputy drove slowly down the street and turned the corner, headed back to Cortez Road.

The front door was unlocked. I had a flashlight and used it to find a light switch. The lights came on and revealed a small, neat living room. Nothing out of place. No dead bodies or signs of struggle. We moved down a short hall and checked out the two bedrooms. The larger of the two was apparently where the old man slept. It had a lived-in look that was absent from the other bedroom. A pair of pajamas was hanging on a hook on the back of the door to the hall, bedroom slippers at the edge of the bed, a hardcover John D. MacDonald novel on a bedside table.

Two eight-by-ten photographs encased in identical silver picture frames sat on top of a bureau. One was black-and-white and obviously taken in a portrait studio. It showed a young woman dressed in the fashion of the late 1940s. She was pretty in an understated way, her smile showing even teeth, her hair cut short and framing a slightly round face. The other photograph was in color, a snapshot taken on a beach somewhere. It showed a young woman so thin she seemed emaciated. She had a big smile on her face and was holding an infant in her arms, the baby turned so that its face was visible in the picture. Everything seemed in order. The kitchen and bathroom were as clean as the rest of the house. We turned out the lights and left the way we'd come in.

A man with the pistol stepped out of the shadows. "Who the fuck are you?" he asked.

"We're friends of Mr. Jamison," I said. "Who're you?"

A flashlight beam suddenly broke the darkness, aimed right at my face. I raised my hand to shield my eyes. "You're Royal," said the man with the gun. "I've seen you around."

"Okay. You got me. Now take that light out of my eyes and tell me who the hell you are."

"I'm a friend of Jimmy DeLuca."

"Okay, so who's Jimmy DeLuca?"

"You know him as Tony. You put him in the hospital."

"Damn. I knew his name wasn't Tony."

"Time to pay the piper, smartass. Mr. Bonino don't like people messing up his guys."

"Don't tell me your name is Guido."

"Fuck you, Royal."

Suddenly, the flashlight was out of my eyes and rolling on the ground. A terrible scream came from the man who had held it. A shot fired, another scream that became a gurgle. Jock was on the attack, and I could only see shadows as my eyes readjusted to the dark. I bent and picked up the flashlight, shined it at the lump on the ground, and saw Guido or whatever his name was, writhing in pain, holding one arm, blood flowing from his mouth and nose, his eyes wide in terror. Jock was standing over him, not even breathing hard. I picked up the pistol. "Want me to shoot him?"

"Might as well," said Jock. "He's not going to be worth much to Mr. Bonino."

"Tell me, Guido," I said. "What's your real name?"

"What the fuck is it to you?" The man still had a little fight left in him.

"I want to put something appropriate on your tombstone."

"Fuck you."

"Shoot him," said Jock.

I put the muzzle of the pistol against Guido's forehead.

"Wait," he said. "Bernie Caster."

"That's your name?"

"Yeah."

"I liked Guido better."

"I'm only Italian on my mother's side."

"I guess that explains it."

"Don't kill me." His tone was pleading, the predator brought low, a sudden appreciation for life, at least for his own.

I heard a siren in the distance. The sound of the gunshot probably had the neighbors calling 911. "Okay. I guess the cops will be right along." I pulled out my cell phone and called J.D. "You might want to get over to Jamison's," I said. "Jock beat the hell out of a guy who was trying to kill me and the fuzz is coming. I can hear the sirens."

"Geez. I can't leave you guys alone for a minute. I'm on my way."

"Better put the gun on the ground, podna," said Jock.

I dropped it and stepped back. The squad car was turning the block, and I could hear another siren in the distance. Jock and I raised our hands as the deputy crawled out of his vehicle, gun in hand.

"Deputy," I said, "I'm Matt Royal and this is Jock Algren. Detective Duncan is on her way from Longboat. She'll vouch for us. This man attacked us."

The deputy kept his gun trained on us as he used the microphone on his epaulet to call for an ambulance. He turned back to us. "How badly is he hurt?"

"Pretty bad," said Jock, "but he'll live. Might lose the use of his right arm."

"What happened here?" the deputy asked.

I filled him in. Told him about my run-in with Tony the day before and what Bernie Caster had told us.

"Did he say Bonino sent him?"

"No. He just said that Bonino didn't like people messing with his guys."

Another sheriff's car, this one unmarked, pulled into the street, blue lights flashing. A man wearing civilian clothes got out of the car. A familiar face. He walked toward us, his gun out. "What've we got here, Walt?" he asked the deputy.

"These two said the one on the ground tried to kill them."

"Actually," I said, "he was only trying to kill me."

The flashlight the plainclothes detective was holding whipped up into my face and then to Jock's. "Shit, shit, shit," he said. "Put your weapon away, Walt. If either one of these guys decided to take it away from you, you'd be on the ground with that yahoo."

"You know these guys, Dave?"

"I do. Every time they show up in Manatee County, something goes terribly wrong."

"Good to see you, too, David," said Jock.

"Hell, I live in Manatee County," I said. "Walt, Detective Sims might be putting you on a bit."

Another car wheeled around the corner, coming fast and braking to a stop in front of the house. Sims looked over his shoulder and said, "And that'll no doubt be Detective Duncan. My life would be a lot easier if you two would stay in her jurisdiction."

"We'd miss seeing you, David," I said. Sims was an old friend who had helped us out in the past.

He gave me the finger and walked over to meet J.D. They talked quietly for a moment. Another siren sounded in the distance. "The ambulance," said Walt. "Dave, you need me to stick around?"

"Yeah. Get another couple of deputies out here. We'll probably need them. I'll take care of these two," Sims said, motioning to Jock and me.

The ambulance drove up as Walt was calling for more deputies. The medics performed a quick examination of the man on the ground and loaded him onto a gurney. He was still moaning and bleeding as Sims cuffed his good arm to the stretcher.

"Have a nice evening, Bernie," I said as they wheeled him away.

CHAPTER TWENTY-NINE

"I wonder how he found me," I said. We were huddled in J.D.'s car parked in Jamison's front yard. A light rain was still falling as we watched David Sims give directions to a couple of deputies who had come to help with the investigation. Sims was concerned about Jamison's absence as well as the attack on me. J.D. had filled him in on her investigation and told him of her fears for Jamison's safety.

"I don't think he was after you," said J.D. "You just turned out to be a target of opportunity."

"How so?" I asked.

"You said he didn't know who you were when he first came at you. He got a look at your face and recognized you. I think he was after Jamison and you just happened to show up. He was going to take the opportunity to get a little revenge for the guy you just about killed in your house yesterday."

I thought about that for a beat. "You may be right," I said. "We need to know a little more about Caster."

"As soon as David Sims gets him checked out, he'll let us know," said J.D. "Let me talk to him. Make sure we can leave." She trudged off toward the harried detective.

We were sitting in my living room when Sims called J.D. She listened, thanked him, and hung up. "David said they found Caster's car a couple of blocks from Jamison's house. Caster is in the hospital and has asked for a lawyer. He won't say anything about why he was at Jamison's. They've run his prints and he's who he says he is. He's been in prison a couple of times for aggravated assault, but that's about it. He was a suspect in a murder in New Jersey, but nothing ever came of it. David sent me a picture of Caster. Maybe we ought to show it to Sammy and see if this was the guy talking to Porter King last night."

"You guys go ahead," said Jock. "I think I'll read a bit and call it a day."

J.D. and I drove the three miles south to Pattigeorge's, the elegant restaurant on the bay where Sammy ran the bar. The streets were quiet, very little traffic. Even the snowbirds stayed in on wet nights like this one.

There were only a few people at the bar, all regulars and most of them year-rounders, those full-time residents of the key who don't go north in the summer. We spoke to several and took our seats. Sammy brought me a Miller Lite and a glass of Chardonnay for J.D.

"Sam," said J.D., "take a look at this picture and see if you recognize the guy." She handed him a copy of the photo I'd printed of Caster. He took it over to his computer terminal and held it under the light. He brought the picture back and put it on the bar.

"That's the guy who was talking to King last night," Sam said.

"You sure?" asked J.D.

"Positive."

"Will you sign an affidavit to that effect?"

"Sure. What do you need that for?"

"I'll take it to a judge first thing in the morning and use it to get a warrant to search King's condo."

"Tomorrow's Saturday," I said. "Where are you going to find a judge that isn't on the golf course?"

"Maybe the rain will keep them home. I know a judge who lives here on the key. He'll probably sign the warrant for me."

"What's 'first thing?'" Sammy asked.

"I'll be at your house at seven, you can sign it, and I'll get it to the judge and get the warrant. I'd like to get to King's place early."

"I don't think my alarm clock will work that early."

"Sammy, this is important."

"Okay. I'll leave the door open. Just come on in and get me out of bed."

"Sammy," J.D. said, "I wouldn't get within a city block of you in bed."

"Hey," he said. "I'm harmless. Besides, I'm afraid of Matt, and I wouldn't want to ruin you for him."

"I'm not worried about you, Sammy. It's me. I may not be able to control myself."

"Well, that happens a lot."

He moved on down the bar to take care of two strangers who had come in, stopping on the way to refresh Murf Klauber's drink. We finished our drinks, ordered a couple more, and enjoyed a night of conversation with friends and banter with Sammy about his girlfriends and his beloved University of Florida Gators.

It was still raining when we left the bar. The wind had picked up and was blowing cold air, dropping the temperature several degrees. It was a night when I appreciated the warmth emanating from the Explorer's heater. Gulf of Mexico Drive was deserted except for a police cruiser sitting in the parking lot of Harry's Corner Store. The Gulf was a black expanse of nothingness. The wind had kicked up an angry surf that roared onto the beach, reminding me that even our placid Gulf could turn ugly. It was not a good night to be on the water, and I was glad to be going home to a cozy bed that I would share with the beautiful woman sitting quietly next to me.

CHAPTER THIRTY

I awoke on Saturday morning to a crystalline sky so blue and deep that I was sure nobody looking at it could possibly be in a bad mood. My bed was empty. J.D. had left before daylight to get to the station to type the affidavit and the warrant. She was going to call the judge and get the warrant signed so that she could execute it before nine.

I heard Jock moving about the kitchen, the banging of cups and saucers providing a pleasant backdrop to the rich aroma of freshly brewed coffee drifting into my bedroom. I washed my face, brushed my teeth, and padded to the kitchen. Jock was sitting on the patio overlooking the bay, bundled up in sweatpants and an old sweatshirt with the Clemson University Tigers logo, the morning newspaper spread on his lap. I went back and put on some heavier clothes and joined him.

We sat quietly in the still air, sipping our coffee, braced by the uncharacteristic cold, the bay calm and tranquil. "J.D. get tired of your snoring?" he asked.

"Maybe, but she left early for work."

"Was Caster the guy Sam saw talking to King?"

"Yeah. J.D.'s using an affidavit from Sammy to get a warrant to search King's condo."

"That'll be interesting."

We sat some more. When you've been friends as long as we have, you don't always need a lot of conversation. "Want to go for a jog?" I asked when I had finished my coffee.

"Sure."

"Better change. We'll be sweating before we get back."

We jogged the beach, dodging the clumps of seaweed that had washed up during the night, discussing the murder case. "None of this makes a lot of sense," Jock said. "Why would a man who legitimately made a lot of money be involved with a snipe like Caster? And why would King want Jamison dead? Was he somehow involved in Goodlow's murder?"

"Sounds like it. He talked to the murderer just before Goodlow was killed. I'm sure he lied to J.D. about that conversation. Now he's tied to Caster and Caster was at Jamison's last night."

"And Caster is connected in some way to the jerk who tried to clean your clock the other day."

"And that guy is connected to the local Mafia who are for some reason stalking J.D."

"But," said Jock, "I think the Mafia connection might be about your hunt for Katie."

"Then the fact that Caster is connected to both the murder of Goodlow and the people upset about my looking for Katie is just a coincidence."

"Possibly."

"I don't like coincidences. Too unlikely."

"I agree," said Jock. "But it's a possibility we have to consider."

We reached our turnaround point two miles down the beach and started pounding our way north, picking up speed. The first bars of "The Girl from Ipanema" sounded from my pocket. "Hold up, Jock," I said. "It's J.D."

We slowed to a walk, and I answered the phone. "King's gone," said J.D.

"What do you mean, gone?"

"Flew the coop. He's not here."

"Maybe he's visiting his girlfriend on the mainland again."

"When he didn't answer his door this morning, I got the manager to let me in. The warrant gives me the right to search the premises even if the owner isn't there. Most of his clothes are gone, the hard drive was stripped out of his desktop computer, no papers to amount to anything left in his desk drawers. Just a few bills."

"That's a bit strange," I said. "Have you talked to any of the neighbors?"

"The manager saw him late last night putting stuff in his car. He said King seemed to be in a hurry, but didn't think anything of it."

"Did the manager see King leave?"

"No. He was still carrying stuff out of his condo the last time the manager saw him."

"What time was that?"

"Near midnight."

"Something spooked him," I said.

"Maybe he found out we'd arrested Caster."

"Could be. What now?"

"I've put out a bulletin for his car and Sarasota P.D. is watching his girlfriend's house. I'm going to talk to her as soon as I finish up here. You want to drive over to Avon Park today?"

"I can. What for?" I asked.

"I got an e-mail from Katie's dad giving me the name and address of the man who took care of Jim Fredrickson's property. I'd like you to talk to him."

"You're not going with me?"

"I've got all I can say grace over right here. Do you mind?"

"No. I'll see if Jock wants to come along," I said.

"I'll text you the name and address. I also got an e-mail this morning from the sheriff's forensic people. They had translations made of some of those documents we found in the car with the guy who killed Goodlow."

"Anything useful?" I asked.

"The German one was strange. It was written in an old-fashioned script that went out of fashion after World War II. I'll have to get you the exact translation, but it said something about the documents containing vital information for the mission and that whoever it was addressed to was supposed to get the courier out of the country. Then there were some numbers that didn't make any sense. It might be some sort of code. The forensic guys think the page we have might just be one of several pages that originally made up the document."

"What about the Arabic documents?"

"They look like correspondence between somebody named Hank and somebody else named Al. They were pretty mundane."

"Could they be in some kind of code?" I asked.

"They thought about that, but they think it's just correspondence. They've sent all the documents to the National Security Agency to see if it might be a code."

"I don't guess you've gotten any more information on the identity of the killer."

"Nada. But it occurred to me that the only indication we have that the killer is an American is what King told us about his accent. If King's involved, you can bet he lied about that. This guy may be some kind of Arab terrorist. Who knows?"

"You going to be home for dinner?" I asked.

"Probably. Call me when you get back from Avon Park."

CHAPTER THIRTY-ONE

"We lost a lot of good groves around here," Frank Cartwright said. "Got turned into subdivisions. Now a lot of those houses are in foreclosure and the neighborhoods are going to hell." He was garrulous in the way of old men. He hadn't stopped talking since Jock and I arrived at the double-wide trailer where he lived with his three dogs. He was tall and spare, his face creased with wrinkles earned by age and hard work in the sun, his white hair mostly hidden by a ball cap with a John Deere logo, his ice-blue eyes rheumy. The jeans he wore were thin with age, his flannel shirt thread-bare. His home smelled of unwashed dog and old cigarette butts. He was drinking from a mug half full of coffee that looked as if it had sat in the pot for the last year or two. Jock and I had declined his offer to join him.

"What can you tell me about Jim Fredrickson's grove?" I asked.

"Wasn't much to it. His ma and pa eked out a living with it. They couldn't afford to hire no pickers, so they did it themselves. Little Jimmy filled his share of boxes before he got that scholarship to college down in Miami. Until a couple of years ago, he never came back here after they got killed in that car wreck."

"I understand they left him the grove."

"Yeah, but he wasn't interested in working it."

"You were the caretaker?"

"If you can call it that."

"What do you mean?"

"He wasn't much interested in citrus. I'd hire a gang of Mexicans to pick the fruit when it was ripe and send it off to a packinghouse. I never had anything else to do with it. He put money in a bank account, and I was supposed to take cash out every day to pay the pickers."

"What do you mean by supposed to?"

"That's what Jimmy told me to do."

"Did you?"

"What? Pay the pickers? I sure did. Every penny. Ain't nobody ever accused me of not being an honest man."

"I didn't mean to imply that, Mr. Cartwright. I understand that Mr. Fredrickson eventually sold the grove."

"Nah. Jimmy didn't sell it. Some lawyer over in Sarasota who's handling the estate sold it after Jimmy got killed."

"Was the grove making any money?"

"I doubt it. It was only ten acres. Was a time a family could make a living out of that kind of acreage, but not no more. You got to have at least twenty acres and then you got to take care of it. Jimmy wouldn't spend no money on that old grove and it was dying. Then that hurricane came along a few years back and knocked down a lot of the trees. Jimmy wasn't about to spend the money to replant."

"What's the property being used for now?"

"Just sittin' there. I heard some developer from Orlando bought it. He's supposed to have plans to put houses on it when times get better. He's still got a few producing trees out there. Something to do with taxes, I heard. He has some locals pull a few oranges off the trees and take 'em to the packinghouse. Don't make no sense to me. He probably clears just about enough to pay his pickers."

"You said Jim didn't come here much until about two years ago. Did he start coming often at that point?"

"Yeah. I'd say he was probably here three or four times a month. I didn't always see him, but I'd hear he'd been around."

"Do you know why he was here?"

"What do you mean?" asked Cartwright.

"You said he didn't have much interest in the grove. I just wondered why he would come here fairly regularly."

"He stayed in the old home place out on the lake. Used to bring his buddies down for the weekend."

"To do what?"

"Nobody knows. Fish maybe. They didn't hunt. They'd bring women sometimes, maybe their wives, maybe not. Nobody around here knows. Come to think of it, his buddies are still using the place. Maybe he left it to them. Or maybe there really is a developer from Orlando and he and Jimmy had the same buddies."

"Where is this house?"

"In the grove Jimmy owned."

"Can you give me directions?"

"Sure, but I don't know why you'd want to go out there."

"Just following up on some legal stuff," I said.

Cartwright told us how to get to the property and said, "Help yourself, but there's a locked gate on the road in. You'll have to park and walk."

Jock and I drove south toward Sebring and then turned off onto a secondary road going east. "You were pretty quiet in there," I said.

"You were asking all the right questions. I didn't want to interrupt your rhythm."

"Well, all that silent intensity you were focusing on Cartwright didn't seem to have much effect."

"Usually doesn't."

We found the locked gate and took care of the combination lock with bolt cutters I had in the car. One never knows when a pair of bolt cutters will come in handy.

We drove down the dirt road, not much more than a rutted path, and parked in the front yard of an old house that had the weathered look that is the consequence of years of neglect. We got out of the car and walked around the house. There was a small lake tucked into the grove and the house sat on its bank. A twelve-foot Jon boat was upside down on the grass that served as a beach. It didn't look as if it had been used for a long time.

"Want to take a look inside?" asked Jock.

"Sure. I hope the law doesn't show up."

"What are the chances of that?"

We went to the front door and Jock pulled his lock picks out of his wallet. We were inside in about two beats. The house smelled musty. The hardwood floors in the living room were warped in places and the uphol-stered chairs and sofa were probably as old as the house, but in surprisingly good shape. No rips or tears. A large window looked out to the lake and a hall ran off to the right, probably to bedrooms. A kitchen was to the left, the appliances fairly new.

I walked down the hall. There were four bedrooms, each with two single beds. A bathroom on either side of the hall. I looked through the drawers of the chests and bedside tables in each room. Nothing. They were empty.

"Matt, better come look at this."

Jock was in the kitchen on his hands and knees, his head stuck into a cabinet that flanked the refrigerator. "What'd you find?" I asked.

"Take a look." He backed out, and I stuck my head inside the cabinet. A safe took up the whole area. What looked like two doors on the cabinet were really one working door and a fake one. The setup provided a large space for the safe. "That's odd," I said. "Who puts a safe in the kitchen?"

"Probably not the cleaning lady," said Jock.

"From the looks of this place," I said, "there is no cleaning lady. There was nothing in the bedrooms or baths, except dust."

"Let me show you something else," Jock said, and motioned me to follow him. We walked through a door and into a laundry room. There was a modern washing machine and clothes dryer, an ironing board folded against one wall, and a door to a closet. Jock opened the closet and switched on a light.

The closet held an arsenal. Half a dozen M-16s and several shotguns and pistols were clipped to a pegboard wall. Boxes of ammunition were stored on shelves. "I don't think this is a hunting lodge," I said.

"Not unless it's used for hunting human game."

"I wonder who owns this place."

"Didn't Katie's parents know who the estate sold it to?" asked Jock.

"I didn't ask."

"Couldn't you find out who owns it at the courthouse?"

"I could, but it's Saturday. The courthouse is closed. I'll pull up the property appraiser's website when we get back to Longboat."

Jock shrugged. "You ready to go?"

"I've seen enough," I said. "Let's get out of here."

CHAPTER THIRTY-TWO

GULF OF MEXICO, JULY 30, 1942

As the U-boat came into torpedo range of the *Robert E. Lee,* Captain Kuhlmann slowed his vessel and called out the range and other coordinates his torpedo officer would need to set up the firing solution. He looked at his watch again. Ten thirty. He wanted to remember the time of the attack so that he could properly insert it into the ship's log. The officer working below advised the captain in the conning tower that everything was in readiness for the attack. "Fire on my count," said Kuhlmann. There was a pause, then, "Three, two, one, fire."

The torpedo blasted out of one of the tubes built into the submarine and was running straight for the freighter. She did not seem aware that her death was moments away. Suddenly, when the torpedo was about two hundred yards from the doomed ship, she started to turn away. Maybe a lookout had caught a glimpse of the onrushing torpedo. But it was too late. The torpedo struck just aft of the engine room.

"Dive. Dive. Dive," the captain shouted into his microphone and motioned to the lookout to go below. Kuhlmann took one last look at the *Robert E. Lee* and knew she was mortally wounded. She had already begun to list to starboard and was slowing in the water, her engines silent. The last view the captain had as he descended the ladder was the patrol craft picking up speed and coming around the bow of the sinking freighter. Coming straight for the U-166.

The next hour was the longest Paulus Graf von Reicheldorf had ever experienced. The patrol craft was dropping one depth charge after another, the sound of the explosions reverberating through the submarine, shaking it like an angry dog with a small animal in its mouth. He could hear rivets pop, the steel hull groan, men crying out in fear, Captain Kuhlmann's orders uttered in a voice so calm they might have been part of a quiet conversation in a local bierstube.

Paulus was afraid he was about to die, but he refused to show fear. He was a German naval officer, and that was a point of pride with him. He came from a seafaring principality in the north of Germany and his ancestors had won and lost great sea battles for generations. Not one of them had ever run from a fight. He was sure of it. He would not be the first of his line to show fear.

He sat at the navigation table with the charts and plotting devices. He was trying to figure the best course out of harm's way. It was difficult with all the shaking, rolling, and pitching of the boat, but he stayed with it. After a few minutes, he advised the captain that the best route of escape was due east. They'd have deep water, and the patrol craft would have to stop chasing them sooner or later in order to help the survivors of the sinking ship.

And then it was over, as quickly as it had begun. The explosions stopped and the men on the U-boat heard the propellers of the patrol craft pick up speed as it ran westward toward the sinking freighter.

Captain Kuhlmann stayed on course for the next six hours, running submerged. He was about twenty-five nautical miles from the site of the sinking when he surfaced. It was still dark, and the fresh night air that began to circulate through the boat was a welcome relief from the terror of the depth charges.

They continued east, running on the surface. "I want to get as far from the shipping lanes as we can," Kuhlmann told Paulus. "We sustained some damage, and I want to get men into the water to check for hull ruptures. And, we need to repair some of the equipment that took a beating during the attack."

"What's our destination?" Paulus had asked.

"I think we can get to a place off the coast of the Florida panhandle that's got enough water if we need to dive, but is far enough off the sea lanes that we ought to be able to lay to on the surface for a few hours while we fix the boat."

After the batteries were charged, Kuhlmann dove again and ran for the rest of the day submerged. By dawn on August second, he was where he wanted to be. There wasn't much activity along this coast, and he could spend a few hours on the surface. He hove to and floated serenely on the flat water, his engines turning over in case he had to submerge in a hurry.

The captain and Paulus stood on the conning tower, alone except for the lookout posted behind them. The sun was rising above the eastern horizon and its brilliance masked the approach of a high-winged twin-engine amphibious aircraft that was homing in on the U-boat, coming fast, unseen by the German crew. The lookout in the tower finally saw the aircraft and shouted a warning, but it was too late, the plane too close. Before Kuhlmann could give an order, the plane had descended to within a couple of hundred feet and dropped its only weapon, a two-hundred-fifty-pound depth charge. It hit the boat's bow and exploded, mortally wounding U-166. The men on the tower braced for another approach by the plane, but it didn't come. The attacker climbed into the sky and headed north.

The explosion had ripped the hull apart and many men died immediately. The boat was breaking up and sinking and nobody was coming out. The lookout was bleeding badly. He'd taken a piece of the submarine's hull in his neck when the shrapnel from the depth charge started to fly. Kuhlmann was pulling at a hatch on the deck of the conning tower. It finally came open and the captain pulled out a yellow two-man rubber life raft, folded into a small square. "Let's get this thing down on the deck," he shouted.

Paulus helped settle the raft on the railing of the tower and then climbed down the ladder. The deck was slanting to starboard and it was hard for Paulus to keep his footing. He looked up. The lookout was hanging over a railing that surrounded his perch. He was dead. Kuhlmann struggled with the raft, letting it slowly dangle from the tower to the deck by its bow rope. Paulus felt the U-boat shudder as it settled farther into the water. He grabbed the raft as it hit the deck. "Paulus, see that little cylinder attached to the raft?"

"Here it is."

"When it's time to launch, pull that cylinder and the raft will automatically inflate. There are provisions for several days in a container in the raft. Water and food."

"I'll wait until you get down here."

"I'm not coming," said Kuhlmann.

"Hans, come on. It's our only chance."

"My men are all dead or dying and going down with the boat. I think I'll join them."

The U-boat rode lower in the water now. The bow had broken off and sunk and the rest of the boat was rapidly following. Nobody had come out of the boat, but men were still alive, trapped in the twisted metal that had only minutes before been a sleek submarine. The screams of the sailors trapped below were pitiful, each man aware that his life was over.

Paulus was about to say something else, to argue with Hans, to remind him of his wife waiting in Flensburg for him to return, when the captain saluted him and said, "Go with God, Paulus. Survive this goddamned war." Then he was gone, disappearing down the hatch.

Paulus stood for a couple of moments at attention, saluting the departing captain, and then activated the raft, pushed it overboard, and got in. In less than a minute, the remaining part of U-166 slipped beneath the waves and Leutnant zur See Paulus Graf von Reicheldorf was alone.

CHAPTER THIRTY-THREE

THE PRESENT

J.D. stopped by the Sarasota police station on her way to see Porter King's girlfriend. She had promised Captain Doug McAllister that she'd return his file on Katie Fredrickson. She wouldn't mention that she'd made a copy of it. She was admitted to the building and directed to the homicide bureau. She was surprised to see Doug in the office late on a Saturday afternoon. He waved her in and pointed to a chair.

"J.D., good to see you," he said. "Want some coffee?"

"No thanks, Doug. I'm surprised to see the boss working on Saturday."

"Murders don't take days off."

She smiled. "I think there was a movie with that title, or something like it."

Doug laughed. "Maybe so."

"I had to come downtown so I thought I'd drop off your file."

"Find anything interesting?"

"Nothing that I didn't already know. I'm afraid Katie's dead."

"Looks that way. What brings you downtown?"

"I'm looking for a suspect in a murder and I want to talk to his girl-friend. She lives on Gulfstream Avenue. One of your patrolmen is sitting on her building."

"I didn't know that," he said.

"I talked to your chief of patrol a couple of hours ago," said J.D.

"The girlfriend lives in high-dollar territory. Who's the guy you're looking for?"

"His name's Porter King. He lives on Longboat. I executed a search warrant on King's condo and found him cleared out."

"Is this about the man gunned down in the condo parking lot out there?"

"Yes. The only murder we've had lately."

"You think King killed him? I heard you had video of the murder."

"We do have the video, and the guy who pulled the trigger is dead. I think King is involved somehow. It looks like he's trying to kill one of our other witnesses."

"Do you have a motive?"

"No. Not for the murder and I can't figure out why King would want to kill a harmless old man, but he was overheard threatening him. We think he sent a lowlife to take care of the witness."

"Do you know who the lowlife is?"

"Yeah. Some idiot named Bernie Caster. David Sims has him in the Manatee County jail."

"Is he talking?" McAllister asked.

"No. Clammed up. He might be mixed up with Sal Bonino."

"The local Mafia. Those guys aren't the sharpest crooks I've run across, but they're well organized."

J.D. looked at her watch. "Gotta go, Doug. Thanks for the file."

"Always glad to help. Call me someday and we'll have lunch again. Let me know if any more of your investigation bleeds over into my territory. I'd be glad to help out."

Josie Tyler seemed nervous, a bit twitchy as J.D. would later describe it. She was tall and blonde and late-twenties and wore a lot of makeup. She was a thin woman with big feet and big boobs, the latter no doubt the work of a plastic surgeon with no sense of proportion. She was sitting primly on a leather sofa, her knees held tightly together, her too-short skirt riding high on skinny thighs. She wore high-heel mules and a sequined T-shirt at least a couple of sizes too small.

J.D. had been a bit surprised when she looked at the address she had for Josie, and realized that it was an expensive high-rise condo on the bayfront in downtown Sarasota. When she knocked on the door and identified herself to Josie, a look of concern briefly crossed her face before she invited J.D. inside. The view from the living room was expansive, taking in the bay, New Pass, Lido Key, the southern tip of Longboat Key, and a large swath of the Gulf. The place screamed money, lots of it.

After J.D. and Josie had taken their seats, J.D. said, "I'm trying to find Porter King, and I thought you might be able to help me."

"Why are you looking for Porter?"

"I'm just following up on something he saw on Tuesday. We talked earlier this week, but he's not at home now, and I have some new information I want to run by him."

"What new information?"

"I'm sorry. I can't talk about that. Do you know where he is?"

"No. He was supposed to be here this afternoon. I thought you were him when you knocked on the door. Did you try to call him?"

"Yes," said J.D., "but his phone goes directly to voice mail. I left a message this morning, but I haven't heard back."

"When I tried to call him this morning, I got his voice mail, too."

"May I ask what your relationship is with Mr. King?"

"He's my boyfriend."

"How long have you been together?"

"A couple of years."

"I thought he only moved to this area a year ago," J.D. said.

"That's right, but he used to visit when he still lived in New York."

"How did you meet?"

Josie sat quietly for a moment as if trying to formulate an answer. "Mutual friends."

"Who?"

"Why are you asking about all this?"

"Ms. Tyler, I'm investigating a murder. Every bit of information can help me solve it."

"You don't think Porter was involved in anything like that, do you?"

"No," J.D. lied, "but every bit of information helps."

"Well, I don't think I want to talk to you anymore."

"Josie," J.D. said, her voice harsh, "I'm going to peel you like a grape.

I'm going to find out everything about you, where you grew up, where you went to school, every job you ever held, every man you ever screwed, and then I'm going to come back here and we're going to have this conversation again. And if I find anything in your background that doesn't look right, we'll be having this conversation in an interrogation room down at the police station."

Josie sat back with a jerk, her face white and wrinkling as if she were about to burst into tears. J.D. almost felt sorry for her, but she was pretty sure that Josie Tyler was holding out on her. And J.D. didn't have time for it. She sat and stared at the blonde, waiting.

"Okay," Josie said, her voice loosening, taking on more of a southern inflection. "I grew up in Live Oak, Florida. You know where that is?"

J.D. shook her head.

"Up near the Georgia border. It's a small town, and I left as soon as I turned sixteen. Didn't finish high school."

"Weren't your parents concerned? Didn't they look for you?"

Josie laughed bitterly, more a croak than a laugh. "I doubt they even knew I was gone. When my old man got horny, he might have wondered where I was. He didn't have anybody to stick it into."

"I'm sorry," said J.D.

Josie shrugged. "Shit happens. I went to Jacksonville and waitressed and cleaned hotel rooms and worked on an assembly line in an electronics plant. I lived with two other girls, and we starting doing some drugs, you know, just to take the edge off."

"Did you ever get arrested for the drugs?"

"No. We never did a whole lot of them. Then I met an older man who started paying my rent, so I moved into a cheap little apartment, and he'd come by now and then and jump my bones. I was still working at the plant, but I was doing okay. Then, out of the blue, the man up and died of a heart attack.

"Then a friend of his came by and offered to pick up where his buddy had left off. In other words, he'd pay my rent if I'd fuck him whenever he wanted it. He wasn't bad looking, and I took the deal.

"This guy owned a topless joint out on North U.S. 1, and he said he thought I could do pretty good if I'd get a boob job. He paid for it and I got these suckers." She put both hands on her breasts and jiggled them. There didn't seem to be a whole lot of play in them.

"I was making pretty good money," Josie continued, "but the owner caught me screwing one of the customers for a little extra dough. He went through the roof, screaming that I put his life in danger. He said you never know what kind of disease the dirtbags who hung out at the club might have. He kicked me out.

"I had a few bucks saved, so I went to Tampa and got a job dancing at a club out on Dale Mabry Highway. A couple of years ago some dude paid me and two of the other girls to party with some high rollers at a hotel on Clearwater Beach. That's where I met Porter."

"He was part of the group of high rollers?" asked J.D.

"Yeah."

"Did he set up the party?"

"No. Somebody else did that."

"Do you remember his name?"

"No. I only saw him one more time."

"Another party?"

"Yeah."

"Where was that?"

"His house, I think."

"You think?"

"I think he owned the house. I'm not sure."

"I take it Mr. King is paying for this place."

"Right. He owns it, I guess. He has a lot of money."

"How did you two hook up?"

"After one of the parties, he made me a proposition. He'd take care of me if I'd take care of him, if you know what I mean."

"I do. Where were you Wednesday?"

"Right here."

"You didn't go to Naples?"

"No."

"Did Mr. King spend Tuesday night here?"

She thought for a moment. "Yeah. He was here. Left early on Wednesday morning."

"Did you see him on Wednesday?"

"No."

"Did he tell you to say you'd gone to Naples with him if anybody asked?"

She hesitated. "You're not going to tell Porter anything we say today, are you?"

"No, but if you don't tell me the truth and I find out, and I will, you'll be charged with impeding a criminal investigation."

"Yes. He told me to say that."

"Do you know if he went to Naples?"

"I don't have any idea."

"Okay, Josie. I appreciate your honesty. I'd like for you to look at some pictures. See if you can identify any of the men who might have been at the parties."

"If it'll help."

"I'll have to get the pictures and bring them by later today or tomorrow. Will you call me if you hear from Porter?"

"I guess so. I don't want to get in any trouble."

"You're doing fine, Josie. You keep cooperating with me, and I promise you won't be in any trouble."

CHAPTER THIRTY-FOUR

Logan Hamilton was sitting in my living room when Jock and I got back to the key. It was late afternoon and he was sipping some of my Scotch and watching a college basketball game on TV.

"Mind if we come in?" I asked as we walked into the living room.

"Make yourselves comfortable. There's some barely passable Scotch in the kitchen, but I wouldn't recommend it."

"I don't drink Scotch," I reminded him.

"I can tell."

"Where've you been the last couple of days?" I asked.

"Practicing for the tournament."

"You mean," said Jock, "that you've actually been out on the golf course? Did it help?"

"Not exactly. I cured my slice, though."

"That's good."

"Yeah. Now it's a hook," Logan said.

"God help us," said Jock. "You're planning to embarrass me, aren't you?"

"Well, not exactly planning to, but it'll probably happen. What's going on with the investigations?"

"Let's wait until J.D. gets here so I don't have to repeat myself," I said.

"Fair enough. Can I have another Scotch?"

"I thought you didn't like my Scotch."

"Beats no Scotch," Logan said. "Barely."

I booted up my computer and found the county property appraiser's website that should show me the owner of the land in Avon Park. The site was down. A banner said that routine maintenance was taking place and the site should be back up by the opening of business on Monday.

My front door opened and J.D. walked in. "You guys been here drinking all day?" she asked.

"We just got back from Avon Park," I said. "Found Logan here depleting my whisky supply."

"Did you find out anything in Avon Park?"

I told her about our trip and what we'd discovered and about not being able to find out who owned the Fredrickson's grove property. "I'm not sure that any of it means anything, but I'd like to know who bought that grove from Jim Fredrickson's estate. They've got more weapons out there than an infantry squad."

"I wonder what's in the safe," she said.

"Me too," I said. "How'd your interview with King's girlfriend go?"

"She's a piece of work, but I think she finally told me the truth. Most of it anyway." She told us about her day, what she'd found at King's and her interrogation of Josie Tyler.

Logan asked, "Have you put together a timeline?"

"In my head," said J.D., "but it might help to rethink it."

"Okay," said Logan, who was in his element. He loved puzzles and his mind worked in ways that were often odd, but always precise. It was as if he could look at a jigsaw puzzle and imagine the whole picture in his mind. "Tuesday," he said, "some dude shoots and kills Ken Goodlow and King was seen talking to the killer just before the shooting. Then the killer drives off a bridge and dies. King leaves the island, spends Tuesday night with his girlfriend, and then disappears for the day on Wednesday. On Thursday, he lies to J.D. about that. Also on Tuesday, J.D. interviews Bud Jamison and thinks he's lying about not knowing why Goodlow would need legal advice. On Thursday evening, King is at Pattigeorge's and Sammy overhears him telling Caster that they have to take Jamison out, or something to that effect. On Friday, J.D. reinterviews Jamison, knowing nothing about the threat made by King, and again she thinks he's lying about something. Matt, you and Jock go to Jamison's house on Friday evening and find him gone, and Caster shows up and wants to kill you. You think it's a coincidence that he wants revenge for his Mafia buddy who attacked you on Wednesday, but he was really there to take out Jamison. Which, according to the theory, may tie Caster into Katie Fredrickson's situation, whatever that is. Now it appears that King has absconded and the grove once owned by Jim Fredrickson has a house on it that contains an armory and a large safe."

We talked it through, going over the last few days in minute detail, rehashing our thoughts and impressions. When we were through, J.D. said, "What about the documents we found in the killer's car?"

"That doesn't make a lot of sense," said Logan. "I can't see how they tie into all this. They might not be relevant to the murder. Anything else?"

"That's about it," I said. "You got any ideas, Logan?"

"Got any more of that Scotch?"

"You keep complaining about it," I said, "but you keep drinking it."

"The more I drink, the better it tastes. Kind of strange, don't you think?"

"I need to get back over to Josie Tyler's," said J.D. "I want to do a photo lineup with Caster's picture and some others who we know aren't involved in this mess. I'm wondering if Jim Fredrickson might have been involved in those parties Josie told me about. I'll slip a picture of him into the mix. See what she has to say."

"What makes you think Fredrickson might be involved?" I asked.

"I don't know, except that according to the caretaker over in Avon Park, there were parties going on at Fredrickson's place. Josie told me she went to a party once at a house. I didn't know about the Avon Park stuff then, and I didn't think to ask where the house was."

"Probably worth a try," said Jock.

"I'm going home for a quick shower," said J.D. "If you guys want to go downtown with me, I'll only need a few minutes with Josie and then we can have dinner."

"I'm in," I said.

"Me, too," said Jock.

"Not me," said Logan. "I'm already pretty drunk. I think I'll stop by and see Sammy and then head home."

"You make another stop, buddy," I said, "and Marie's going to kick your butt when you get home."

"You're probably right. We're going to dinner with her aunt tonight. I better not show up with a load on."

CHAPTER THIRTY-FIVE

Jock and I were sitting in the Explorer parked in front of a high-rise condo complex on Gulfstream Avenue in downtown Sarasota. J.D. had asked us to wait in the car while she went up to talk to Josie Tyler. We'd stopped by the Longboat Key Police Station to pick up the pictures J.D. needed. She had been gone about three minutes when my phone rang. "Matt," J.D. said, "you and Jock get up here on the double. Twelfth floor."

"What's up?"

"Now," she said and hung up.

"Let's go," I said. "Something's up with J.D."

We took the elevator to the twelfth floor. The doors opened and I saw J.D. standing about twenty feet down the hall in front of an open door, her weapon drawn. I pulled my pistol from the holster in the small of my back. The one I'd been carrying since I went to meet Appleby in Tampa. Jock's pistol was in his hand.

We trotted down the hall. J.D. had her finger to her lips, signaling us to be quiet. She moved to meet us. "What's the matter?" I asked.

"Maybe nothing," she said, "but the front door was wide open. I didn't want to go inside without backup."

We moved toward the door and followed J.D. into a small foyer. A kitchen was to our left and the living room in front of us. It was night now and the lights of the living room reflected off the dark windows. A leather sofa came into view as we moved forward. A blonde woman was sitting upright, her head resting on the cushioned back. She looked like she was asleep, except for the bullet hole in her forehead.

I saw an open door in the wall on the right side of the living room, probably leading to the bedroom. I moved quickly that way, holding my pistol in front of me. The lights in the room were on. I eased through the doorway, alert for any movement. I ignored the mess on the bed and slipped toward the door to the bathroom. I reached carefully around the doorjamb and found the light switch, turned it on. Empty. I turned back to the bedroom and to the king-size bed that took up a large part of it. A body lay sprawled on its back bleeding onto the coverlet, a large red splotch staining the left side of his shirt. I didn't know the man, but I was pretty sure of his identity. A pistol that appeared to be a .22, an assassin's weapon, was on the floor at the foot of the bed. A silencer was attached to the muzzle. I didn't touch it. "J.D.," I called. "You better come see this."

She walked into the room and looked at the body, shook her head. "Well," she said, "we found Porter King."

We were back in the hallway when a young Sarasota patrolman arrived in response to J.D.'s 911 call. She identified herself and introduced Jock and me. "There're two bodies in the apartment," said J.D. "We went in, but came right back out. We haven't disturbed the crime scene."

"Okay," said the young cop. "Captain McAllister's on his way."

"Captain McAllister himself?" J.D. asked. "Does he usually roll on homicides on weekends?"

"I don't think so," said the cop. "But my boss called me on my way here and said to be on my toes because the captain was on his way."

We stood awkwardly while quietly waiting for the detective. In a few minutes a man in a suit and tie came up the elevator and walked toward us. "Doug McAllister," J.D. said under her breath, and went to meet him. They talked for a minute or two, J.D. explaining what we found and who the victims were.

She led the captain over and introduced Jock and me as friends from Longboat. "We were on our way to dinner," she said, "and I stopped by to have Josie look at a picture of Caster to see if she recognized him." I noticed she didn't mention the picture of Jim Fredrickson she'd slipped into the pile. I wondered about that, but figured she'd explain later.

"And you just went busting in there like the Three Stooges?" asked the captain.

"No," said J.D. "They were waiting downstairs in the car when I came up. I saw the door standing open and called them in for backup."

"Are you out of your mind, Detective?" asked McAllister, his voice rising in anger. "You called a couple of civilians for backup? Why didn't you call us?"

"I did call you," J.D. said, a bit of steel creeping into her voice. "I didn't know what we had here, whether someone was hurt, whether there were others in the apartment or what. I sure didn't want to be facing down more than one killer, if that's what it was, by myself."

"So you called on a couple of useless civilians to back you up?" The captain's voice had gotten louder, incredulous.

"Hold the phone," I said angrily. "Just who the hell—"

J.D. broke in. "I've got this, Matt."

I knew I'd better shut up. I'd stepped into that minefield that was J.D.'s sense of self. She didn't need some man coming to her rescue. She was able to take care of herself and didn't need my protection, or my outrage at the way she was being treated.

She looked back at McAllister. "You're out of line, Captain. I would suggest that you wait until you know the facts before jumping to conclusions. Now, if you want my cooperation on this little mess you have here, you'll shut up and listen for a change." Her voice was low and flat. She was irate, but holding it in. I'd seen her do this before. She had a steely control of her emotions when needed, and I wouldn't want to be on the receiving end of the tongue lashing she was capable of meting out. I thought McAllister had better be careful.

"I noticed a security camera in the elevator," said J.D., trying to lighten the mood, to move away from a confrontation.

"Yeah," said McAllister, the heat gone from his voice. "I've got the manager on his way over to let us have a look at the video. You might as well go on to dinner. We'll want statements, but we can get those by phone. I'll have a detective contact you later this evening."

"Maybe I should stick around until the manager gets here," J.D. said. "I might recognize somebody on the video."

"You don't have to stay. I'll send you a copy of it on Monday."

"What's up, Doug? You know if I can identify somebody on the video you can start looking for him immediately. Why wait until Monday?"

"Look, Detective," McAllister said, his voice tight, "this is my jurisdiction, my murder, my case. I'll run it however I see fit. Now, y'all go on."

"If you say so," J.D. said curtly, and turned on her heel and walked toward the elevator. Jock and I followed.

"J.D.," McAllister called after us, "I'm sorry. Can you guys stop back by here after dinner? I'll have the video and a detective to take your statements."

"Okay, Doug," J.D. said. "We'll be back."

The restaurant was crowded and we had to wait half an hour for a table. Saturday night during season at Two Senoritas. We were lucky we had such a short wait. The hostess gave us a pager and we stood on the sidewalk in front of the restaurant. "What the hell was that all about with McAllister?" I asked.

"I don't know," said J.D. "That's not like him. And I didn't like being treated like a rookie."

"He seemed a little nervous," said Jock, "and angry. It sounded like he was trying to control himself and then the anger would take over again. I wouldn't expect that behavior in an experienced detective."

"I wouldn't either," said J.D. "I was surprised that he showed up on the scene."

"Maybe," I said, "it was the address. A couple of murders on Gulfstream are quite different than a murder in some other parts of the city."

"That's probably it," said J.D. "A lot of political heat can come down on a case like this. Rich guy from Longboat Key, stripper girlfriend being kept in an expensive downtown condo. The newspapers will be all over it."

"Maybe the pistol will give them some leads," I said.

"I'll be surprised if it does," she said. "I think whoever killed them knew what he was doing. I don't think he'd have left the murder weapon unless it was on purpose. I doubt they'll ever be able to identify it."

"I wonder why he would leave the weapon," I said. "Why not take it with him?"

"Maybe he didn't want to get caught with it on him," said J.D. "If the gun can't be connected to him it'd make sense to leave it rather than take a chance on getting stopped with a murder weapon in his pocket."

When we finished dinner, we drove back to Gulfstream Avenue. McAllister was waiting for us outside Josie Tyler's condo. The bodies had been removed.

"Sorry about earlier, J.D.," McAllister said. "I guess I'm just having a bad day. But I still don't understand why you put these two civilians in danger."

J.D.'s voice was cold. "Your apology's accepted, Doug. But don't ever do that again. I'm not some rookie. I've probably handled more murders than you have, and I damn sure don't appreciate being talked to like that."

I was surprised at J.D. She almost never used curse words, and if she did, she was really pissed. I guess McAllister caught that, too. He said, "It won't happen again, J.D. I've got too much respect for you. I hope we can still be friends."

She smiled at him. "I don't see any reason why we can't. And these two civilians? They're not as dumb as they look. Call my chief or Detective Sims in Manatee. They'll vouch for them. Can I see the video from the elevator now?"

"There isn't one." he said.

"I don't understand," said J.D. "This isn't the kind of place to put up fake cameras."

"The camera is real. The video feed goes into a computer in the manager's office. Somebody disabled the damned thing."

"How?" J.D. asked.

"The video camera is wireless and the images are sent to a router in the manager's office and from there to the computer. The router runs on electricity and somebody unplugged it. The video couldn't make it to the hard drive in the computer because the router shut down."

"No battery backup?" asked J.D.

"None."

"Sounds like somebody had to know his way around," J.D. said.

"Maybe not," said McAllister. "The cleaning people were in earlier today, and they might have accidently knocked the plug out of the wall."

"What about the gun on the floor?" J.D. asked.

"No prints and the serial number had been obliterated by acid. No way to trace it."

"Do you know yet if the gun is the one used in the murders?"

"No, but our ballistics people are working on that."

"Did you find anything else?" J.D. asked.

"Not yet. Our forensics people are still in the condo. They'll be finished soon."

"Doug," said J.D., "I know these murders aren't in my jurisdiction, but they touch on my case. I'd like to be kept in the loop on this."

"Not a problem," said McAllister. "I'll make sure you're copied on everything."

"How do you think it went down?" J.D. asked.

"It looks like the killer just walked in the front door, found Josie on the sofa and shot her and went to the bedroom. Maybe she didn't lock the door, or maybe the killer had a key. Maybe Josie didn't have time to get off the sofa when the guy opened the door, or maybe he motioned her to sit back down.

"I think King had probably been in the bathroom and was walking toward the living room when the killer came through the door and shot him. He fell backward onto the bed and the killer dropped the gun and took off. He probably went down the stairs."

J.D. was silent for a moment, biting at her lip the way she does when she's thinking. "Why do you think he went down the stairs?"

"No evidence of it," said McAllister, "but I think it makes sense. Why take a chance with the elevator?"

"He might have come up that way, too."

"The stairwell doors are locked from the inside. You can get out but you can't get in. He would have had to have come up the elevator."

"Too bad about the video," said J.D. "What about those statements?"

"Detective Harry Robson is finishing up inside the condo. He'll be with you in a few minutes. I'm going back to the station."

Robson was a tall, gangly man who wore a bottlebrush mustache and smiled a lot. He shook hands all around and said, "I overheard some of the conversation between McAllister and J.D. I'm sorry about that. He's seemed unusually tense lately."

"Thanks, Harry," said J.D. "It's no big deal. We all get frazzled from time to time."

"Mr. Algren," Robson said, "I've met Matt before and I know both of you by reputation. All good. Bill Lester speaks highly of both of you. I know you're not just a couple of civilians who get in the way. Sometimes the captain speaks before he knows the facts."

Jock grinned. "Don't blow my cover, Harry."

CHAPTER THIRTY-SIX

GULF OF MEXICO, AUGUST 1942

Paulus Graf Von Reicheldorf was floating in a field of debris from the sunken U-boat. Pieces of the hull bobbed in the oil slick that was spreading over the surface, painting the water with a multicolored sheen. He rummaged around in the small compartment that contained his rations and found a compass. He pulled the folding paddle from another pocket, locked it into place and headed north.

The sun was brutal, leeching hydration from his body, blistering his skin. Paulus was wearing the duty uniform he'd been in when the attack occurred, long pants, a short-sleeve shirt, and hat. He knew his face and arms would not fare well in the sunshine. He sipped his water carefully, aware that he might be in the raft for days. He had plotted the U-boat's position just before the attack, so he knew he was about twenty-five nautical miles south of St. George Island in the Florida panhandle. There was a lighthouse on the island that at night could be seen from fifteen miles at sea. He decided to paddle north and hope that by dusk he would be in sight of the light, if it hadn't been darkened because of the war.

Paulus set a schedule for himself. He'd paddle for an hour and rest for fifteen minutes, sip his water, and use his bailing bucket to soak himself with water from the Gulf. By the time the first hour was up, his hands were blistered from the paddle and his arms were bright red from the sun. He rested as much as he could and then set off again, paddling north.

He was young and strong and during the weeks in the submarine he'd kept in shape by working out with sit-ups and push-ups and other exercises. He could make it ashore if the sun didn't kill him first. He kept to his schedule, but had no sense of how far he traveled during each hour. A slight wind was blowing from the south, and the current seemed to be flowing northward, but he wasn't sure. The seas remained flat and he knew that whatever current might be present was minimal. He pushed on through the long day, checking his compass every few minutes, making sure that he was on course. At noon, he ate one of the rations. He thought about it and decided that if he didn't find land within the next couple of days, he'd die from exposure, and the rations would be wasted. The sun was too hot, and his arms were going limp from the strain of the paddle, the blisters on his hands open and painful. He needed the energy provided by the rations, so he ate another one, drank some more water, and rested for thirty minutes.

The August days are long in that part of the world. The attack had occurred at seven in the morning and full darkness would not fall until nine in the evening. He had about thirteen hours of paddling before he'd be able to see the light from the St. George lighthouse. If it was there. If he was on the right course. If he was still alert. A lot of ifs.

He knew this part of the Florida coast was virtually deserted and he also knew he had to find people. He expected to be arrested and taken to a prisoner-of-war facility. As long as he was in uniform, he wouldn't be seen as a spy. He thought his best bet was to simply knock on the lighthouse keeper's door and surrender.

There was no reasonable way for him to complete his mission. He was a long way from San Antonio, and he didn't have the documents he was supposed to deliver. They were still in the submarine's safe at the bottom of the Gulf of Mexico. If he was able to make it to San Antonio, there was no way to identify himself to the agents there. They would not open their escape route through Mexico to a stranger with no identification and nothing to explain his appearance in San Antonio other than his word that he was an Abwehr agent.

Paulus didn't like the idea of surrendering, but he had thought a lot about his beloved fatherland during the long trip from France. His country had been taken over by a bunch of hooligans and murderers. He and Captain Kuhlmann had discussed the rumors that were circulating through the military about death camps where the SS, the dreaded black-uniformed Schutzstaffel, were murdering Jews and Eastern Europeans in numbers that were impossible to comprehend.

Hitler had taken them into a war that was already lost. Once the Americans declared war, Germany had been assured of defeat. Sure, the Afrika Korps was still taking care of the British in North Africa, but the army had become bogged down in Russia after making great strides in the first months after the invasion the year before. The generals were learning the lessons of Napoleon's campaign. Russia was just too big and its winter too long and too cold. The Germans had also begun to realize that Stalin was willing to shed rivers of his people's blood in order to defeat them.

America was tooling up, training a great army, turning its industrial might into war production. They would strike soon, and the beginning of the end for Germany would be apparent to anybody with a brain. Hitler and his idiot advisers would be able to prolong the war for a few years, wasting the resources and youth of a great culture, but in the end they would succumb to the overwhelming might of the United States. And if the rumors of death camps were true, Germany would become a pariah among civilized nations and would never regain its rightful place in the world.

His thoughts turned to the young U-boat captain with whom he'd spent long evenings discussing the war and Germany, what their country had been, what it had become and what it might be in the future. Paulus would visit Kuhlmann's wife when he returned to Germany. He wanted this young woman who had meant so much to the captain to know that he'd died a hero, had lived up to the code of the sea and gone down with his ship. Such a waste. A crew of forty-nine good men lost in a war that couldn't be won.

The young graf had decided that he'd rather spend the next few years in a prisoner of war camp, than waste his life in a lost cause that he had never believed in. He paddled on, his thoughts of a lost Germany bringing a sadness that he couldn't shake.

The night brought relief from the relentless sun and a glimpse of a light on the horizon. He watched it for several minutes until he was sure that the light was flashing with a rhythm that had to be the lighthouse. He was too tired to go on. He lay back in the raft staring at the stars that blanketed the dark sky. A sliver of a moon hung among the stars like the one in the pictures in the fairy-tale books his mother had read him as a child. He wondered if she was looking down on him now with that smile that she seemed to reserve just for him. He hoped so. He sipped some more water and then dropped off to sleep.

He awoke with a start and looked at his watch. Almost midnight. He'd only slept a couple of hours, but he felt refreshed. He ate two of the ration meals and drank some of the water and started paddling toward the light blinking on the horizon. He stuck to the schedule he'd set for himself that morning, one hour of paddling, followed by fifteen minutes of rest.

The night was hot, but better than in the sun. He slogged along for several more hours, the light becoming brighter and more defined. Just before dawn, he heard the surf and knew he was close to shore. Soon, the bottom of the boat scraped along the sandy Gulf floor and the surf began to take control of his little vessel. He jumped overboard, grabbed the painter, and pulled the boat up onto the beach. The sun was still below the horizon to his right, but the sky was lightening with every minute that passed. The beach and the dunes behind it began to take shape. Paulus was perhaps a half kilometer west of the lighthouse, just about where he had planned to be.

He found a large piece of driftwood and tied the raft's painter to it. He then walked west for another half kilometer and then up into the dunes. He was looking for a landmark of some kind, something that would mark a spot that he could find later if he needed to return. He came upon a lone pine tree just landward of the dunes. It stood like a sentry among the low palmetto scrub that seemed to cover most what he could see of the island. He went to the tree, turned, and walked fifty paces due north, consulting his compass the whole way. He sank to his knees and used his hands to dig a shallow hole. There he placed his waterproof money belt, the one that held all the documents that would make him an American citizen. He wasn't sure why he decided to keep them, but it didn't make much sense to throw them away.

When he finished, he tamped down the spot and picked up a dead palmetto branch. He backtracked to the pine tree using the branch to wipe away his tracks. He walked back to the beach, still wiping away his tracks, and trudged eastward toward the lighthouse keeper's quarters, his back straight, his pride intact. He was a German naval officer and he was about to do what none of his seafaring ancestors had ever done. Surrender. But the country that his forebears had so honorably served was no more. It had been subsumed into the Nazi empire and until that fell, his Germany, the nation of his ancestors, had ceased to exist.

When the war was over, when Germany lay in ruins, Paulus Graf von Reicheldorf would go home and help lead his people out of the darkness. It would be a big job.

CHAPTER THIRTY-SEVEN

We were quiet on the drive back to the key. I was not happy with McAllister and his surly attitude. I think my feelings were hurt by his calling Jock and me dumb civilians. I decided not to say anything to J.D. I didn't want to get into a conversation about why I had tried to intervene with McAllister. Actually, I wasn't intervening. I was ready to put a fist in his mouth. Not a very good idea. One does not assault a detective captain at a homicide scene without consequences.

J.D. broke the silence as we were driving through St. Armands Circle. "I think I'll stay at my place tonight. Give you two some bonding time."

"We bonded in junior high school," I said.

"Still, you guys need some time to hang out and get drunk and tell lies, or whatever you do when I'm not around."

"We mostly talk about you," said Jock.

"Be careful," she said. "I have a gun."

"Yes, ma'am," said Jock.

J.D. dropped us at my cottage, and Jock and I went to Tiny's. We took seats at a high-top table across the little room from the bar. "That Detective Robson seems like a good enough guy," said Jock.

"He is. J.D. and I met him back in the fall. He called Bill Lester about me, and Bill told him I was okay and if you showed up to treat you like family."

"I gathered you guys knew each other."

"Robson's an old-fashioned detective who thinks before he opens his mouth," I said. "He knows about J.D.'s background as the assistant homicide commander in Miami and seems to have a great deal of respect for her."

"He took a chance on really pissing off McAllister by apologizing to us," Jock said.

"He did, but he's been on the force for a long time. I don't think he has to worry too much about the captain. Robson will always do the right thing, no matter the consequences."

"What do you think is going on with McAllister?" Jock asked.

"Who knows? I've heard he's not a favorite of the chief of police. He's a little rough around the edges, and there's always been a suspicion that he's not above stepping over the line if it'll help put the bad guys away."

"Why do they keep him on?"

"He closes a lot of cases. He's very good at what he does."

"It'll catch up to him someday," said Jock. "He's going to make a mistake, screw over somebody with the power to take him out."

"That may be his problem now. The press is going to be all over him on this one. The reporters have all heard the rumors about the tactics he's used. He might be worried that the heat will get too high. This is one murder he's got to solve and he's going to have to do everything by the book."

Logan came through the door, strangely sober for so late on a Saturday evening. "Where've you been?" I asked.

"I told you. Marie's aunt is visiting from Jacksonville, and we went to dinner."

"You didn't drink?" I asked

"Marie said she'd kill me if I did. Her aunt thinks anybody who touches alcohol is going to hell."

"You're probably going there anyway," Jock said.

"Yeah, but Marie's aunt doesn't know that."

Susie brought a tall glass of amber liquid to the table. "A triple, just like you ordered."

"You didn't put too much water in that, did you?" asked Logan.

"Just a splash."

"You're a lifesaver, Susie," Logan said.

"Be careful," she said. "You've got to drive home."

"Aw," said Logan, "the cops are okay. If the town commission hadn't meant for people to drive drunk they wouldn't have insisted on all those parking spaces for a bar."

"Go easy on that," said Jock. "You and I are playing a practice round in the morning."

Logan smiled. "Okay. Guess you need the practice. Any luck finding old Mr. Jamison?"

"No," I said. "J.D. ran him through the system and turned up nothing, not even a traffic ticket. He's lived in the village since World War II, in the same house he bought when he got married. Worked the fishing boats most of his life. He lives on Social Security and his savings and drives a twenty-year-old car that he bought used fifteen years ago."

"Somewhere along the line, he must have run afoul of somebody," said Logan. "Why else would a punk like Caster be after him?"

"I think the better question," Jock said, "is why somebody like Porter King would be after him."

"Maybe if J.D. can find King, she'll get some answers," Logan said.

"Small problem there," I said. "King's dead."

"Well, there goes that idea. How did he die?" Logan asked.

"Somebody shot him earlier this evening at his girlfriend's condo on the mainland," I said. I told Logan how we came to find King and his girlfriend and the strange reactions we'd gotten from McAllister and our speculations about his demeanor.

"You're probably right about McAllister being spooked by the press on this one," Logan said. "I wouldn't read too much into his bullshit."

"I didn't," I said.

"Does anyone have any thoughts about who might have killed King and his girlfriend?" asked Logan.

"If McAllister does, he didn't share it with us," I said.

"Could it have anything to do with J.D.'s visit to her this afternoon?" Logan asked.

"I doubt it," I said. "Who would know about it other than J.D. and Josie and, possibly, King?"

"Based on what J.D. said about her interview with Josie," said Jock, "I don't think Josie would have mentioned it to King. She was too concerned that King would somehow find out that she'd told J.D. that King had lied about going to Naples the day after Goodlow was killed."

"Then," said Logan, "maybe J.D. should concentrate on finding anybody Josie might have told about J.D. coming to see her."

"That's a good point," I said. "McAllister will probably get her telephone records. Hopefully, he'll share that with J.D. At least it'll be a start. If we find out who she told about J.D.'s visit, we might be able to track back to the killer."

The conversation turned to golf, which bored me and seemed to be beyond Logan's understanding, and then morphed into tales of our fishing prowess. All lies. Locals came and went, the late night filled with staff from local restaurants and bars, finishing their day with a libation or two or three. A typical night at Tiny's, old friends laughing and telling big stories, a few of them true. Logan finished his tall drink and left. Jock and I had another drink and called it a night.

CHAPTER THIRTY-EIGHT

Sunday was one of those days that we islanders live for, temperature in the low seventies, very little humidity, a clear sky, and flat seas. Jock had finally talked Logan into a practice round, and they left early for the golf course. I was drinking coffee and reading the morning paper on my patio, thinking that the day was too beautiful to waste. I'd go for a run later, maybe call J.D. and see about taking the boat to Egmont Key for a picnic. There was a knock on the front door, and J.D. walked through the living room and out to the patio.

"Good morning, sunshine," I said.

"Sunshine?" she asked. "That's a new one."

"Ain't no sunshine when she's gone," I sang.

"Bill Withers didn't do it better," she said, laughing, and leaned down and planted a kiss on my forehead.

"Miss me?" I asked.

"Sort of. I want you to hear something. Where's Jock?"

"He and Logan just left for the golf course."

"I'm afraid they're headed for disaster in the tournament."

"Probably. Want some coffee?"

"I'll get it."

She returned from the kitchen with her mugful of steaming coffee. "I didn't think to check the voice mail on my cell phone until this morning. Listen to this." She punched a few buttons on the phone and held it up so that I could hear the message.

"Detective Duncan, this is Josie Tyler. I just got a disturbing call that I think you should know about. I think I may be in danger. Please call me as soon as you get this message."

"Uh-oh," I said. "When did that come in?"

"Five thirty-two yesterday afternoon. She probably called while I was in the shower."

"That tells us that she was killed between the time she made the call and when we got to the condo. What? About an hour?"

"I checked my phone. I made the 911 call at 6:23, so it was a little less than an hour. We probably just missed the killer."

"We need to know who called her," J.D. said.

"Can you get the phone records?"

"I can try, but I'm going to need a warrant, and I don't know that I have enough to justify that to a judge."

"McAllister should be able to get them," I said. "Can't you get them from him?"

"I guess, but I'd sure like to see them fresh from the phone company."

"Do I detect a little suspicion of McAllister?"

"Not really. I think he was just stressed out last night. He's a good cop, but you never know."

"Are you going to tell him about the call from Josie?"

"I want to see the phone records first. We know she got a call from somebody who spooked her. And we know about what time the call came in. I'd like to see if it shows up on the records."

"Your number is going to show up there, you know. From when she called you."

She chewed on it for a moment. "You're right. I'd better come clean up front on that."

"I agree. You don't want McAllister thinking you're holding back on him. Not if you expect cooperation from him."

"I'd sure like to see those phone records before I talk to Doug."

"Jock can help. He's got resources that neither you nor McAllister have."

"I don't know, Matt. I don't want to put Jock in a tough position."

"It won't hurt to ask. Let me give him a call."

She nodded. I dialed Jock's cell phone.

"Jock," I said, "J.D. needs the phone records on Josie Tyler today. She doesn't want to put you out, but I don't mind. Can you get those for us?"

"It'll be easier if I had her numbers," he said.

I asked J.D. and she rattled off both Josie's cell phone and home numbers. I gave them to Jock.

"How much time do you want me to cover?" he asked.

I asked J.D. "Just for Saturday afternoon," she said.

I relayed that to Jock. "How're you hitting them?" I asked.

"I'm doing fine. My partner stays in the rough and cusses a lot."

"I'm not surprised. Call me when you get something."

"I'll have the records e-mailed to you. Probably take an hour or so." He hung up.

"Can he just do that?" asked J.D. "He doesn't need a reason?"

"No. Jock's been around a long time, knows a lot of people. They never question him when he wants something."

"I'm not sure I like this, Matt. I'm going behind the back of a good cop."

"But you're having some doubts about McAllister."

She was quiet for a couple of beats. "Yes. He was way out of line last night. Maybe it was the stress, but he's been in stressful situations before."

"Harry Robson didn't seem too surprised that McAllister was being an asshole."

She smiled. "No. I guess most cops can be that way on occasion, but there was something more to his tirade last night. Like it was personal and aimed directly at me."

"Can you think of anything that might have set him off?"

"No. When I saw him in the afternoon, he was his normal cordial self."

"Let's see what the phone records show. If McAllister will give you his copy tomorrow, we can compare them and see if he's left anything out."

"What if he refuses to let me see them? I don't really have any right to be involved in his investigation."

"Either way, we'll know he's not playing it straight with you."

"I'd better call him," J.D. said. "Let him know about the voice mail message from Josie."

A half hour later, my computer dinged, letting me know I had an e-mail coming in. It was from a sender I'd never heard of, but it was a printout of Josie Tyler's phone records. Her home phone had not been used for either incoming or outgoing calls during Saturday afternoon. The cell phone record showed an incoming call at 5:29 in the afternoon. It lasted for one minute. Three minutes later, Josie called J.D.'s cell phone.

A typed note attached to the printout identified the second call as going to J.D. and the first call originating from a prepaid cell phone that had been bought at a Wal-Mart in Sarasota. It had been a cash transaction and it would be impossible to determine the name of the buyer.

"It looks like the call from the prepaid is what spooked Josie," said J.D. "She called me as soon as she hung up."

"She said she *thought* she might be in danger. Like she wasn't sure. Maybe the call came from somebody she knew."

"That's a reasonable hypothesis."

"Is a hypothesis like a hunch?"

"Pretty much," she said. "If the call came from somebody she knew, she might have let that person into the apartment."

"I wonder when King showed up."

"We'll never know for sure, but my guess is that she wouldn't have called me if he was there."

"You're probably right. He must have come in after she made the call."

"Think about this scenario," she said. "Josie gets a call from somebody she knows and has some reason to fear. He says he's coming over and she panics, calls me. King arrives and she tells him that the caller is on his way, so they leave the door unlocked. King is in the bathroom when the caller walks in, shoots Josie, and goes to the bathroom. King is coming out of the bathroom and the killer shoots him, drops his weapon, and leaves by the stairwell."

"That would work," I said, "but there's a missing piece. I think Josie would've told you about somebody that she was that afraid of when you met with her. Either she didn't know she had to be scared of him when she talked to you, or he said something to her that caused her to panic."

"Maybe King was the target and Josie was just at the wrong place at the wrong time."

"Or, maybe the other way around. What if Josie told someone about your visit to her? Could that have attracted the interest of the killer? Was he afraid of what Josie may have told you or would tell you?"

"But, she didn't make any calls after I left her."

"Unless she had a cell phone we don't know about. Or maybe she had a visitor, somebody she trusted enough to tell about your conversation."

"If she had a prepaid cell phone," J.D. said, "we'll never find it without a number. But, I don't think that's the case. The only reason somebody with a cell phone would buy a prepaid would be to hide the calls she made. But at this point, I can't see any reason she'd have to do that."

"I don't guess you've heard anything more from Katie," I said, changing the subject.

"No, but I've been thinking about that. I may have a way to narrow down the area where the building with the graffiti is located. There was a number on the rear quarter panel of that Tampa squad car. I'm pretty sure that's the number assigned to that particular vehicle. If we can figure out the patrol area that car operates in and the cop who usually drives the car, we might be able to get a location on the building. Maybe Katie lives near the building and the picture of the car and the building was a clue she was sending. "

"It's worth looking into. Can you touch base with Tampa P.D.?"

"I'll do that first thing in the morning."

"Would Katie have any way of knowing that you've gotten involved in the investigation of her disappearance?"

"I doubt it, but she probably knows I would. Especially once I moved here."

"How would she even know you're here?"

"My name pops up in the newspapers now and then. She could have seen one of those articles. Or she might have tried to call me in Miami and was told I'd moved over here."

"I've been wondering why she would text you the first two pictures and then go to the trouble to e-mail you the picture of the car. Why not just text that one, too?"

"Maybe she was trying to get my attention with the texted pictures.

The chances of anybody seeing those pictures other than me were miniscule, unless I showed them to somebody. Plus, they were pretty esoteric. If they'd somehow gone to the wrong phone, nobody else would have been able to figure them out. If it hadn't been for the word 'Jed' in the first picture, I might not have recognized her. The e-mail, on the other hand, had a much better chance of being seen by any number of people. She wouldn't have my personal e-mail, so she sent it to the office. That e-mail address is posted on the town website. Without the texted pictures, the e-mail wouldn't have made much sense to anybody but me."

"I wish we could figure out what she's trying to tell us," I said.

"I don't get the impression she's in any immediate danger, but maybe somebody's looking for her."

"I wonder why she doesn't just contact me directly," said J.D. "If she's trying to tell me where she is, it'd be a heck of a lot easier to just call me and tell me to come get her."

"Maybe she's afraid somebody has hacked into your cell phone and would intercept any calls she made to you."

"It'd take somebody powerful to do that, wouldn't it?"

"I don't know," I said. "We'll have to ask Jock."

"If my phone is bugged, somebody would also intercept the text, wouldn't they?"

"Yes, but you said the picture didn't look much like Katie and the message surely wouldn't have set off any alarm bells. It's more like a gag photo."

"What about the second picture she texted? The one with 'U166' written on her hand?"

"Maybe that didn't mean anything," I said. "Or maybe she thought it would mean something to you, but not to anybody else."

"I'm at a complete loss on it."

"I wonder what the hell 'U166' means. She went to some trouble to send us that."

"I Googled it," said J.D. "The only references I could find were to a German submarine that was sunk in the Gulf of Mexico during World War II. Katie's certainly not connected to that."

"I wouldn't think so," I said. "You up for a boat ride?"

"What've you got in mind?"

"We could run up the Manatee River to the Twin Dolphin Marina. Pig out on crab cakes at Pier 22."

"Sounds like a plan," she said.

And that's what we did.

CHAPTER THIRTY-NINE

The ride back from Pier 22 was pleasant. Tampa Bay was quiet, the water flat, and the sun warm, but the wind kicked up by our passage was cool enough to make us glad we were wearing sweatshirts and jeans. We decided to exit the bay through Passage Key Inlet and run south in the Gulf. I took *Recess* out about a mile offshore, set the autopilot for the sea buoy at Longboat Pass, put my feet on the dash and cruised toward home. J.D. and I sat quietly, enjoying each other's company without any conversation.

As we cruised south along the length of Anna Maria Island, dark clouds were building to the southeast over the mainland, piling atop each other like so many blocks of spun granite, dark and foreboding. A bolt of lightning flashed in the distance. I pointed toward the storm. "We'll have some rain. Maybe before we make it home."

"It's pretty, isn't it? Even bad weather has a certain beauty when you live in paradise."

"Yes, it does, but if that storm hits us before we get home, you won't think it's so beautiful. There's lightning in those clouds."

"It's pretty far off," she said.

"It's moving fast, coming toward us." It was one of those rapidly moving thunder cells that we see so often in the summer. They're rare in the winter, but they do pop up on occasion, and this one looked dangerous.

I disengaged the autopilot and pushed the throttles forward. I angled in closer to the beach and made for the rock jetty that juts off the southernmost tip of Anna Maria Island, defining the northern edge of Longboat Pass. There was a swash channel at the end of the jetty that was deep enough for *Recess*. I would save a lot of time by not having to go all the way to the sea buoy and then back through the marked channel to the bridge.

I took the swash channel at speed and slowed as I passed under the bridge and turned toward the channel that runs between Jewfish Key and Longboat Key. I moved as fast as I could without leaving a wake that would rock the boats at anchor in the lee of the island. I moved toward the dock in back of my house. The storm was moving faster than I'd thought and just as I eased *Recess* into her slip, the rain hit us with such ferocity that I couldn't see more than a few yards. J.D. jumped off the boat with the lines and was wrapping them around the cleats when thunder boomed close.

"Get down," I shouted to J.D.

She didn't hesitate. She fell prone on the dock as I reached for the pistol I'd stowed in the canvas bag I always carry aboard. My Glock 9mm was stowed in a plastic sandwich bag to keep the water out. I stuffed it in the front pocket of my jeans.

I hadn't heard thunder. I'd heard a gunshot. I don't know what made me realize that. Maybe it was the absence of lightning just before the noise, or maybe something deeper, a fading memory of enemy soldiers shooting at me.

"What is it?" she asked. Maybe two seconds had elapsed since the shot.

"Somebody's shooting at us." I'd taken cover behind the helm seat, knowing that was no protection, but trying to make myself as small as possible.

Another shot. This one took out part of *Recess's* windshield. J.D. had rolled off the pier and was swimming under the short leg of the T-dock to the seaward side of the boat. She'd be protected and out of danger. I recovered my cell phone from the dash and dialed 911, identified myself, and told the operator someone was shooting at me. I gave her the address, hung up and crawled to the stern, keeping my head below the gunwale. I opened the transom door that was designed for bringing fish aboard and slipped out of my boat shoes, jeans, and sweatshirt. The big outboard engines were between me and the shooter. I held onto my pistol, still in its plastic bag, as I slithered across the small swim platform and into the dark water.

The cold hit me like a blast of snow. J.D. was holding onto the swim platform, protected by the big outboards, already shivering. She had removed her sweatshirt, jeans, and shoes and placed them in the engine well.

"I'm going to swim around the bow and come up on the other side of the dock," I said. "Once I get into shallow enough water to stand, I'll go after the shooter."

"I'm coming with you," she said.

"You're not armed."

"I've got my pistol."

"Where?"

"It was in my ankle holster."

"It's wet. It might not even fire."

"I'll take that chance."

"Stay here," I said. "I called 911. The cops should be here soon."

"Yeah, and they'll all see me cowering here in the water while my manly rescuer is taking on the bad guy. That's not going to happen."

Sometimes, loving a cop is hard work. I looked at her for a moment and then began to breaststroke toward the bow, holding the pistol in my right hand. I heard her right behind me, but knew I'd better keep my mouth shut and keep swimming.

Recess was tied port side to the short leg of my T-dock. My plan was to swim around the bow and under the dock's short leg and then ease myself toward the beach until I could stand. I wanted to move toward shore with just my head showing. The dark clouds and hard rain obscured the daylight and turned mid-afternoon into dusk.

As I reached the shallows and my feet touched bottom, I felt J.D. at my side. God, she was tough. The gunfire had stopped after the first two shots. Maybe the shooter was waiting for one of us to show ourselves. Maybe he was gone. No luck. Another shot rang out. I heard it plunk into the *Recess's* fiberglass hull. He didn't know where we were.

I duck walked toward the shore, keeping my head just above the surface. J.D. was right behind me, her pistol in hand. The bottom rose as we neared shore, and we were crawling on all fours and then on our stomachs. The rain was still falling hard and lightning blasted the sky, thunder rumbling right behind it. I could see the house, looming like a silhouette through the pelting rain. A man stepped around the corner, holding a rifle, and let loose another round, just as a bolt of lightning flashed nearby, illuminating the shooter and giving me a pretty good look at him. He was a stranger, a man I'd never seen before. The round hit my boat. Another hole in the fiberglass. This guy was really starting to piss me off.

I pulled my pistol out of the plastic bag and held it out of the water. We waited. The man stepped around the corner again, and I let go with three quick shots. He bounced back behind the corner of the house. He popped back out firing the rifle, answering me with three shots in quick succession. The rounds hit the water near us, sending us scurrying beneath the dock.

"My gun is useless," said J.D. "How much ammo do you have?"

"A full clip. Seventeen rounds plus the one that was in the chamber. I've got fifteen left."

"He can sit up there for hours with that rifle and hold us off."

"The cops are on their way," I said. "He can't stick around for long."

The man sprayed the dock with automatic fire, kicking up splinters and making little plopping sounds as the rounds hit the water all around us.

"He's got an M-16," I said. "Stay here." I crawled out the other side of the dock and onto the grass of my backyard. I fired three quick rounds in the direction of the house and then made a run for it. I wasn't going to wait while the son of a bitch picked us off.

I saw him stick his head around the corner. I fired again and dropped to the grass. I heard sirens nearby, probably the cops turning off Gulf of Mexico Drive. The man appeared again, fired at me, missed. Then quiet. I heard a car crank in the distance and then the fading sound of an engine. I called to J.D. "I think he's gone, but let's stay where we are until we're sure."

"No sweat," she said, her voice quiet and close.

I was startled. She was about three feet behind me, lying in the grass. "I thought I told you to stay put," I said.

"Yeah. Like I'm going to pay attention to some dumb civilian."

I laughed, the tension broken. "You sound just like Doug McAllister. You cops are all alike."

I saw a man coming around the corner of my house, a gun in his hand. A cop. "Matt," the cop called. "The shooter's gone."

Steve Carey walked toward us. The storm was moving on and the rain was diminishing, the sky lightening perceptibly. J.D. was standing next to me, wearing only her bra and panties.

"You realize you don't have any clothes on," I said.

"Yeah. We probably look a little silly."

I laughed again, partly with relief at having survived and partly at the absurdity of us standing in my backyard in our underwear, shivering and holding guns. "You know you can see through that flimsy stuff you're wearing."

She looked a bit embarrassed, a faint smile playing on her lips. "I can't do anything about that now."

Steve was smiling as he walked up. He pulled off his windbreaker as he approached. "You're a bit out of uniform, Detective," he said as he handed her his jacket.

"I better not ever hear another word about this," J.D. said. "Not ever."

Steve laughed, threw a sloppy salute her way, and said, "Yes, ma'am."

J.D. laughed too. "It *is* kind of funny, though."

Another cop came around the corner of the house. "All clear," he said. "Whoever was here is long gone."

"Okay," said Steve. He looked toward J.D. and me. "How many shots were fired?"

"A lot. I didn't have time to count them," I said.

"What kind of weapon?"

"Rifle," J.D. said.

"I agree," I said. "Probably an M-16."

"Could you tell where the fire was coming from?"

"Not at first," said J.D. "I thought the first shot was thunder."

"He was at the corner of the house," I said, pointing.

"Did you get a look at him?"

"Yeah. I didn't recognize him, but I'll know him if I see him again."

Steve turned back to the other cop, pointed toward where I thought the shots had come from. "See if you can find any brass over in that area."

"I'm freezing," said J.D. "Let's get inside."

•   •   •

J.D. disappeared into the bedroom, mumbling that she needed a hot shower. I was left standing in my undershorts dripping bay water on my carpet. I told Steve to have a seat and I went to put on dry clothes. When I came back into the living room, Chief Bill Lester was sitting and talking to Steve. "I heard you were trying to get my star detective killed," the chief said to me.

"I don't know what's going on, Bill," I said. "Who the hell takes a shot at us in the middle of a Sunday afternoon?" ·

"I don't think it's just some crazy," said Bill. "I wonder if the Mafia guy is behind this."

"I think it's time to have a chat with him," I said.

"We don't have any real basis to do that," said Bill. "Even if we could find him."

"The guy who tried to beat me up said Bonino sent him."

"That's not really enough to go after him," said Bill. "And we have no idea where Bonino lives. He has an office downtown, but Sarasota P.D. tells me he's never there. He's never been arrested, and the police don't even know what he looks like. He's a ghost. And the guy who tried to beat you up, DeLuca, isn't talking."

"Is he still in the hospital?"

"Yes. Under guard. He's going to be there for at least another week."

"What about Caster?"

"He's not saying anything either," said Bill. "I called Detective Sims as soon as I heard about King's murder and asked that he put Caster in isolation. I wouldn't want whoever killed King to get to Caster in lockup."

"I wonder if we can put some kind of pressure on Caster to get him talking. Maybe tell him the reason he's in isolation is that we have good intelligence that somebody has put a contract on him."

"That might work. I'll talk to Sims."

J.D. came into the living room wearing a pair of shorts and a T-shirt. She was barefoot, her hair wrapped in a towel. She handed Steve his wind-breaker, smiled, and said, "Thanks, Steve. You're a gentleman."

"Don't feel like you've got to dress up for us," said Bill.

She stuck her tongue out at him and took a seat next to me on the sofa.

"How can a guy like Bonino stay off everybody's radar?" I asked.

"I don't know. The intelligence guys at all the police agencies in the area have been trying to figure that out. We first started hearing about Bonino about five years ago. The word on the street was that he was taking over and consolidating a number of illegal businesses that had been run by low-level gangs. A lot of the gang members began to disappear, and the agencies let the whole thing slide. The idea was that if Bonino was cleaning up our streets, more power to him.

"The problem began when Bonino infiltrated some legitimate businesses and over a period of a couple of years took them over. The owners quietly disengaged, sold their interest, and moved out of town. One of the legitimate owners talked to an FBI agent a couple of years ago and told him that the Bonino people just showed up one day with pictures of his house, his wife, his car, and one of his sons being delivered to a middle school by a school bus. The owner was offered a price for his business and told that his family might be better off if he accepted the offer and moved to California."

"Was the offer fair?" I asked.

Bill chuckled. "It was for about fifty percent of the fair value of the business. The owner took the money and left town."

"What kind of business was it?" I asked.

"A large used car dealership."

"Why would the Mafia want a used car dealership?" I asked.

"It's a great way to launder money. Comes in dirty, goes out clean. The dealer has no legal obligation to ask the buyer where he got the money. Of course, the car buyer was always somebody who worked for Bonino, but the title would be issued in the name of somebody with no ties to the dealership. The cars were recycled through dealerships all over the country."

"What do you mean by recycled?"

"Guy comes in and buys a car from Bonino, pays ten grand. He drives the car to Alabama, alters the vehicle identification number, and sells it, for one grand to another dealership that is either owned by Bonino or one of his cronies. The car is then resold to another buyer for ten grand and he moves on to Tennessee and sells the car again for one grand."

"Slick. They leave a paper trail of buying and selling cars and the money comes into the dealership clean as a whistle."

"Bonino also took over some other businesses that he used to make money. He's a mini conglomerate and nobody's ever seen him."

"Surely his employees have met him."

"Nope. Everything is done through managers who deal with Bonino only by e-mail. Nobody ever sees him."

"Not even his thugs? His enforcers?"

"Not even them."

"I'll be damned," I said.

CHAPTER FORTY

The policemen left just as Jock and Logan were coming in. "Did you guys have a nice round?" I asked.

"I don't want to talk about it, podna," said Jock.

"It wasn't that bad," said Logan. "We had finished the second round and were in the clubhouse when the rain hit."

"Why were the cops here?" asked Jock.

I told them about our afternoon and our speculation as to who was shooting at us.

"I think it's time to have a chat with Mr. Bonino," said Jock.

"Nobody knows where he lives or works or even what he looks like," I said.

Jock grinned. "I'll bet DeLuca does," he said. "I think I might pay him a visit in the hospital."

"The sheriff has him under guard," I said.

"I'll make a call," said Jock.

"Jock," J.D. said, "what are you going to do?"

"Have a little chat with DeLuca."

"Come on, Jock," said J.D. "You can't beat him up in a hospital surrounded by cops."

Jock looked puzzled. "Who said anything about beating him up?" he asked.

"J.D.," I said, "let it go."

"Sorry, Jock. I'm a suspicious person," J.D. said.

"I noticed," Jock said, grinning.

"Anybody up for Tiny's?" Logan asked.

J.D. shook her head. I said, "Not us. I think I'd just as soon stay in and do nothing."

"I'll go with you, Logan," said Jock. "If it's all right, I think I'll stay at your place tonight. Matt, keep your pistol handy. The shooter might come back."

"Maybe J.D. will stay and protect me," I said.

"Maybe," said J.D. "If I don't have to cook."

"What's Jock going to do?" J.D. asked after they'd left.

"Whatever he has to," I said.

"I'm still not comfortable with his methods."

"He's not either, you know. But he does what he has to do to keep the country safe. And sometimes, when his family's threatened, he does it to keep us safe."

"We're his family," she said.

"Bingo."

"How big a family are we? How many people does he consider family?"

"There's you, me, and Logan," I said. "I think his director, Dave Kendall, fits in there as well. It's a small group. Jock can't afford to get too close to anybody. It might bring harm to them."

"Then how did we get into such a select group?"

I laughed. "Jock and I have been closer than brothers since we were twelve. We both came from very dysfunctional families and I think we kind of clung to each other as kids. Our high school buddy, Fran Masse, once said that Jock and I challenge each other every day. Not in a confrontational sense, but by each of us inspiring the other to seek excellence. We are each part of the other's success. We've taken care of each other for a very long time.

"You and Logan sort of married into the family. Jock knows I love you and he knows that Logan has become more than just a friend. Other than you and Jock, Logan is my best friend, and Jock isn't going to let anything happen to any of us."

"He's a very strange man," said J.D. "He's gentle and warm and funny, but every now and then I get a glimpse of a side of him that's so cold it makes me shiver."

"There's another side you've never seen," I said. "The side that brings on the cleansing time."

"I never want to be part of that," she said. "It would embarrass him and I think maybe diminish him in some way. When the time comes for that, I'll disappear. Let you two do what you have to do to get him back to sanity."

"I'm glad you understand. I worry that a time will come when he won't be able to get back. When the horrors of what he has seen and done will outweigh what he sees as the good in it."

"What then?"

"I don't know. I've heard of pet dogs who grow old and one day disappear. They leave the owners who have cared for them and loved them all their lives and they go off somewhere to die. I'm afraid that may be what's in Jock's future. One day he just won't come back."

J.D. got up from her chair and came over to the sofa and hugged me for a long time. "I hope you're wrong," she said, finally. "For all our sakes."

CHAPTER FORTY-ONE

Jock followed Logan in his rental car and sat outside Tiny's while he made a phone call. He hung up and went inside to join Logan. He was on his first O'Doul's when his phone rang and he stepped back outside. He talked for a couple of minutes and reentered the bar.

"I have to go," Jock said to Logan. "I'll be back at your place before too late."

Logan gave him a knowing look. "Be careful, Jock."

Jock nodded, turned, and walked out the door. He drove to Blake Hospital and took the elevator to the third floor. He walked down the corridor to a deputy sheriff sitting in a folding chair next to a door.

"Afternoon, Deputy," Jock said, as he walked up. "My name is Jeff Washington. I think you probably got a phone call about me from Detective Sims."

The deputy stood. "I did, Mr. Washington. Go on in."

Jock walked into a typical hospital room. DeLuca was in the bed, both legs in some kind of contraption with ropes and pulleys that held them off the bed. Monitors were hooked up and beeping, IV lines running to his left arm, cuffs around both wrists and attached to the bedrails. He looked up as Jock walked in.

"Are you the new doctor?" DeLuca asked.

"I'm Dr. Washington," said Jock. "I just need to check your vitals." He walked toward the bed and gently pulled a pillow from under DeLuca's head, looked at him for a moment, and then forcibly pushed the pillow into DeLuca's face, holding it down tightly, depriving the man of air.

DeLuca tried to scream, but the pillow muffled the noise so that it couldn't be heard outside the room. He jerked around in the bed, but his arms were locked down by the handcuffs and the contraption holding his legs in place allowed for almost no movement. Jock kept the pressure on DeLuca's face until the struggles subsided some and then leaned in close. "Listen to me," he said. "I'm going to remove the pillow, but if you try to scream it goes back on your face and it'll stay there until you're dead." He let up the pressure and could hear DeLuca gasping for breath. "Nod if we have a deal."

DeLuca nodded and Jock removed the pillow. DeLuca looked up at Jock, fear contorting his face. "Who are you?" he asked.

Jock was still holding the pillow near DeLuca's head. One quick move and it'd cover his face again. "I'll ask the questions. If I don't like the answer, you'll die right here, right now. Understand?"

DeLuca nodded.

"Where is Bonino?"

"I don't know."

Jock gave him a cold stare and began to move the pillow back into position. "Okay," he said. "Sorry we couldn't have communicated better."

"No," DeLuca said, his voice trembling in fear. "Honestly, I don't know where he is, but I think I know who he is."

"That's better. Give me a name."

"Dwight Peters."

"Who's that?"

"He's the man I reported to. I think he might be Bonino."

"Tell me about him," Jock said.

"I don't know where he lives. I always met him in a restaurant in downtown Sarasota or talked to him on the phone."

"How often did you meet with him?"

"Not a lot. Maybe three or four times. Everything else was on the phone."

"Why haven't you told the cops about this?"

"Peters will have me killed if I rat him out."

"You just did."

"Yeah, but you were going to kill me if I didn't. Cops don't do that."

"Did he tell you why he wanted you to beat up Matt Royal?"

"I never talked to him about that little job."

"Little job? It just about got you killed."

"Nobody told me Royal was that tough."

"If you didn't talk to Peters, who gave you your marching orders?"

"A guy named Norwood. Cal Norwood. He's Peters's right-hand man."

"Did he usually give you your orders?"

"No. They usually came straight from the boss."

"Why not this time?"

"Mr. Peters fired me a couple of months ago."

"Why?"

"I don't know. It may have had to do with his wife."

"Peters' wife?"

"Yeah."

"How so?"

"She was with him when we met one time and she is hot. I might have mentioned that to Mr. Peters the last time I saw him. He fired me on the spot."

"You're lucky he didn't kill you."

"Yeah. I thought about that."

"Why do you think Peters is Bonino?" Jock asked.

"Bonino runs things, but nobody's ever met him or even seen him. Peters seems to be in charge, and sometimes I think he might really be Bonino."

"How many people work for him?"

"I don't know. Norwood's the only one I've ever met. He's usually with Mr. Peters. I think he's some kind of bodyguard or something."

"How many people have you killed, DeLuca?"

"I've never killed anybody. I just beat people up sometimes. I think Norwood and some other guys he works with do the killing."

"So you know about the killings?"

"Not really. I just know there have been some."

"How did you find out about them?"

"Just gossip. I go to some of the car dealerships sometimes and hear people there talking about somebody who disappeared right after Norwood came around asking about them."

"Why did you go to the dealerships?"

"Sometimes Mr. Peters needs me to tap on some of the guys a little."

"Tap on them? You mean beat the shit out of them."

"Yeah."

"Why?"

"Don't know. Mr. Peters never told me why."

"Are you smart enough to know that you'll probably be killed the first night you're in the jail's general population?"

"Why would that happen?"

"Because you know more than you should about Peters's operation."

"Yeah, but I ain't talking."

"You just did."

"That's different. Are you going to tell Peters I've been talking to you?"

"No. But if anything you told me isn't true, I'll come back and kill you myself. If I ever hear that you've told anybody about our little discussion today, I'll take you out."

"How did you get by the guard at the door?"

"Think about it. I can get to you anywhere. If you're willing to tell Detective Sims what you've told me, I may be able to get you into the federal witness protection program where you'll be safe."

"Okay. I'll do it."

No hesitation, thought Jock. The bad guys could always make quick decisions when it involved their well-being.

Jock sat in his car in the hospital parking lot and called David Sims. "Did you learn anything?" Sims asked.

"A lot, and DeLuca is willing to testify if you can get him into witness protection."

"I'll work on that. Do you need anything else?"

"Yeah. I need all you can get me on a man named Cal Norwood. I'd also like to know about any known associates."

"Norwood has been around for several years. He's been arrested a few times, but we've never been able to make anything stick. I think our organized-crime unit will have some stuff on him. I'll get right back to you. Five minutes at the most."

Jock sat quietly, listening to a smooth jazz station, letting his mind empty. It was a form of relaxation he'd learned long ago. His phone rang. Sims. "I've got an address and phone number if you need it for Norwood and I'm texting you a picture of him. I'll send some more information on his buddies within the next half hour. The organized-crime unit is digging it up for me."

Norwood lived in a subdivision off University Parkway near its intersection with I-75. Jock looked at his watch. He had about an hour and a half of daylight left. It'd have to do. He drove east on Cortez Road, south on Tamiami Trail to the airport, and then east on University Parkway. He pulled into the subdivision and found the address Sims had given him for Norwood. He parked two doors down.

Norwood's house was ranch style, probably built in the '60s. The yard was neat and recently mowed. There was a single-car garage, no toys in the yard. Jock knew from the information sent by Sims that Norwood was single and had no family. The house seemed to confirm this.

Jock picked up his phone and called the number Sims had given him for Norwood. It was answered on the second ring by a gruff voice. "Yeah?"

"Mr. Norwood, you don't know me, but I'm going to kill you tonight. First, I'll take out Peters. Then I'll come for you. Before daylight. If you need to say good-bye to anyone, now's the time."

"You some kind of comedian? Who the fuck are you?"

"You'll never see me coming. Neither will Peters." Jock closed the phone and waited.

Five minutes later, Norwood's garage door opened and a black Lincoln Town Car backed out, Norwood at the wheel. Jock let him get around the nearest corner and then fell in behind. Norwood turned east on University Parkway and drove to Lakewood Ranch. He turned into an upscale neighborhood where the houses backed up to a golf course and parked in front of one of them. He got out of the car and walked to the front door, went inside.

A few minutes later, Norwood came out and got into his car and sat, waiting. The garage door at Peters's house glided up and a red Corvette backed out, turned into the street, and left the neighborhood. Norwood followed close behind. Jock followed the Town Car and the Corvette to the little shopping village a half mile away and watched as Norwood parked directly in front of the restaurant. The Corvette pulled into a nearby parking slot, and the man Jock assumed to be Peters joined Norwood. They disappeared inside.

Jock checked in the bag he kept in the trunk of the rental and retrieved a digital camera with a long telephoto lens. He put on a navy blue blazer that sported an American flag in the lapel. A wire ran from the flag pin, behind the lapel, and through the jacket and down the coat sleeve to Jock's hand. He drove back to Peters's neighborhood.

Jock used the long lens to take a couple of pictures of Peters's house. He put the camera in his car and walked up the sidewalk and knocked on Peters's door. A pretty blonde woman in her mid-thirties opened it.

"Mrs. Jackman?" Jock asked and squeezed the trigger mechanism for the lapel camera.

"No, I'm Mrs. Peters. You must have the wrong house."

Jock looked at a piece of paper he was holding. "This is the address I was given. Do you know where the Jackmans live?"

"I don't think I know them," she said.

Jock could hear children laughing and squealing somewhere in the house. "Sounds like you've got a houseful," he said. "I guess they gave me the wrong address. I'm sorry to bother you."

The woman smiled. "Not a problem," she said. "I hope you find the Jackmans."

Jock walked back to his car and sat and uploaded the pictures from the digital cameras to his phone. Then, he sat some more.

An hour later, Jock walked into the Polo Grill in the little shopping village in Lakewood Ranch. He was wearing jeans, a white golf shirt, a navy blazer, and a baseball cap with the logo of the Tampa Bay Rays. He had a mustache glued to his upper lip and a small goatee on his chin. He told the hostess he was expected by Mr. Peters. "I can find my way," he said and stepped into the dining room. He saw Norwood sitting at a table in the far corner, his back to the wall, talking to a middle-aged man.

Jock walked to the table and pulled out a chair and sat. Norwood and the other man watched him in stunned silence for a moment. "This table's taken," Norwood said.

Jock looked at the towheaded man and said, "Mr. Peters, we need to talk."

"I'm afraid you have the advantage, sir. You know my name, but I don't know yours."

"Tell your thug to back off, Peters, and we'll talk. I want to show you some pictures."

Peters grinned. "That's not going to happen."

"Look at the pictures and then you can ask him to leave us alone." Jock said.

"Dirty pictures? Naked women?" Peters asked, and he and Norwood laughed.

"Pictures of your family," Jock said.

Peters suddenly sobered. "Let me see."

Jock showed him the pictures on his phone. One was of Peters's house, another, a close-up of a pretty woman standing in the doorway of the house, smiling.

Peters stared at them. "What the hell is this?"

"Tell your thug to go play with himself in the men's room," Jock said. "I've already talked to him today, and I really don't have anything else to say to him."

"I'll tear your fucking head off," said Norwood.

Jock looked at him, staring into his eyes. "No, Mr. Norwood, you won't," he said in a quiet voice.

Surprise spread across Norwood's face. "You know my name?"

"You're a button man for Peters here. You've killed a lot of people, but you're no match for me. You'll die here on the floor of this pretty restaurant and ruin dinner for a lot of nice people. Then Mr. Peters here will do what I say, or I'll kill all the people in that big house of his."

"Mr. Peters, this is the man who called me earlier and threatened to kill both of us."

"Go," said Peters. "Wait for me outside."

Norwood didn't like that, but neither did he like the murderous stare he was getting from the strange man sitting at his table. He said, "You're sure, Mr. Peters?"

"Yes. I'll be all right."

As Norwood was leaving, Peters turned to Jock and said, "What's the meaning of this?"

"Mr. Peters," Jock said, "or do you prefer Bonino?"

Peters paled, sat back in his chair. "Who are you?"

"It doesn't matter. I know who you are and I know what you do. I also know that you have kids in that house. If you want them to stay safe, you're going to do exactly as I say."

"I'm a businessman. That's what I do."

"Let's not waste my time, Peters. I know you control a lot of the drug business around here and use other legitimate businesses to launder money. That'll be coming to an end real soon."

"Right," Peters said, disdainfully. "You don't know who you're fucking with."

"Indeed I do, but the real question is whether you know who you're fucking with."

"I don't know who you are or who sent you. But my guess is that you're just some pussy who thought he could bully me. You won't get out of this building alive. My man who just left will meet you outside with some of our friends. Now get the fuck out of my face. I'm hungry."

Jock stood. "Mr. Peters," he said in a quiet voice laden with steel, "I'm going to kill your friends and then I'm coming back to get you. Sit tight and enjoy your meal." He turned and left the dining room.

Jock didn't go out the front door. He went into the bar and through a door that led to the kitchen. He passed the food preparers without speaking and left through the back door. He stood for a minute in the shadow of the big Dumpster, thinking. He pulled his pistol from its holster at the small of his back and attached the silencer he carried in the pocket of his blazer. He walked to the corner of the building, and in the glare of the security lights he spotted three men standing nonchalantly near cars parked about thirty yards away. The welcoming committee. They were wearing suits, and Jock could tell from the slight bulges in their jackets that they were carrying pistols in shoulder holsters.

Norwood was standing next to the Lincoln Town Car parked about ten feet away, near the front of the restaurant, his back to Jock. "Norwood," Jock said, "I've got a gun pointed at your back. I want you to turn around slowly, keeping your hands where I can see them."

Norwood turned, facing Jock. "I've got men watching me," he said. "One wrong move and you're dead."

"Give me your cell phone," Jock said.

"What?"

"Cell phone. Reach into your pocket and pull it out. If I see anything other than a phone, I'll shoot you."

Norwood did as he was told. Jock saw one of the men in the parking lot start to walk toward them. "Put the phone on the pavement," he said.

Norwood placed the phone at his feet. "You're a dead man," he said. He pointed. "My men are just over there. You shoot me, and they'll kill you before you can move."

Jock shot Norwood in the forehead, the gun making no more sound than an air rifle. He stepped back around the corner and waited for a reaction from the three men in the parking lot. Jock recognized them from the pictures Sims had texted him. All were known shooters for Bonino.

Nothing happened for a couple of seconds. Then the one who'd started walking toward Norwood began to run toward the Town Car, a pistol in his hand. As he ran, he shouted something to the other two men in the parking lot, and they followed at a run, pulling pistols from the shoulder holsters concealed by their suit coats. Jock shot the running man in the chest and then turned and shot both of the other men who were fast approaching the Town Car. They were dead before they hit the pavement.

Jock moved out of the shadows and picked up Norwood's phone. He quickly darted back behind the building, unscrewed the silencer from the muzzle of the pistol and returned it to his jacket pocket. He replaced the pistol in its holster and walked to the restaurant's back door, let himself in, and returned through the bar and to Peters's table.

Peters looked up from his steak. He laughed. "I guess you saw my friends outside. You want to tell me who sent you?"

"Your friends are dead," said Jock.

Peters laughed again, took a sip of his wine. "Right," he said.

"I'll be at your house, Mr. Peters," Jock said. "When you get finished with dinner, come on by, and we'll talk."

Peters laughed some more. He was in a jolly mood. "I don't think you'll make it to my house."

"Mr. Peters," Jock said, "In about five minutes somebody is going to find Norwood and three other bodies in the parking lot and they're going to raise a stink. You might want to keep our little conversation to yourself. See you in a bit."

Jock stood and left through the back door, stopped for a minute to affix the silencer to the pistol and wiped it all down with a handkerchief. He dropped the weapon by the corner of the building and walked a couple of blocks to his rental car. He wouldn't need the pistol anymore and it was untraceable. He didn't want to take the chance that for some reason he'd get stopped by the police and they'd find a murder weapon on him.

He drove toward the neighborhood where Peters lived. He parked two blocks away and let himself into an empty house he'd spotted earlier. It sat across the street from the Peters home. Jock had been there earlier, taking the pictures that he'd shown to Peters. He'd watched the house for an hour after he took the pictures and then used his lock picks to let himself inside. Someone lived there, but they seemed to have been away. A couple of days' worth of mail was stacked in the mailbox and the garage had only one car inside. Tire tracks laid down by a larger vehicle were visible in the empty space. The car had run through some clay just before coming into the garage and the floor had not been swept of the remaining dirt that outlined the tires. The air-conditioning was set on low, too low for people to be comfortable on February nights. A couple of table lamps were set on timers so that they came on when it got dark. People didn't use timers when they were living in the house. It was a pretty good bet that the owners were on vacation somewhere.

An hour went by and Peters's Corvette pulled into the driveway of his house. He got out. Jock dialed Peters's cell phone and watched as Peters pulled it out of his pocket, answered it.

"Sorry about your friends," Jock said.

"Who the fuck are you? How did you get this number?"

"It seems Norwood had you on speed dial. I want you to listen very carefully to me, Mr. Peters. Can you do that?"

"Yes. What do you want?"

"I'm watching you. You just drove into your driveway. You're standing beside your car right now. I want you to raise one of your arms or legs, and I'll tell you which one. It's just a little test to let you know I can truly see you."

Peters stood stock still for a couple of beats, then raised his right leg.

"Good boy," said Jock into the phone. "You raised your right leg. Are you listening very carefully?"

"Yes."

"Good. There's a bomb in the trunk of your Corvette. A pretty big one. I can set it off remotely, so if you don't do just what I tell you, well, you know, ka-boom. It'll take out your car and your house and everybody in either one. Are we communicating now?"

"Yes."

"Okay. Tell me why you were trying to hurt Matt Royal."

"Who the hell is Matt Royal?"

"Remember, Mr. Peters? Ka-boom."

"I don't know anybody by that name. Honestly."

"How about Jimmy DeLuca?"

"Yeah. I know Jimmy. He used to work for me."

"He doesn't anymore?" Jock was checking what DeLuca had told him.

"No."

"Since when?"

"A couple of months ago."

"He quit?"

"No. I fired him."

"For what?"

"Inappropriate remarks about my wife."

"That'd get him killed in most Mafia circles."

"His dad's a friend of mine. So I let it go."

"Do you have any idea why DeLuca would try to beat up Matt Royal last week and tell him you ordered him to do it?"

"None. I swear. I thought Jimmy was down in Miami."

"Okay, Mr. Peters. Here's what you're going to do. Get back into your Corvette and drive to the Manatee Sheriff's Operations Center over by the DeSoto Square Mall. You know where that is?"

"Yes."

"You're going to meet with a Detective David Sims. He'll be waiting for you. You're going to turn yourself in, tell him who you really are, and give him any documents he'll need in order to bust up your little operation. And you'll waive your right to a lawyer."

"You're crazy."

"Ka-boom, Mr. Peters. There's another bomb in your garage. My associates will be watching your house, both front and back. If your family tries to leave, they'll activate the bomb. Your wife and kids won't stand a chance. I'll be behind you. If you deviate from the route to Sims's office, I'll blow the bomb in your trunk. If everything goes like it's supposed to, I'll remove the bomb from your garage, and the sheriff will take the one out of your car."

There was quiet on the other end of the phone. Then, "Okay. I'll do it. I've never heard of anything so filthy in my life. To threaten a man's family."

"Don't be an ass, Peters. You use it as a business tool. Threaten a man's family and take his business."

"I would never have harmed any of their families."

"The men you extorted didn't know that. Now, get your ass in the car and get moving."

Jock watched as Peters pulled out of his driveway and then dialed Detective David Sims. He answered on the second ring. "A man will be at your office within about thirty minutes," Jock said. "He's the elusive Bonino. He wants to spill his guts and give you any documentation you need to bust up his operation."

"And why would he do that?"

"Just being a good citizen, I guess. He might be calling himself Peters.

Call me when he's in custody. And impound his car and his cell phone. He might tell you there's a bomb in his car, but there isn't. And I don't want him talking to his wife or anyone else. He'll waive his right to a lawyer and will allow you to search his house."

"What the hell's going on?" asked Sims.

"Do you really want to know?"

Sims was quiet for a moment. "I guess not," he said.

"I don't think his wife has anything to do with Bonino's business enterprises, and they have at least two small children in the house. I don't want them upset. It's going to be a long hard time for them while Bonino spends the rest of his life in prison."

"We'll go easy on them. If we find any evidence that the wife's involved, that's another story."

"Thanks, David. Call me when Peters is in custody and isolated."

"Is this number good? The one you're calling from?"

"It'll be good until I hear from you."

"Where are you?"

"Out doing the Lord's work, David. Talk to you soon."

Jock hung up and sat and waited to hear that Peters was a resident of the county jail.

CHAPTER FORTY-TWO

In the real world, Monday is the day when people trudge off to work trading the ennui of the weekend for the rush of earning a living. For retired people, Monday is just another Saturday. You can sleep in, take your time reading the paper and drinking coffee, hit the golf course or the fishing grounds or just do nothing. My Mondays were usually spent doing mostly nothing. This wasn't going to be a normal day.

J.D. and I were up early. We ran on the beach, took a long shower together, and ate a leisurely breakfast. The morning air was cool, the sun bright, the Gulf calm. "JAPDIP," as we islanders smugly say; "Just Another Perfect Day In Paradise."

The *Sarasota Herald-Tribune* headline was large and black. "FOUR MEN SLAIN IN LAKEWOOD RANCH." The story told of a restaurant patron walking toward his car when he found the body of a man shot through the head in the driveway of the restaurant. He alerted the hostess on duty in the restaurant and she called the sheriff's department. Deputies arrived and found three more bodies, all men, all wearing suits, all shot in the chest. A nine-millimeter pistol with a silencer attached was found at the corner of the building where deputies speculated the killer had stood when he shot the men. The kitchen staff reported seeing a man come through the kitchen, but nobody paid any attention to him. Some said he wore a ball cap, others said he was bareheaded and had dark hair, some said clean shaven, others saw a beard. There were no suspects and no motive. The dead men had been identified, but their names weren't being released until the next of kin were notified.

J.D. left for work shortly after seven, and I booted up my computer and tried the Highlands County property appraiser's website. It was up, the maintenance finished. I looked up the Avon Park property using the street address that Frank Cartwright, the grove keeper, had given us. The property had been sold by the estate of James Fredrickson to a corporation named APL Property, LLC for ten thousand dollars. I assumed the APL stood for Avon Park Lake. Not very original. The transaction had taken place about six months after Jim's death.

I logged off the site and went to the Florida Secretary of State's website and found the Corporations Division's site. APL Property, LLC had been organized about a month before it bought the property from the Fredrickson estate. It had one manager/member, a man named Robert Hammond with an address in Orlando. The agent for service of process was Wayne Evans whose address was in Sarasota.

That name rang a bell. I went to the website of the Fredrickson's old law firm. Evans was a partner in the firm's Probate and Estate Planning section. A quick search of the Sarasota County Clerk of Court's website brought me to the case file in Fredrickson's estate. Bingo. Evans was the personal representative, the administrator, of the estate.

I Googled Robert Hammond. I found a man by that name who was a developer with offices in Orlando. His website consisted of one page that had a few graphics, a picture of Hammond, and some verbiage that said his company developed subdivisions and built houses. That was it. No descriptions of projects or available properties; not even an address or phone number. I wondered why he even had a website.

My phone rang. "Matt, this is David Sims."

"Good morning, Detective."

"Is Jock with you?"

"No. He's staying here, but he's out right now."

"I need to talk to him. Will you have him call me as soon as he shows up?"

"Sure."

"Thanks, Matt. Have a good day."

That was a puzzling call. Why would Sims be looking for Jock? I guess I'd find out as soon as Jock showed up and returned the call.

Jock walked in the door ten minutes later. He looked haggard, as if he hadn't slept well. "Logan keep you up all night?" I asked.

"No. I had a long night, but the good news is that you won't have to worry about Bonino anymore."

"What's the bad news?"

"I don't think he was the one who put the thugs on you."

"Uh-oh. What did you do?"

"I had a little conversation with the man."

"Come on, Jock. Talk to me."

"I killed four of his goons."

"I'm guessing this little conversation took place in Lakewood Ranch."

"You've read the paper."

"Yes. Was it necessary?"

"I'm not sure 'necessary' is the word I'd use. All four of those guys were murderers. They've killed lot of people and they'd kill again. I also wanted to send a message. At the time I shot them, I was pretty sure Bonino had sicced the thugs on you, but he pretty much convinced me he wasn't the one. Says he's never heard of you, and I think he was under enough pressure that he'd have told me the truth about anything."

"Where is he now?"

"David Sims has him."

"How did you find him when the cops can't come up with anything?"

"I had a little conversation with DeLuca and he gave me the name of one of Peters's men, a guy named Norwood. I made a call, threatened him and his boss, and followed him to a meeting with Bonino. And Bonino is actually a man named Dwight Peters who lives in Lakewood Ranch. He has a pretty wife and at least a couple of small children."

"That's not good."

"No. They're going to suffer a lot because of Peters. I wish I could do something about that."

"You can't, Jock. I'm sure there're a number of families out there suffering because of what Peters did."

"That's for sure, but the Peters kids didn't have anything to do with it."

"You can't cure all the world's ills, my friend. I'm still a little puzzled about the reason for killing the guys in the parking lot."

"I needed to make a point with Peters. He seemed to think he was bulletproof. I made the point and took out some bad guys that needed killing. And Peters is in jail and will stay there for the rest of his life."

"Are you all right?"

"Yeah. I think so."

"Sims called about fifteen minutes ago. Wants you to call him as soon as you can."

"I'll get back to him."

"What time do you tee off?"

"Ten. We've got a couple of hours."

Jock and Logan were playing in a foursome with Mike Nink and Randy LaFlamme. Their chances of winning the tournament ranked right up there with whatever patsy football teams the Florida Gators played in their first two games of every season. In other words, it'd take a miracle.

My job as the beer cart driver required that I bring two coolers full of beer and ice and cheer my team on at the appropriate moments. We hoped the beer would last for the first nine holes and I could replenish the supply at the clubhouse. I didn't expect to have to do a lot of cheering, but I'd get to drink some beer and enjoy the weather. A great Monday on our island. Too bad it didn't work out that way.

CHAPTER FORTY-THREE

J. D. Duncan sat in her office looking at Josie Tyler's phone records; the one sent to her by Captain Doug McAllister. It was identical to the one Jock's people had sent her the day before. She put the printout aside and called the Tampa Police Department and asked to speak to the patrol commander. He was in a meeting and would call her back. She hung up and called Captain McAllister.

"Doug, it's J.D. Thanks for sending Josie Tyler's phone records over. Do you know who made the incoming call to Josie Friday afternoon?"

"No. It's a burner phone. A dead end."

"I'm thinking that call is probably what spooked her into calling me and leaving that message."

"I've been thinking about that. You're probably right, but I doubt we'll ever find out who made the call."

"Did forensics turn up anything else?"

"No. The crime scene was clean as a whistle."

"Any better idea on how the elevator security camera got screwed up?"

"No. Somehow the router became unplugged. Nobody can figure out how that happened unless the cleaning people did it."

"Okay. Thanks. Will you keep me in the loop?"

"I will. And listen, J.D., I'm sorry about the way I acted on Friday."

"Water under the bridge, Doug. Don't worry about it."

"Are we okay?"

"We are. Talk to you later."

She hung up and walked across the hall to Chief Bill Lester's office. "Got a minute, Bill?"

"Sure."

"How well do you know Doug McAllister?"

"Pretty well," the chief said. "I've known him for a long time. Why?"

"I don't know, exactly." She told him about McAllister's actions on Saturday evening at the murder scene. "He's been very apologetic about it, but I was surprised at the way he blew up."

"Doug's a complicated guy. He's a good detective, but sometimes I think he steps over the line. There have always been rumors about him using excessive force on some of the perps he's arrested. Once, some years ago, when he was working undercover, he supposedly got involved with a woman who was closely connected to the drug trade. She disappeared before they took down the gang, and everybody thought she was dead. A year later she was arrested in Jacksonville and claimed that she was a confidential informant for McAllister."

"That sounds odd," J.D. said.

"On a couple of levels. How did she even know that McAllister was a cop? He was working undercover and his life would have been in danger if anybody had found out he was the police. And how did the woman manage to avoid getting arrested with the rest of the druggies? Advance information?"

"What came of that?"

"Nothing. The girl was written off as a flake and ended up in prison on the charges out of Jacksonville."

"Wasn't anybody interested in how she knew McAllister was a cop?"

"She had a story, of course. Said they were lovers, but McAllister denied it. His story was that she disappeared before the bust, and he thought she was dead. Apparently the gang wasn't above killing its own members if they stepped out of line."

"I still don't understand how she knew he was a cop."

"Nobody ever figured that out. I think most of it just got swept under the rug. McAllister was a hero for taking down that drug operation. It was a big one, and he got a lot of career mileage out of it."

"Do you know anything about those four dead guys in Lakewood Ranch?"

"Only what I read in the paper. That's Manatee Sheriff's bailiwick. Glad it's not our problem."

"Me, too. Thanks for the insight on McAllister, Bill."

"J.D.," the chief said, "you've got to work with him, but you don't have to trust him."

CHAPTER FORTY-FOUR

My phone rang at nine. J.D. "I talked to the patrol commander at Tampa P.D., and he put me in touch with the cop assigned to the car in the picture. I had our geek blot out Katie's image, but otherwise keep the picture intact. I texted it to the cop, and he recognized the building. He just called back with an address. Can you go up there this morning and look around?"

"I've got beer cart duty."

"You think those guys can't play without beer?"

"Well, they won't play as well without beer."

"Will it make much difference in their score?"

"No, but they'll be happy with whatever they get. Without the beer, it's going to be pretty depressing."

"Listen, Matt. This is important, and those guys are used to losing."

"You've got a point. I'll get right back to you."

I discussed the problem with Jock, and we decided that we should ask Les Fulcher to fill in for me. I called Les and he agreed to do it, but warned that he would expect a beer allowance for himself. I told him I had an extra cooler, and he said that'd probably hold him for the first nine holes.

I drove to Tampa and followed my GPS to the address the Tampa cop had given J.D. I found the building from the picture in one of those neighborhoods that had deteriorated over the years, but seemed to be coming back. Gentrification, it was called. Houses had been rehabbed and new stores were moving in. There was a grocery store, a couple of restaurants, a bar, all in recently renovated buildings. A Kmart store took up most of one block fronting the main street, but it looked as if it'd been there a while. A new McDonald's restaurant stood in a corner of the Kmart parking lot.

The building I was looking for was abandoned and apparently forgotten. It sat on a corner of the major street that ran through the area and a secondary street that meandered through the adjoining neighborhood. The graffiti I'd seen in the picture Katie had sent was sprayed over a large portion of the wall facing the larger street, standing in sharp contrast to the neat facades of its reconstructed neighbors. Perhaps whoever owned the building was waiting for the urban renewal efforts to catch up with his corner.

I drove around the area looking for anything that might give me a lead to Katie. Most of the rehabs seemed to be on the north side of the main street. The south side looked as if gentrification hadn't yet reached it. I doubted that someone on the run, as Katie presumably was, could afford the north side.

I drove into the southern part of the neighborhood and found a small apartment complex about two blocks from the building with the graffiti. It looked better built than its neighbors and held ten units on two floors. Four cars were parked in the lot in front of the building. I wrote down the tag numbers and called them to J.D. She said she'd run them and call me back.

Katie had grown up in an affluent family, in a home situated in one of the most desirable areas of Greater Orlando. She'd lived lavishly on the bayfront in Sarasota, married to a prominent lawyer who had ten million dollars in cash in the bank. It'd be hard for her to settle for living in a dump, but with the exception of the apartment complex, that's about all there was south of the main street.

I drove back to the McDonald's and ordered a Big Mac, fries, and a Diet Coke and returned to the apartment complex. I parked on the street in front of the house that was next door to the apartments, ate my lunch, and waited.

J.D. called to tell me that none of the cars in the lot were registered to Katie. I finished lunch and sat some more. I had the radio tuned to a local talk show and was learning more than I needed to know about the underside of Tampa politics as seen by people who had nothing better to do than listen to the idiot who hosted the show. I switched to NPR and listened to people talk of things that they knew even less about than I did. Finally, I found an easy-listening station and settled in for a long wait.

There was little activity on the street. An old man walked his yappy little dog, a woman brought her garbage bags to the curb, the occasional car or pickup drove by. I sat some more and then some more. I was bored and wishing I hadn't gotten the large Diet Coke. I had to go to the bathroom. Finally, I gave up and drove to the McDonald's to use their restroom. It was mid-afternoon, and I'd wasted the day sitting outside an apartment complex where Katie probably did not live and where I didn't see one resident come or go. They were probably all working.

I decided to make one more pass by the apartment building. Maybe there'd be a new car in the lot. Maybe the place had burned down while I was in the bathroom. I just wanted something to happen to make up for my wasted day.

As I turned into the street on which the apartments were located, I noticed a woman walking southward on the sidewalk. She was thin with short dark hair. She was wearing shorts and a T-shirt and running shoes and one of those little carryalls known as fanny packs. Hers was turned so that the large pocket was in front. Katie? I couldn't be sure. I drove past her and pulled to the curb half a block away. I got out of the Explorer and began walking toward her. I was wearing cargo shorts, a golf shirt, and boat shoes. I didn't think I presented a threatening image. The closer I got to the woman walking toward me, the more I was convinced it was Katie. She kept walking, never breaking stride. She didn't seem concerned about me, but I noticed that her hand was now inside the pocket of the fanny pack.

As I came abreast of her I kept walking and said in a quiet voice, "J.D. Duncan sent me."

I was almost past her. She stopped abruptly and turned toward me. I stopped. She said, "I've got a gun in my hand. Do you need to see it?"

"No. I believe you."

She wanted to make sure I knew she was armed. She pulled the pistol partly out of the pack, showing me the butt of it. "Who are you?"

"My name is Matt Royal. I'm a friend of J.D."

"Who's J.D.?"

"Your friend from college. The one you call Jed. The Longboat Key detective."

She stood quietly, fidgeting a bit. She was about to take off.

"Katie, listen to me," I said. "J.D. got the two text pictures you sent and the e-mail with the police car. She's shared them with no one but me. She did what you probably meant for her to do and tracked down the location of the building. I came up here to find you. I drove around the neighborhood and figured you probably lived in the apartment house down the street. I've been sitting outside most of the day waiting to see you."

"I don't live in the apartments."

"Use my phone. Call J.D. You know her number. She'll tell you who I am and why you should trust me. I'm pulling my phone out of my pocket. Okay?"

"Let me see the phone."

I slowly pulled the phone out and handed it to her. She took it with her right hand, her left still in the fanny pack holding the pistol. She backed up about three steps, putting some distance between us.

"I can reach my pistol before you can reach me," she said.

I backed up a couple of steps, my hands in front of me, palms down.

She dialed the phone. Waited for it to be answered. "Jed, it's me." She was quiet for a moment and then, "I'm fine. Did you send some guy named Royal to find me?" More quiet. "I'm standing on a street in Tampa with a pistol trained on him." She laughed. "Okay. I won't shoot him. I'll talk to him and get back to you."

"J.D. says you're her honey."

"She used that word?"

"Yep."

"I'll be damned."

"Let's go to my house. It's in the next block."

The house was as old and as rundown as the others on the block, but the inside was immaculate. The furniture was new, the walls painted, the terrazzo floor covered with expensive carpets. "Have a seat," she said. "Can I get you something to drink?"

"I'm fine, thank you."

"Tell me about yourself," she said.

"Not much to tell. I'm a retired lawyer and live on Longboat Key and I'm in love with your friend J.D."

"You look way too young to be retired."

"Long story. Let's talk about you."

"What do you want to know?"

"Where have you been for the past year?"

"I lived in Atlanta for a few months and came here about six months ago."

"What about Detroit?"

"What about it?" she asked.

"The texts you sent J.D. came from Detroit."

"Yeah. A bit of misdirection."

"How did you manage that?"

"Another story for another day. I may have to keep that channel open."

"Why did you run away?"

"Long story."

"Try me."

"Not yet."

"Okay," I said. "Why are you in Tampa?"

"I've had to keep moving."

"Somebody chasing you?"

"Probably."

"Who?"

"I'm not ready to tell you that."

"Why not?"

"I have to figure out whether I can trust you."

"Didn't J.D. vouch for me?"

"Yes," she said, "but can I trust J.D.?"

"Your parents do."

"They don't know the whole story."

"What story?"

"The one I'm not ready to tell you about yet."

"Why did you get in touch with J.D. if you don't trust her?"

"I'm tired of running, and she's the only person I think I can trust. But I've got to be sure."

"Are you going to run again after I leave?"

"No. Like I said, I'm tired of running. If somebody comes after me, I'm prepared. I can get out of here in a hurry and nobody will ever find me. If I have to spend the rest of my life looking over my shoulder, so be it. But I felt like I had to take this chance to come home, maybe my last chance."

"You're playing a dangerous game, Katie."

"Maybe."

"How have you stayed lost the last year?"

"My husband had a suitcase full of cash in our house. I took that with me. I don't have a job or a car or a house or credit card or a bank account. I pay cash for everything. I use different names for different things with different people at different times. I'm off the grid, as they say, and as long as I've got cash, I can stay that way."

"Where did the cash come from?"

"Jim was involved in illegal activities. He kept a lot of cash around the house."

"What kind of illegal activities?"

"Not now, Matt. Maybe later. You go on home and tell J.D. I love her and that I'll be in touch soon."

"One more question, Katie. What does U166 mean?"

She smiled. "You're pretty sharp. I hoped J.D. would pick up on that."

"What does it mean?"

"I honestly don't know. I heard my husband and another man talking about it like it was some really big deal. Drugs, maybe. I thought J.D. could figure it out."

"Not so far."

"Go home, Matt. We'll talk more later."

I got up to leave. "Katie, I know you're probably worried about somebody being able to hack into J.D.'s phone. I want to give you a number of a friend of mine whose phone is absolutely unhackable."

"All phones are at risk," she said.

"Not this one. My friend is an intelligence agent for the federal government. His phone is completely safe, and no one who would want to hurt you even knows he exists. You can call him if you need help. Anytime of the day or night. He's staying with me on Longboat, and I promise you any message you want to send will be instantly conveyed to J.D."

"I don't know," she said.

I wrote Jock's cell phone number, the one very few people had, on the back of one of my business cards and handed it to her. "It's just in case of an emergency. If you really need help. If you're in that much trouble, you've already been found by whoever is chasing you."

"You've got a point. Now go home."

She ushered me out the door, and I drove back to Longboat Key. It had been a very strange meeting. Maybe J.D. could make more out of it than I could. She'd known Katie for a long time. I called her and she said she'd be working late and that I could bring her up to date when she got home. She'd order pizza from Ciao's and pick it up on the way to my place.

It was nearing dark as I pulled into the parking lot at Tiny's. The golf foursome and the beer cart driver were sitting at a table in the corner. They'd been there a while and were cheerful in the way of drunks the world over. Except for Jock. He had an O'Doul's in front of him and sat quietly listening to his friends.

"Did you win?" I asked.

"Not quite," said Logan.

"We might have if Logan could ever hit a fairway shot," said Randy.

Mike Nink laughed. "I shot close to par. These yahoos ruined it for me."

"Yeah," said Jock dryly. "Mike was only about thirty over."

"I did my part," said Les, the beer cart driver. "Even received some accolades."

"From whom?"

"Logan, mostly," said Les. "He said I was a much better beer cart driver than you are."

"Was he drunk when he said it?" I asked.

"Well, uh," said Les. "Yeah."

That was about as good as the conversation got. I had a couple of beers and announced that I was headed home. Jock followed me out the door. "I talked to Sims," he said. "He's not going to announce the arrest of Peters until he has all the information he can squeeze out of him."

"That's probably a good plan. Does he know you were responsible for the killings in Lakewood Ranch?"

"He doesn't know anything, but he suspects it. Peters wouldn't talk about that. Told Sims his family was in danger if he said anything. But, Sims knows I was in the area because I was the one who called to tell him Peters was going to turn himself in. But there's something else."

"What?"

"It seems that Peters is not Bonino."

"I don't get that."

"Peters is a go between. One more layer of security. He says he doesn't know who the real Bonino is. They communicate by e-mail and burner phones. Peters is a smoke screen."

"How do we know that?"

"Sims says Peters is scared enough to admit to anything. He also agreed to take a lie detector test. He answered all the questions truthfully, according to the examiner. Including the one about whether he was Sal Bonino."

"Peters must have been a damn good smoke screen."

"He was. I think Bonino, whoever he is, set this up so that Peters would take the fall if it ever got that far. Bonino must have had something to hang over Peters's head. My guess would be that Peters's family was at risk if he didn't take the fall once he was discovered. My threat to his family was more immediate. Maybe Peters figured he'd neutralize the most imminent threat, me, and deal with Bonino later."

"I need to talk to J.D. about all this," I said.

"I know. She's cool."

"I'll leave a light on for you."

"I'm going to bunk in with Logan again and give J.D. and you a little privacy. See you in the morning."

That worked for me.

CHAPTER FORTY-FIVE

Darkness was creeping over the island as I arrived home. J.D. showed up five minutes later with the pizza and a bottle of red wine. We sat on the sofa eating pizza as I told her about my afternoon with Katie.

"She's playing it pretty close to the vest," said J.D.

"She's scared, doesn't know whom to trust."

"I'm a little hurt that she doesn't trust me."

"She'll get there. I'm thinking there must be some pretty powerful people after her to make her so cautious."

"What do you think we should do?" she asked.

"Let's give her a little time. I gave her Jock's number in case she needs us. I told her nobody would be able to hack his phone. She also has my number, but I don't think she'll be calling it. Not yet, anyway."

"What if I went to see her?"

"That might spook her into running."

"Let's think about that. I'd like to sit down with her, talk this thing out."

"I've got something else to tell you," I said.

She looked at me for a moment. "It's bad, isn't it?"

I'd thought a lot about how much to tell her. She was a law enforcement officer and that carried certain obligations, ones she took very seriously. I wasn't sure she could overlook the shooting death of four people, even if they deserved their fate. "I know something about the shootings in Lakewood Ranch last night. I want to tell you, but I can't do it unless you'll promise me you won't start acting like a cop."

"What does that mean?" There was a sharpness to her tone that I didn't like.

"It means that if I tell you what I know, it won't go out of this room. The information will stay with us."

J.D. stared at me, her green eyes flashing, a look of anger that set me back on my heels. I'd seen that look before, but never directed at me. She said one word, "Jock."

"I can't tell you without your promise that it stays between us."

"What if I told you that your silence on something this big could cause an irreparable rupture in our relationship?"

"That would break my heart." My breath caught in my throat.

"We can't have what we have if there are secrets between us," she said.

"That's exactly the reason I want to tell you about this."

"But you put stipulations on it."

"The only stipulation is that you keep it between us. If you weren't a cop, that wouldn't be an issue."

"But I *am* a cop. That's part of the package. It's who I am."

"And I love the whole package, but this is a matter of honor. I've never done anything in my life that violated that sense of honor, of my under-standing of what honor is all about. That's who *I* am."

"I don't understand how telling me about four murders can somehow violate your sense of honor."

"You'd understand if you knew the facts."

"Then, we're at a stalemate," she said. "I'm a cop and I can't agree to hold back information I know about a crime, and you can't tell me about the crime without breaching your sense of honor. Maybe I'd just better go home."

"Don't leave, J.D. We've got to work this out. Now. I wouldn't have brought it up if I didn't think I owed you total honesty. And that includes telling you things that affect us, things that lovers should never keep from each other. But sometimes, that honesty might carry dire consequences for someone we both care about. If either of us can't consider that factor in how we process the information, what we do with it, then we may not have much of a future. We'll have other issues, other times in our lives when we have to be honest with each other and risk a breach of our rela-tionship. We each have to know that the other is committed above all else to us, to this entity that is us, the one that makes us unique in the world."

J.D. sat quietly, her eyes downcast, thinking. It reminded me of the many times I'd sat in a courtroom waiting for a jury to return with a verdict that would change the life of my client, either for good or ill. If the trial was on criminal charges, a jury decision one way would send my client to jail, while a different decision would free him. There's an old saying that no matter what the jury decides, the lawyer goes home. I might not be going home from this one. J.D. literally held my life in her hands. If she decided that we were done, my life would be done. There was no way to start over again. Self-pity is not a desirable trait in a man, but there you have it.

"One question, Matt."

"Yes?"

"If this involves Jock, was he protecting his family?"

I thought about that for a minute. "I'm not saying that Jock is involved at all, but if he were, the answer would be yes. He would have been protecting his family. In the only way he knows how. Direct confrontation."

"Okay, Counselor," she said. "You've made your case. You win. We have a deal."

"J.D., it will never be a win-lose proposition with us. We both win. We still have us. And that's the most important thing in my life."

"And in mine," she said.

"You want all the details?"

She nodded, and I told her about Jock's evening. When I finished, she asked, "What about Peters? I haven't seen anything about his arrest."

"Sims is keeping that under wraps. Jock talked to him this morning. Sims is pretty sure that Jock took those guys out, but he thinks Jock did society a favor. He wants to wring Peters dry before anything comes out about his arrest. And it turns out that Peters is not the big boss. Bonino is still out there. Peters says he doesn't know who Bonino is and Sims believes him. So does Jock."

"If it wasn't Peters who sent the thugs after us, who was it?"

"That's an interesting question," I said. "Maybe the real Bonino just bypassed Peters and came after us. Sims had a heart-to-heart with Caster and all he knows is that King hired him to find Bud Jamison. And Peters says he never heard of King."

"Is Sims pretty sure he got everything out of Caster?"

"Yeah. David's been at this a long time. I won't say there wasn't some coercion applied to that little snake Caster, but I think he gave it all up."

"Matt, I feel lousy about this. I know Jock did what he did to protect us, but it's still murder."

"I don't think so. I could make a hell of an argument to a jury that it was self-defense. If he hadn't taken the gunmen out, they'd have killed him."

"They probably would have," said J.D., "but Jock set the whole thing in motion. The dead guys wouldn't have been after him if he hadn't confronted Peters."

"Call it a preemptive strike. Based on all the facts Jock had, Peters was Bonino and Bonino was trying to kill you and me. And remember, those facts all led to the reasonable conclusion that Jock reached, that Peters and Bonino were the same person. Besides, Jock did not commit a crime by confronting Peters, and when the bad guys came after him, guns drawn, mind you, he had a right under Florida law to kill them. He would have been immune from prosecution."

"What about the first guy?" she asked. "He was standing next to his car not bothering anybody."

"But he had threatened Jock in the restaurant, and Peters had told Jock that the man was waiting in the parking lot to kill him. If Jock had just walked out of the restaurant without a weapon, he'd have been the one lying dead on the driveway."

"He could have taken the facts to law enforcement instead of going all vigilante."

"Put yourself in the position of the cops who Jock would have gone to see. He couldn't tell them how he came upon the information he had without compromising DeLuca and probably getting him killed. Even if he could tell them what DeLuca said, Jock had no way to prove it. What would you have done in those cops' position?"

She sat quietly staring at me, biting her lower lip. "I would have started an investigation," she said.

"And by the time the investigation was finished, you and I would be dead, and Peters would be untouchable because the police would never have been able to prove anything."

She nodded. "You're probably right. I bet you were hell on wheels in front of a jury."

I laughed, relief pouring over me. "I had my moments," I said. "And, Peters is in custody and spilling his guts to David Sims. A lot of mangy heads are going to roll before this is over, a lot of bad guys are going to be guests of the state for a very long time."

"I'm glad you told me. Maybe I overreacted. I'm sorry."

I felt like I'd dodged a bullet. You never know when a heap of trouble is going to drop in on you. It always comes as a shock. Sometimes you can fix it and sometimes you can't. I thought I'd fixed this one. For now, at least. "Nothing to be sorry about," I said. "I didn't expect anything less of you."

"This was our first fight."

"I didn't like it."

"Do you think you'd like a little makeup sex?" she asked.

"That seems a bit shallow, but if it'll make you feel better, I'm game."

She laughed, that big one that turns me into Silly Putty, and then she led me into the bedroom.

CHAPTER FORTY-SIX

I was running hard, the packed sand squeaking beneath my shoes. Tuesday morning was enveloping the key, the early light gentle and the air cool as I raced south on the beach. I pulled up at my usual turnaround point and began to walk back north. I was perspiring heavily under the sweatshirt I wore, breathing hard, trying to slow it down, catch my breath.

J.D. was sleeping in, drained, I thought, from the rigors of the day before. She had a lot on her mind, and I hadn't helped with the revelation about Jock's part in the deaths in Lakewood Ranch. We still had no idea where Bud Jamison was and, a week after Ken Goodlow's murder, we were no closer to a solution.

I decided to spend the day looking into the ownership of the property in Avon Park. I wasn't sure what significance that had to anything, but a cabin full of weapons on property owned by a man in Orlando, who may or may not exist, raised a number of interesting questions. When I added in the fact that Wayne Evans, the personal representative of Jim Fredrickson's estate, was also involved in some manner with the owner of the property, a bevy of questions began to swirl around in my prefrontal cortex.

I was troubled by the fight J.D. and I'd had the night before. The problem was that we were both right and somebody had to give in. It was the kind of situation where compromise was impossible, the positions of each of us too important and entrenched. One of us had to surrender, and I felt strongly that it couldn't be me. I wouldn't put Jock in danger. At the same time, J.D. had a job to do. She was a cop and knowing about a crime and not reporting it went against everything she believed about her role in law enforcement.

I thought I'd convinced her that Jock probably could not have been prosecuted under the circumstances, but I knew J.D. was never at ease with Jock's methods. They came from different worlds. J.D.'s had rules and procedures and protocols and statutes and constitutions and it was the one to which every civilized society aspired. Jock's world was a jungle where only the fittest and wiliest survived, a place that J.D. saw as an alternative universe, a murky and deadly and lawless realm. Sadly, Jock's world was the necessary counterweight to J.D.'s, a place where good people did bad things to ensure that a society governed by the rule of law could survive and flourish. It was hard to reconcile the two worlds, but each was indispensable to the other. Jock and J.D. understood the dichotomy, but only Jock had accepted the essentiality of both. I wasn't sure that J.D. would ever be able to reconcile herself to a world where the law was meaningless and death was a cheap commodity.

I picked up the pace, settling into an easy jog, and headed for home. J.D. was puttering around in the kitchen making coffee. "Good run?" she asked.

"Yeah. It's going to be a beautiful day."

We ate bowls of cereal and finished our coffee, and J.D. left for the police station. I showered and as soon as nine o'clock rolled around, I called Evans's law firm and asked to make an appointment to see him as soon as possible.

"I'm sorry," said the overly officious secretary, "but Mr. Evans is tied up the rest of this week."

"I'm a lawyer," I said, "and I think Mr. Evans would want to meet with me. Can you see if he can squeeze me in today for about fifteen minutes?"

"May I tell him what this is in reference to?"

"No."

"I'm sorry, sir. He'll need to know why you want to see him."

"Put him on the line and I'll tell him."

"Sorry, sir. I can't do that."

I remembered a time when lawyers weren't such stuffed shirts that you couldn't get through to them on the phone. I think the ones who hide behind a phalanx of receptionists and secretaries and paralegals are insecure little weasels who think their law degrees confer some special aura on them and they're not sure anyone else sees it. Thus, they surround themselves with sycophants who limit access to those who are used to paying their outrageous fees, those poor fools who equate their lawyer's ability with the amount of money he is able to extort from his clients. Guys like that just piss me off.

"Please tell Mr. Evans that I will be in his office in one hour. I have some pictures of him taken over in Avon Park. He probably looks better in clothes than he does in these pictures. If he won't see me, I'll give them to an enterprising reporter at the *Herald-Tribune.*" I hung up. I didn't have any such pictures, of course, but I was betting that Evans had been in that old house in the grove and that he'd been naked at least part of the time while the women were visiting.

The law firm was housed in a new building designed by an architect with no vision. It was essentially a three-story cube set in an expanse of asphalt parking lot just off Main Street in downtown Sarasota. Inside, the furnishings were plush and homey. A beautiful woman, probably in her early thirties, manned the receptionist desk. "May I help you, sir?"

"I'm Matt Royal to see Mr. Evans."

She smiled. "He's expecting you. Have a seat, and I'll let him know you're here."

I sat in a brocaded wing chair while the receptionist dialed a number and murmured into the phone. "It'll be just a few minutes, Mr. Royal."

Geez. This guy wanted to play games. Make me wait for a while. It would show me who was in charge. "Never mind," I said. "Please tell Mr. Evans that I have an appointment with a newspaper reporter and I can't wait." I turned and walked out the door. I stopped at the edge of the parking lot. I was pretty sure someone would be coming out the door shortly.

Sure enough, the front door opened and a harried middle-aged woman came trotting out. "Mr. Royal?" she called to me. "I'm Joyce, Mr. Evans's secretary. He can see you now."

I walked over to her. "Joyce," I said, "I want you to give your boss an exact message. Do you need to write it down?"

"Oh, dear. I don't have anything to write on."

I tore a sheet of paper from the yellow legal pad I was carrying and gave it to her. I pulled a ballpoint pen from my pocket, handed it to her. "Write this, please. 'Evans, you've got two minutes to get your sorry ass down to the parking lot. Get a move on.' You got that, Joyce?"

"Yes, sir." She was smiling. "I got it down verbatim."

"He's a bit of an ass, huh?"

She smiled some more. "More than a bit," she said, "but he pays well." She turned and walked back toward the building.

In less than two minutes, a diminutive man came hurrying out of the door. He was wearing a white dress shirt, red patterned tie, and beige trousers held up by suspenders. He stood about five feet six and didn't weigh one hundred-thirty pounds. He had bright brownish-orange hair that was going quickly to gray, dark bags under his eyes, and a scowl on his face. He looked a bit like an aging Pekingese dog. He stormed up to where I was leaning on my Explorer. "What's the meaning of this?" he asked, waving the yellow sheet of paper in my face.

"The meaning of this is that you'd better not ever keep me waiting again. I'm used to dealing with assholes, so I take people like you in stride. But you try to fuck with me again and I'm going to take you down. You got that?"

"Take me down?" His voice was rising. He wasn't used to being confronted by anybody, much less in a parking lot by a guy wearing cargo shorts, boat shoes, and a ratty sweatshirt with a picture of a boat on it. "What the hell do you mean, take me down? You said you were a lawyer."

"I *am* a lawyer."

"You don't look like one."

"Neither do you," I said. "You look like a little boy playing dress up."

"Do you really think insulting me is going to get you anywhere?"

"Mr. Evans, I'll be surprised if you still have your law license by the time we get finished. You'll probably be in jail, and I assure you those big ole boys in your cell block are going to be, shall we say, intrigued by you."

The color drained from his face. One minute it was red with anger and agitation and the next minute it was as pale as a corpse. He looked smaller, deflated, beaten. I'd have felt sorry for him if I didn't suspect he was hip deep in some illegal activities that may have led to the death of Jim Fredrickson and the disappearance of his wife, Katie.

"I'll pay you for the pictures," he said. "But this is extortion. You could go to jail, too."

"Mr. Evans," I said, "the pictures aren't for sale. What I want is for you to explain to me why you're the personal representative of Jim Fredrickson's estate, why you haven't completed probate yet, why you sold the grove property for such a pittance, what your relationship is to Robert Hammond, the man who bought the property, what you've done with the ten million dollars in cash that should be in the estate, and what you do at the grove house over in Avon Park when you and a bunch of your buddies get together."

"Who do you represent?" he asked.

"Nobody right now," I said. "But I think you're screwing with the Fredrickson estate and are probably involved in a bunch of other activities that the police will want to know about."

"I don't know what you're talking about," he said.

I grabbed him by the tie with one hand and used the other to open the rear door of the Explorer. I threw him into the backseat and said, "If you move, dickhead, I'm going to shoot you."

"What're you doing? Where are you taking me?" Panic had crept into his voice, but he didn't move from the seat.

I stood there for a moment, reality sinking in. I was about to kidnap this little moron and that could result in me losing my law license and the next several years of my life. I crawled in beside him on the back seat. "I just want to get you out of the sun, Mr. Evans."

"Let me out of here."

"You're free to go."

"What about the pictures?"

"I think I'll sit on them for now. Give you time to think things over a little."

"What do you want from me?" he asked.

"I just told you. Information."

"How do I know that you've really got those pictures?"

"You don't."

"Why should I believe you?"

"You can trust me, Mr. Evans. I'm a lawyer."

"Right," he said with a hint of incredulity.

"Are you going to get out of my car?" I asked.

He looked at me a bit sheepishly and got out without another word. I got in the front seat and drove out of the parking lot and toward Longboat Key. Other than rattling that arrogant little piece of dog droppings, I hadn't accomplished a damn thing.

CHAPTER FORTY-SEVEN

I crossed the John Ringling Bridge just before noon. I called Jock and got his voice mail. "It's almost lunchtime," I said, "and I'm going to the Old Salty Dog. Meet me there if you're hungry."

I drove a quarter way around St. Armands Circle and headed south, crossing the causeway to Lido Key. I turned right on Ken Thompson Parkway just before the New Pass Bridge, crossed onto City Island and found a parking spot about a block from the restaurant. I wasn't surprised. It was, after all, *the season*, and half the people in the Midwest had come to the Suncoast for the winter.

The Old Salty Dog is a throwback to a time when waterside restaurants flourished in coastal Florida. It sits on the edge of New Pass, which separates City Island from Longboat Key. The view is of green water and the flora of the Quick Point Nature Preserve that takes up the south end of Longboat. The pass is always heavy with boat traffic, fishermen heading for the man-made reefs, and people just out enjoying the weather. The restaurant's deck is open on all sides and the gentle February breeze off the water was cool enough to make me glad I was wearing a sweatshirt. I had to wait for a table and was standing near the bar watching the boat traffic and sipping from a bottle of Miller Lite when Jock strode up.

"Hey, podna. Got your message. How long do we have to wait?"

"They said about ten minutes, but who knows," I said. "You got anywhere you're supposed to be?"

"Nope. Just asking."

"Where were you?"

"I was in a meeting with one of our agents at a Starbucks in Sarasota.

I'd turned my phone off and got your message just as I was getting back into my car."

"What is the world coming to?" I said. "Secret agents meeting in Starbucks."

"You might be interested in our conversation."

"Oh?"

"I called my director last night to see if the agency had anything on this Bonino ghost."

"Why would your agency be interested in a bunch of Mafia thugs?"

"We keep tabs on all kind of career criminals. They have a tendency sometimes to get tied up with terrorists. Usually in the drug trade. It's a way for the jihadists to make a lot of money and move it around."

"Was there anything on Bonino?"

"No. But the director called me this morning and said an agent from Tampa was coming to Sarasota to meet with me. He had some information he wanted to pass on."

"Not about Bonino."

"Not directly," Jock said. "The agent I met with spends a lot of time looking into organized crime in this part of Florida. He's the agency's resident expert, I guess. He told me that he'd heard about Bonino, but he wasn't sure he really existed."

A waitress came out of the covered deck area and called my name. Jock and I followed her to a table overlooking the pass. She took our drink orders, left us menus, and walked off, promising to return quickly.

The wind had picked up a little, and I could see small waves breaking on the shoal that lay outside the inlet and just north of the channel markers. Boats were making their way through the chop and into the calmer waters of the pass. Several had anchored on the sandbar just seaward of the bridge and a few hardier souls were standing in waist-deep water drinking beer.

"Did the agent have anything useful?" I asked.

"He did. He has a mole in the group that runs most of the rackets in the entire state of Florida. The mole's a trusted member of the inner circle and he's been a part of the mob for a long time. About five years ago, this mole was in love with a woman who was feeding information to a Tampa police detective. Nobody knew that our mole was in a relationship with the woman. The big boss found out that the woman was talking to the cops and he put a hit on her. He later bragged to the mole that he'd personally overseen her murder."

"So," I said, "the mole becomes the mole."

"Yeah, in a roundabout way. See, and this is the good part, the mole's sister is married to the big boss."

"Wait a minute," I said. "The mole is the big boss's brother-in-law?"

"Yep. And he's also the second in command of the operation."

"Wow. Talk about an insider."

"The mole plays things very close. He only gives us information that he wants us to have. There's a lot we don't know."

"Why don't you squeeze the guy?"

"We've come to an agreement. We won't disrupt his organization as long as he keeps us apprised of what's going on in the other groups he deals with."

"I'm not sure I understand," I said.

"We made a deal with the devil. The mole didn't know his girlfriend was dealing with the Tampa detective until after she was killed. It seems that the detective was on the organization's payroll and he was the one who fingered the woman to the big boss."

The waitress returned and I ordered the Old Salty Dog, a beer-battered deep-fried foot-long wiener on a bun with cheese and bacon. I only allowed myself one of those per month. Jock grinned and ordered a salad and looked smug.

"What happened to the detective?"

"That's where things got interesting. The mole figured that if the boss was telling him about having the woman killed, the boss didn't know about the mole's relationship with her. If the boss didn't know, then he was pretty sure the cop didn't know. But the mole knew the cop from some past dealings, so the mole invited the cop on a fishing trip. Told the cop the boss would be along and that the cop shouldn't say anything to anybody about where he was going."

"I take it the detective never made it back from the trip."

"Right. The mole had a big sportfisherman at a marina in Clearwater. When the cop showed up, the mole told him the boss was below in the cabin nursing a hangover and didn't want to be bothered. They went out about fifty miles into the Gulf and the mole pulled a pistol and told the detective about his relationship to the woman. Then he tied him up, attached an anchor to him and threw him overboard."

"The big boss wasn't involved."

"No."

"How did your agency get the mole?"

"He wanted to get back at his brother-in-law without completely ruining his operation. He didn't trust the cops and didn't like the FBI, so he went to the CIA."

"How does one *go* to the CIA?"

"He walked into the CIA headquarters in Virginia and told a security guard he had some very sensitive information that he was sure the CIA would like to have. The guard sent him up the line until some guy met with him. When he realized the information was about Mafia activities in the U.S., he called us in. The CIA takes itself very seriously and doesn't like to step outside its charter and operate inside the U.S. The mole's been working with our guy in Tampa ever since and thinks he's dealing with the CIA. He doesn't know that we're working with the FBI."

"So what's your deal?"

"We're squeezing his organization. Revenues are down and some of the underlings are getting restless. The mole thinks it's just a matter of time before somebody stages a palace coup. He figures his brother-in-law is a real short-timer in this world. When the boss is dead, the mole will take his sister and disappear into the witness protection program and the FBI will dismantle the organization."

"Why wait? Why not just take the whole organization down?"

"The FBI is stockpiling evidence that will put the whole gang in jail. In the meantime, we're also learning a lot about the inner workings of some of the other groups, and we're taking them down one at a time."

The waitress came back with our meals, and I dug in. That dog probably wasn't doing my arteries any good, but my taste buds were in heaven.

"What about Bonino?"

"Apparently, Bonino doesn't have anything to do with the Mafia. He's a relatively small-time operator, and since he's not infringing on the real organization's territory, they leave him alone. They're aware of him, but don't know who he is. They're not even sure he's real."

I was disappointed. "So we didn't really learn anything," I said.

"Maybe we did. The Mafia crowd used a lawyer in Sarasota from time to time to represent one of their people who got arrested. He was killed about a year ago. The word the mole hears is that he was killed by Bonino because he got too greedy."

"Fredrickson?"

"Yes. The mole's group has kept pretty close tabs on Bonino's people to make sure they don't start encroaching into Mafia business. They're pretty sure that Fredrickson and Bonino were in business together. They'd stopped using Fredrickson as a lawyer because of that connection."

"I'll be damned," I said. "That changes a lot of things."

"Yep. If Fredrickson was in bed with Bonino, we have to think that maybe Bonino had him killed."

"Why would Bonino do that?" I asked.

"Maybe Fredrickson got greedy or had a change of heart and was going to expose the operation. Who knows? The criminal mind works in mysterious ways."

"Did the mole know anything about Katie?"

"No. He assumes she's dead."

"Well, your morning was a lot more productive than mine. I went to see Wayne Evans."

"And?"

"And nothing. He's obviously been to the Avon Park house, but he wouldn't tell me anything."

"How do you know he was at the house?"

"I implied that I had pictures that were taken there of him naked. He was pretty worried about that."

Jock laughed. "Where do we go from here?"

"I don't know. I think Evans may be the key to finding out who killed Fredrickson and is looking for Katie. I almost kidnapped him today, but common sense got the better of me."

"Maybe," said Jock, "I ought to have a go at him. I'm pretty much under the radar."

"I don't know, Jock. Evans may be a snake, but he's a prominent lawyer in this town and you can't just go after him like you would some lowlife."

"Why not?"

He had me there. "No reason, I guess, except that he'll put up a huge squawk about it. I'm thinking I might hear something about my meeting with him this morning."

"That's not likely, if he's engaged in something illegal. You're pretty sure he's dirty, aren't you?"

"Yes."

"Suppose I arrange a little meeting with him tonight."

"Okay, but stay out of trouble with the law."

Jock looked at me as if I'd lost my mind. I laughed. "Sorry," I said. "Didn't mean to insult you."

CHAPTER FORTY-EIGHT

It was almost noon and J.D. was on her fifth cup of coffee. She'd been going back over the file on Goodlow's murder, trying to find some tidbit she'd overlooked, some tiny fact that might send her in another direction. It was a frustrating exercise and one that wasn't bearing any fruit. The phone on her desk rang. Bert Hawkins, the medical examiner for the three-county Twelfth Judicial Circuit.

"J.D.," the deep voice rumbled. "It's Bert Hawkins."

"Good morning, Bert."

"I've got some disturbing news for you, I'm afraid."

"Bert, my day's already so lousy that a little more bad news isn't going to make much difference."

"A couple of hunters found some human remains over in DeSoto County a couple of weeks ago."

"That's in your jurisdiction, isn't it?"

"Yes. There wasn't much left of the body. Scavengers had gotten to it and only a few bones and the skull were left. There was a bullet hole in the skull, which is probably the cause of death. There wasn't enough of the body left to find any other cause, but there was enough to tell that the body was female. We were able to extract some DNA for comparison purposes in hopes of identifying the body. I just got the DNA results back from the state crime lab in Tampa."

"We don't have any missing persons out here on the key," J.D. said.

"A femur was among the bones recovered. That told us that the woman stood about five feet three inches tall."

"Okay," said J.D. She was confused. Why would Bert call her about this?

"Katie was a good four inches taller than this woman," said Bert.

"Yes. That means it isn't Katie."

"It does. But here's the disturbing thing. The DNA matches Katie's, or at least it matches the blood we thought was Katie's."

"Wow," said J.D. "That kind of changes things. Have you talked to McAllister about this?"

"No. I wanted you to know first. I'll call Doug when we hang up."

"Bert, is there any way that lab report could get lost for a couple of days?"

"What do you mean?"

"I'd like you to hold off on passing this information on to Sarasota P.D."

"What's going on?" Bert asked.

"I'm not sure, but I'd like a couple of days to dig into this thing a little further."

"I need more than that, J.D."

"Okay. I know Katie's alive. I can't tell you how I know that, but I can tell you that I just confirmed it yesterday."

"Then what's the problem with passing this on to McAllister?"

"Bert, do you ever have one of those feelings about a case? A hunch, intuition, educated guess, whatever you want to call it, and when it's all said and done, you were exactly right? But at the time you made the leap there were absolutely no facts to base it on."

Hawkins was quiet for a moment. "Yeah," he said. "I've been there. Can you tell me how you know that Katie is alive?"

"If you'll agree to hold the DNA results for a couple of days and swear that what I tell you about Katie won't go any further. That it's our little secret."

"Suppose I agree to hold the lab report for forty-eight hours. Can you do what you need to do in that time frame?"

"Yes, I think so. But if I can't, I still need to protect Katie. You'll have to agree not to tell anybody about Katie until I say it's okay. And I may not ever be able to say that."

"Agreed. I trust you to do the right thing."

"Thanks, Bert. She contacted me last week. I wasn't sure it was her until Matt met with her yesterday."

"Did she tell Matt why she disappeared or what she knows about her husband's murder?"

"No. She said she wasn't sure she could trust me. I have to wait for her to contact me again. In the meantime, now that we know the blood wasn't Katie's, we have another murder to solve, and this one is surely tied to Jim Fredrickson's death."

"I agree. You've got forty-eight hours. I'll touch base with you before I call McAllister."

"Thanks, Bert. I'll keep you posted."

J.D. went back to the Goodlow file, bored but hopeful. Ten minutes later she spotted it in her typed notes. She didn't think much of it at the time, but now that things were coming into a little better focus, it might have some importance. Barb at Moore's had told Matt that she'd walked into Annie's one afternoon and found Goodlow and Jamison at the little bar. Before they noticed she had come in, she heard Goodlow tell Jamison, "They'll kill us all if you don't give them what they want." She remembered writing the quote exactly as Matt had told her.

But, what did they, whoever they were, want from two old men? Barb had overheard the conversation after the two men who were the coffee regulars at the café had died. Could Goodlow have been talking about their deaths? Were the four of them, Jamison and Goodlow and the other two old men, involved in something that was getting them killed? If so, that would be a reason for Jamison to disappear. He was the last one.

The Goodlow file didn't contain the report she'd requested from IBIS, the Integrated Bullet Identification System, maintained by ATF, the Bureau of Alcohol, Tobacco, Firearms and Explosives. She looked at her watch. The lunch hour. Well, maybe somebody in Washington was eating at his desk. She pulled up her computer's Rolodex and found the number she was looking for and dialed it.

"AFT IBIS lab," a feminine voice said. "This is Agent Weatherington."

"This is Detective J. D. Duncan in Longboat Key, Florida. I sent you a request for a possible match on a bullet last week. I was wondering if you had anything on it."

"Let me see, Detective."

J.D. heard the tapping of fingers on a keyboard and then quiet. Weatherington sighed. "I'm sorry, Detective. I have it and it should have been e-mailed to you on Friday. We're a little backed up on paperwork here. Give me your e-mail address, and you'll have it in a couple of minutes."

"Thank you, Agent Weatherington." J.D. gave her the e-mail address and sat back and waited for the report. The e-mail popped up on her screen within minutes and J.D. downloaded the attachment. There was one hit. A man named Rodney Vernon had been killed by the same gun two weeks before in Toms River, New Jersey.

The victim's name rang a vague bell in J.D.'s mind. She started thumbing back through the file. She was pretty sure it had come up in an interview with Jamison. She reread his statements and there it was. Rodney Vernon was the man in one of the old pictures of the picnic taken shortly after the war. The one who had moved to New Jersey in the early fifties and who Jamison said he hadn't heard from since he left Cortez. Jamison said he didn't know if Vernon was dead or alive.

J.D. remembered that conversation. There had been something in Jamison's demeanor that made her suspect he was lying. She remembered asking Jamison about that, telling him she had a vague feeling that he knew more about Goodlow's murder than he was telling her. Jamison denied it.

J.D. went to her computer and pulled up the website for the Toms River Police Department. She called the number listed for the Criminal Investigation Bureau and dialed it. She identified herself and asked to speak to Captain Leonard Garner, the man who commanded the unit. He was out of the office, but the detective who answered asked if he could have the captain call her.

"Yes," J.D. said. "Tell him I'm calling about the murder of Rodney Vernon. We have a murder here on Longboat Key that apparently was committed by someone using the same gun that killed Vernon."

The detective said he'd get in touch with Captain Garner and have him call her immediately. No more than five minutes later, J.D.'s phone rang. "Thanks for calling me back, Captain," J.D. said. "We had a murder here on Longboat Key a week ago. I just got the IBIS report. It seems that the same gun that killed my victim killed Mr. Vernon. I wonder if you could fill me in on what happened up there."

"Did you get your shooter?" Garner asked.

"Yes. He drove off a bridge while fleeing the scene. He's dead."

"Who was he?"

"We don't know. His prints aren't in the system, and he didn't carry any identification. The car he was driving was stolen a couple of days before the shooting."

"Dead end. What can I tell you about our shooting up here?" asked Garner.

"First, was Mr. Vernon an elderly man?"

"Yes. Late eighties, I think. I don't have the file in front of me."

"What can you tell me about the murder?"

"That was very strange. One of his neighbors called us after she hadn't seen him for a couple of days. We found his body tied to a chair in his dining room. It looks as if he'd been tortured before he was shot in the forehead."

"How bad was the torture?"

"That's one of the odd things about this case. It looks like the bad guys didn't get too far with Vernon before he died of a heart attack. I guess the bullet to the head was just to make sure he was dead."

"Do you have any thoughts on a motive?"

"No. The old man had been retired for more than twenty years. He puttered around in his garden and hung out some at the American Legion post. He didn't seem to have much of a life but, according to everybody we talked to, he was happy."

"What can you tell me about him?"

"Not much to tell. He grew up around here, went off to fight in World War II, came home, and worked for years for a boat builder down in Egg Harbor."

"Was he married?"

"No. His wife died a couple of years before. He had one daughter and a son who live out of state, the son in Connecticut and the daughter in Atlanta."

"Any friends?"

"Not really. All his buddies have died. We did turn up one strange coincidence, though. The old boy had come into the computer age. Had a laptop and used e-mail. The laptop was missing, so we figured the killers took it. His son told us about the computer, so we got access to the old boy's e-mail service provider. He used it to keep up with his son and daughter and grandchildren. But he also had regular e-mail exchanges with a man in Germany. Every six months or so for the past several years. They all seemed to be about family things, but neither Vernon's son nor daughter had ever heard of the man. Turns out he was a retired German government official named Paulus von Reicheldorf. Thing is, he'd been tortured and killed."

"When did that happen?" asked J.D.

"That's the oddity here. He died about a week before Vernon was murdered."

"You checked it out?"

"Sure did. We could find absolutely no connection between Reicheldorf and Vernon. Except for the e-mails, of course. Reicheldorf had been well known and highly respected in German political circles. He apparently was one of those guys who works behind the scenes and let the elected officials be the show horses."

"Did the German cops come up with a motive for his murder?"

"They think it was the work of some of Germany's homegrown terrorists. He had been pretty outspoken about his opposition to allowing more Muslims into the country. He felt that the terrorists had infiltrated many of the mosques in Germany and were a danger to the future of the country."

"Why the torture? Why not just kill him?"

"The German detective who was investigating the case told me that he'd seen that before in situations where the terrorists went after somebody they thought might be a danger to them. He thinks they torture people for the fun of it and to set an example for others who might get in the way of their jihad."

"That's cold," said J.D.

"So was driving passenger planes into the Trade Towers in New York," said Garner.

"You've got a point. Still, it seems strange that a man in Germany who was corresponding with Vernon would be killed about the same time and both men were tortured."

"I agree, but neither my department nor the German police were able to find anything that connected the men, except a few e-mails."

"What about Vernon's wife? Do you know where she was from originally?"

"No. That didn't seem like pertinent information."

"I'm sure it wasn't," said J.D. "But I think I may know something about Mr. Vernon and I'm wondering if his wife was from Cortez, Florida."

"Where is that?"

"Do you know where Longboat Key is?"

"I'm guessing it's somewhere near Key West."

"No," said J.D. "We're a barrier island off the coast of Sarasota, south of Tampa. Cortez is a fishing village on the mainland across Sarasota Bay from Longboat Key."

Garner laughed. "Could've fooled me."

"It's a common mistake," J.D. said. "Would you mind giving me the names and phone numbers of Mr. Vernon's children?"

"Not at all, Detective. I'll e-mail them to you as soon as I get back to the office. Can you keep me posted? We don't have a lot of violent crime around here, and I'd sure like to close this file."

J.D. gave him her e-mail address and hung up.

CHAPTER FORTY-NINE

My phone rang as we were walking out of the restaurant. Logan.

"Have you had lunch yet?" he asked.

"Just finished."

"Where are you?"

"Jock and I are just leaving the Old Salty Dog on City Island."

"Meet me at the Hilton for a drink."

"Isn't it a little early for booze?" I asked.

"It *is* after lunch."

"You've got a point. We'll be there shortly."

When we arrived at the Hilton, Logan was sitting at the outside bar talking with Billy Brugger, the longtime bartender. He usually worked nights, and I guessed he must be covering a shift for somebody.

"Little bright out for you, isn't it, Billy?" I asked.

He grinned. "Yeah, but the customers are a bit more sober this time of the day. Even Logan."

It was the kind of day that brought the islanders out, and many of them, with nothing else to do, came to sit on the deck of the Hilton and drink the afternoon away. I saw several familiar faces at the tables that sat under the ancient Banyan tree that shaded the area. We took our drinks to a table in the far corner of the deck, out of earshot of the other customers.

"I've been thinking," said Logan. "The guy who shot old man Goodlow had some papers on him that were in German and then some code. The German script went out of style after World War II, meaning that the documents were probably prepared before or during the war. The only reference I could find to U166 was a German submarine called the U-166 that was sunk in the northern Gulf of Mexico, up near the panhandle, in the summer of 1942. That was the only U-boat ever sunk in the Gulf. The wreck was found and noted by some federal agency several years ago. But suppose somebody had found it before and suppose there was something in the boat that was so valuable people could get killed over it."

"That seems a little far-fetched," I said.

"I agree," said Logan. "But I did a pretty detailed search for U166 and the only thing that comes up is the submarine. Katie says she doesn't know what it means, but her husband and the people he was dealing with mentioned U166 several times. Then we have Goodlow's shooter in possession of some documents that probably date back to World War II and a caption that says they contain vital information and that the recipient should help get the courier out of the country. The rest of it is in code. It begins to sound like the documents were important and had maybe been sneaked into this county."

"What's that got to do with a submarine?"

"The Germans used their subs to bring spies into the country. They'd drop them off near the coast and head back to sea. Maybe the courier mentioned in the papers was aboard the U-166 when it was sunk."

I said, "But then we have to make the assumption that somebody found the sunken boat, retrieved the documents, and somehow knows that they're valuable. It seems a little hard to swallow."

"How else can you tie the documents, the submarine, Katie's disappearance, and her husband's murder together?" asked Logan.

"Maybe they're not tied together," I said. "Maybe U166 has nothing to do with that sub. Who knows why Goodlow's murderer would have some of the documents with him or where he got them? Katie doesn't know what U166 means, but she thought it might mean something to J.D."

"Why would Katie think that J.D. would know anything about an esoteric letter-number combination like U166?" asked Logan. "Maybe she wasn't telling you the truth when she said she didn't know what it meant."

"I hadn't thought about that," said Jock. "I think we all just assumed that Katie was being straight with us. Maybe she wasn't."

"I think we should get J.D. in on this," I said.

Jock and Logan nodded in agreement. I looked at my watch. Almost two. I called her cell. "You had lunch yet?"

"No," she said, laughing, "I forgot about it."

"Why don't you come down to the Hilton? Jock and Logan are here, and you can get a burger or something."

"Okay. I'll see you in a few minutes." She hung up.

Our conversation drifted into island gossip, the upcoming baseball season, and other useless talk. In a few minutes I saw my sweetie make her way from the parking lot to the bar. She stopped for a moment to speak to Billy. She placed her lunch order and then joined us.

"You guys been here a while?" she asked.

"Not long," said Logan. "I'm still on my first drink."

She laughed. "Before we get into that, let me tell you about my conversation with Bert Hawkins this morning."

"The medical examiner?" asked Logan.

"Yes. Turns out all that blood at Katie's house the day she disappeared didn't belong to her."

"How did he determine that?" asked Jock.

"Some hunters found a bunch of human bones and a skull over in DeSoto County a couple of weeks back. Turns out, the DNA in the blood found at Katie's matched the DNA in the bones the hunters found."

"We know Katie's alive," Logan said. "So the bones obviously don't belong to her."

"Not a chance. Bert was able to determine the victim's height by measuring a femur found with the rest of the bones. This victim was four or five inches shorter than Katie. Bert knew before he called me that the bones didn't belong to her."

"I guess Sarasota P.D. will reopen its investigation," I said.

"Not until noon Thursday, at least. I traded information with Bert, told him we knew Katie was alive and where she was. In return, Bert agreed to hold off notifying the police for forty-eight hours. That's how long we have to wrap all this up before McAllister takes over and I have to tell him where Katie is."

"We can't do that," I said. "We promised her confidentiality."

"I know," she said, "but if I hadn't told Bert what we know, he wouldn't have agreed to give me time to solve this before McAllister gets involved."

"Are you sure that McAllister is a problem?" asked Logan.

"No," said J.D. "I just have a gut feeling that he knows more than he lets on."

"Why is that?" asked Logan.

"His theory is that Katie is dead. All the evidence points to that. Yet, McAllister regularly calls Katie's parents and asks if they've heard from her. It's like he doesn't believe his own evidence. If that's the case, I wonder what he knows that nobody else knows. And, I'm beginning to wonder if Goodlow's murder is somehow connected to Jim Fredrickson's murder and Katie's disappearance."

"Maybe he's just concerned," said Logan. "He and Jim Fredrickson were good friends."

"You may be right," J.D. said. "I've had a busy morning on another front. IBIS came through on the bullet that killed Goodlow. It seems that the same pistol was used in a murder in Toms River, New Jersey, a couple of weeks ago. And get this, the victim was Rodney Vernon."

"Who's Rodney Vernon?" I asked.

"Do you remember that Bud Jamison told me that one of the men in Goodlow's old photographs moved to New Jersey in the early '50s? That was Rodney Vernon."

"Are you sure it's the same person?" Jock asked.

"Yes. I called his daughter in Atlanta after I talked to the cops in Toms River. She told me that her dad was stationed at Sarasota Army Airfield for a couple of months in the summer of 1942."

"I didn't know we ever had a military base here," said Logan.

"It's now the Sarasota-Bradenton Airport," J.D. said. "Vernon was a mechanic in a fighter squadron that was only at the base for a couple of months before moving on. He met his wife during the time he was here. The daughter wasn't sure how they met, but thought it was at a USO event. They corresponded during the rest of the war and after Mr. Vernon was discharged, he came back to Cortez and married the girl. They lived in Cortez for several years and then decided to move back to Vernon's hometown, Toms River."

"I'll be damned," I said.

"There's more," said J.D. "It seems that Vernon was tortured before he was shot in the head. He'd died of a heart attack before he was shot."

"There's got to be a connection there," said Jock, "but Goodlow wasn't tortured."

"No, he wasn't," said J.D. "Whoever killed Vernon wanted some information from him. Maybe whatever it was, it led the shooter to Goodlow."

"Do the Toms River cops have any leads?" I asked.

"No. They can't come up with a motive or anybody with a reason to kill him, much less torture him. He had some e-mail correspondence with a retired German politician who was tortured and killed just before Vernon was, but there was no connection between them except for several e-mails over a number of years."

"That's too much of a coincidence," I said. "There's got to be a connection."

"I think so, too," said J.D., "but I don't see how the murder of man in Germany has anything to do with our problems here."

"The gun connects Vernon and Goodlow and the e-mails connect Vernon and the guy in Germany," Logan said. "Do we know anything more about the German?"

"I Googled him," said J.D. "He was some sort of hereditary count named Reicheldorf who began working for the new German government right after the war. He was a real behind-the-scenes type, but he was well respected and ended up holding high positions in all the postwar governments, no matter which party was in power."

"I don't think we're going to get anywhere with this," I said. "If it turns out that the count was connected to Goodlow's death or Jamison's disappearance, we can follow up on it later. We've only got two days to figure some of this out or McAllister takes over and we lose what little bit of head start we have."

"Then the question is what did Goodlow know that caused somebody to kill him," Logan said.

"Logan, tell J.D. your theory on the U-166. If I remember my history, there was a lot more U-boat activity off the Atlantic coast than there was in the Gulf. Maybe there's a connection there."

Logan told J.D. what he'd related to us. "Based on what J.D. found out today, maybe the documents weren't found in the wreckage of U-166. Maybe the sub dropped the courier off near the New Jersey coast on its way to the Gulf, and the documents were delivered, or lost somehow, and Vernon came across them."

"If the 'U166' written on Katie's arm in that photograph is a reference to the submarine, there'd have to be a connection," said Logan. "It's a bit tenuous, but it's there. Goodlow was killed by a gun that killed Vernon in New Jersey. The man who killed Goodlow had German documents in his possession. If those documents came from the sub named U-166, and Katie's husband and his buddies were talking about it, you have your connection. And now we find out that Vernon was connected to a German politician who was killed just before Vernon was."

"But your scenario falls apart if the documents didn't come from the U-boat," I said. "And even if they did, the only connection between Goodlow's murderer and Katie's disappearance is that the murderer had one page of what had to be at least several pages of one or more documents and Katie had heard someone mention the sub."

J.D. laughed. "So all I have to do," she said, "is find the documents, find out why they're important, prove that they came from a German submarine that was sunk in the Gulf and didn't leave a trace of wreckage that anybody has ever found, prove how Goodlow's killer came across the documents, find out the killer's name, find a motive for why he or someone else would torture and kill Vernon and kill Goodlow and Jim Fredrickson, find out who else might be involved, who Katie might be afraid of and why she dropped out of sight for a year, and why people are being killed more than a year after Fredrickson's murder. Did I miss anything?"

"Yeah," said Jock. "Bonino has got to be involved in this. Caster was looking for Jamison and had some ties to DeLuca who worked for Bonino, or at least worked for Peters, who reports to Bonino. Since Porter King sent Caster to find or kill Jamison, we can be pretty sure King is tied into Bonino, who may have ordered the hit on King and his girlfriend. The only reason anybody would be after Jamison is because of his relationship with Goodlow and maybe Vernon in New Jersey. Which maybe brings us back to the U-boat and the documents and the fact that the only reason DeLuca would have tried to beat the tar out of Matt is because Matt made contact with Katie's parents."

"And," I said, "we have no idea who the hell Bonino is. He's a ghost."

J.D. sat back in her chair, a look of consternation on her face. "We'll never untangle that ball of conjecture."

"Well, J.D.," said Logan, "you *do* have two days to figure it out. And you've got us to help. I don't see a problem."

CHAPTER FIFTY

J.D. went back to work and Logan said he'd stay awhile and keep Billy company at the bar. Jock said he had some things to do and would see me later. I made my daily trek to the island post office, pulled my mail from the box, and, without looking at the stack of bills and other junk mail, drove home. Once inside, I shuffled through the mail and came to an envelope addressed to me in a feminine hand. It was marked "Personal" and had no return address. Probably somebody trying to sell me an annuity. I left it with the rest of the mail on the kitchen counter and found a beer in the refrigerator.

I sat on my patio, taking the warm winter sun, sipping beer, and thinking. I got up, went into the kitchen and retrieved the letter with no return address. It had been postmarked in Tampa on Monday, yesterday. I opened it and found a letter addressed to me in the same handwriting as that on the envelope. I shuffled the pages and found the signature at the bottom. It said, "Fondly, Jed."

I went back to the patio and read the letter from Katie and sipped beer and thought some more. I called J.D. "Katie's gone."

"What do you mean?"

"I just got a letter from her. Postmarked yesterday in Tampa. She apparently wrote it on Sunday right after I left her."

"What did she have to say?"

"She said that after I left, she read the morning newspaper and saw that Porter King had been murdered the day before. She knew him, and under the circumstances, she didn't feel safe having anyone know where she was. She would be moving so there was no reason for us to look for her at the house she'd been living in. She said she'd be in touch."

"That's a shocker. She knew King. I wonder what that connection is."

"I don't know, but his murder spooked her. Maybe King was connected to her disappearance somehow."

"We know he was connected to the attempt on old Mr. Jamison," she said, "and that was probably Jamison's reason for disappearing."

"Either that, or he's dead."

"That might be the case if somebody else was after him, but King sent Caster, so he would have thought that Jamison was alive. I think the old man somehow figured out that people were after him and went into hiding."

"Maybe he heard about the murder in New Jersey."

She was quiet for a moment. "That's a possibility. But how would he have known? Jamison said they hadn't been in contact in years."

"Yes, but you thought Jamison was lying," I said.

"Suppose he was in touch with Vernon in New Jersey. Vernon was killed two weeks ago. Why would Jamison just now be running?"

"Maybe he just found out about the murder."

"I guess that's possible. Still, I'd like to know what connection Katie had to Porter King. And is she connected to Jamison in some way?"

"Lots of good questions."

"Did Katie say anything else in the letter?"

"She said she loved you and asked that you trust her. She'll get back to you. Soon."

"That's it?"

"Just that she thought you were lucky to have a stud like me."

"She didn't say that."

"No, but I think it was implied."

"And what led you to that conclusion?"

"Truth will out."

"Geez," she said. "I'll talk to you later."

I went back to the patio and sat and sipped beer and thought some more. Was the murder of Ken Goodlow connected in some way to Jim Fredrickson's murder and Katie's disappearance? The murders happened more than a year apart. And then there was the torture and murder of Rodney Vernon in New Jersey. There was a definite connection between

Goodlow and Vernon. They had known each other a lot of years ago, and they were killed recently by the same gun. But why would somebody be killing harmless old men? And who was after Bud Jamison? Probably the same people who'd caused the murders of Goodlow and Vernon. How did Porter King fit into that? And why?

I decided it was time to jog the beach. See if a little oxygen would clear the mental cobwebs. I changed into shorts, a sweatshirt, and running shoes and began to jog toward the North Shore Road beach access. I was on Broadway, less than a block from its intersection with Gulf of Mexico Drive when I saw J.D.'s car turn the corner. She pulled up beside me and said, "Get in."

"I just got started on my jog."

"We've got to talk. Get in."

I got in. Never argue with a woman when she wants to "talk." It's been my experience that nothing good ever comes from the "talk." "What's up?" I asked.

"Wait until we get home."

"Am I in trouble?" I asked.

She glanced at me. "Have you done anything to cause you to be in trouble?"

"Not lately."

"Hmmm. We'll explore that later, but I want to discuss a phone call I got from Harry Robson a few minutes ago."

"The Sarasota detective?"

"Yes," she said as she pulled to a stop in front of my house. "He gave me some very disturbing news."

"What?"

"Let's go inside."

We went into the living room, and she plopped down in an armchair. "I'm scared to death for Katie."

"What's going on?"

"When she said she was afraid somebody was trying to kill her, she wasn't just being paranoid."

"What did Robson have to say?"

She sat back in the chair, her face a mask of concern. She was holding back on me, but I knew she'd get to it eventually. Sometimes, you just have to let J.D. talk it out. "After you called about the letter, I tried to figure out how Katie would know Porter King. I didn't come up with anything, and I went back through her file on the off chance I'd missed a reference to King. There wasn't any."

She stopped talking and sat quietly, her head resting on the back of the chair, eyes closed. A minute passed, two. Her eyes opened and she took a deep breath. "Harry Robson is old school. He's honest, never takes shortcuts and almost always gets a conviction or a guilty plea out of his arrests. He's worked in the shadow of Doug McAllister for a long time. He never complains, just does his job. If McAllister goes off the tracks occasionally, Harry just takes it in stride." She was quiet again.

"I didn't think you knew Robson that well," I said.

"I didn't. Don't. But after I met him last year, I ran into him a couple of times on a case. I checked him out with a friend of mine in Miami who worked for Sarasota P.D. for a number of years. He moved to Miami and joined Miami-Dade P.D. about two years before I left and came here. He knew Harry well during his years up here and had nothing but good things to say about him." She sat quietly again. Something was really bothering her.

"Okay," I said, gently. "He told you something that's got you upset. Talk to me. Maybe I can help."

She looked at me for a moment and then said, "Harry called to tell me that when they ran the ballistics from the gun that killed Porter King and his girlfriend, Josie Tyler, through IBIS, they got a hit."

"I don't see the problem."

"McAllister had already sent me over the IBIS report. It was in the stack of mail I got this morning. The report said the gun was clean. There was nothing in the IBIS database that indicated it had ever been used in a crime."

"An error somewhere in the paperwork?" I asked.

"No. Harry called to tell me that the report from McAllister was a fake. Harry had gotten in to work early this morning and saw the fax from the ATF's IBIS lab. He didn't think anything about it and put it in McAllister's in-box. It was Doug's case and Harry figured he'd take care of it."

"What happened?"

"McAllister showed the bogus report to Harry after lunch. He said he'd sent a copy to me the day before and asked Harry to file it. When Harry looked at the report, he realized it was a fake. The real report had been faxed in during the night, not the day before. Therefore, McAllister could not have sent it to me yesterday. Harry figured that maybe the captain had had a phone conversation with the lab the day before and made up the report so I could get it as soon as possible."

"But that's not what happened," I said.

"No. When Harry read the report I'd been sent, he realized that I had a bogus report. He stewed on it for an hour and called me. He told me that IBIS had gotten a hit and that he was concerned about his boss sending me a fake report and, even worse, putting the fake one into the official investigation file."

"Why in the hell would McAllister do that? Could Robson be wrong?"

"I don't think so."

"What other crime was the gun used in?"

She sat stock still for a beat, staring intently at me. "It's the same gun that killed Katie Fredrickson's husband."

CHAPTER FIFTY-ONE

I sat back in my chair, stunned. I hadn't seen that one coming. "To state the obvious," I said, "that ties Jim Fredrickson to Porter King. What the hell were they into and why is Captain McAllister lying to you?"

"I wonder if it has anything to do with the ten million bucks that Fredrickson had in the bank. That's a lot of money and that lawyer Evans is in control of it right now."

"I've been thinking about that," I said. "If Fredrickson got that money illegally, it doesn't make much sense that he would have deposited it in his checking account or any other account with his name on it. I'd sure like to know when he deposited that money."

"What difference would that make?"

"What if Jim didn't put that money in the bank, but somebody deposited it just before he was killed? If Evans is dirty, it might be a way for him to get control of money that he couldn't have gotten any other way without alerting law enforcement. Suppose this whole estate thing is an elaborate money laundering setup."

"But wouldn't the deposit of the money by Fredrickson have alerted the authorities as well?"

"Yeah," I said. "But what if the money had been wired into the account for the purchase of real estate? Think about it. Suppose Jim sold the land in Avon Park for ten million bucks and the purchaser wired the money to his account. That happens every day. Money is wired from one account to another to pay for real estate transactions. I don't think that would get the Treasury Department or whoever worries about these things in an uproar."

"That property in Avon Park surely isn't worth ten million dollars."

"It doesn't have to be. We're not talking about having the property appraised by a bank. Even if somebody were to check back there'd probably be fake appraisals and all kinds of documents to back up the purchase price."

"But that wouldn't work if Jim were alive."

"No. It wouldn't."

"So, maybe somebody killed him to help in a money-laundering operation."

"Not that far-fetched. People will do a lot for ten mil."

"We need to get the bank records. It'll take me a couple of days to get a warrant, and by then McAllister will be involved. Can Jock help?"

I called Jock's cell and explained what we were thinking. "Can your people get those records? Like today?"

"No sweat. I'll get the ball rolling. They'll be e-mailed to you."

"When?"

"Within the hour."

"Thanks. Where are you?" I asked.

"Sarasota. I've got a meeting in a little while. I'll be home late."

I hung up and said to J.D. "We'll have them in about an hour."

"Okay," she said. "Now, what if we find something weird? How do we follow up?"

"I'd like to find out what we can about the man who supposedly bought the property. That developer in Orlando, Robert Hammond. His website didn't have a lot of information and I never followed up on it."

"Call Katie's dad. He might know Hammond."

"J.D., I'm about to say something that might make you mad. Will you let me explain?"

"What?"

"I'm a little concerned about George Bass. There's something that just doesn't ring true with him."

"What do you mean?"

"I'm not sure. I think he knows McAllister better than he lets on. And if they're buddies, I'd just as soon not let George know our thinking."

"I think you're wrong, Matt, but there are other ways to find out about Hammond. Let me get the department's geek onto this."

She called the station and talked to the police department's computer whiz, giving him Hammond's name and website address. She told him this was important and she needed the information as soon as possible. He told her he'd stay late if necessary and call her as soon as he found out anything.

I looked at my watch. Five o'clock. "We can't do anymore until we get the records from Jock and hear back from your geek. Want to take a nap?"

She laughed. "I'm onto your naps. Somehow we never get much sleep."

"Yeah," I said, "but I've never heard you complain. Besides, Jock will be here tonight." I tried to wiggle my eyebrows. It's harder to do than you might think.

"Well," she said, "it might refresh us. You know, give us enough energy to review the bank records and such."

I agreed and we made our way to the bedroom.

CHAPTER FIFTY-TWO

It was a little after five o'clock and twilight was creeping over the small city of Sarasota. It would be dark before long and that suited Jock Algren. He preferred darkness when he was working and this evening would be what passed for a workday in his world.

He was sitting in his rental car, engine idling, parked in the shadows cast by the large live oaks that draped a quiet residential street just south of downtown. The big houses that lined the street were older and had a comfortable look that you don't find in the newer, more pretentious neighborhoods. It was not a place where cars were parked at the curb. They were all tucked away in garages behind the homes. It was a neighborhood for physicians and lawyers and successful businessmen. The third house down from where Jock was parked was the home of the very successful, and probably dirty, lawyer, Wayne Evans.

Jock had been sitting for five minutes. He knew he couldn't stay long. A strange car would be noticed and police would be called and he would have to explain his presence. He'd give it five more minutes and then leave, drive around the block, and pick another parking spot on a different part of the street.

He realized that wouldn't be necessary when he glanced in his rearview mirror and saw Wayne Evans's car driving slowly up the street. As the car closed on Jock, he dropped the transmission into drive, pulled in front of Evans, and stopped, partially blocking the street. The lawyer slammed on his brakes but wasn't able to stop before the front of his Mercedes crunched into the rear quarter panel of Jock's rental.

Jock punched the button that opened his trunk and got out of his car. Moving quickly, he got to the Mercedes before Evans had time to get completely out of his car. Jock pulled the partially opened door all the way out and stuck his pistol into the left side of Evans's neck. "Get out," he said.

Evans's face went instantly from annoyance to fear. "What's the meaning of this?" he said, his voice quavering.

"Get out or I pull the trigger," Jock said.

Evans climbed out of his car, hands up. Jock motioned to him to the open trunk of the rental. "Get in," he said.

Evans didn't argue. He climbed into the trunk, and Jock slammed the lid shut, got into the rental, and drove out of the neighborhood just as the neighbors started coming out of their houses. If anyone got a tag number, it wouldn't matter. He'd stolen it earlier from a car parked in a downtown parking garage.

He drove to an abandoned service station on nearby Tamiami Trail and replaced the stolen tag with the one that belonged to the rental. He tossed the stolen tag into the grass and drove south to Clark Road. An hour later, in full darkness, he pulled up to the gate that blocked the road to the old house in the grove near Avon Park.

The chain holding the lock had not been replaced. He opened the gate and drove through and closed the gate, replacing the chain. He pulled a small device from the canvas bag on the front seat of the rental and used duct tape to affix it to a tree at waist height. He flicked a small switch on the device and got back into his car. He parked near the front of the house, picked the lock, and went inside. He switched on the lights and saw no evidence that anybody had been there since he and Matt had discovered the place. He searched each of the rooms. The weapons were still in the closet in the laundry room, and the safe was in the kitchen cabinet.

Jock went back outside and walked the property, looking for signs that anybody was nearby or had been there recently. Nothing. He went back to the house and stood on the porch, listening. It was quiet. He checked the small plastic receiver that was clipped to his belt. If a car came down the road, the laser device he'd attached to the tree would let him know.

He went to the car and beat on the top of the trunk. "You ready to get out, Evans?"

"Yes."

Jock inserted the key and opened the trunk and helped Evans out.

"Where are we?" Evans asked.

"Shut up," Jock said. "Put your hands behind you." He used a flex tie to bind the lawyer's arms and led him toward the house and into the living room and told him to sit on the sofa. Jock pulled a chair close and used another flex tie to bind Evans's ankles. "Know where you are now?" Jock asked.

Evans looked around and nodded. "Who are you?"

"That doesn't matter. You and I are going to have a little conversation, and then I'm going to take you back home."

"Conversation about what?"

"Let's start with what happened to Jim and Katie Fredrickson."

"I don't have any idea."

Jock's hand shot out quicker than a blink and slapped Evans in the face, opened-handed. He watched as shock and fear twisted Evans's facial features. "Wrong answer."

"What do you want?" Evans asked.

"I want to know about Jim and Katie Fredrickson."

"I honestly don't know."

Jock slapped him again. "Look," he said, "I didn't drive all the way out here just to shoot you, but I will. If you don't cooperate, I'll leave your body here to rot. When your buddies come back and find you, I suspect you'll end up in an unmarked grave out in the grove."

"Ask me something else," said Evans. "If I know the answer, I'll tell you."

"Why are all those weapons stockpiled in the laundry room?"

"For the war."

"Which war?"

"The one that's coming."

"What the hell are you talking about, Evans?"

Evans breathed out a deep sigh. "Look, we've gotten ourselves involved in some things that could get us killed."

"Who's we?"

"Some friends and me."

"What've you gotten involved in?"

"Drugs."

"Okay."

"We've stepped on some toes."

"Tell me about it."

"We apparently encroached into the territory of some very bad people who are planning to kill us."

"What people?"

"I don't know."

"Tell me what you do know," said Jock.

"If I don't tell you, and you shoot me, you'll never find out what I know."

"And if you don't tell me and I let you live, I still won't know anything."

"I'd say we're at a Mexican standoff," Evans said, grinning.

"Not really. Here's how it'll work. I'll shoot you and then go talk to Sal Bonino." It was a shot in the dark, but Jock watched the color drain from Evans's face. He'd hit a nerve with Bonino's name.

"You know about Bonino?"

"Yeah," said Jock, "and a lot more. Lie to me and you're dead."

"I'm dead anyway if I tell you what I know."

"Yeah, but you won't be dead today. Besides, there may be a way to get you out of the line of fire if you cooperate."

"You can do that?"

"Yes."

"Who are you?"

"I told you, that's not important. Just believe that I have connections that can make you disappear. Either dead or alive. It won't make any difference to me."

Jock's phone rang. Matt Royal. "I've got to take this. Sit tight." He moved out to the porch leaving Evans bound and on the sofa.

"What's up, Matt?"

"I'm sorry to intrude on your meeting, but if it's with Wayne Evans, I thought you'd like to have this information."

Jock laughed. "What makes you think I'm meeting with Evans?"

"I can read you like a book, old friend. Where are you?"

"Mr. Evans and I are having a nice chat at the grove house over in Avon Park. What did you turn up?"

"Your people sent me those bank records. Fredrickson's bank account received a wire transfer in the amount of ten million dollars on January tenth of last year. The wire came from a bank in Orlando from the account of a developer named Robert Hammond. It was for the purchase of the grove where you're sitting right now."

"This place can't be worth ten million," Jock said. "Do we know anything about Hammond?"

"The computer whiz at the LBK police department came up with some interesting information. We don't think the guy exists. There is no record of him anywhere except for that little website we saw and the bank account that wired the money to Fredrickson's account. Turns out the website was set up by a freelance web designer in Sarasota. J.D. is going to have a talk with him. Tonight, if she can find him. Do you think your people can find out more about Hammond's account?"

"I'll get right on it. You said the money was wired in on January tenth. When did Fredrickson die?"

"The night of January tenth."

"I'll be damned."

"Yeah."

"I'll let you know what Evans has to say. This shouldn't take long."

"Don't hurt him," Matt said.

"Right."

CHAPTER FIFTY-THREE

It was eight o'clock. J.D. and I had eaten a meal of frozen Chinese food and iced tea. Most of the meal was sitting like a lump in my stomach. She was getting dressed so that we could go find the web designer. We had a name and an address. Bret Zanders lived in an apartment complex off University Parkway, not too far from the airport. We took J.D.'s car, the official police vehicle, and headed south on the key, stopped at the Starbucks on St. Armands Circle, and sipped our coffee as we drove through the night.

We found the complex and then the apartment, climbed one flight of stairs, and knocked on the door. I was expecting a small bespectacled young man with frizzy hair. The guy that opened the door was about my height, totally bald, and probably fifty years old.

J.D. showed him her badge and said, "I'm Detective Duncan from the Longboat Key Police. This is Mr. Royal. Are you Bret Zanders?"

"I am. How can I help you?"

"May we come in?"

"Of course. I'm afraid I'm forgetting my manners. Can I get you something to drink?"

J.D. smiled as we followed Zanders into his living room. "No thanks. I don't think we'll be but a few minutes. We're trying to find out who retained you to design a website for a man named Robert Hammond?"

"Please, sit down," Zanders said. "That name doesn't ring any bells to me. Do you have a date for when it was set up?"

"March of last year, I think," said J.D.

"Are you sure I set it up?"

"Our department tech says you did."

"Excuse me for a minute. I'll see if I can find it in my files."

We sat quietly for the few minutes it took Zanders to return with a file folder. "This is the file on the Hammond website, but I never dealt with Mr. Hammond. Everything was done through his business manager, a man named Jim Smith."

"How were you paid?" J.D. asked.

"By check. I always keep copies of checks." He handed J.D. a sheet of paper with the image of the check, both front and back. It was a cashier's check drawn on a small community bank in Orlando.

"Do you have a copy machine here?" J.D. asked.

"Take this one," he said. "I made two copies."

"Do you always require a cashier's check?" I asked.

"No, and I didn't this time. This is what he sent me."

"The website is pretty skimpy," I said.

"It sure is, but that's all Mr. Smith wanted."

"Did you ever meet Mr. Smith?" asked J.D.

"No. Everything was handled on the phone. Can you tell me what this is about?"

"I'm sorry," said J.D., "but no. It's an ongoing investigation. Would you happen to have a phone number for Mr. Smith?"

Zanders looked at his file and read out a number to J.D. She jotted it in her notebook and looked at me. I shook my head. I didn't think we were going to get anything else out of him. I was pretty sure he'd told us everything he knew.

We stood, shook hands all around, and J.D. handed him one of her business cards. "If you think of anything else, I'd appreciate your giving me a call."

"I'm guessing that Jim Smith is as bogus as Hammond," I said as we drove away from the apartment complex.

"And I'm guessing you'd be right. That was kind of a dead end."

"Not completely. We got some more information on the bank the cashier's check was drawn on. I'm betting it's the same one that wired the ten million dollars to Fredrickson's account."

"But we still don't know who Hammond is."

"Hammond doesn't exist and neither does his manager Jim Smith. But somebody's out there stage managing this whole charade."

J.D. handed me her notebook. "Call the manager's number. Let's see what we get."

We got nothing. There was no such number. We drove on through the night, anxious to get back to the key.

My phone rang. Jock. I put him on speaker. "Hey, podna," he said. "This thing's starting to unravel a bit. Evans told me that the money wired into Fredrickson's account was drug money. They set it up to look as if Hammond had bought the Avon Park property for ten mil. Evans handled the transaction so all the paperwork is in order. The property was transferred to the limited liability company that we found on the property appraiser's website, but the ownership of the LLC has since been transferred to a corporation controlled by Evans. It all looks clean as a whistle on paper."

"Who's playing the part of Hammond?" I asked.

"Evans doesn't know, and I think he's telling the truth. This whole operation is run like a spy ring with cells of people who don't know anything about the people in the other cells. Somebody is in charge of the whole thing and nobody knows who that is."

"Bonino?" I asked.

"Maybe. Evans knows Bonino and is scared to death of him. He's never met the man, but he thinks it was Bonino who had Fredrickson killed. The little group in the Fredrickson cell had been threatened by somebody who said he was working for Bonino. They were told to get out of the drug business or they'd be killed. Nobody took it seriously until Fredrickson was murdered."

"Are you coming home tonight?" I asked.

"I'm on my way."

"What about Evans?"

"I'll drop him at his house. He's riding in the trunk."

CHAPTER FIFTY-FOUR

It was nearing ten o'clock and the key was quiet as we drove north for home. The night was chilly, the result of yet another cold front drifting south. The weatherman said that Wednesday's high would be in the low sixties, but Thursday would see the temperature move back into the mid-seventies. Winter never lasts long in our paradise, a day or two usually, but it brings a somnolence to the island, with people staying indoors and off the streets. The bars and restaurants close a little earlier and the traffic is almost nonexistent. We met an occasional car going south, but the usual hustle and bustle of the season was absent. As we passed Harry's Corner Store, a car pulled out of the parking lot and followed behind us. Somebody had made a stop for beer or bread or some other convenience item that Harry sold.

J.D. turned off Gulf of Mexico Drive onto Broadway. Almost home. As we neared the second cross street, I saw a large truck with no lights moving from our right. As it came under the streetlight I could see that it was a large garbage truck, the kind that should not be working late at night.

"J.D.," I said.

"I see him."

I felt the car slow as her foot came off the accelerator. The truck was still moving, not slowing for the stop sign. J.D. began to brake hard. The truck blew the stop sign and came to rest blocking the road. The car from Harry's had turned onto Broadway behind us and was pulling to a stop. I saw the truck driver climb down and come toward us. He carried what looked like an Uzi machine pistol in his right hand.

"He's armed," I said as I opened the door and rolled onto the pavement. J.D. ducked down in the seat and was trying to free the shotgun that was mounted on the dash rack, its butt on the floorboard.

I stood behind my open door and fired two shots from my little nine millimeter. Tap, tap. Two in the chest. The gunman went down, sprawling face-first. I looked to my rear. Two men had exited the car that had stopped behind us, both carrying pistols. They were walking toward us, apparently not aware that we were armed. Maybe they hadn't heard the shots that got the garbage truck driver. I didn't have time to sort it out.

The man on the left let loose a round that whizzed by my head. Close. I dropped to the ground near the rear tire of J.D.'s cruiser, but there was no place to take cover. I had to get him with my first shot. I was raising my pistol to return fire when I heard the shotgun blast and saw the chest of the man on the right explode in a plume of blood and bone.

The man on the left turned to run and I shot him in the back. Tap, tap. Two right between the bastard's shoulder blades. Sportsmanship be damned. I wanted him dead. He went down without trying to catch himself. One of the shots may have severed his spinal cord, instantly paralyzing him, or perhaps blew out his heart. I'd let Doc Hawkins figure that one out.

"J.D. You okay?"

"Yes. Are they dead?"

"I think so. I'll check. You cover me."

"Go."

The entire incident had taken only seconds. I ran to the man I'd shot in the back. He was dead. I turned and ran back to the garbage truck driver. Dead. I turned to see J.D. falling to her knees. Was she hit? No. She was doubled over, sobbing and retching, spewing the remnants of the bad Chinese meal onto the pavement. I put my arm around her shoulder and held her. The sounds of a siren cracked the cold air. One was coming from the north, from Anna Maria Island, and the other from the south.

I held J.D. and my pistol and waited for the cops. The car coming from Anna Maria, blue lights painting the dark night, turned onto Broadway and came to a stop behind the car that had been following us. An officer got out and stood behind his open door, his weapon in his hand, headlights pinning us like captured moths. "Let me see you," he said. "Hands in the air."

J.D. was on her feet, trying hard to regain her composure. "I'm Detective Duncan," she said.

"J.D.? Who's with you?"

"Matt Royal."

"What the hell happened?"

"We got ambushed," she said.

"Are you okay?"

"Yes. We've got three dead bad guys."

Another patrol car turned onto Broadway and came to a stop, its light bar adding to the cacophony of blue-and-red shadows bouncing off the nearby houses, its headlights illuminating the first police cruiser with the Bradenton Beach P.D. logo on the door panel. I thought the second car would be from Longboat. The officer had probably been patrolling near the south end of the island, and asked for help from Bradenton Beach.

The Bradenton Beach cop holstered his weapon and waved to the second cop getting out of his vehicle. "It's J.D. She's fine."

Lights had come on in the houses that lined Broadway. The flashing blue lights of the police cars gave the people the confidence to come out onto porches and stoops and sidewalks. They stood quietly, watching the action, not interfering. One of the men in the group called out. "I'll put the coffee on. Matt, you and J.D. okay?"

"Yes," I said. "Thanks."

The investigation would take a while and involve forensics people and other cops. They would all be supplied with coffee and food by the neighbors. The village was that kind of place.

I recognized the Bradenton Beach cop, but didn't remember his name. The Longboat officer was my friend Steve Carey. "Damn, Matt," he said. "What the hell have you gotten yourself into?"

I shrugged. "Beats me. Can you put a light on these dead guys?"

Steve shined his flashlight on the face of man who'd been driving the garbage truck. I recognized him. "I'm pretty sure that's the guy who tried to kill us at my house on Sunday," I said.

"Pretty sure?"

"Real sure, Steve. I got a good look at him."

We walked over to the one J.D. had hit with the shotgun. Part of his face was shot away and his chest was a mess of internal organs, bones, and blood. He was unrecognizable.

The third man, the one I'd shot in the back, was lying facedown near the right front tire of the car they'd arrived in. I couldn't get a good look at his face without disturbing the body and that would really piss off the forensics techs.

"Any idea on the other two?"

"Can't tell much about them. The one I shot is facedown, and I didn't want to move him until the medical examiner's people get here. The other guy lost part of his face to the shotgun."

"J.D. looks a little ragged," Steve said. "Take her home. I'll come by in the morning and get your statements."

"I'm all right," J.D. said. "Let's get the statements out of the way while it's all fresh."

"One of these guys was shot in the back," said Steve. "Y'all go home and think about your statements. I'll get J.D.'s squad car back to the station and come by in the morning for the statements."

We were only two blocks from my house. I gathered J.D. up, put my arm around her, and we walked through the dark and cold and were glad to be alive. When we got into the house, she said she was going to take a shower and disappeared into the master bedroom. I fished a beer out of the refrigerator and poured some white wine into a plastic cup. I took the wine to the bathroom, opened the glass shower door, and handed it to her. She mumbled her thanks and I left.

In a few minutes she came back into the living room wearing a robe, her hair wrapped in a towel. "That's better. I'm sorry I blew apart out there."

"Come here. I want to just hold you for a bit."

She sat on the sofa and cuddled up to me. "I've never shot anyone with a shotgun. I don't know what I expected, but seeing that guy sort of explode got to me. I know he was trying to kill us and that shooting him was necessary. But still, the reality of it. I don't know. I'm glad there weren't any other cops out there to see me turn into a girl."

I laughed. "You *are* a girl. You're my girl and you're tough and strong and very good at what you do. And if you hadn't shot that bastard, he'd have shot us and never missed a wink of sleep over it. You did good and I'm proud of you."

She reached up and kissed me on the cheek. "Let's go to bed. Maybe a good night's sleep will make things better."

CHAPTER FIFTY-FIVE

The night was long and neither J.D. nor I slept well. I felt her fidgeting in the bed, dropping off to sleep with a slight snoring sound, and then waking with a start. She moved close and put her arm around me and relaxed for a while before jerking awake again. I wasn't any better and got very little sleep. I heard Jock come in at some point, his shower running, and then quiet. Finally, at four o'clock on a cold Wednesday morning I got out of bed and in the dark slipped into sweatpants and an old, soft sweatshirt. I put on boat shoes and listened for a moment to the steady breathing that indicated that J.D. was finally asleep.

I walked out into the living room and jerked to a stop. Somebody was reclining on the chaise longue on my patio. He was wrapped in a heavy jacket with a hood obscuring his face. He wore jeans and tennis shoes. He appeared to be asleep, with his knees drawn up in a fetal position. For a moment, I wondered if he was dead. Then I saw movement. He was stretching, as if just waking. I walked back into my bedroom and retrieved a pistol from the closet shelf. I returned to the living room, walked softly to the sliding glass doors that led to the patio, and jerked one open and switched on the overhead floods that turned the patio into daylight.

The person on the chaise sat up quickly, took one look at me, and said in a feminine voice, "Don't shoot. I come in peace." And then Katie Fredrickson pulled the hood off her head and smiled.

"Come in," I said. "You must be freezing. How long have you been out here?"

"A couple of hours." She picked up a backpack that I hadn't seen in the shadows and walked into the house.

"Why didn't you knock? Wake us up. Or call. You have my numbers."

She smiled again. "I wasn't sure what kind of welcome I'd get. I was actually hoping J.D. would be the first one up."

I laughed. "She usually is. You want some coffee?"

"I'd kill for a cup."

"Have a seat. I'll put the coffee on and get J.D. up."

I didn't have to bother. J.D. came padding out of the bedroom, barefoot and wrapped in an old robe I kept in the closet. "I thought I heard you," she said as she rushed to Katie, "but I thought I was dreaming."

"No, Jed. It's me. In the flesh."

They hugged for a long time and when J.D. pulled away she was smiling. "You've changed, little sister," she said.

Katie laughed. "I guess I have. More than you can see."

"Bad times, huh?"

"Terrible times, but I'm ready to put it behind me."

"We just got your letter yesterday," I said. "I thought you'd decided to move on. I was afraid I'd said or done something to spook you."

"No. Reading about Porter King's murder is what spooked me. I was planning to disappear, but I decided I was going to have to face this sooner or later so I took a Greyhound from Tampa to Bradenton then got a city bus out to the beach on the other side of the bridge. I think I got the last one of the day. I walked from the bus stop here. I wasn't sure that I wasn't followed, but I think that was my paranoia kicking in."

"How did you know where I live?" I asked. The business card I had given her listed only my post office box.

She chuckled. "You can find out almost anything with computers."

"You want to talk about it?" J.D. asked.

"That's why I'm here, J.D. It's a long story and I think you might find some of it unbelievable, but I want you to hear it. You make the decision if I'm nuts or lying and I'll live with it. If you want me to disappear again, I'll do it. But I'm tired of running and hiding and looking over my shoulder all the time."

"Do you mind if Matt sits in?"

"He's your guy?"

"He's my guy. He's *the* guy, the one I've been waiting for all my life."

I went to the kitchen, feeling quite smug, and brought them coffee in two mugs and went back for my own. They had settled onto the sofa and I took the chair across from them. "Katie," I said, "if you'd rather talk to J.D. alone, I'll understand."

"Sounds like you're family now, Matt. That means you have to put up with the crazy little sister."

"There's one more member of my and J.D.'s family asleep in his room. He's the one I told you about, the one to call if you needed anything. I don't know of anybody who is better situated to help you get out of whatever you're in. I'd like for him to sit in on this if you don't mind."

Katie looked at J.D who nodded. "I agree, Katie. Jock has resources that a mere cop can't touch."

Katie nodded. "Okay. Wake him up."

J.D. laughed. "Oh, he's awake. He sleeps like a cat." She got up and went to Jock's door, knocked and said, "Jock, come meet Katie Fredrickson."

Jock opened the door and followed J.D. back to the living room. She introduced him to Katie. "I've heard a great deal about you, Katie. I'm sorry you've had a bad time, but I think we can fix it. Let me get a cup of coffee."

"Start at the beginning, Katie," said J.D. "Tell us about Jim's death. I'm guessing that whoever killed him was somebody pretty powerful or you wouldn't have run, cut yourself off from your friends and family. Who killed Jim?"

Katie looked at J.D. for a couple of beats, as if mulling over something in her mind. She seemed to snap out of whatever reverie she had escaped to and said simply, "I killed Jim."

CHAPTER FIFTY-SIX

"Do you think you caused his death in some way?" J.D. asked.

"Yes," said Katie. "I pulled the trigger and sent a bullet into his worthless head."

J.D. sat back in her chair. "Katie," she said, "I'm a cop. I'm also your friend, but I'm a cop first. Maybe you shouldn't tell me anything more."

"No. I've got to tell the whole story. It's sordid and you're going to think a lot less of me when I'm finished, but it's time everything came out. When I've finished, if you have to arrest me, I'll understand."

"What happened?" J.D. asked, her voice soft, as if she were speaking to a child. "Whatever it is, we'll work through it. I promise."

"It all started about a year before Jim's death," Katie said. "He had gotten mixed up with some bad people. They were dealing in drugs in a pretty big way."

"Why would Jim do something like that?" J.D. asked. "He had a good law practice."

"He did. But he also had developed some expensive tastes. We were having trouble making the mortgage payments on that big house he insisted on buying. His Mercedes was about to be repossessed, and he was going to be deeply embarrassed in front of his friends and colleagues."

"How did he get involved in the drug trade?" I asked. "That's not the kind of thing you just decide to do one day. You've got to have a source and customers."

"Jim had represented some underworld types on criminal matters and got to know them pretty well. Most of their money came from drugs, and Jim and one of his law partners, who was also in financial trouble, indicated that they would like to get into the business. One day Jim got a call from one of the bigwigs in the drug business and offered to cut him in if he would do all their legal work, including a lot of transactional stuff about buying and selling businesses and real estate. He agreed and they were off to the races."

"Sal Bonino offered him the deal," Jock said.

Katie looked shocked. "Yes. How did you know?"

"And the lawyer partner who joined the deal was Wayne Evans," Jock said.

"Right again," Katie said. "It sounds like you know as much as I do."

"Not really," said J.D. "But when I got your first text message, I knew that either you were in big trouble or it was some kind of hoax. The reference to 'Jed' made me think it wasn't a hoax. We've been trying to put some of the pieces together. One of Sal Bonino's thugs tried to beat up Matt the day after he went to Winter Park to see your parents."

She looked at me and something moved across her face. Fear, shock, regret? I couldn't tell. "You went to see my parents?" she asked.

"I did, but I didn't tell them we'd heard from you. I was trying to figure out if they knew anything. If they'd heard from you."

Katie breathed a sigh of relief. "Thanks for that."

"So what happened after Jim got involved with Bonino?" I asked.

"They began to sell drugs. They'd pick them up from Bonino and store them in the Avon Park house where Jim grew up until they could get them to the street dealers. They had a big safe out there where they kept cocaine and money."

"Did you ever meet Bonino?" Jock asked.

"No. I don't think Jim did either. There were always go-betweens."

"Who did Jim sell the drugs to?" J.D. asked.

"Bonino had a ring of dealers in Sarasota and Bradenton. Jim thought the main reason Bonino brought him and Evans in was that Bonino needed help with the distribution to the street dealers."

"So, you knew Jim was dealing drugs," J.D. said.

"Not at first. But I began to suspect it when Jim took me to the Avon Park house and tried to sell me to one of the bosses."

"Sell you?" J.D. asked.

"Yes. The boss offered to pay Jim ten thousand dollars to sleep with me."

"Tell me how that happened," J.D. said.

"Jim took me to Avon Park to what he called a party at his old house. I hadn't been there in years and was surprised to see that Jim had done a lot of remodeling and fixing up. There were five men there that night, including Jim. There were also four women, probably prostitutes. They were drinking and snorting cocaine. I was pretty upset that Jim would bring me into such a situation, but he said they were businessmen that he was working with on some projects that would make us a lot of money."

"Tell me about him trying to sell you," J.D. said.

"One of the men held up ten one thousand dollar bills and said he would pay them to Jim if I'd sleep with him. I was standing right there when he made the offer. I expected Jim to slug him, but Jim said it was all right with him as long as I agreed. I told him to go to hell. I said it was time for us to leave. The man said, 'Look, honey. Just go in the room at the end of the hall and get naked. I'll be right there and do you.' Jim laughed and I started for the door. Jim stopped me and asked what I was doing. I told him that either he took me home, or I was going to start walking."

She sat quietly for a moment, probably thinking about her humiliation that night in Avon Park. "What happened?" asked J.D.

"He took me home. I was crying, almost hysterical. He kept telling me it was a joke and that he was sorry. I slept in the guest room that night and the next. But then I started to feel better, even euphoric. Every day was brighter than the day before. Sex with Jim was better than ever. A couple of weeks went by, three maybe, or four. I don't really remember. The days all ran together. I didn't care. Life was grand. And then the bottom fell out. I found myself dropping off a cliff, hitting bottom, and not bouncing back. I craved the euphoria of the weeks before. I stayed in my room curled up in the bed, crying, hurting. I told Jim I needed to see a doctor. He told me to ride it out. I was like that for two days, and then Jim gave me some medicine that turned me completely around. The euphoria came back, not as exquisite, but still so much better than the two days in bed.

"The next day, I began to drop again. The cliff was back, and I was falling into the abyss. Jim gave me more medicine, and I almost immediately soared back to the top, or almost the top. I couldn't seem to get all the way back, but still, it was good."

"He was drugging you," said J.D. "Do you know what he was using?"

"No. Later the doctors I saw figured it was some sort of cocaine-based substance, but by the time I got to them, there wasn't enough in my system to measure or to identify."

"What happened with the drugs Jim was giving you?" J.D. asked.

"Jim finally told me that he had drugged my food. I never did know whether he was telling me the truth or if the drug got into my system some other way. It didn't matter. I was hooked. Without the drugs, I'd crash and want to die. He told me he'd continue to supply me with the 'medicine' but I had to do exactly what he told me to do. I agreed. Hell, at that point I'd have agreed to anything."

"What did he want you to do?" J.D. asked.

Katie put her head in her hands and choked back a sob. She didn't look up, but said, "He made me sleep with his buddies."

"It's okay, Katie," J.D. said. "Do you want to stop?"

"No," Katie said, and looked up, defiance on her face. "That bastard made me undress in front of his friends, the same ones from the house in Avon Park. I'd take one of them into the bedroom. Jim took pictures of them screwing me."

"God," said J.D. "I'm so sorry, Katie."

"This went on for weeks," Katie said. "One of the men made me do unspeakable things. Things I won't talk about. But I did them. I'd do anything for the next high. I knew what was happening and I was so ashamed I wanted to die. I thought about suicide, but couldn't do it." She was quiet then, her hands clenched together in her lap, her head down.

J.D. touched Katie's arm, a calming gesture, or one of condolence for lost innocence, a bit of human contact. "Do you know who the man was?" she asked in a soft voice.

"Oh, yeah. I remember him like it was yesterday." She raised her head, her eyes blazing, a look of disgust crossing her face. "I was never so glad to see somebody dead. The day I read about his murder in the paper was one of the best days I've had since I got off the drugs. The sorry bastard was named Porter King."

CHAPTER FIFTY-SEVEN

"Let's take a break," J.D. said. "I'll get some clothes on and fix breakfast. Katie, why don't you use the guest room, it's the one in the middle down the hall. You make yourself at home there. You'll stay with us until we get this sorted out. Take a shower if you like. Breakfast will be ready in thirty minutes."

Katie picked up her backpack and said, "Thanks, Jed. I'll be out in a few minutes. The worst of the story is almost over."

We finished a breakfast of eggs, grits, toast, and bacon just as the sun began to emerge from the mainland. It was going to be a beautiful day. We put our dishes in the sink and went back to the living room, taking our coffee.

"Are you up to continuing?" asked J.D.

Katie smiled. "Yes. I need to get this out of my system."

"How long did this ordeal last?" J.D. asked.

"Several weeks. Jim was getting rich, and all his buddies were getting me on a regular basis. I was as high as a kite and deathly afraid that my loving husband would withhold the drugs I needed. I did whatever he told me to do. Until one evening in January of last year. I don't know what happened. Maybe the drugs were wearing off and I was having a lucid moment before the fear and depression set in. The big boss, the one who reported directly to Bonino, was at the house with a girl whom I think was a prostitute. They were all naked and the girl and the boss were having sex on the sofa. Jim was standing there with an erection, watching. I was dressed. Jim told me to get naked. He said the boss would deal with me as soon as he got finished with the girl on the sofa.

"I noticed a pistol on top of the clothes Jim had left on a chair. It was the one he'd begun carrying regularly. I'd never fired a gun, never even picked one up. But I'd watched enough TV to know you just pulled the hammer back and pulled the trigger and the gun would fire. I picked it up and pointed it at Jim's head and pulled the trigger. He went down and the boss started screaming at me.

"Jim had left a backpack on the floor next to his clothes. I'd seen the boss give it to him when he first came in with the girl. There was cash in the bag, lots of it, although I had no idea how much. It turned out to be almost a hundred thousand dollars in various denominations. I picked up the bag and ran out the front door."

"Why didn't you shoot the boss?" I asked.

"I don't know. Jim was the cause of my becoming," she paused, "whatever I was. I guess I just thought that if he was dead, my troubles would be over. Or at least Jim wouldn't be around to keep me in some sort of drug-induced stupor."

"How did you get away?" J.D. asked.

"When I got to the street in front of my house, I saw an elderly man in a car. I think he might have been parked in front of one of the neighbors because he was just pulling away from the curb. I called to him and he stopped. I told him I'd give him a thousand dollars to drive me to Tampa. He took me there to the Greyhound station, and I got on the first bus headed north. The old man wouldn't take any money. Just wished me well.

"When the bus got to Atlanta early the next morning, I put some cash in my pocket and stashed the backpack in a locker and took a taxi to the nearest hospital. I was in pretty bad shape. I'd been without drugs for about twelve hours and I was going to pieces. I told the emergency room doctors that I'd been on drugs and needed to get clean. They recommended a treatment center and a driver in a van came and took me across town to a pretty place on the north side. I checked in and told them I could only stay a few days. I knew I had to get back to the bus station and get the money I'd left in the locker. I didn't know how long it was going to have to last me, and I knew the boss had a lot of power and resources to find me. I had to establish a new identity right from the start. I gave the people at the center a false name. I didn't have any identification and told them I'd probably lost it somewhere. I don't know if they believed me, but they took me in and worked hard to get me clean. After a few days, I got one of the drivers to take me back to the bus station and I retrieved the money and spent the next three months in the center. It was the most peaceful time I've known in years."

I could tell Katie was running down. She'd been talking nonstop for the better part of an hour. She seemed to be in a rush to get it all out, to tell us what her life had been like for the past year. I said, "Maybe we ought to let Katie get some rest."

"I'm okay," Katie said. "Let me get this done and then I'll rest. Ask me something. They're probably blanks I need to fill in."

"Why did you wait so long to contact me?" asked J.D. "Didn't you trust me to help you?"

"I killed a man, J.D., and you're a cop. I wasn't sure what the police knew. Had they figured out that I had killed Jim? I just didn't know the lay of the land. I assumed I was a fugitive."

"How did you get the pictures texted from Detroit?" I asked.

Katie laughed. "I guessed that you'd figure out where the pictures originated and I didn't want to let you know that I was in Tampa. My best friend in the center was a young man who was going home to Detroit when he finished his rehab. He left before I did. I went to a Wal-Mart and bought seven disposable phones and paid cash for enough minutes on each to last for a couple of years. I labeled each phone with a day of the week and told him that if I needed him, I'd call on the phone that matched the day I was calling.

"When I decided to send J.D. the picture, I sent it to my friend through my computer, and he then texted it to J.D. I knew you'd run into a dead end when you tried to track where the text had come from."

J.D. said, "Let's stop for now. You take a nap. We'll make sure you're not disturbed and we can finish this when you're not so tired."

"Okay," said Katie. "You're probably right."

"I do have one question," J.D. said. "Do you know the boss's name? The one who was there when you shot Jim?"

Katie smiled ruefully. "You won't believe me."

"Try me," said J.D.

Katie shrugged, as if she didn't care whether we believed her or not. She said, "He's a Sarasota policeman. Captain Doug McAllister."

CHAPTER FIFTY-EIGHT

When Katie was gone, I said, "Jock, somebody tried to take J.D. and me out last night." I told him about the shoot-out on Broadway. "The guy driving the garbage truck was the same one who tried to kill us on Sunday."

"You're sure it's the same guy?" Jock asked.

"Positive."

My doorbell sounded and I went to open the door. It was Chief Bill Lester and Officer Steve Carey. I invited them in, offered coffee, which they declined, and told them to take a seat. Jock went into the kitchen and returned with another cup of coffee.

"How're you holding up, J.D.?" asked Lester.

"I'm fine, Chief, considering I killed a man with a shotgun less than twelve hours ago."

"You did the right thing, but you know you'll have to be on administrative suspension until the sheriff's office sorts this out."

J.D. made a face, but she knew the rules. Any officer-involved shooting requires a thorough investigation by another police agency, in this case the Manatee County sheriff's office. "How long will that take?" she asked.

"A few days," Lester said. "I'll try to hurry them along."

"What do I do in the meantime?" she asked.

"I'm putting you on paid leave until the investigation is done."

"Wait, Chief. You don't think I did anything wrong here, do you?"

"Absolutely not. But if you're on leave, you don't have to sit in the office and do paperwork. You're free to pursue any activities you want as long as it's not official business." He winked.

J.D. laughed. "Okay. Thanks, Bill. I'll try not to embarrass you. Have you come up with IDs on the bad guys yet?"

The chief looked at Carey who said, "Yeah. You'll be surprised to know they were all in the system. The one who went after you and Matt on Sunday was a local named Carlton Owens. He was picked up last year for trying to intimidate one of our citizens who owned a used car business that our friend Sal Bonino was trying to buy. The man sold his business and refused to press charges. The other two were strangers to the local law. They had records in New Jersey. We don't know how long they'd been here, but they haven't gotten into trouble since they left Jersey."

Bill Lester stood up. "Steve needs to take statements from you. I'll be on my way. Call me if you need anything, J.D."

Steve put a digital voice recorder on the coffee table and began to question J.D. and me. I told him that the man I'd shot in the back had almost got me with his first shot, but turned to run when J.D. let loose with the shotgun. I thought he was running for the cover of the open car door. If he made it, I'd be a sitting duck. He'd have a clear shot at me and I had no place to take cover, at least no place I could get to before he settled in and killed me. Steve smiled. When we finished, he shut down the recorder and said, "Self-defense, Matt. If the shooter had reached the door of his car, you'd be dead."

"You know that wasn't what I was thinking when I shot the bastard."

He grinned. "I just deal with the facts, sir, and I have the facts on my trusty recorder."

After Steve left, Jock said, "We've got to take McAllister out."

"I agree," I said.

"What about due process?" J.D. asked. She had always had a problem with Jock's methods. What he did for his country was almost always extralegal. He didn't have time to follow laws that were made for normal people living in an orderly society. He operated in a jungle that was beyond J.D.'s understanding.

"You mean like the due process he gave Katie?" Jock asked.

J.D. was quiet for a moment. "I don't like it," she said. "You know that, Jock, but I'm beginning to see that sometimes your way might be the only way. McAllister is so wired with the Sarasota P.D. that he might walk. It'd be Katie's word against his, and Katie has already confessed to killing her husband. McAllister's a decorated police officer. It wouldn't be much of a contest."

"Do you believe Katie?" I asked.

J.D. thought about that for a beat. "Absolutely," she said. "She'd have no reason to make any of that up."

"It could be a complex excuse for Jim's murder," I said.

"Then where did the money in the backpack come from?" J.D. asked. "And what about the Avon Park house, the weapons, and the safe? And how would you explain a pitiful ten-acre grove with a few producing trees going for ten million bucks in a bad economy?"

"You should've been a lawyer," I said.

She grinned. "Couldn't do it," she said. "The minute they found out I had principles, I would've been kicked out of law school."

"Well," I said. "There's that."

"I agree," said Jock. "I believe Katie. I think we need to confront McAllister when he's out of his element. Where his badge doesn't protect him. Do you know where he lives, J.D.?"

"No, but I can probably find out."

"I'm thinking we take him at home," said Jock. "Tonight."

"What's your plan?" I asked.

"I want to put the fear of God into the bastard," Jock said. "If we go in at night, late, after he's asleep, I think I can do that."

"I'd bet on it," said J.D., sardonically.

"Do you know if he's married?" I asked.

"Divorced," J.D. said, "and I don't think he has anyone living with him."

"We still need to find out a few things from Katie," I said. "Like what she knows about U166 and why she would have given us that clue in the last text."

"I'd also like to know who the other two guys were," Jock said.

"Other two?" I asked.

Jock said, "Katie told us there were five guys, including Jim, at the Avon Park house the first time Jim tried to get her to join the fun. We know that McAllister and King were there. Who are the other two?"

"Good question," said J.D.

"Another thing," I said. "I was surprised at Katie's reaction when I told her I'd been to see her parents."

"So was I," said J.D. "At first, I thought it might just be her fear that if they knew she was alive, they might mention it to McAllister. But then, why wouldn't she trust them enough not to tell anybody if she asked them not to?"

"We still don't have a lot of the answers, Jock."

"I don't want to overdo this," said J.D. "Katie's been through a lot. She's pretty fragile."

"You're right," I said, "but I think she's tougher than you give her credit for. What could be worse than what she's already told us?"

J.D. shrugged, but the answers to that question would make me despair of the human race.

CHAPTER FIFTY-NINE

Jock and I went for a run on the beach. J.D. stayed at the cottage to watch over Katie and be there when she awoke. The late-morning temperature had barely climbed into the sixties. The beach was deserted and we made good time on the hard-packed sand. We were finishing up and walking toward the North Shore Drive beach access when I saw a tall angular man standing at the beach end of the boardwalk. He waved at us.

"That looks like Harry Robson," I said.

"Careful," said Jock. He put his right hand behind his waist, touching the pistol he always carried in a holster in the small of his back. Even when he was wearing sweatpants.

"He's okay."

"You're probably right, but this has been one strange day so far."

We walked toward the ramp. "Good morning, Harry," I said. "What brings you to paradise?"

Harry said, "I stopped by your house. J.D. told me I could find you here. I need to talk to you guys. I'm not happy about the way my boss is handling the King investigation."

"As your boss pointed out," I said, "we're just a couple of civilians. I don't see how we can help."

"I filled J.D. in this morning," Harry said. "Jock, I don't know exactly what you do, but I know you do it for the federal government and you're the best we have at whatever it is you do." He grinned ruefully. "I know from Bill Lester that you two get involved in all kinds of things that you probably shouldn't and always come out smelling like roses."

"Talk to us, Harry," said Jock.

"Can I buy you lunch at Mar Vista?" he said.

"Do we have time to get cleaned up?" I asked.

"No. I've got to get back. Come on. I'll give you a ride."

The restaurant was busy but, at our request, we were seated at a table under the trees away from the other diners. We ordered drinks and looked briefly at the menus. "What's up, Harry?" I asked.

"The press has been all over the King case. That always happens when we have a murder in the high rent districts."

"You're not surprised, are you?" I asked.

"No. But what does surprise me is how McAllister is handling it."

"How's that?" Jock asked.

"He's telling the reporters that all the evidence leads us to believe that the murders were the result of a random robbery that went bad. There's absolutely no evidence pointing to anything other than that this was an execution."

"Maybe he can't say that without causing a panic among the downtown residents," I said.

"That's a point, but why is he trying to pass that story off on me and the other cops?"

"Have you called him on his story?" Jock asked.

"This morning. I sat down with him and asked what the hell was going on. He said I just had to trust him on this one because it involved some very highly placed people. I pointed out that King and his girlfriend were not exactly high-profile folks."

"No they weren't," I said. "Did you see the report J.D. sent to McAllister about her conversation with the girlfriend on the afternoon of the murders?"

"No. It's not in the file. I assumed she hadn't sent it."

"Did he tell you that Josie Tyler called J.D. and left a voice mail just before the murders?"

"No. Did he know that?"

"I was there when J.D. told him," I said. "I think the call is probably on the printout from the phone company as well."

"I never saw the printout. It's not in the file."

"I can see why you're concerned," I said.

"There's more," Harry said. "I talked to the people who cleaned the manager's office on the afternoon of the murders. They were both adamant that they did not knock the router's plug out of the wall. They said it was under a table and a couple of feet off the floor. They would have run the vacuum cleaner under the table, but they couldn't have knocked out the plug. They were aware it was there and that it was important. I think somebody unplugged it on purpose."

"Who do you think did it?" Jock asked.

"I don't know, but it has to be somebody with some juice with McAllister. The cleaning people told me that McAllister never talked to them. That's just not something that an experienced detective would forget to do."

"Maybe he thought somebody else was handling it," I said.

"I doubt it. He was playing this one very close to the vest, not involving me or any of the other detectives."

"Is that unusual?" asked Jock.

"Very much so. We usually work as a team and just report back to McAllister. If he ever does get involved in the investigation, he just becomes another member of the team. He's never taken one over before and not involved the rest of us."

"What was J.D.'s take on all this?" I asked.

"She thought it very odd. She wanted me to tell you about it, but she also seemed a little anxious to get me out of the cottage. I guess she's still reacting from last night."

"You know about the attack last night?" I asked.

"Yeah. McAllister mentioned it this morning. I'm glad you two are all right."

"What did McAllister tell you?" I asked.

"Just that some shooters tried to take you and J.D. out last night, but that you managed to kill all three of the bad guys."

"How would McAllister know about that?" I asked.

"It was a pretty big story down at the station. The word gets out quick anytime a cop is involved in a shooting. I'm not concerned that McAllister knew about it."

"Anything else?" I asked.

"Only that it happened near your house."

"Harry," Jock said, "what do you want us to do about this?"

Harry shook his head. "I don't know, Jock. I thought I ought to tell J.D. about my suspicions, and she wanted me to tell you two. She has an interest in the murders since they're tied into a case she's working here on the island. I can't go to anybody in my department. McAllister's been around a long time and is owed a lot of favors. I just thought J.D. ought to know. And she thought you and Matt should know."

We finished our meal, talking about inconsequential things. Harry left and Jock and I walked home to find J.D. and Katie sitting in the living room. Katie was sobbing, spasms shaking her whole body, struggling to catch her breath and then sobbing some more. J.D. was sitting across from her, a stunned look on her face, a rictus of horror and disgust and unfathomable sadness.

CHAPTER SIXTY

Katie got up as we walked in, excused herself, and went into the guest room and slammed the door. "Is she all right?" I asked.

"No, but I think she'll be better now that she's got some of that out of her system."

"Some of what?"

"The reason she didn't want her parents to know she's alive is that she's as much afraid of her dad as she is of McAllister."

"Tell us about it," I said.

"George Bass abused her as a child. Sexually. She doesn't think her mother knew anything about it, and Katie tried to put it behind her when she left for college. I guess that's one of the reasons she fell for Jim Fredrickson. She wanted to be independent of her father."

"Did Katie ever confront George?" I asked.

"Yes. A week before her disappearance. She went for a short visit to talk to George. She didn't want her mom to know what was going on with her, so she went at a time that she knew her mother would be out of the house volunteering at the hospital. Katie asked George for help. She told him that she was addicted to some kind of drug and told him what she'd been doing in order to get the drugs. She wanted George to help her get away from Jim and into rehab."

"He refused?" I asked.

"Not only did he refuse, he blew a gasket. He told her that she was nothing but a whore, selling herself for drugs. She was no better than the streetwalkers. Apparently things got real tense, real quick. Katie asked George if he'd thought her a slut when he was sneaking into her room late at night when she was a little girl."

"And George's response?" I asked.

"He laughed. He told her that she wasn't his child, that he and Betty had adopted her when she was an infant. Katie didn't believe him, so he brought her the adoption papers. She asked why they hadn't told her before now, and he said that it was because Betty didn't want to raise the issue. Ever."

"That must have been devastating," I said.

"It was. Katie told George that she was going to the cops. She knew that her husband and his cronies were involved in some bad stuff and she was going to turn them in and get herself into rehab."

"George's reaction?" I asked.

"He said he'd kill her if she went to the police. He told her that he and Jim were in business together and there was a lot of money to be made. If she upset that apple cart, he'd kill her. Betty, too. 'You've got your mother's life in your hands,' he told her. His exact words. The last thing George said to her before she left, and I'm quoting Katie directly, was, 'You fuck up and she dies.' "

"Katie's father was working with her husband?" Jock asked.

"Apparently, so," J.D. said.

"Then George Bass would have known that Katie was alive," Jock said. "McAllister would have told him."

"Maybe not," J.D. said. "Katie was the only one who could put McAllister at the Fredrickson house the night Jim and the woman died. If he let on to George that he knew Katie was alive, he, McAllister, would have to explain his presence at the time of Jim's death."

"And," said Jock, "there was always the chance that George Bass would try to protect Katie from McAllister."

"You might be right, Jock," said J.D. "McAllister wouldn't have known about the abuse. That's not the kind of thing George would have told him. He might not have even known that George was not Katie's birth father. In that case, McAllister couldn't be sure that George wouldn't do whatever he could to protect his daughter."

"J.D.," I said, "did you ask Katie about the other two men who were raping her on a regular basis?"

"Yes. The lawyer, Wayne Evans, was one and the other was Dwight Peters, the man Jock thought was Bonino."

"Damn," said Jock. "I think I'd better talk to David Sims and see if I can get some more time with Peters. I guess he's still in the Manatee County jail."

"He probably is," said J.D., "but let's take care of McAllister first. He's the real threat."

"What about the U-166?" I asked.

"I didn't get to that yet," said J.D.

"Maybe McAllister can enlighten us," said Jock.

J.D. said, "I also want to know why King was interested in Bud Jamison, and we still don't have a clue as to who killed old Mr. Goodlow."

J.D. stood up. "I need to check on Katie," she said.

"What are you thinking about how to take McAllister?" I asked Jock.

"We go in hard and fast and quiet about three in the morning, wearing ski masks. He'll be sound asleep. We wake him up with a couple slaps, show him our weapons, and drag his ass out of bed. He'll be a bit disoriented. We throw him in the trunk of the rental and drive out somewhere to the woods, drag him out, tie him to a tree, and throw a hood over his head. Then we start asking questions."

"Sounds like a plan," I said. "Only one hitch. Where the hell do we find ski masks in Florida?"

Jock grinned. "I have a couple in my suitcase."

I never ask about those things. Who knows why he'd be carrying ski masks around with him in his luggage? It's probably better if I don't know.

Katie had composed herself and followed J.D. back into the living room. "Sorry about that," Katie said. "I've never told a soul about what my father did to me. Talking about it brought back some terrible memories. Things I'd buried a long time ago."

"Are you up to some more conversation?" I asked.

"Yes. I'm not sure how much else I can tell you."

"Talk to us about U166."

"I don't know much about that. I heard the men talking about it several times. I thought it might be a street drug, one of those things the kids cook up. Like Ecstasy or meth. I just assumed that J.D. would know what it was and would maybe be able to connect it to somebody. It was a shot in the dark."

"Do you remember any of the conversations?" Jock asked.

"No. Sorry. They just talked about making a lot of money out of it."

"Katie," I said, "I'd like you to close your eyes, and really think about the answer to what I'm about to ask you. The question might sound a little weird, but it might jog your memory some."

"Okay." She shut her eyes.

"Do you remember the men ever talking about a submarine, specifically a World War II German submarine?"

She was quiet for a moment or two. Thinking. Her eyes popped open. "Yes," she said. "They were talking one night and not paying any attention to me. I must have been less drugged than usual. Anyway, I heard Porter King talking about a submarine. Something about stumbling over the wreckage, but they needed a key. I don't know what to, but it sounded important. Like they had put a lot of effort into the deal and without the key, they wouldn't be able to make the money they planned on."

She held up her hand, as if holding us off, and closed her eyes again. We sat quietly. She opened her eyes and shook her head. "I'm sorry," she said. "I can't remember anything else about that conversation."

"Did you ever overhear them talking about the submarine after that?" I asked.

"No. Not that I can remember. Sorry."

J.D. said, "Logan might be right about the submarine after all."

CHAPTER SIXTY-ONE

We were sitting in the living room of Captain Doug McAllister's home on a large tract of land out near Myakka City. The place had once been a working farm, but now was just a large house isolated by the fallow fields surrounding it. It was four o'clock on Thursday morning and McAllister was tied naked to a straight chair facing us, a black hood covering his face and head.

J.D. had found the address and we looked it up on Google Maps. The house sat back from the highway, shielded from the traffic by a grove of old-growth live oaks. A driveway led from the main road through the trees to the house. The location and isolation of McAllister's home led us to a change of plans. Why not be comfortable while discussing matters with Mr. McAllister?

We drove the rental with its crumpled rear quarter panel and stopped at the entrance to McAllister's property. Jock doused the headlights, and we turned quietly into the trees. When we were sure our car wouldn't be spotted from the road, we parked. We were dressed in jeans and black sweatshirts and black running shoes. Jock handed me a ski mask, a pair of latex gloves, night-vision goggles, and a rifle from the trunk. He picked up a shotgun and a small satchel and we walked carefully toward the house.

We weren't sure if the house had an alarm system, but Jock had some sort of electronic gadget that he said he could use to disarm one if necessary. In the event, we didn't have to use it. The house wasn't even locked. We walked carefully through the front door and stopped, listening for any sound. We heard loud snoring coming from a hallway that ran off the living room. We moved that way and found ourselves standing in front of an open door of a bedroom. The snoring was coming from a large lump under a blanket. Jock went quietly through the other rooms while I waited outside McAllister's bedroom.

Jock returned. We were alone in the house. He nodded at me and we went to either side of the bed. McAllister was lying on his back. The smell of old booze emanated from the sleeping man's mouth with every snore. Jock poked the shotgun under McAllister's chin and I grabbed a handful of his hair, lifted his head, and shoved the hood over his face. He was coming awake like a disturbed rhinoceros. Jock poked harder with the muzzle of the shotgun and said, "Calm down or I'll blow your head off." McAllister got the message and lay still.

"Who are you?" McAllister asked.

"Not important," Jock said. "Get out of bed. There are two of us, and if you make one false move, they'll be picking parts of you out of the furniture for the next week. Understand?"

"Yes," said McAllister and slowly began to get out of bed. He was naked and said, "I gotta pee."

"Where's the bathroom?" Jock asked.

McAllister said. "Through the door."

"Go ahead. I've got a twelve-gauge pointing at your back. If you make a wrong move, you're dead. I better not see your hands move above your waist."

"I can't see to pee with this hood covering my face."

"Just pretend it's dark," said Jock,

McAllister murmured his understanding and felt his way toward the bathroom, bumping briefly into a chest of drawers near the bathroom door. When he'd finished, Jock led him into the living room and sat him in the chair. He used flex ties to bind McAllister's legs and arms to the chair. Jock then opened the satchel he carried and pulled out a small blowtorch. He used a lighter to activate it. It lit up with a whooshing sound of escaping gas. He held it near McAllister's right ankle, not close enough to do any damage, but close enough for McAllister to feel the heat.

"Do you know what this is?" asked Jock.

"Blowtorch?" asked McAllister.

"Right. I'm going to ask you some questions. If you refuse to answer or lie to me, I'm going to burn your dick off. Understand?"

"Yes." McAllister's voice was shaking. I think he was just coming to the realization that he was in big trouble. "Are you going to kill me?"

"Depends," said Jock.

"On what?" asked McAllister.

"On how much you cooperate."

"Are you from the competition?"

Jock turned off the blowtorch. "You might say that. Do you have a safe in the house?"

"Yes."

"Where is it?"

"In the bedroom closet. Under the floor. You have to pull up the trap-door under my shoes."

"What's the combination?"

McAllister gave it to him. Jock looked at me, and I went into the bedroom, found the trapdoor, and opened the safe. There was a stack of currency wrapped with a rubber band. Mostly hundred dollar bills. Several thousand dollars' worth. There was also what looked like a book bag. I opened it and found a loose-leaf notebook full of what appeared to be copied documents. They were all typed in English. I opened the book and glanced at the first page. The heading said, simply, "U-166." I left the money and took the book bag back to the living room. Showed the first page to Jock. He nodded.

"Okay, McAllister," he said. "Tell me about U-166."

"Shit."

"I know some of it," Jock said. "You'd better not lie to me."

"Not a problem. It turns out the whole deal was worthless. What do you want to know?"

"Everything. From the get-go."

"At first, this was a deal that a guy named Porter King had set up. He was looking for investors. He'd found a sunken German sub up near the panhandle."

"Where?" asked Jock.

"I don't know. Somewhere south of St. George Island."

"How did he find a sub?"

"He was in the business of surveying pipe lines for oil rigs. His company would figure out the best route to get crude oil from the platforms drilling in the Gulf to the refineries. His people came across the U-166 in about three hundred feet of water."

"Weren't they required to notify the government of the find?"

"They did," said McAllister, "but not before exploring it. They found the safe in the captain's cabin. It'd been torn loose during the explosions that sunk it. It was just lying there. Two of his divers hooked it up to a float device and raised it. They opened the safe and found nothing but the ship's log and some documents stored in a waterproof metal container with a name etched into the top."

"What were the documents about?"

"King didn't know. They were in some sort of numerical code. He hired a cryptologist to figure it out and the guy told him it was impossible. He said the code was a simple one based on page, line, and word numbers in some book. Without the book, it was indecipherable."

"Why would King be looking for investors for something like that?"

"It got a bit complicated. He told the divers that there was nothing of value in the safe, but that they had committed a major felony by not leaving the safe with the wreck. A lot of people in his company knew about the wreck, but only King and the two divers knew that the safe had been found. King told the divers they had to keep quiet about the safe, or they would go to prison for a long time."

"And the divers bought that?" asked Jock.

"They did for a while. But then one of them started making waves. He wanted some of whatever King got out of it. King had them both killed."

"When did all this happen?"

"King found the wreck about two years ago. The murders happened about six months later," McAllister said.

"Okay, then why did King want investors?"

"He thought the documents must be worth something if they were in a virtually unbreakable code. He hired a researcher in Europe to see what he could find out about the sub. Apparently, those records aren't that difficult to find. It turns out that the sub was on a routine patrol in the Gulf of Mexico when it was lost. The Germans didn't know if it was sunk in the Gulf or somewhere in the Atlantic. They just knew it was gone.

"It turns out that as far as the U.S. Government knows, we only sank one U-boat in the Gulf during the entire war. The last log entry on the U-166 was August first, 1942, so it was reasonable that the sinking took place about that time. It just so happens that the U.S. Coast Guard has always maintained that the only sub sunk in the Gulf was the result of an attack by one of its planes on the morning of August second, 1942."

"How did King determine that the sub was U-166?" Jock asked.

"U-166 was embossed on the cover of the logbook."

"So, what did the researchers in Europe find that made the documents so valuable?"

"The sub was carrying a passenger, an officer named Paulus von Reicheldorf. It turns out that he was some sort of spy."

"How do you know that?"

"The researchers found a document in the folder for U-166 ordering Reicheldorf aboard. It would have been very unusual to simply have a passenger along on a war patrol. That sent the researchers to the files of the German intelligence agency, the Abwehr. One of the major documents in that trove is the diary of the head guy, an admiral named Canaris. Looking back from the date the U-166 left Lorient, France, for the Gulf, they found a reference indicating that Canaris had sent Reicheldorf on the patrol to take some documents to German spies in San Antonio, Texas. Canaris knew Reicheldorf's family, apparently, and was worrying about whether he'd sent his friend's son to his death. King thought that the mission, and therefore the documents, must have been very valuable for Canaris to send this particular officer on such a dangerous mission."

"So King needed the money for the research," Jock said.

"Right."

"I thought he'd made a bundle when he sold his business."

"Not really. The company was deep in debt and most of the money from the sale went to pay that off. King ended up with some money, but he was quickly running through it."

"How did you get hooked up with him?"

"Through my lawyer," McAllister said.

"Jim Fredrickson."

"Yes." There was a hint of surprise in McAllister's voice. I could almost hear the wheels turning in his simian brain. Jock must know a lot more than McAllister thought he did.

"Tell me about that," said Jock.

"King was living on Longboat Key and played golf at the same club that Jim and I did. Somehow, he and Jim got friendly and one day King mentioned to Jim that he needed some backing to hire the researchers and find out more about what he'd found. Jim brought him to me."

"You're a cop. Why would Jim think you could fund such a thing?"

"I inherited some money."

Jock reached down and picked up the blowtorch. He made a production of lighting it, getting the sound of the gas escaping and igniting. "Whoa," said McAllister. "I'm cooperating."

"Inherited money?" Jock said. "You think I'm an idiot? Talk to me about the drugs and the house in Avon Park and the armory you have over there and what's in the safe. Tell me about the parties with the women."

"Jesus," said McAllister.

Jock moved the blowtorch closer to McAllister's crotch. Close enough that McAllister could feel the heat. "No," he screamed. "Honest to God, I'll tell you everything."

Jock moved the blowtorch back and said, "You lie to me again, and I'm going to light up your gonads. Do we understand each other?"

"Yes. Please." McAllister was breathing hard, gulping for breath, sobbing. He was near panic and Jock had to calm him down.

"Look, Captain," Jock said. "Burning your nuts off isn't going to get me anywhere. So let's make a deal. You tell me the truth, and I'll let you keep your equipment."

"Okay. God, yes. Okay."

"Now, tell me why Jim Fredrickson came to you."

"Jim and I were in business together. We were buying and selling drugs. We had established a network of street-level dealers and we were getting our product from some very bad people. We'd put a lot of money aside. We couldn't figure out how to launder it, get it in our accounts without the feds finding out.

"Jim and his law partner, Wayne Evans, came up with a solution of sorts. We'd invest in King's deal, but it would show up on all the documents as an investment in a new oil-drilling venture. King was in the business, so that might pass muster if it was ever looked into. It wasn't a lot of money, a couple hundred thousand, and Jim and I salted our accounts with low-level deposits over several months. Then we gave the money to King, and he got the information from Europe."

"When did you get the answers from Europe?" Jock asked.

"A couple of months ago. Those guys took over a year to dig it up. But once we got the information, we felt that we were onto something big."

"Why? The documents were indecipherable."

"Maybe not. The man Admiral Canaris sent on the sub? He was some sort of hereditary count, and they found him in Berlin."

"How?"

"Easy. He was some kind of big shot in the government. He was retired, but he wasn't hard to find."

"Is this the guy you killed a few weeks back?" asked Jock.

"Hey, I didn't kill him. I never left the U.S. You can check it out."

"But you killed Rodney Vernon up in New Jersey," Jock said.

"If you know so much, why are you asking me?"

"Don't get surly with me, McAllister, unless you want your wienie roasted."

"Sorry," McAllister said.

"What happened to Vernon?"

"That was King's doing. He sent some men to talk to the guy in Berlin. They thought they could get him to give up the name of the book that was the key to the documents and maybe explain what was in them. He was a tough old bird, I guess, and didn't give up anything. He said he didn't know what the hell the men were talking about."

"So," Jock said, "the count wouldn't talk, and King's men killed him."

"That's the way I heard it."

"Who did you hear it from?"

"Porter King," McAllister said.

"What about Vernon in Jersey?"

"King said his men in Germany found some e-mails on the old man's computer. They were correspondence with the guy in Jersey. King thought Vernon might know something, maybe the name of the book that was the key to the code."

"Why would King think that?"

"In one of the e-mails, the old man in Jersey said something about books and how they were the key to learning. King just thought that might be some kind of code the two old guys were using, maybe to let the count know that Vernon had the book. King was grasping at straws."

"Canaris's diary didn't mention the name of the book that was the key?"

"No, and there was nothing else that the researchers found that would give him that information."

"Why did you kill King?" Jock asked.

McAllister reacted as if he'd been hit by a rifle butt. "What?"

"Lie to me," said Jock, "and I'll barbeque your nuts."

"Okay. Look, his girlfriend was talking to that bitch detective out on Longboat Key. I was afraid she might incriminate me. I had to take her out. Unfortunately, King was in the condo when I got there. I hadn't expected that. I had to get rid of him, too."

"He was the guy who was going to make you rich. Why kill him?"

"I'm already rich. King was going to be my vehicle to launder the money. That wasn't going to happen. We'd hit a dead end with finding the key to the code. Wayne Evans had come up with another idea on how to move the money and we'd already done that, so we didn't really need King. We just thought if he was able to figure out those German documents, we'd maybe make some real money."

"What did you think were in the documents?" Jock asked.

"King thought they might identify a bank account with lots of spy money in it. Or maybe the names of people who were helping the spies. He said that there were a lot of prominent people who were sympathetic to the Nazis before we got into the war, and maybe some of them had continued to work for the Germans."

"So what? Most of them would be dead by now."

"But their descendants would still be alive. A lot of those people were rich, and we thought their children and grandchildren would pay some money to keep us from going public with the documents identifying them."

"In other words," said Jock, "you didn't have a clue. Was King milking you for more and more money?"

"Yes. He was sort of obsessed with the documents. But we'd brought him into the drug business, so he was doing okay and nobody really needed the fucking documents. We just couldn't get him to see that."

"Why did you leave the murder weapon at King's condo? Surely, you knew that it would be connected to Jim Fredrickson's murder."

"Yeah," said McAllister. "Who the hell are you and how do you know all this?"

"Doesn't matter who I am. Why leave the weapon if you were going to cover up the IBIS report?"

"Shit. Do you know everything?"

"Most of it."

"I thought even if the gun was connected it would be a bit of misdirection. It would tie King into Fredrickson."

"Why would you want to do that?" asked Jock.

"With both of them dead, I thought I could guide the investigation so that it would appear that they were the ones involved in the drug business and leave me out of it. It would look like a professional hit. Somebody from organized crime taking them out. I'd get my money out of the business, all washed and everything. Then I'd get out of the drug business and in five years or so retire from the department and find myself an island someplace."

"Who was the prostitute you killed at Fredrickson's house the night he died?"

I could see McAllister shaking his head beneath the hood. "Geez," he said. "You know every goddamned detail."

"Who was she?"

"She was a dancer at a joint up in Tampa. She used to come to some of our parties. Said her name was Amber Wave, but that was bullshit. I never knew her real name."

"So when Katie Fredrickson shot her husband and ran out of the house," Jock said, "you killed the girl and set it up to look as if Katie had been killed."

"Yes." I heard the voice of a completely defeated man.

"Are you Sal Bonino?" Jock asked.

McAllister let out a bitter little laugh. "I'm surprised. There's finally something you don't know. But no, I'm not Bonino."

"Who is he?"

"He's the boss of the whole thing, I never met him, don't know who he is. And think about it before you fire up that torch again. If I knew, what would I have to gain by not telling you?"

"How did you contact him?"

"I didn't. He always contacted me. Usually by phone."

"Why even bother with him if you had the network all set up?"

"It was his network. He recruited us. There was one of the original guys who came in with us and he got greedy. One day he turned up dead at the Avon Park house. He'd been beaten and mutilated before he was killed. We buried him on the property. There was a DVD in the house on the kitchen counter with a note signed by Bonino that said we should watch it in case we ever got any big ideas of our own. It was a recording of our guy being tortured to death. It wasn't pretty, but we got the message."

"You got any beer in the refrigerator?" Jock asked.

"Yeah. A six-pack of Bud."

"Thanks," Jock said and motioned for me to follow him to the kitchen.

"I need some water," McAllister said.

"Maybe later," Jock said.

"You drinking beer?" I asked Jock.

"No. Can you think of anything else we need to ask him?"

"We need to ask him about the ten million dollars that showed up in Fredrickson's bank account," I said. "I also want to know what he has to say about Katie's dad, George Bass, being in business with Fredrickson. And I'd like to search the place before we leave."

"Go for it. I'll give our good captain a little time to stew."

CHAPTER SIXTY-TWO

I tossed the place without taking pains to be tidy. I figured McAllister would never be coming back to the house. He was going to spend the rest of his life locked up and possibly finish it at the end of a needle up at the old Raiford Prison. I found a large manila envelope hidden in his underwear drawer and a couple of pistols in the master bedroom closet.

The envelope contained a number of bank statements on four separate accounts in the name of somebody I'd never heard of whose only address was a post office box in Parrish, a small town near Bradenton. Each account held several hundred thousand dollars. The police would be able to trace the ownership of the accounts, and I was pretty sure they all belonged to McAllister.

The envelope also held a thumb drive that probably had a lot more documents relating to McAllister's drug business. I went back to the kitchen and found Jock sitting quietly at a small dining table. He had learned patience over many years of lying in wait for bad guys, and I had often wondered where his mind went when he was so absorbed. Knowing his brainpower, I wouldn't have been surprised to learn that he was doing quadratic equations in his head. Whatever a quadratic equation is.

I put the bank statements on the table. "Have a look at these," I said. "I think our boy has gotten rich."

"What's on the thumb drive?"

"I don't know. I saw a laptop in his living room. Let's find out." I brought the computer to the table and fired it up only to find it password protected.

Jock called into the living room. "Hey, McAllister, what's the password for your computer?"

"Open sesame," said McAllister.

Jock made a face. "You're kidding me," he said, but typed the words into the computer. It came alive and I put the thumb drive in the port. A file marked "fun and games" popped up on the screen. I clicked on it and a large number of thumbnail pictures filled the screen. I clicked on the first one and saw a completely naked Katie Fredrickson lying on a bed. The next picture showed her having sex with McAllister. I was taken by the expressions on their faces. McAllister was laughing and looking past his shoulder, as if he were joking with the photographer. Katie's face showed nothing. Absolutely nothing. She could have been dead. Maybe part of her, the thinking part, was dead. I hoped so.

I let my eyes scan across the thumbnails without opening any more. "Jock," I said, "there're a lot of pictures here of Katie in sexual situations."

"I don't want to see them. Is McAllister there?"

"In at least one of the pictures. I don't want to open the others."

Jock got up and I followed him back into the living room. "McAllister," he said, "I'm about one inch away from using the blowtorch on you."

"Hey, man, I'm answering all your questions."

"How many times did you screw Katie Fredrickson?"

McAllister slumped in his chair. "We had a little affair. That was all. Didn't mean anything."

I slugged McAllister in the solar plexus and when he bent over struggling for breath, I hit him with an uppercut to the mouth, knocking him back into the chair. I knew what was happening. The Rage. That's what I called it. Sometimes, when I was very stressed, usually when somebody was trying to kill me, the Rage would take over. I could almost see red. It was like it was on the periphery of my vision, slowing spreading like a puddle to cover my entire visual field. I was standing off to the side somehow, knowing what was happening, watching myself being consumed, knowing it was wrong, and helpless to stop it. I wanted to kill, take no prisoners. I watched myself pick up the blowtorch, struggle to find an ignition source. I knew I was about to use it on his face. I wanted to wipe away the smirk I imagined was under the hood that covered his head.

Jock pulled the torch from my hands and wrapped me in a bear hug, restraining me. "It's okay, podna," he said softly in my ear. "It's okay. Let me take it from here."

It was over. The Rage left as suddenly as it had appeared. I felt drained and stumbled back to the sofa and slumped onto it. "I'm sorry, old buddy. I'm so goddamned sorry."

McAllister was gulping air. "You broke my nose. I'm bleeding all over the place. Get this hood off me. Untie me. Your buddy's a lunatic."

"Shut the fuck up," Jock said, low, quietly, menacing, "or so help me, I'll light you up with the blowtorch."

McAllister fell quiet. Jock looked at me and I nodded. The Rage wasn't a stranger to Jock. He'd seen it before. We'd talked about it. I never knew when it was going to come over me and I'd never discovered where it came from. J.D. thought it was probably rooted in my lousy childhood and maybe my war experiences. She'd urged me to talk to a shrink, to try to understand it, and, by doing so, banish it forever. I didn't take her advice. I didn't think I could talk to a shrink without revealing a lot more of myself than would be prudent.

The Rage had never taken me unless somebody was trying to kill me or kill a member of my family, which consisted of Jock, J.D., and Logan. Not until now, anyway. I'd have to think on that some.

"Okay, asshole," said Jock, leaning in close to McAllister. "Maybe you want to revise that last statement. You didn't have an affair. You raped the girl."

"No. It wasn't rape," McAllister said. "She never resisted."

Jock laughed. "How could she? You had her drugged to the gills."

"Have you found Katie?" he asked.

"Yes. She's safe."

"I'm glad," McAllister said.

"You're glad?"

"Yeah. I would've killed her if I could've found her, but I guess I'm done, so I'm glad she's okay."

"She's the one who's going to sink you when you get to a court of law."

"Maybe, but I doubt I'll live to see that."

"If you give me everything, I won't kill you," Jock said.

"I hear you."

"Tell me about the bank accounts," Jock paused to look at the bank statements, "in the banks in Tampa and Orlando."

"Nothing to tell. That's where I keep the drug money."

"Somebody would be looking into that if you made a bunch of large deposits."

"Most of the money was electronically deposited by some dummy corporations that were supposedly my employers, and some of it was deposited a few thousand at a time. Never more than ten grand, not enough to get the feds excited."

"Where did the ten million dollars wired to Jim Fredrickson's account the day before his death come from?" Jock asked.

"That was actually sent the day after his death. Evans simply changed the date of death on the estate documents he filed so that it appeared as if the deposit was made before he died. Otherwise, there would have been questions. Evans altered the death certificate that's part of the file. Check the date in the probate file against the police report. They're different, but Evans didn't think anybody would look that closely at it."

"Why the transfer?"

"We needed to get the money laundered. The submarine didn't work out and there was only so much we could feed into bank accounts like mine without somebody taking a look at it. Evans thought we could move the money into Fredrickson's account by showing it as compensation for the sale of the Avon Park property. All the paperwork had been done before he died, but Evans said that if the money had to be paid to the estate instead of to Jim, it could create a probate problem and the money might get tied up and take us a long time to get to it. We decided to simply move Jim's death forward a day."

"But you still don't have the money."

"No, but we know where it is and Evans controls it. Katie was the only beneficiary under the will and as soon as Evans can get her declared legally dead, we'll get the money."

"Are you sure?" I asked. "The probate court really controls it."

"Evans says if nobody contests any of the assets, we won't have any trouble."

"Who is Hammond, the guy who bought the property?" Jock asked.

"I think Hammond is Bonino, but I don't know that."

"What's your relationship with George Bass?"

"Only that he's Katie's dad. I talked to him every now and then to find out if Katie had been in touch with them."

"Are you telling me that you didn't know that Bass was part of the drug trade?"

"He wasn't."

"He told Katie that he and Fredrickson were in business together in the drug trade."

McAllister was quiet for a beat. "That's funny," he finally said.

"What's funny?" asked Jock.

"Jim must have told his father-in-law about what we were into, but that doesn't make sense."

"Why?"

"Jim hated the old man. Said he'd screwed up Katie in the worst possible way."

"Do you know what Jim meant by that?"

"Not really. He said that Katie had told him some things. Apparently she and Jim were having some problems in their sex life, and he attributed it to her old man. I assumed there had been some sexual abuse going on, but Jim never actually told me that."

"Then how else would Bass even have known that Jim was in the drug business?" asked Jock.

"I honestly don't know."

"Are you aware that Bass thinks he's going to inherit the ten million in the estate?" I asked.

"How would Bass even know about the money?" asked McAllister.

"Under state statutes," I said, "if Katie is dead, then George and Betty Bass are the remaining beneficiaries. They get the money."

"Evans didn't mention that."

"Maybe Evans doesn't know," said Jock.

"I don't understand," said McAllister.

"Not your problem," said Jock. "Did you send a goon named DeLuca to rough up Matt Royal?"

"No. I don't know anybody named DeLuca. And I didn't know Royal until I met him at King's condo the night of his death."

"The night you killed King and his girlfriend," Jock said.

"Yeah. That's what I meant."

"What did you have to do with Ken Goodlow's death?" Jock asked.

"Who's that?"

"A harmless old man who was killed on Longboat Key last week."

"Oh. That was King's deal."

"Tell me about it."

"The guy in New Jersey, the one who King had killed, said that there was an old man in Cortez who would know the answer. He said that he and the old man had been friends as young men back just after World War II."

"Did he give up a name?"

"No. He died. Apparently, a heart attack. He just keeled over dead, and King didn't get a name."

"How did Goodlow come into the picture?"

"There were only two old men in Cortez who were still alive and were around right after World War II. Goodlow and an old guy named Jamison. King put a couple of his men on them, surveillance, you know, and they followed them around. The day before the shooting on Longboat, the guy following Goodlow overheard him talking to a bartender about finding a lawyer. By then, he knew that the old man in Jersey had been killed. I guess he and Jamison were getting worried. Goodlow planned to see the lawyer the next day, so King had his button man follow him that day and make sure that he didn't get to the lawyer. He found the old man and shot him and then died when he went off the bridge."

"Who was the killer?"

"Somebody King knew from New Jersey."

"Was he Arabic?"

"Might have been. I heard King refer to him as Youssef."

"Any terrorist connections?"

"I doubt it. This guy was as American as I am. King said the guy was gay. Had a boyfriend in New Jersey."

"Did you ever see the documents from the sub?"

"I saw copies."

"A lot of pages?"

"No. Five, maybe."

"Did you know that Youssef had a copy of the first page of the coded message with him when he went off the bridge?"

"I don't know."

"Can you think of any reason he would have that with him?"

"I think King had cut Youssef and his boyfriend into the deal. They'd get a small piece of the action from the documents instead of cash."

"That seems a little odd, doesn't it?"

"Not if you knew King. He was a cheap bastard."

"I still don't understand why King was willing to kill Goodlow," said Jock. "If he was one of the men who might have the key to the code, wouldn't killing him destroy any chance of finding out what was in the document?"

"King was sure that Jamison was the one with the key. He thought killing Goodlow not only would keep him from talking, but send a strong message to Jamison. But he got caught short. King didn't expect Youssef to end up dead, so he had to import another hood to kidnap Jamison. Once he was in King's control, Jamison would give up the key."

"How was Jamison supposed to know the name of the book that was the key to the code?"

"We think he knew Reicheldorf some way. They may have gotten to know each other after the war. We weren't sure Jamison had the key, but he was the most likely suspect. He was also our last chance to figure out the documents."

Jock was quiet for a moment and then looked at me. "You got anything else?" he asked.

"No."

"I'll be right back," said Jock, and stepped out onto the front porch, pulling his phone from his jeans pocket.

He was back a couple of minutes later. "Captain," he said. "I'm going to give you a bottle of water from your refrigerator. I'll hold it to your mouth so you can drink as much as you want. If your hood comes off, you're dead. I'm going to cover you with a blanket and leave. In a couple of hours some men will be here to take you someplace where you can cool your heels until we figure out which law enforcement agency to turn you over to. Understand?"

"Yes," McAllister said just above a whisper. I was listening to a man whose life was over.

We packed up our things, including the documents from the safe and the thumb drive with the pictures and left. I knew Jock had called some men from his agency who would come down from Tampa and keep McAllister incommunicado until we were ready to put him in jail.

CHAPTER SIXTY-THREE

The ride into town was quiet, each of us lost in his own thoughts. We had a lot of the answers, but they had come at a cost to Jock and me, not to mention McAllister. I wasn't going to waste any time on sympathy for McAllister. He was a cretin, a dirty cop who sold his soul to the drug dealers. I would have been perfectly happy killing him for what he did to Katie, but I knew it was better to let the law handle this one. McAllister would spend the rest of his life in prison.

We needed to talk some more to Evans. I was sure that the pictures on McAllister's thumb drive would include some of Evans raping Katie, and I thought he hadn't told Jock everything he knew about the drug operation.

I was a bit puzzled by the situation with Bud Jamison. Who was he running from? On the other hand, he might have been taken by some of King's cronies. In that case, if Jamison knew the key to the code and had given it to the bad guys, he'd probably be buried in an orange grove in Avon Park.

"Jock," I said, "we need to talk to Evans again."

"That we do, podna. I'm thinking that it might be easy to meet him in his office. Maybe you ought to go see him. I don't think he'll try to bullshit you if he has an inkling as to how much you already know."

"It's worth a try." I looked at my watch. It was nearing six o'clock. "You want some breakfast?" I asked.

We pulled into the parking lot of a Denny's on Tamiami Trail and went inside. We were just finishing a breakfast that had a lot of grease and other things bad for the circulatory system when Jock's phone rang. He answered and then listened silently for a few moments.

"You're kidding me," he said, finally.

More quiet, then Jock said, "Okay. Make sure you don't leave any traces of your visit and get out of there. Use a secure phone to call the Sarasota Sheriff's office and give them some story that'll get deputies headed that way."

There was a little more conversation and Jock clicked the off button on the phone. "Bad news, podna," he said. "Somebody killed Captain McAllister."

"How?"

"Gunshot to the forehead. He still had the hood on. He never saw it coming."

"He got what he deserved," I said. "Do you think the killer knew we were there?"

"I don't think he was there when we were. He would have put a stop to our interrogation if he'd known about it. Finding McAllister trussed up like a Christmas turkey would have given the shooter good reason to think the captain had talked to somebody. The only reason to kill McAllister is to shut him up."

"Bonino, you think?" I asked.

"Bet on it."

"I'd better call Harry Robson and get some protection on Evans. He may be next on the list."

"I don't think that's a good idea," said Jock. "We're not supposed to know about McAllister's death and, without that, we'd have no reason to suspect that Evans is in danger."

He was right, of course, but I felt impotent, sitting there over the remains of breakfast while Evans might be about to be murdered. "Maybe we ought to go sit on him," I said.

Jock agreed. We paid our check and drove to Evans's house. Dawn was just beginning to lighten the sky when we turned onto Evans's street. Lights were on in all the neighboring houses. Two police cruisers were parked in front of Evans's house. An unmarked police car sat in the driveway behind a coroner's van. Uniformed cops were milling about in the front yard, bored, waiting for orders. "We're too late," Jock said, and kept driving.

"Somebody's cleaning up loose ends," I said. "Either we've got two killers or the one stopped here before going after McAllister."

"The cops look like they've been here a while. The killer probably took Evans out and then went for McAllister. If he'd done it the other way around he'd have found us with the captain. We got lucky."

"I wonder if he killed Evans's family."

"Let's get back to the key and get J.D. working on this. We need to know what happened."

I'd hardly gotten that out of my mouth when my phone rang. J.D. wanting to know where the hell we were. I told her that both McAllister and Evans were dead and asked if she could follow up and find out what the cops knew.

"Later," she said. "I need you back here to babysit Katie. I've got to go to a meeting. I just got a call from Bud Jamison."

CHAPTER SIXTY-FOUR

J.D. was waiting impatiently on the sofa, drinking coffee, when we walked into the house. She got up, kissed me on the cheek, and said, "See you later."

"Wait," I said. "What's going on?"

"Jamison called me an hour ago. He wants to meet me at seven in the Cracker Barrel Restaurant out on I-75. It'll take me forty-five minutes to get there and I'm already late. I'll fill you in when I get back."

"Take me with you," I said. "I can fill you in on the way about our meeting with McAllister."

"He said to come alone, and I'm not going to take the chance of spooking him. I'll call you when I get to the mainland. My duty phone is secure. I'll call you on Jock's phone, and you can tell me about McAllister. I've got to go."

Ten minutes later, J.D. called. She told me that Jamison had called about six o'clock, waking her up. He said he had to meet with her, but he wanted the meeting to be somewhere public, far enough away from Cortez that nobody would recognize him. They'd agreed on the Cracker Barrel.

I told her what McAllister had told us and about the photographs and documents I had. She agreed that we needed to find out about the bank accounts. She was particularly interested about the part dealing with Jamison and the submarine and the coded documents. I also told her that someone had killed McAllister after we left him and that something was going on at the Evans house.

"He fooled a lot of people for a long time," J.D. said. "I wish we could have brought him into a courtroom and put him in jail forever."

"Jock and I think Evans is probably dead, too."

"I wouldn't be surprised. I'll call Harry Robson at Sarasota P.D. later and see what he can tell me."

J.D. said she'd call me again after she talked to Jamison. She was planning to come straight home after meeting with him.

Jock's phone rang again thirty minutes later. He handed it to me. "J.D.," he said.

"Matt, I'm on Highway 64 almost to the Cracker Barrel. Jamison called and when I told him where I was, he told me to get on I-75 and drive south at exactly seventy miles per hour. He said he would time me and would call again when I should be nearing the exit that he wanted me to take. He's changing things up."

"It sounds like he's just being cautious," I said. "Call me as soon as you know where you're going."

I heard Katie stirring in the guest room and in a few minutes she walked into the living room. "Good morning," she said. "Is J.D. up yet?"

"She had to leave," I said. "What can I fix you for breakfast?"

"If you've got cereal and milk, that would be fine. And some coffee, please."

J.D. called back while I was getting another pot of coffee going. "He just called. Told me to exit at University Parkway and drive west. He's going to call again. I'm pulling off the ramp now."

"Do you have your gun?" I asked.

"Of course."

"Be careful. Stay in public view."

"I'll be fine," she said. "I'll call you when I get new instructions." She clicked off.

"He's running her all over the east county," I said to Jock.

"He's a careful man. He's thinking J.D. may be bringing the cops, or worse, with her."

"What's going on?" asked Katie.

I told her about the meeting with Jamison and how careful he was being.

"Who's Jamison?" she asked.

"An old man who was a friend of another old man murdered on the key last week. He disappeared a couple of days after the murder. We were afraid he was dead."

"So, he doesn't have anything to do with the drugs and Captain McAllister."

"Only tangentially," I said. "King and McAllister and the others had a side deal going. They were trying to find a key to decode some documents King found on a sunken World War II submarine. It was kind of a crazy scheme, but King apparently thought that Goodlow, the man murdered on the key, and Jamison were involved somehow. We think King was after Jamison, but it doesn't have anything to do with the drugs."

"If Mr. Jamison was involved with either McAllister or King," Katie said, "he's probably in trouble."

"Katie," I said, "I need to tell you something. We don't know the details yet, but we'll find out when J.D. gets back."

"This sounds bad," said Katie.

"Actually, I think it's a good thing. McAllister is dead and we think Evans is, too."

She sat back in the chair. "Tell me what you know," she said.

"Jock and I met with McAllister early this morning. He confirmed everything you had to say, by the way."

"Did you kill the bastard?"

"No. When we left, he was alive. But somebody put a bullet in his head shortly after we left him. We think Evans may have been killed by the same person, but we don't really know that. When we drove by his house an hour or so ago, there were cop cars all over the place. Something happened there. We'll know when J.D. can check in with the Sarasota cops and the sheriff's office."

Katie breathed out a long breath. "I guess that is good news," she said. "In a way. I'd like to have killed the bastards myself."

"It means you won't have to worry about them anymore."

"I guess," she said.

"Or face them in a courtroom."

"That would've been hard, but I planned on doing it. I was mostly afraid that McAllister, being a cop and all, would get away with everything. That nobody would believe me."

Jock's phone rang again. He answered and held it out to me. J.D. said, "He directed me to the short-term parking at the airport. I just got here, but don't see him. It's full daylight, so I'll just wait."

I heard the ding of the alarm signaling that one of the car doors in J.D.'s Camry had opened. "Never mind, he's here. Hang on for a minute."

A male voice came on the line. "Good morning, Mr. Royal. This is Bud Jamison. I assure you my intentions are benign. I need to talk to Detective Duncan. This won't take long and she's safe. She's got a gun and I don't."

"Tell her," I said, "to call me in fifteen minutes. If not, I'll call the cops."

"Not to worry," he said and hung up.

But I did worry. Calling the cops would be useless. In fifteen minutes, J.D. could be dead or so lost in the tangle of roads near the airport that we'd never find her. But then, she had her gun and she was a good cop. Tough and resilient. And she was in a very public place with cars and people coming and going.

I was too nervous to do much but pace the floor. Five minutes went by and my phone rang. J.D. "We're coming to your house," she said.

"We?"

"Jamison and I. You're not going to believe what he has to tell us."

CHAPTER SIXTY-FIVE

J.D. walked through the door, followed by a tall, slender man who, while obviously elderly, didn't look like he was in his nineties. She introduced Jock and me to Bud Jamison.

"Where's Katie?" she asked.

"In her room," I said. "She didn't want to get in the way."

"She's a part of this," J.D. said, and went to knock on Katie's door.

When we were all seated in my living room, J.D. said, "I wanted you to hear what Mr. Jamison has to say. He told me some of it, but I haven't heard all of it. I wanted to wait until we were together so he only has to go through it one time."

Jamison said, "This is a long story that covers a lot of years. I'll tell it all and answer any questions you have."

"Why did you disappear?" I asked.

"Some very bad men were looking for me."

"Then why resurface now?" I asked.

"One of the men, Porter King, was killed last weekend. I thought about it for a few days and decided that I needed to talk to Detective Duncan about the other man that would want to do me harm. I wasn't sure she wouldn't turn me over to the bad guy, so I went through some machinations today to make sure she wasn't bringing somebody with her."

"But you're here," I said.

"I told Detective Duncan that the leader of a group of very bad people was a cop; Captain Doug McAllister. When she told me that he was dead and what he'd said about King, I thought I could tell her the rest of the story and come out of hiding."

"Tell Katie who you are," said J.D.

He turned to look at Katie. "Do you recognize me?" he asked.

"I've seen you somewhere, but for the life of me, I can't remember where or when."

"I once drove you to the bus station in Tampa."

Surprise, or shock, or something suffused Katie's face. "Of course," she said. "You were in front of my house the night my husband was killed."

"Yes."

"I don't understand," Katie said.

"Let me show you something," Jamison said. He pulled a small photograph from his shirt pocket. It was a duplicate of one I'd seen in his bedroom when Jock and I searched the place, the one of the skinny woman standing in the surf holding an infant.

Katie took the photograph and looked at it for a moment. "Okay?" she said, a question in her tone.

"That's you and your biological mother," Jamison said, "taken when you were five days old."

This time the look on Katie's face was one of skepticism. "I don't understand," she said.

"Your mother was dying of cancer when that picture was taken. Your father was the captain of a long-line fishing boat and was lost at sea a few months before your birth."

"I don't understand," said Katie. "What happened to her?"

"She died a month after that picture was taken."

"How did you get this picture?"

"I took it."

"Who is the woman?"

"My daughter," Jamison said.

Now Katie looked puzzled. She was quiet while she worked it out. "I'd like to hear the story," she said.

Jamison smiled. "Your mom's name was Melanie. Melanie Jamison. My wife died in childbirth, bringing Melanie into the world. I raised her by myself, with a lot of help from the people of Cortez. I left the sea and took work in the fish houses. Sometimes, I had to go back to sea for a few weeks to make enough money to keep us in food. When I had to leave, Ken Goodlow and his wife took Melanie in and took care of her.

"She grew up to be a wonderful young lady, smart and full of life. She graduated from high school and went up to Tampa to the University of South Florida. When she finished, she came home and took a job teaching at Manatee High School. She got married and within a year was pregnant with you."

"What happened?" Katie asked. She was intent now, focused on Jamison, intrigued by the story, but perhaps still skeptical, not believing what Jamison was telling her.

"As I said, her husband, your father, was the captain of a long-line fishing boat that would be at sea for several weeks at a time. One day, the boat didn't return. A bad storm had come up the Gulf from south of the Yucatán. There was no warning. It developed fast and moved north with tropical storm winds. We're pretty sure your father's boat was caught in the storm. There was no more radio contact and the Coast Guard couldn't find any trace of the boat. A few months after the boat disappeared, when your mom was in the last stage of her pregnancy, some debris washed ashore down on Marco Island. They were able to identify it as coming from your father's boat."

"Tell me about the cancer," Katie said.

"Your mom was pretty sick during the pregnancy, but it got worse, and the doctors did a lot of tests. They found the cancer, but it was too late. They told us that if your mom underwent chemo and radiation treatments, she had a slim chance of beating it. But, the treatments would kill you. She thought it would be better to save you than try to hang onto life. I have to tell you that I argued with her about the decision. I didn't want to lose her."

"But you did," said Katie. "Lose her."

"Yes."

"Why not keep the baby?" Katie asked. I noticed that she didn't refer to the little girl as "me," just "the baby." She still wasn't convinced.

"I was in my fifties," Jamison said, "and still working the boats some. I knew I couldn't raise a child the way she should be. Melanie and I talked it over and decided to put you up for adoption."

Katie smiled. "I think you have the wrong girl, Mr. Jamison," she said. "I was left at a fire station in Orlando."

"No," said Jamison, "you weren't. I contacted a lawyer I knew in Bradenton, and he arranged a private adoption. Melanie and I took you to his office right after that photo was made. It was the hardest thing I've ever done, other than burying my wife and daughter."

"My adoptive father told me I was left at a fire station."

"I can see your skepticism, but if you'll think about it, you'll see that I could have no motive whatsoever to make up such a story. A simple DNA test will confirm that I'm your grandfather."

"Who was my birth father?"

"His name was Brian Fox. Melanie met him at the university. He'd been in the Coast Guard before starting college and when Melanie brought him to Cortez, he was able to get a job as a captain on one of the boats."

"Are his parents still alive?" Katie asked.

"No. They probably died years ago. They lived in Michigan, and I don't think Melanie ever met them. There had been some friction between Brian and his parents, and he never even told them about Melanie being pregnant. I was never in touch with them."

"So," said Katie, "my mother's name was Melanie Jamison Fox."

"Yes," said Jamison. "But even that was a lie."

"I don't understand," said Katie.

"My name is not Jamison."

"What, then?" I asked. I wasn't sure if what he was telling Katie was true, but I couldn't see any reason for him to lie, either. The fact that he had been living under an assumed name might shed some light on the whole mess.

Jamison laughed. "It's a long story," he said, "but my real name is Paulus Graf von Reicheldorf."

CHAPTER SIXTY-SIX

"Reicheldorf was killed in Germany a few weeks ago," I said. "What the hell are you selling?"

"The dead man in Germany," said Reicheldorf, "was my cousin, the son of my father's younger brother."

"You didn't tell me about this," J.D. said to the old man.

"Sorry, Detective," Jamison or Reicheldorf said. "I didn't think it important. I wanted to go to my grave as Bud Jamison."

"Tell me about this cousin," I said.

"My cousin was known by his middle name Ernst. In our family the firstborn sons carried the first name of Paulus, the name of the first graf in our line, but, except for the heir to the title, each son was called by his middle name. If for some reason one of the other sons succeeded to the title, he was thereafter called Paulus. When I was lost at sea in 1942, my cousin inherited the title."

"You were lost at sea?" J.D. asked.

"Yes. In 1942."

"What's a graf?" asked Katie.

"It's the German equivalent of a count," said Reicheldorf.

"I thought you grew up in the Washington, D.C. area," J.D. said.

"I did. My father was an officer in the German Navy during World War I and later, during the Weimar Republic, became a diplomat assigned to the German Embassy in Washington. We came to the U.S. when I was about four years old and stayed for ten years. When the Nazis took over the German government, my father resigned and we returned to Germany. I had gone to American schools and spoke English with an American accent."

"What happened when you returned to Germany?" asked Katie.

"My family was ostracized from the government, but we had varied business interests that my father and his brother oversaw. We weren't poor. I finished school and enrolled at Heidelberg University."

"Ah," I said. "Thus the dueling scar."

He touched his left cheek and laughed. "Yes, the foolishness of youth. I guess we were proving our manhood, but we were headed into a war that would test that with much more severity than a game of fencing."

"How in the world did you end up in Cortez?" I asked.

"After Naval Officers School and a tour of sea duty, I was assigned to the Abwehr, the German Intelligence Agency. My parents were killed in an air raid on Hamburg right after I joined the navy and one of my father's old comrades from World War I had become the head of Abwehr."

"Admiral Canaris," I said.

"Yes. He felt that it was his job to shield me from the horrors of war. I disagreed. I hated the Nazis, but I thought it my duty to fight for Germany. We were an old civilization and tyrants had come and gone. I didn't think Hitler would last more than a few years, certainly not the thousand-year reign he envisioned for the Nazi party.

"I talked the admiral into sending me on a mission which turned out to be a fatal one. I was ordered to act as a courier for some documents that were going to a German spy ring in San Antonio, Texas. I boarded a U-boat that would drop me off the coast near Galveston. As it turned out, we were sunk by an American plane near St. George Island up in the panhandle. I was the only survivor. I rowed a lifeboat ashore and gave myself up to a lighthouse keeper on St. George."

"You walk with a limp," said J.D. "Is that a souvenir of the U-boat sinking?"

Reicheldorf smiled ruefully. "No," he said, "that was inflicted on me by some Nazis in a prisoner-of-war camp at Camp Blanding up in north Florida near Jacksonville. There were two groups of prisoners, those like me who had no use for the Nazis and those who were rabid about the cause. There was a big riot one evening, with the groups fighting each other. I got hit in the knee by some kind of heavy bar. It caused a lot of damage, and the American doctors at the camp didn't have the tools or knowledge to do much about fixing it."

"How long were you in the POW camp?" J.D. asked.

"Only about three months. It became apparent that I was marked for death by the Nazis. An informer told one of the guards, an American military policeman, that I would be killed in another riot that was to take place soon. The MP came to me to discuss it. He spoke very little German and I had not revealed to anyone that I spoke English. Once I got the gist of what the MP was trying to tell me in German, I responded to him in English. He helped get me out of the camp. The records were a bit chaotic that early in the war, so I don't think anyone ever really knew I had been there, much less that I was gone."

"How did you survive with no identification and no money?" J.D. asked.

"The Abwehr had provided me with some very good forgeries, passport, driver's license, birth certificate, all kind of documents to make me appear American."

"You had them with you in the POW camp?" Jock asked.

"No. Before I turned myself in at the St. George lighthouse, I buried the documents. I went back and got them."

"How did you get back to St. George?" J.D. asked.

"Hitchhiked. The MP had given me twenty dollars, which amounted to almost a month's pay for him. It was enough to keep me going for a while. He'd also hidden some old clothes outside the camp's wire, so once he got me out, I buried the prison uniform, put on the clothes, and started walking west. Nobody questioned me except one man in a small grocery store where I stopped to buy food. He was wondering why I wasn't in the service. I showed him the scars on my knee and told him I'd crashed a motorcycle and wasn't physically fit for the military.

"Once I retrieved my identity documents, I was home free. From that moment on, I was John Jamison, nicknamed Bud."

"How did you find out about Cortez?" Katie asked.

"The MP who saved my life at Camp Blanding was born and raised in Cortez. His name was Ken Goodlow."

CHAPTER SIXTY-SEVEN

The room was silent. I think we were starting to see the threads of two disparate mysteries come together. "Did anyone else in Cortez know who you really were?" I asked.

"Not at first. Ken knew, of course, but he was sent overseas right after he helped me escape. I got a job with old Captain Longstreet and fell in love with his daughter, Bess. Ken came home when the war was over and we decided that we'd keep the whole thing secret. The only other person who knew the story was Bess Longstreet, and I didn't tell her until just before we were married. If she'd backed out of the wedding, I would have left Cortez."

"You must have told Rodney Vernon," J.D. said. "Otherwise, how would he have been in contact with your cousin in Germany?"

"After the war, the Allies restored some of my family's business holdings. Ernst was running them and beginning his rise in the new political atmosphere. He'd spent the war years in Sweden and had become friendly with Willy Brandt, who after the war, became mayor of Berlin and then chancellor of Germany. After Melanie was born, I began to think about how I was cutting her off from a family that she might someday want to know. I decided to make contact with Ernst, but I didn't want him to know my assumed name or where I was living. I was perfectly happy with my new life and didn't want to go back to Germany. I was also afraid that I'd probably violated a bunch of American laws by coming into the country the way I had and living under a false identity. I didn't want to be prosecuted and deported.

"Rodney and I had become close friends and when he moved back to New Jersey, I asked him to mail a letter for me. I figured no one would be able to trace a New Jersey postmark back to Cortez. I wrote Ernst and told him I was fine and would stay in touch. I mentioned some things in the letter that only he and I would have known about so that he would know that I was really writing the letter. I gave him Rodney's address and told him he could communicate with me through him. I told Rodney that it was very important that my name and whereabouts be kept secret, and he honored that. Ernst honored my request as well, and never tried to find me or to question Rodney about me. We corresponded once or twice a year, first by letter and much later by e-mail. I'd send an e-mail to Rodney, he'd copy and paste it and send it on to Ernst."

"Whoever killed Vernon took his computer," I said. "The killers were Porter King's people, so that's probably how King made the connection to you. The e-mail exchanges."

"You're probably right, Mr. Royal," said Reicheldorf. "The only connection between Ernst and me was through Rodney."

"And," said J.D., "the Toms River detective told me that the only people Vernon emailed were his children, you, and your cousin. That had to be the connection. But why would they kill Ken Goodlow?"

"That was my fault," said Reicheldorf. "Ken knew about my correspondence with Ernst and Rodney's connection to it. I had no idea why Ernst and Rodney had been killed, but the only connection between them had to do with me. The only reason I'd be important to anybody would be my time in the Abwehr. When I began looking into it, I found an article on the Internet about U-166 being discovered a couple of years ago. The U.S. government took a look at it with a submersible and then left it alone as a gravesite.

"I was presumed dead, lost at sea. The German government would have made that decision when U-166 didn't return from its patrol. But, if the killers thought Ernst was me, they might have come after him for some reason. Maybe they became convinced that Ernst was exactly who he said he was, but told them about our correspondence through Rodney. They then went to Rodney and found my name and made the connection that I was the one corresponding with Ernst and therefore must be the Abwehr agent."

"Did you figure out why they might be looking for you?"

"Not at first. I read some of the German newspapers online and saw an article about Ernst's death. I tried to call Rodney, but didn't get an answer. I left a voice mail, but he didn't call back. After a couple of days, I went to the online version of the *Toms River Times* and found an article about Rodney's death. I figured that somebody was looking for me and would know where I was.

"A couple of days later, two days before Ken's murder, a man came to my door and introduced himself as Porter King. He asked if I knew Rodney and Ernst. I told him I knew Rodney, but didn't know Ernst. I didn't have any idea what they might have told King when they were being tortured, but I knew neither one of them would have given me up if they could have helped it.

"King showed me a document that I recognized instantly. It was the first page of the documents that I was delivering to San Antonio when U-166 was sunk. I told him I had no idea what it was. He asked me if I knew anybody named Reicheldorf. I told him I didn't. I don't think he believed me."

"What did you do after King showed up?" I asked.

"I called Ken and told him what had happened. We decided that King was looking for the key to the code. The key was a book and without knowing which book, the code is virtually unbreakable. King, or somebody, must have discovered the documents in the U-166's safe. I had no idea what was in those documents, but it must have been important for somebody to torture and kill two old men."

"Do you know why Mr. Goodlow was killed?" J.D. asked.

"I think it must have been because Ken was planning to talk to a lawyer. He thought that I should meet with one and see what we could do about the documents and my immigration status."

"How would the killer have known that?" J.D. asked.

"I don't know. Ken thought somebody was electronically eavesdropping on us. I didn't put much credence in that, but maybe somebody was. After he died, I remembered that he had gotten the name of a lawyer from Nick Field over at the Seafood Shack. Maybe somebody overheard the conversation and didn't want Ken talking."

"I understand," said Jock, "that a couple of your friends died during the last year or so. Ones you had coffee with every morning. Were they involved in this?"

"You're talking about Mack Hollister and Bob Sanders. The answer is no. They had been my friends since the war, and I watched them wither and die."

"You don't think their deaths were suspicious?"

"No. Mack died of pancreatic cancer. Took him five agonizing months to die. Bob had a bad heart and it caught up with him. He dropped dead walking to the post office."

"What made you run?" I asked.

"If they killed Ken, I assumed I'd probably be next. They'd torture me until I gave up the key and then kill me. I got in my car and went to the airport, parked it in long-term and took a taxi to downtown Sarasota, another one to the Manatee Memorial Hospital in Bradenton, and one more to a hotel at I-75 and Highway 64. I've been hiding out there ever since."

"Do you remember the name of the book that was the key?" Jock asked.

Reicheldorf nodded. "The instructions were in German, but the code was based on English. The book was part of the King James Version of the Bible. Fitting, as it turned out. The key was the Book of Job."

CHAPTER SIXTY-EIGHT

"Why were you in front of my house that night?" Katie asked. She'd sat quietly during Jamison/Reicheldorf's story. I had watched the hard edge of skepticism drain slowly from her body language. Her face, at first tight with a look of disbelief, had relaxed into some kind of partial acceptance. Was she beginning to believe that Reicheldorf was really her grandfather?

Reicheldorf smiled. "I stopped by there on a regular basis," he said. "I could never stay long without attracting attention, but occasionally I'd see you walking the dog or driving out of your driveway. Just glimpses, really, but I sometimes caught flashes of your mother in the way you carried yourself or bent over to pet your dog or smiled at a neighbor."

"Were you stalking me?" Katie asked.

Reicheldorf laughed. "Probably," he said. "But I meant no harm. I was in the audience the day you graduated from Winter Park High School and again when you walked across the stage to get your diploma at Florida International University. I watched a number of your volleyball games when you were competing in high school. I couldn't be part of your life, but I could stand on the edges and admire the young woman you'd become. Your mom and grandmother would have been so proud."

"Were you ever going to tell me who you were?" Katie asked.

"I don't know. I assumed you knew you were adopted, but I didn't know how you would feel about meeting me, or hearing the story of your biological mother."

"My parents never told me I was adopted," Katie said. "Not until my dad blew up and threw it in my face. If you really are my grandfather, how did you find me?"

"I never lost you. The lawyer in Bradenton who handled the adoption was a friend of mine and he told me from the beginning that you had been adopted by the Basses. He made me promise not to interfere in any way, and I kept that promise. Well, mostly." He chuckled. "Aside from stalking you."

"Why were you so interested in me?" asked Katie.

"Except for my cousin Ernst, you were the only family I had left. Ernst was gay, so he would never have children. You were it. And I'd loved my daughter so much and missed her so much. You were a link, a tenuous one to be sure, but still a link to that bright little girl I raised from birth and buried before her twenty-fifth birthday."

"This is hard for me to get my head around," Katie said.

"I'm sure it is," said Reicheldorf. "When we get things cleared up around here, we can run DNA tests. If you're not my granddaughter, you'll never hear from me again. And if you are, you'll set the parameters of our relationship."

J.D.'s phone rang. She looked at the caller ID, excused herself, and walked out to the patio. I looked at my watch. Almost eleven. The morning was slipping by. When J.D. returned, she said, "That was Harry Robson, the Sarasota detective. He told me that Captain Doug McAllister was shot to death this morning at his home and the body of Wayne Evans was found in his home. They were shot by the same pistol. Robson found some documents in Evans's house that were similar to the one we found on Ken Goodlow's murderer. He wants me to take a look at them."

"What about Evans's family?" I asked.

"They weren't home. They were visiting family over on the east coast. Vero Beach, I think Robson said."

"I'd like to get my hands on those documents," Jock said. "My people can run them through a computer program and have them translated very quickly."

"Harry scanned them," said J.D. "He's e-mailing them to me this morning."

"I can't imagine that they're of any importance today," said Reicheldorf. "I wonder how something so useless could bring about so many deaths."

"King seemed to think they might contain references to money or bank accounts. Something he could use to find money. Or maybe names that he could use to blackmail the families of Americans who were Nazi sympathizers."

"That seems like a long shot," Reicheldorf said.

"King was probably insane," I said. "McAllister said he was obsessed with the documents. In the end, they got him killed. Sometimes justice takes some strange twists."

CHAPTER SIXTY-NINE

It was late in the afternoon, two days after the meeting with Reicheldorf, when Jock and a FBI agent named Lisa Coyle pulled to a stop in the parking lot of a branch office of a medium-size community bank. They were chasing ten million dollars.

The Sarasota police department had found documents in Wayne Evans's files that indicated that the wire transfer to Jim Fredrickson the day after his death had originated with the specific branch of this particular bank. The wire had been sent by a loan officer, the only loan officer assigned to this branch.

The branch office was on the first floor of a two-story red brick building located in an upscale section of Orlando. The bank would be closing in minutes. Jock and Lisa walked through the front door and went to a teller. Lisa showed her credentials and asked to speak to the branch manager. The teller went to a phone, returned, and said the boss would be right out. In a couple of minutes a blonde woman in her mid-thirties came into the lobby. "I'm Laura Hargrove, the branch manager," she said. "What can I do for you?"

"I'm Special Agent Lisa Coyle and this is Jock Algren. We need to talk to you privately."

Hargrove led them into a small office off the lobby and took a seat behind her desk. "Can I get you something to drink?" she asked.

"No, thanks," said Lisa. "This shouldn't take long. You have a loan officer here named Travis Watson."

"Not anymore," Hargrove said.

"May I ask why he left?" asked Lisa.

"It was a mutual agreement."

"Ms. Hargrove," said Lisa, "I can get a bunch of bank examiners in here before dinner this evening and I'll have a warrant for all your personnel records by breakfast tomorrow. I think it would be in your best interest and that of your bank to answer my questions. Do I make myself clear?"

"Yes," said Hargrove, "I get it. Your tone sounds just like my mother did when she was in a bad mood. I asked Watson to resign. If he hadn't, I would have fired him."

"Why?"

"He opened a business account for a customer with a little over ten million dollars in it. That was good for the bank, of course, but it wasn't too long before ten million was wired out of the account, leaving a couple hundred dollars. There were never any other deposits made, and after about six months, I asked Watson what was going on. He gave me some malarkey about the business falling on hard times, but I couldn't find any references to the business anywhere. It started to look to me like a scam of some sort, and I couldn't get any straight answers out of Watson. I talked to the president of the bank and we agreed to let Watson go."

"You didn't alert the authorities?" Lisa asked.

"No."

"Why not?"

"The president said that what was done was done, and he didn't see any reason to open a can of worms."

"Do you know where Watson is now?"

"No."

"Is the account still active?"

Hargrove pulled out a keyboard, typed a bit, and peered at the monitor. "Yes," she said.

"We'll need to see all the information you have on that account," Lisa said.

"I'm not sure I can give that to you without a warrant."

"You might want to call your president. Mention to him that the FBI is in your office and that the agent is a bit pissed that nobody in this bank saw fit to let anybody in law enforcement know about the bogus account. Tell him that the government frowns on money laundering."

Laura Hargrove turned ashen, all the color leaving her face. She stood.

"Give me a moment," she said and walked out of the room. She returned in about ten minutes with a stack of paper. "This is the entire account history, including the initial application. It's not much."

"I'm glad the president saw the light," Lisa said.

"He didn't," said Hargrove. "He said to tell you to go piss up a rope. I quit, downloaded the documents, and I'll start looking for work tomorrow. I won't be a party to anything illegal. I try to run a squeaky-clean operation."

"Thank you, Laura," said Lisa. She laid one of her business cards on the desk. "Let me know if I can be of any help in your job hunting."

"Thanks. I may go back to teaching school in Atlanta. Not as many headaches."

Back in the car, Jock said, "We've got to find Watson. Do you want to have my people look into his whereabouts?"

"You can probably get it quicker than I can."

Jock made a phone call, was put on hold for a couple of minutes, and hung up. He turned to Lisa and said, "He lives south of town in the Conway area."

The house was large and new and took up several hundred feet of lakefront. A very expensive piece of property. There was no answer to Lisa's knocks on the front door. She and Jock walked around to the side of the house and peered through a window into a two-car garage.

"Two cars inside," said Lisa. "Let's check the back."

The backyard sloped down to the lake, a massive expanse of manicured grass spotted with flower beds. A large, screened swimming pool was part of a patio that was attached to the rear of the house. A man's body, clad only in a swimsuit, lay with the upper torso in the water and the rest of the body on pool deck.

Lisa took out her phone and dialed 911. She identified herself as an FBI agent and said that she'd found a dead man and would like for Orlando police officers to respond as quickly as possible. Less than two minutes later, Lisa and Jock heard the sound of sirens and a few minutes later two uniformed police officers walked into the backyard. "What've you got?" one asked.

"I'm FBI Special Agent Lisa Coyle." She showed the cop her credentials. "We're looking for a man named Travis Watson who lives here. I don't know if that's him in the pool. We didn't want to disturb anything until your crime-scene people clear the area."

"Good thinking," said the officer. He looked at Jock. "Are you an agent as well?"

"Yes, but not FBI."

"May I see some credentials?"

Jock handed him a small case with a picture ID card that identified him as a special representative of the president of the United States.

"Political?" asked the cop.

"No. Intelligence," said Jock.

The officer handed the case back to Jock. "Thank you, sir," he said and stood almost at attention.

The other cop said, "I've called for the detectives and the crime-scene unit. They should be here shortly."

"I don't think we need to wait around and get in the way," Lisa said. She gave him a business card and asked that he call her as soon as they had any information. "I won't interfere with your murder investigation," she said. "I'm simply looking into some bank-fraud matters. Mr. Watson was a witness to some of that. If that's him in the pool, I'm probably finished."

CHAPTER SEVENTY

Two hours later, Jock's cell phone rang. Agent Coyle had dropped him at his hotel in downtown Orlando and gone back to her office in the federal building a few blocks away. She was on the phone.

"I just got a call from the Orlando detective working the Watson homicide. It was definitely Watson. He was shot in the head with a .22-caliber pistol. The medical examiner's initial estimate is that Watson had only been dead a couple of hours when we found him."

"I'm not sure where we go from here."

"We may not be dead in the water yet," Coyle said. "No pun intended."

"Right," said Jock, laughing.

"It looks as if Watson had been tortured. He had some knife slices on his belly. They weren't deep, but probably hurt like hell."

"Sounds like somebody wanted some information."

"Does the name George Bass mean anything to you?"

"Yes, it does. Why?"

"Watson made several calls to Bass in the three or four hours before his death."

"What makes you think Bass is involved? He may just have been a good friend."

"Well, if that's so, Watson's good friend was killed an hour ago in a hit-and-run accident in downtown Winter Park. The police found the car within ten minutes. It was abandoned on the Rollins College campus. It was stolen earlier this afternoon."

"Prints?"

"Wiped clean."

"Maybe Bass was just in the wrong place at the wrong time," said Jock. "Got run over by some kid out joyriding in a stolen car."

"That might be true, but then what would the kid have been doing in Watson's neighborhood at about the time he was killed?"

"Crap. Too much of a coincidence. Who saw the car in Watson's neighborhood?"

"The lady who lives across the street. She described it exactly. Didn't get a tag number, so we can't be positive it was the same car, but I don't think that kind of a coincidence happens."

"I agree," said Jock. "Bass has been on our radar for a while now."

"You didn't mention this to me for what reason?"

"I didn't want you to get too far out in front of the investigation. If you knew Bass was possibly a target, you might have overlooked something that would have led us in a different direction."

"I'm a better cop than that," said Lisa.

"I know that now. I'm sorry."

"Apology accepted. Do you want to talk to the Winter Park detective who's investigating the hit-and-run?"

"Absolutely."

"He'll meet us at the scene in thirty minutes. I'll pick you up in front of the hotel."

George Bass had been run over as he crossed Park Avenue in front of city hall. He'd just left a SunTrust Bank branch. There were a number of witnesses, all of whom saw something different. No two stories matched. It was a shocking event to have happen on a tranquil street late on a Friday afternoon.

Dark had fallen by the time Jock and Lisa arrived and the Winter Park police had blocked off two blocks of the street. Light wagons had been arranged around the scene and forensic technicians were crawling around on all fours looking for evidence.

"Several people said they thought the car may have been waiting for Mr. Bass," said the Winter Park detective. "Nobody paid much attention to the car, but it was idling in a parking space in front of the old theater building just up the street. That's not unusual around here, but this guy shot out of the space at a high rate of speed, hit Mr. Bass, and kept going. He turned right onto Fairbanks, but must have doubled back onto the Rollins campus, because that's where we found the car."

"You don't think it was an accident," Lisa said.

"Doesn't look like it," said the detective.

"Have you notified his family?"

"Yes. He only has a wife. No children."

"How's she taking it?" asked Jock.

"Surprisingly well," the detective said. "I was caught off guard. I was expecting a lot more grief."

"Do you mind if we go by and speak to her?" Jock asked.

The detective hesitated. "Just what is your interest in this?" he asked.

"Like I told you on the phone," said Lisa. "We're investigating a bank-fraud case and Mr. Bass was tied to the man killed in Orlando today, Travis Watson. Watson was a target of our investigation. It's just too coincidental that both were killed on the same day and there's no connection."

Jock spoke. "I'm hoping she can shed some light on what kind of activities her husband may have been engaged in that could have gotten him killed."

"I'm not sure I understand your involvement in this, Mr. Algren," said the detective. "Why would a federal intelligence agent be interested in a murder in Winter Park?"

"The FBI is looking into bank fraud, and I'm interested in money laundering. We think that might have been going on here and may have been what got Bass and Warner killed."

"Well, then, be my guest," said the detective, "but don't forget, the homicide investigation is mine. Let me know if you come across anything that'll help me find a murderer."

CHAPTER SEVENTY-ONE

Betty Bass seemed unruffled when she answered the door a little after eight o'clock that evening. Special Agent Coyle introduced herself and Jock. "I'm sorry to intrude at a time like this, but I need to talk to you about your husband."

"Come in. Now's as good a time as any. I can't say I wasn't expecting you."

"You were expecting the FBI?" asked Lisa Coyle.

"You or some other law enforcement people."

They followed her to the living room and took seats. "Why were you expecting us?" Lisa asked.

"My husband was a crook. I don't know what he was into, but it had to be illegal. I can't say that I'm sorry he's dead."

Lisa leaned in, her voice quiet, sympathetic. "You want to tell us about it?"

"I can tell you what I know, but I'm afraid it's not a lot. Five or six years ago, George began to have very good years with his brokerage business. There was a lot more money coming in than there had been in the years before."

"And that made you suspicious?" Lisa asked.

"Not at first. That business always has ups and downs, but even when the stock market took a big hit, George kept making more and more money. I began to think it was coming from somewhere other than the brokerage business."

"How much money are we talking about?" Lisa asked.

"I don't know. We were doing fine and George spent a lot of money on refurbishing the house, bought a new and expensive car, that sort of thing. Not spectacular amounts, but more than we'd had to spend in the past."

"And that made you suspicious?"

"Not really, but one day I found a briefcase full of cash. It was sitting on the desk in his office here at the house, and I moved it to dust under it. It was heavier than I suspected, and I dropped it. It wasn't locked and it fell open when it hit the floor. The briefcase was stuffed with cash. Bundles of one hundred dollar bills. A lot of bundles."

"Did you confront your husband about it?" Lisa asked.

"I did, but he told me it was some money a client had given him to invest and he hadn't gotten around to putting it in the bank."

"Did you find that suspicious?"

"Sure. I'd never heard of a client, an honest one at least, handing out briefcases full of cash. That's usually handled by check, isn't it?"

"Usually."

"It was about this time that George became abusive," Betty said. "He'd always been a bit distant, but suddenly he just got mean. He'd be gone for days at a time, without explanation. If I asked where he'd been, he'd tell me it was none of my business. He had a short temper and nothing ever seemed to satisfy him. He began to talk about moving to an island somewhere, crazy talk like that. We couldn't afford to move, and we've been in this house for years. I didn't want to go anywhere at my age. He told me he'd go without me. Things like that."

"Was he physically abusive?" asked Lisa.

"No. He never hit me."

"Why didn't you leave him?"

"I was thinking about it. I even went to see a lawyer, but then our daughter was killed last year. Murdered. That took the heart out of me. I didn't want to live. George seemed not to care that Katie was dead. I was so devastated that I couldn't get out of bed some mornings."

Jock spoke for the first time. "Mrs. Bass," he said, "I understand that a man named Matt Royal came to see you last week."

"Yes." She smiled. "He's a nice man. The boyfriend of a detective who was almost like a daughter to us."

"Did you tell him any of this?"

"No. He was helping J. D. Duncan, that's the detective over on the west coast, look into Katie's murder. It didn't seem pertinent."

"Was there any tension between Katie and your husband?" Jock asked.

"A lot. Katie wouldn't come visit much when George was here. If he was out of town, she'd come over for a day or two. We never spent more than one night at a time with her in Sarasota, because there just seemed to be something between George and Katie."

"Did you ever ask either one what that was all about?" asked Jock.

"Yes, but they only said that it was nothing, that they just didn't get along well. They'd just grown apart. It was more than that, but I never did figure it out."

"Was there anything else that made you suspicious of your husband?" Lisa asked.

"He always had several cell phones with numbers in the 941 area code. The Sarasota area code. I asked about them once and he got so angry that I was afraid to bring them up again. He seemed to conduct a lot of business on them."

"Do you know a man named Travis Watson?" asked Lisa.

"Yes. He's George's banker."

"Did the money continue to come in?"

"That's one of the funny things. After I found the briefcase full of cash, the money seemed to dry up. We had enough to live on, but that was coming from retirement accounts that George had set up years ago. It was like the faucet was turned off. Then one day a couple of years ago, when George was on one of his out-of-town trips, I found a file on his desk. He usually kept that in a safe, and I didn't have the combination. The file was full of bank statements under different names in different banks. I didn't understand them, but they all had a post office box address in Winter Park. The same address. And there was a lot of money in each one of them. It totaled millions of dollars."

"Did you ask your husband about them?" asked Lisa.

"Yes. He exploded. Told me if I ever mentioned them again, he'd kill me. I took him seriously. I went to see a lawyer the next day about a divorce."

"Katie was adopted, wasn't she?" asked Jock, changing the subject abruptly.

Betty looked surprised. "Yes," she said. "How did you know?"

"Did Katie know that she wasn't your birth child?" Jock asked.

"No."

"Why didn't you tell her?"

"We thought it would be best if she didn't know. What good would it have done for her to know that?"

"Did you go through an adoption agency?" Jock asked.

"No. It was a private adoption. All legal and everything. The lawyers handled it. We went to court and got the adoption approved. What's this got to do with George's legal problems?"

"Maybe nothing," Jock said. "Does the name Sal Bonino mean anything to you?"

Betty Bass's jaw literally dropped, her eyes widened in shock. "Yes," she said. "How do you know that name?"

"Who is he?" Jock asked.

"Salvatore Bonino was a little boy who lived in Italy and was horribly abused by his parents. When he was four years old, his parents were killed in some sort of gang murder. Little Sal was taken in by an American couple who worked in Rome toward the end of World War II. They brought him to the U.S. right at the end of the war, gave him their name and raised him as their own. It was all very secretive because Sal was never adopted legally."

"How do you know about Sal?" asked Lisa.

"The couple who brought him to this country was named Bass. They gave Sal an English name. George."

CHAPTER SEVENTY-TWO

February passed into history and, as it does every March, spring slipped early onto Longboat Key. The jacaranda, frangipani, and begonias were all in bloom, giving the island a tropical feel. Sunbathers were back on the beach, the air was dry and warm and spiced with the scent of flowers. Walkers and joggers smiled and greeted each other and chugged on their way, getting the exercise they had been robbed of by our colder mornings. We were done with winter and even as mild as the season is our latitudes, the islanders were glad to see the temperature inch into the high seventies.

Katie was still staying in my guest room, venturing out only in the evening for walks with either me or J.D. She was getting a bad case of cabin fever, but we didn't think it was safe for her yet; not until we solved the Bonino equation.

Reicheldorf had gone back to his house in Cortez and was still living as Bud Jamison. He and Katie had confirmed their relationship through DNA testing, and she was becoming more at ease with the idea of having a grandfather. Bud visited us every couple of days, often staying for dinner. He and Katie talked for hours, filling the gaps in their lives. Katie was amused by the fact that she was now a German countess.

Jock had called from Orlando on Friday of the week before and told us about George Bass's death and that there was a connection to an Orlando banker named Travis Watson who'd been murdered. He said he thought he'd solved the Bonino puzzle, but wanted some time to confirm what he'd been told. He planned to be back on Longboat Key with all the answers by the end of the following week.

On the last day of the first week of March, Jock showed up at my cottage, a big smile on his face, the kind he gets when all is right in his world. That usually meant that he'd just broken ninety in a round of golf. This day was different. He'd solved the Bonino puzzle and wanted to talk to J.D. and me outside the presence of Katie.

I called Logan Hamilton and asked him to come over and stay with Katie while I took Jock and J.D. to lunch. I didn't think she was in any danger, but Logan was a tough guy and, if needed, he could protect her as well as I could.

We walked the two blocks to Mar Vista and took a table under the trees. The place was crowded on this glorious Saturday, the snowbirds basking in the warm sun, soaking up memories to sustain them in their northern cities until they returned in the fall. We ordered our lunch and, after the server had gone off to the kitchen, Jock said, "I think I've got the whole story, including the U-166 documents."

"Was there anything in them that would justify King in killing all those people?" I asked.

Jock shook his head. "Sometimes, man's greed astounds me. King figured that if the documents were in a safe aboard a submarine at the bottom of the Gulf, they had to be important. I guess they were, but not in any way that would make King rich."

"What were they?" I asked.

"Instructions, mostly. The Germans were trying to set up a new way to get spies into the U.S. through Mexico. The borders were pretty tight then, and it was almost impossible to get anyone into the country from Mexico. The documents had the names of some corrupt U.S. border guards and some bank account numbers from which they could be paid. It was a pretty elaborate scheme, but there's no record that it was successful. Maybe when the documents didn't reach San Antonio, the Abwehr just gave up on the exercise. Maybe the men on the border didn't turn out to be corrupt. One of them was killed in action during the Normandy invasion, and the rest of the people involved have all since died of natural causes."

"What about the bank accounts?" I asked.

"They were stripped of cash and closed during the war. We suspect that the spies used the money for living expenses."

"So there was no treasure and no one to blackmail," said J.D. "What a useless reason for good people to die."

"How did Katie react to the death of her father?" Jock asked. After he'd called us from Winter Park to tell us about George Bass. J.D. and I had told Katie.

"She had a lot of emotions rolling around," said J.D. "Part of her was sad that he was gone. After all, he was the only father she'd ever known. I guess even a bad father can be better than no father."

"Not always," Jock said.

"I know," said J.D., "but his death was still a shock to her. She worried about her mother. She was afraid that George's death only a little over a year since her own supposed death would be devastating to her mom. She wanted to go to Winter Park and let Betty know that she was alive. Matt and I talked her out of it."

"An FBI agent and I spent some time with Betty Bass on the night George was killed," said Jock. "George Bass was Sal Bonino. Betty showed us a safe where he kept a lot of incriminating documents. The FBI somehow got somebody out on a Friday night to open the safe. Everything was there."

"I can't believe that," J.D. said.

"I'm afraid it's true," said Jock.

"I believe you," said J.D., "but that's a real shocker. I've known him for years."

"What did Betty have to say?" I asked.

Jock told us about his and Lisa Coyle's conversation with Betty, what they'd learned and what they suspected. The trove of documents in the safe confirmed everything they had suspected. "That P.I. from Tampa, Appleby, was on Bass's payroll. We found a copy of a check Bass sent to him. So was DeLuca, the one who tried to beat up Matt."

"Did you find any tie-in to the guy who took shots at us at my house on Sunday?" I asked.

"One of Bass's cell phones showed a contact with a cell phone registered to the shooter."

"Then that means Bass also set up the attempt with the garbage truck," said J.D.

"Looks like it," said Jock.

"Why would Bass want us dead?" I asked.

"We'll never know for sure, but I think it was because you were digging into Katie's death. I suspect Bass at least had some suspicion that McAllister was somehow involved in Jim Fredrickson's death and Katie's disappearance. He was probably afraid that whatever you found might lead back to McAllister and maybe to himself. At the very least, if you tied McAllister into the drug running, it would cause Bass to lose an awful lot of money."

"So," J.D. said, "it's over."

"Yes," said Jock.

"We have to tell Katie," she said.

"Yes," said Jock.

"I'll do it," said J.D. "Did you tell Betty that Katie is alive?"

"No," said Jock. "I thought that decision should be left to Katie."

"Do you know who killed George Bass?" I asked.

"The Tampa Mafia, as it turns out. Our agent, the one who's working with the mole in the organization, said that the boss had figured out the name of the banker who was moving money around for Bonino. When some of his goons went after the banker, this guy Watson, he pretty quickly gave up Bass as the man he was dealing with. Watson had never heard of Bonino, but it was pretty clear that Bass was Bonino. Or at least that he was a top lieutenant. They took Bass out. They figured if he was Bonino, they'd solved a competition problem, and if he wasn't Bonino, at least they'd be rid of somebody who ranked high in Bonino's organization."

"We still have the problem of Katie having killed her husband," said J.D. "How do we handle that?"

"I think we leave it alone," I said. "It was self-defense."

J.D. thought about that for a minute. "I guess you're right. After Doc Hawkins figured out the DNA and McAllister was killed, it was just assumed that McAllister had something to do with her disappearance. It also looked like McAllister killed Jim Fredrickson, so why not leave it at that?"

"I agree," said Jock. "Katie is going to have some money from the estate, so she'll be fine."

"I thought the government would get all that money," J.D. said.

"The government will get the drug money, but they've agreed to only take the ten million. Katie will end up with a couple of million that was legitimate. The proceeds from the house, Jim's IRA and another retirement account, some legitimate cash they had in a savings account."

"Will Katie feel safe enough now to come back to life?" I asked.

"I'm sure she will," said J.D. "She's a survivor."

"What about her mother?" Jock asked. "Will Katie be ready to see her?"

"More than ready," said J.D. "She's really looking forward to it."

We finished our lunch and walked home through the soft spring afternoon. We were alive and Katie was about to restart her life. Jock would stay a few days and then return to Houston and the dark world in which he lived so much of his life.

My and J.D.'s world was slipping back into the languid rhythms of island living and we were content. We had lots of sunshine and friends and a deepening love affair to look forward to in the coming months. As we walked, I felt her hand slip into mine, a simple act that confirmed that all was right with the world. We were happy and you just can't ask for more than that.

AUTHOR'S NOTE

I believe it is the fiction writer's prerogative to take occasional liberties with history, changing the hard facts so that they conform to the plot. However, it is also the novelist's duty to set the record straight when the story is finished.

Part of this book was written with World War II as a backdrop. I've been diligent in researching the history of that time as it relates to my story. The wonderful people at the Manatee County Library main branch in downtown Bradenton have been most helpful in bringing the Cortez of the 1940s into reality for me. Their collections of Cortez, Anna Maria Island, and Longboat Key memorabilia have been of immeasurable help in putting this story together. The curator of this trove of memories, Pam Gibson, who has lived on Anna Maria Island her entire life, made the period come alive for me. All mistakes in the historical record are mine.

There really was an *Unterseeboot*, the famed or infamous German submarines known as U-boats, designated as U-166 and it was sunk at the end of July, 1942, about forty-five miles south of the mouth of the Mississippi River. It was the only U-boat sunk in the Gulf of Mexico during World War II. The boat was captained by twenty-eight-year-old Oberleutnant zur See Hans-Gunther Kuhlmann, born in Cologne and married to Gertrude Wee of Flensburg for two years when he started on his fateful journey from Lorient, France, on June 17, 1942. Leutnant zur See Paulus von Reicheldorf is a figment of my imagination, but the U-boats did on occasion infiltrate German spies and saboteurs into the United States.

U-166 was a class IX C boat, launched in 1941. She was two-hundred-fifty-one feet in length and had a cruising range of thirteen thousand nautical miles.

This first war patrol of U-166 under the command of Captain Kuhlman was essentially as I described it. On July 11, 1942, Kuhlmann sank an eighty-four ton Dominican flagged schooner off the coast of the Dominican Republic, using cannon fire. On July 13, he encountered the 2,309-ton U.S. steam freighter *Oneida* off the Cuban coast and sank her with a torpedo. On July 16, he encountered a small, motorized fishing boat about forty-five miles north of Havana and sank it with gunfire.

On July 30, 1942, U-166 found the American passenger freighter, the *Robert E. Lee,* about forty-five miles southeast of the mouth of the Mississippi River. The *Robert E. Lee* was launched in 1924 and was owned by the Eastern Steamship Company of Boston. She was home ported in New York and under the command of Captain William C. Heath. On the night she died, the *Robert E. Lee* was carrying a crew of one hundred thirty-one, two hundred seventy passengers and forty-seven tons of cargo. She was cruising at sixteen knots on a northwesterly course to the Mississippi River in water that was approximately five thousand feet deep.

She was escorted by an American navy patrol craft, PC-566, under the command of Lieutenant Commander H. G. Claudius, U.S. Navy. She was 178 feet long with a top speed of twenty knots. She'd been launched in Houston in March 1942, and commissioned on June 15, 1942, two days before U-166 left Lorient on her final patrol.

The fatal encounter between U-166 and the *Robert E. Lee* occurred at ten thirty on the evening of July 30, 1942. There is no way to know what actually was happening aboard the U-166 during her attack run or during the depth-charge attack that followed. I could find no information as to whether the U-boat attacked on the surface or submerged, but German captains preferred to attack on the surface at night.

Once Captain Claudius of the American patrol boat realized there was a submarine attack on the *Robert E. Lee,* he went after the U-166, dropping a number of depth charges. PC-566 ended her attack when the crew saw an oil slick on the surface of the water. Captain Claudius turned his vessel and went to rescue survivors of the *Robert E. Lee.* Twenty-five crewmen died in the sinking, but the rest of the crew and all the passengers were rescued by the PC-566.

Captain Claudius claimed that his ship had sunk the submarine, but there was no debris on the surface and, because of events two days later, PC-566 did not get credit for the attack.

On the afternoon of August 1, 1942, two days after the sinking of the *Robert E. Lee*, a U.S. Coast Guard Widgeon aircraft, crewed by Chief Aviation Pilot Henry Clark White and Radioman First Class George Henderson Boggs, Jr., spotted a U-boat on the surface south of Houma, Louisiana, while flying a routine patrol south of Isles Dernieres, Louisiana. The U-boat had apparently spotted the Coast Guard plane and was crash diving when White and Boggs attacked with their single three-hundred-fifty pound depth charge. The Coast Guardsmen circled the site of the attack until they saw an oil slick on the surface. They reported by radio that they had sunk a U-boat. After the war, when it was determined that the only unaccounted for U-boat in the Gulf of Mexico was the U-166, White and Boggs were credited with its sinking.

The reader will note in the story that I moved the site of this encounter eastward to near the Florida Coast and while the Coast Guard attack occurred in the afternoon, I moved it to sunrise. Moreover, I have written the story as if the attack by the Coast Guard aircraft actually sank the U-166. Even though this sinking became part of the Coast Guard tradition and was accepted as fact for many years, the truth was discovered in 2001, when a U-boat wreck was found near the wreck of the *Robert E. Lee* in five-thousand feet of water. In 2003, this wreckage was positively identified as the U-166. It had indeed been sunk by the American patrol boat, PC-566.

Further investigation of German records revealed that the U-boat attacked by White and Boggs south of Houma was U-171 that had been in the area at the same time. While the U-boat sustained some superficial damage, it escaped and completed its patrol in the Gulf. The U-171 was sunk when it struck a mine near its home port of Lorient, France, while returning from its only combat patrol. Most of the crew survived.

I am not aware of a German spy ring in San Antonio during the war. However, there was a rather large ring in St. Louis, so we know that such groups existed in the United States during the entire length of the war.

The deep-water boats did not come to Cortez until several years after the end of the war. The fisherman who lived there during the war years fished for mullet in small boats and came home every night. It was a hard life and the men who lived it worked the bays and sounds for days on end with no respite. They were a tough bunch of guys.

Camp Blanding, Florida, now a Florida National Guard Base, was an army training post during World War II. It also contained a large prisoner-of-war camp, with the first German submariners arriving in September 1942. There was never a successful escape from the POW camp, so I had to fictionalize one. I also moved the date of the first submariner's incarceration back a few weeks, since the loss of U-166 occurred in late July, or in my fictionalized version, August 2, 1942.

I trust that I have not overstepped the bounds of my literary license in making the changes to the historical record. If I have, I hope my readers will forgive me.